INTERSECTING DREAMS

A Novel of Mystery, Romance, and Redemption

Linda Edmister

ISBN 979-8-9863138-2-5 (Paperback)
ISBN 979-9-9863138-3-2 (Digital)

where fiction meets fun and faith

www.misteredbooks.com

Books in the *Intersections* Series
Intersecting Lives
Intersecting Dreams
Intersecting Beliefs
Intersecting Destinies

Author's Note:

With "Intersecting Dreams," the continuing saga of Tinkers Well not only follows the mixed fortunes of its now familiar players, it also addresses critical societal concerns. Readers may find themselves challenged to examine the questionable ideology surrounding these issues as they impact our children and our world. I trust no offense will be taken at the sparing use of very mild, colorful language in keeping with the equally colorful characters. The scripture passages, which begin each chapter, are intended to be read as poetic pointers rather than taken contextually. All other passages relate to the storyline. A map has been provided to help readers navigate the mythical metropolis of Tinkers Well, Kansas so that they might make it their own.

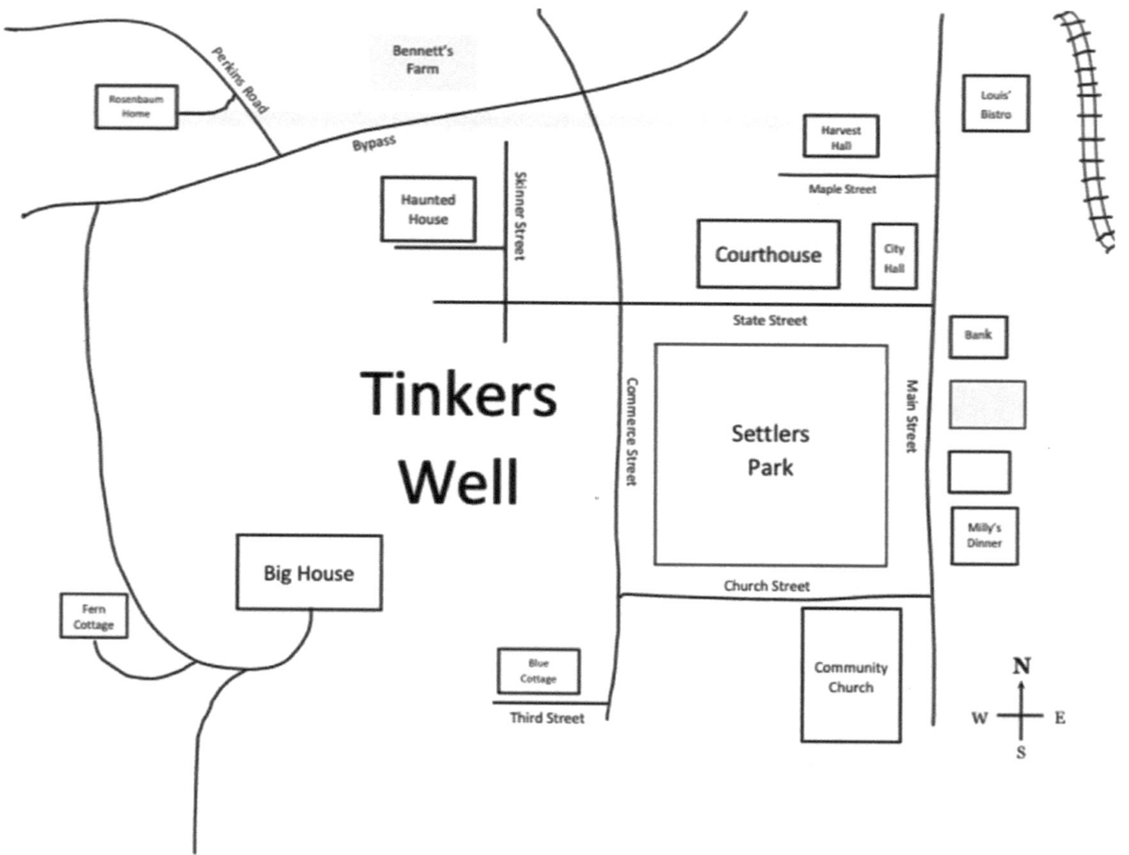

Perkins Road
Bennett's Farm
Rosenbaum Home
Louis' Bistro
Bypass
Harvest Hall
Maple Street
Haunted House
Skinner Street
Courthouse
City Hall
State Street
Bank
Tinkers Well
Commerce Street
Settlers Park
Main Street
Big House
Milly's Dinner
Church Street
Fern Cottage
Blue Cottage
Community Church
Third Street
N
W
E
S

PROLOGUE

Blessed are they that mourn: for they shall be comforted.
Matthew 5:4 (ASV)

From a distant past.

A distraught young woman in her early twenties frantically pulled out drawer after drawer, grabbing indiscriminately at clothes and stuffing them into an already bulging suitcase. She managed to get a few hanging things on top before forcing the latches closed. The once natural loveliness of her face was twisted by despair. Tears ran down her cheeks, smearing her mascara, before dripping off her trembling lips, their pink color washed unusually pale by grief.

"You can't leave," pleaded her companion, a man, not much older, whose emotion manifest itself more in angry appeal than sorrow. "I *love* you! You're my wife and I *need* you!" As she walked toward the front door, laden with luggage, he grabbed her arm and swung her around to face him.

Dropping the suitcases as she spun around, the girl shrugged off his hand and tried to blink away the tears drowning her soft, blue eyes. She forced herself to look into his, now hard and dark.

"And I love *you*, or at least, I love the man I married, but I don't see him anymore when I look at you. I haven't seen him for a very long time," she added with bitter regret. "I can't stay here and watch the kind, clever, caring man I fell in love with become an unfeeling, ruthless... opportunist blinded by... ambition and... and spite."

"*Spite?*" he cried, his self-assurance momentarily shaken. He knew the accusation was true, but he refused to admit it – had *always* refused to admit it.

"Yes, spite. You *never* forgave your father for insisting you start at entry level in the company when you finished grad school. You rejected the idea of working your way up through the ranks, so that you could learn humility and an appreciation for all the employees, just as he had. That's when you started to change. It's as if you decided that you would succeed *despite* his help, or anyone else's, mine included."

"That's not fair," her husband responded, stung by the knowledge that every word she spoke was true. "You knew when we started dating that I was ambitious."

"Ambitious, yes, but not at any cost. I *know* how hard you worked in school to excel so you could make a good life for us, and I respected you for it."

She looked away, ashamed to admit her own willful blindness to his character flaws. As a shy freshman coed, she had been irresistibly drawn to the outgoing assurance of a young upperclassman who exuded confidence and purpose. He had been resolute in setting the world on fire with his ideas and sheer determination, often leaving her feeling like a buoy bobbing in his wake. She sometimes worried about his single-minded purpose, but as an insecure girl, who had been raised by her grandparents in a sheltered environment, she couldn't help falling for him. He had promised her the moon on a silver platter, and she had blindly followed him into that glittering unknown, only seeing his shining qualities, and loving him for them.

"I… I guess I never realized, maybe never wanted to realize, that you expected to accomplish that goal by stepping off the graduation stage with an MBA and straight into a Vice-President's office. I loved the man who embraced challenges; the man who enjoyed meeting new people who would become friends and future colleagues. Not the man who now treats those same people as faceless names to be stepped over on his relentless march to the top of… of… some undefined… pinnacle of success."

The young wife fought to control her emotions. Her breathing came in a series of short, heaving sobs. After a brief inner struggle, she tentatively stepped closer to her husband and raised her hand to gently stroke his furrowed brow and caress his hard, lean cheek. Her voice, barely audible through the constriction of her throat, spoke words of parting. "I am *so* sorry, my love. I truly am, but I just can't do this anymore."

His shaking hand covered hers briefly as he looked into the lovely eyes whose image had so often floated through his dreams, filling them with happiness and contentment. Gazing at her beloved face, now distorted with tears of his making, he let his guard down for a split second, and allowed her to see the very real pain and regret he felt. Then, as if a switch had been flipped, his face hardened, and he retreated behind a shell she could not penetrate. Even though she had witnessed the transformation many times, especially in recent months, it frightened her now in its finality.

Thrusting her hand away, he strode quickly to the hall table where he scratched his signature several times on a document lying there. He held it out to her and spoke in a steely cold voice devoid of emotion. "Go, then, and take your filthy divorce papers with you. I don't need you. I don't need *anyone.*"

She retrieved the fallen bags and stepped through the apartment door. Before closing it and heading to the waiting taxi, she glanced back at the handsome solitary figure now wrapped in a cloak of indifference. Her dreams shattered, she closed the door and was gone.

CHAPTER 1

Through wisdom a house is built, and by understanding it is established; By knowledge the rooms are filled with all precious and pleasant riches.

Proverbs 24: 3-4, NKJV

The uncertain present.

A wounded, vulnerable young woman, stood at a critical crossroads. It was one that even someone with a seemingly limitless imagination could not have foreseen despite having largely, though unwittingly, brought the crisis upon herself. She could hardly turn back, for that way was liberally sprinkled with the ashes of her delusions now lying in ruins. She might have considered heading down a side road, back to Kentucky and home and the stability of an ordinary existence. The future there promised none of the adventure her spirit craved, but neither did it threaten unseen pitfalls and devastating heartbreak. Yes, she might have considered that course but for the encouraging vision she saw in the opposite direction. A new home, and new friends who challenged her limited understanding of trials and hardships by showing her how they could be faced with humility and courage.

It was that vision that forced Rose Thompson to look ahead, to move forward. The unknown future held no guarantees, but she had been reminded that, regardless of what she encountered along the way, she would not face it alone.

With only her dreams to inspire her, Rose had been on a lifelong quest. Her trouble had always lain in identifying a direction to follow, and being prepared to deal with whatever she encountered at the end of the journey. Though no Don Quixote or Joan of Arc, fired with noble vision and purpose, Rose longed for adventure and romance – a dreamer with a capital "D." The opportunity to drive her 82-year-old grandmother, Gertrude Gunn, to the small town of Tinkers Well, Kansas in mid-June had appeared, if not as an adventure, at least as a break from the monotony of one failed employment attempt after another. None of the jobs had been life callings – coffee shop attendant, dog walker, admin assistant – but it is difficult to find meaningful work with a B.A. in English Literature. So, she had willingly offered her services as chauffeur to the outwardly fierce but inherently kind Granny Gert who welcomed Rose's company on a visit to an old school chum from her own college days of decades past.

During the two-day journey, which began for Rose in her hometown of Winchester, Kentucky, she had pumped her grandmother for information about Aletha Mason, the old school chum Rose had never met. Aletha was twice widowed, both times of successful entrepreneurs who had built their fortunes with hard work and acute business acumen. She met her second husband while visiting mutual friends who had left New York for a job opportunity in Chicago. The friends became her family. Peter Ludlow was employed by Martin Mason for many years, while his wife, Marilyn, served as a surrogate daughter for Aletha, long estranged from her only child. When some undisclosed health problem finally necessitated that the Masons move to Kansas, Martin's home state, the Ludlows soon followed. Leaving the windy city behind, they all made a home in Tinkers Well.

With the passing of both Martin and Peter, the two widows were left to comfort one another. Eventually, Marilyn returned to her profession of teaching to fill the void of loneliness. No such option was open to Aletha. Though grateful for Martin's foresight in providing her with Prince, a canine companion who became her constant guide and friend, Aletha faced the prospect of another empty summer with dismay. Knowing her old college friend had lost her husband the year before, Aletha was inspired to invite her for a visit, thinking they could provide solace and companionship for one another. She was equally delighted to include Rose in the invitation, so the two ladies from Kentucky set off on their journey.

Rose and her grandmother had always been close, but the time spent together on the road, sharing their struggles and dreams, cemented the bond. It also gave Rose a much better appreciation for the challenges of the elderly and their determination to overcome them. Upon their arrival at Aletha's home, the two learned that some challenges must simply be born.

The home in question was a modest but beautifully furnished Victorian bungalow liberally adorned with ferns, aptly named *Fern Cottage*. Upon entering the cottage, Rose and Gert discovered that Aletha's undisclosed health problem was blindness. She made little of it in the happiness of welcoming guests to her home and the simple life she enjoyed there, surrounded by friends, young and old, who quickly assimilated Rose and Granny Gert into their society. It was an inspiration for Rose to witness the transformation of her usually brusque grandmother into a laughing, ostensibly younger woman through the sharing of long-buried memories. The two old friends also shared a common goal – one Rose was not privy to until its success came almost too late.

All might have gone smoothly, Rose content to follow along in the wake of their daily routine, had it not been for a chance meeting on the journey west. At a dinner stop, Rose had encountered, if only in passing, the pinnacle of masculine perfection. A stranger so handsome (not a soft brown hair or dark eyelash was out of place), so debonair (he drew the eye of every woman wherever he went), and so charming (his smile and casual greeting alone could have served as a declaration of undying love) that he set a new standard for what Rose considered the ideal man. He surpassed the image of every hero in her mental vault of classic literary characters, eclipsing even the most personable and attractive of everyday members of the male fraternity.

When she met three of the latter on her arrival in Tinkers Well, she couldn't help comparing the men to the unforgettable stranger and found them all somehow wanting. They were friendly enough, except for Tim Ludlow, who had appeared either unwilling to talk to her or needlessly tongue-tied during an early encounter. Rose quickly came to the conclusion that he was certainly no self-assured man of the world. She learned to admire them all, though, as she got to know them and formed welcome friendships with the Army vets-turned-building-remodelers. Their value grew in her estimation as she learned of their courage in facing their own trials while supporting each other.

Tim Ludlow, with his broad shoulders, chiseled jaw, and deep blue eyes, held the rank of reserve captain in the Army Corps of Engineers. Leaving active duty after the death of his father, he relocated to Kansas and started a building renovation business. Derek Warner had followed suit after a devastating firefight left him riddled with survivor's guilt and PTSD. He tried to hide his pain behind a perpetual broad smile that lit up his smooth, black face. Comical posturing of his body builder muscles only served to emphasize his short stature compared to his two buddies. Ahmad "Abe" Yousef, only a few inches taller than Tim, was thinner and more lanky. Curly black hair shadowed his hooded eyes and accentuated his olive skin. He wore his scars outwardly as a combat amputee who had been cast adrift by his family after his conversion from Islam to Christianity. When they learned of Abe's troubles, Tim and Derek invited him to join them in their renovation business, gladly handing him all the technological and logistical issues, and *Three Brothers Construction Inc.* was born. They were good men, honorable men, and Rose developed real affection for each of them. She would have done well to follow their examples of humility and integrity, but those sterling qualities abruptly took second place in her estimation.

The chance met handsome stranger miraculously turned up on the doorstep of *Fern Cottage* three days after her arrival in Tinkers Well.

Rose *knew* it was fate that had brought Simon Applegate, alias Atherton[1], into her life, and she fell for him like the proverbial ton of bricks. Confused by the blatant hostility and suspicion directed at Simon by both Granny Gert and Tim Ludlow, Rose blithely ignored it and accepted wholeheartedly any invitation to spend time with the charming Englishman. While Rose was engaged in living out her fairytale romance, those who had her best interests at heart, Gert and Aletha, hatched a plan to separate the two. They were joined by Marilyn Ludlow, who worried over her son's growing affection for Rose, and by Aletha's friend Angelica Warner, a Jamaican immigrant who provided practical care and much needed company for the elderly woman.

Their plan succeeded only in as much as Rose eagerly welcomed the prospect of rebuilding the formal gardens surrounding a dilapidated Victorian mansion at the same time Simon was skillfully manipulating her emotions for his own ends. The parallel endeavors occupied a mere two weeks, which, in the course of human events, signified less than nothing. But for Rose, they marked the greatest triumph and the greatest humiliation of her young life. For while she readily compared Simon's devastating charm to that of Jane Austen's elegant Mr. Darcy, she blindly overlooked his closer resemblance to the nefarious George Wickham.

On what should have been a languorous day of innocent dalliance filled with sunshine and light flirtation, the hero of her dreams toppled headlong from his pedestal when he was unmasked as a lying undercover private investigator. For some obscure reason, his real object appeared to center on Aletha Mason, and he had masterfully used Rose to get close to the old woman. No one knew for what purpose, though Aletha had her suspicions. For Rose, it was enough to know that she meant nothing to him – had

---

[1] *Intersecting Lives*

merely been a pawn in his game. The knowledge of Simon's betrayal came to Rose after she discovered the rotting carcass of Aletha's companion dog. In a blinding flash, she made the connection between Prince's death and Simon's guilt. After confronting him with her revelations, she was spared Simon's physical retaliation by a merciful and unforeseen rescue. Lost in a pit of degradation, Rose failed to appreciate the romantic timing of Tim's arrival and the subsequent dispatch of a badly beaten Simon. All she knew was pain and guilt for her part in perpetuating the horrible masquerade.

Disappointment, humiliation, grief, betrayal, loss. Pain, in whatever form, comes into every life at some point. But when it crashes unceremoniously into the midst of a golden summer interlude that promises perfect happiness and a resolution for doubts about an uncertain future, its effect can be devastating. Dreamers find the solid ground of reality difficult to traverse at the best of times. When those dreams are shattered and halcyon days of fanciful bliss become dark days of misery in the blink of an eye, reality can become almost unbearable. Rose, however, was not forced to bear the unbearable alone.

Tim had immediately taken her to *Fern Cottage* and Granny Gert's comforting arms. After a night of tears and self-recrimination, Rose was certain she would never be able to face the world again. It wasn't until the following day – when her three friends showed up unexpectedly at the cottage – that she was profoundly reminded of the power of forgiveness and the promise of new beginnings. Fortunately for Rose, she had a greater capacity for honest self-evaluation than others in her situation. Her supporters reminded her that all wounds can heal in time, and for every traitor that crossed her path, there were true friends tenfold waiting to stand by her. She did not awaken on Monday with a spirit wholly refreshed, or a mind free of painful memories. But the blessed memory of sitting at a make-shift communion table the day before, with her flawed but faithful brothers in Christ, bolstered her courage to face the future.

And the rhythm of life brings its own healing: the impetus to greet a new dawn, the need for nourishment, the gathering of family and sharing of each other's lives. Rose couldn't help but smile as she entered the kitchen to find Granny Gert and Aletha, who addressed each other with their college nicknames "Trudy" and Letha," arguing over who would prepare breakfast. Just then Rose's cell phone rang. It was Angelica.

She had been surprised that morning by Derek telling her he planned to go to the VA hospital in Leavenworth to enroll in Psychiatric counseling. She was even more surprised when he invited her to accompany him. Angelica called the cottage to let Aletha know about her change in plans, and to share thanksgiving for the miracle in her son's heart. Instead, she heard only Aletha's voicemail message telling her that she was not at home and inviting her to leave a message. She knew that was nonsense, so she called Rose's cell phone.

Rose, experiencing a moment of true happiness for the first time in days, congratulated Angelica on Derek's decision and assured her that Aletha and Granny Gert were both at home and well, and that the two were already engaged in good-humored rivalry over cooking honors. "And I'll try to find out why you got voicemail instead of one of us." After short contemplation, she added, "You know, I don't even remember hearing the phone ring. That *is* strange. Oh well, give Derek a hug for me and tell him I'm *really* proud of him."

Rose soon joined Granny Gert and Aletha in meal prep, with each contributing their part. Rose cooked the sausage and eggs. Gert cut up a delicious fresh fruit salad, and Aletha made the coffee. After breakfast, the older ladies insisted on doing the washing up, suggesting that Rose could use a little sunshine and exercise.

"You just run up to the main house and make sure that new-fangled sprinkler system is working proper," Gert said. "I'd hate to think that all those plants and the new lawn are drying out in the morning sun." Rose might have argued, but she knew it was time to venture out of the security of the house, and the prospect of checking on the status of her new plantings was as good an excuse as any. Besides, there was little chance of encountering anyone on the now deserted job site, so she changed her shoes and walked out into the welcoming sunshine.

She was instantly assailed by a wave of sadness as she thought about her missing four-legged walking partner, Prince. She was about to turn back, unbidden tears flooding her eyes once again, when she realized that an explanation of her action might bring pain to Aletha too, so she brushed the tears from her eyes, squared her shoulders, and continued on her way. She even smiled a little as she thought of Tim's comment from the Friday before when she, like Aletha, had been distressed over the missing dog. "Keep your chin up, Thompson."

Her smile may have gone a little awry at the thought of Prince, but it failed to nullify any of her natural, unaffected beauty. Soft auburn ringlets fluttered in the morning breeze around a rosy, heart-shaped face and even rosier lips. Her soft round eyes, always open in frank wonder and appreciation at the beauty of nature around her, were fringed with long, curling lashes. They almost rivaled those of the egregious Simon, had he ever cared to notice. He *had* noticed her petite figure with every curve in the right place, though he had, thankfully, been thwarted in his attempt to take advantage of it.

Arriving at the main house, Rose was gratified to note that the sprinklers had indeed done their work. All the paved walkways were wet, and water dripped from leaves and petals as roots stretched into the rich, damp soil. While admiring the fledgling Eden, its young plants reaching toward the sun's radiance, Rose felt a sense of peace and tranquility pour over her troubled soul. She walked slowly toward an old stone wall under an ancient willow tree. Sitting there, watching the graceful sway of the willow branches in the morning breeze, she allowed her mind to drift over the events of the previous weeks.

In the light of day, Rose forced herself to examine her relationship with Simon, false as it had been. Passing quickly over her own cringe-worthy moments of self-exposure, she faced the fact that after the initial infatuation and wonder at his interest in her, she had never felt completely comfortable in his company. He had often set her senses whirling with his polished touch and tender words of affection. Though, just as often, he had embarrassed her by his critical tongue and dissolute behavior. She also realized that her lack of disappointment over his absence on her second weekend there had probably been due more to the comfort she found in more congenial, like-minded company than to the distraction of simply being busy. After much consideration, Rose was compelled to admit that the sum of all their meaningless conversations added up to a lot of posturing and verbal diversions. Simon had implied much but promised nothing.

With many hours having intervened between the harrowing events of Saturday and the calm of a Monday morning, she also found the courage, though with reservation, to evaluate her response to Simon's physical demands. She felt sick when she considered the way her near unwitting surrender had betrayed her naiveté before she had awakened to the reality of fear and revulsion. It had been a painful lesson, and she resolved to never allow herself to be so moved by any man again. When, if ever, she met a man truly worthy of her love, she would be wiser and more guarded in her response. Sighing, Rose looked up into the heights of the old willow and said aloud, "But that isn't likely to happen any time soon, is it?"

It took several minutes before the sound of a power saw, humming away somewhere inside the house, managed to penetrate her thoughts. It was the silence which followed that finally caught her attention. She hadn't seen Tim's or Derek's trucks anywhere around the front or side of the house, so she walked around toward the garage where she found the big white pickup. Tim had spent so much time helping her finish the garden the previous week that Rose had forgotten he still needed to complete work on a second operational bathroom for the upcoming church picnic. She knew from personal experience that a functional toilet was in place in the tiny powder room just inside the back door, but she had never penetrated further into the house. Her curiosity aroused, she stood on the small covered back porch and peered inside through the screen door. Not so much as a fleeting second of hesitation impeded her eager expectation of meeting Tim. Without realizing it, over the past two weeks he had gone from being an awkward, surly acquaintance, to brother in Christ, to trusted friend. Whether consciously or not, Rose knew herself to be safe with him.

"Hello! Anybody home?" Receiving no answer, she waited a few minutes, knocked loudly on the doorframe, and tried her hail again. "Hello! Tim, are you in there?" Still no answer. Welcoming an excuse to explore the house, she let herself into the kitchen. In the dim light that filtered into the room through tattered window blinds, she noticed again the regrettably worn condition of the room. Some of the cabinets had doors that were missing or hanging at odd angles from broken hinges. Dingy linoleum, peeling in the corners, revealed solid wood underneath. The old farmhouse sink was scratched and stained with decades of mineral deposits, and a single hanging light fixture emitted a pitiful attempt at illumination. As she was completing her inspection, Rose heard steps approaching from the front of the house and ducked just in time to avoid being coldcocked by a load of freshly sawn 2x4s. Perusal of the butler's pantry would have to wait.

"Tim!" she called. She had to repeat herself twice before her voice penetrated his thoughts. He swung around so quickly he knocked loose the hood mounted over an ancient gas stove.

"Rose!" he said in surprise, quickly dropping his load and removing his hearing protectors and earbuds. "I am so sorry. I didn't know you were here. Please tell me I didn't hit you."

"No. You missed," she said, smiling. "My radar was fully engaged." She couldn't resist adding, "Though it doesn't look like that stove hood faired quite as well."

"The good news is that its days were numbered anyway," he responded with a laugh, then asked diffidently, "What brings you over here today?" As soon as the words left his lips he thought, *Ludlow, you idiot! Why would you even ask? Just be thankful she's here.*

Rose noticed nothing untoward in the question and merely responded that she had walked over to check on the garden, had heard sounds from the house, and noticed the truck in the garage. "To be honest, I was kind of hoping you might give me a tour of the interior. I've been so intent on bringing beauty to the *outside* of the house lately that I've never actually seen any of the beauty *inside*."

"It'll be some time before *this* room looks even *passable*, but sure, I'd be happy to show you around."

All plans for project completion were immediately pre-empted by her request. He removed his work gloves, dusted off his arms and legs and ran his fingers through his hair to dislodge most of the sawdust nesting there. She couldn't help laughing. "You really get into your work!"

"That I do," he said, with an unabashed grin. He surveyed the room, blew out his cheeks, and said, "Phew! Where to begin?" Looking pointedly at Rose, he asked, "You have a pretty good imagination, right?" Her simple affirmative nod qualified for understatement of the year.

"Good. You'll need it." And the tour into another world began.

Tim was once again on his hobby horse just as he had been when he took Rose over Tom and Lucy Bennett's renovated farmhouse, but this time it was personal. He took pride in any job, especially for friends like the Bennetts, but this house was almost a calling for him. Not only did it belong to the Masons, who had practically been grandparents to him all his life, it represented the epitome of the Queen Anne period of Victorian architecture. It was the ultimate challenge for a craftsman who believed in maintaining the beauty of the past while incorporating modern safety and energy measures. Tim was committed to reusing or repurposing as much of the original structural material as possible. With that goal in mind, he had spent countless hours sketching ideas for opening up living areas and adding more functional space such as bathrooms and closets. He was never able to share his ideas with Aletha because the house layout was only a distant memory for her by the time he'd left active duty and moved to Tinkers Well.

Now he had the pleasure of sharing his dreams with someone who appreciated the old place as much as he did. He longed to share so much more with Rose, but he was trying to put his trust in God's plan for his life, with or without her. For now, he chose to be content with her friendship. He would leave the rest to time.

Rose was enchanted by every room, viewing all through the eyes of wishful thinking, and with open appreciation for the obvious craftsmanship exhibited from floor to high, soaring ceilings. She marveled at hand carved fireplace surrounds depicting the four seasons – summer in the light-filled conservatory, autumn in the dining room, winter in the library, and spring in the front parlor. She was amazed at the effortless movement of massive double pocket doors connecting the main living areas – dining room and parlor. Another pair of doors allowed access to the expansive foyer. She was delighted to see more of the 'wooden lace' millwork she had noticed on the exterior of the house crowning the entry to the main hallway, and she stood in awe of the grand staircase rising in flights from the foyer. Tim's descriptions of the artistic details were filled with intriguing terms such as *spiral turned baluster, beaded spindle, scroll-sawn cutouts, newel caps,* and *face string* – and that was just for the stairs! The rich wooden framed doors and trim work included *incised cornices, rosettes, paneled stiles,* and ornate *bevels* and *pendant drops.*

Having hit his stride, Tim guided Rose from room to room, commenting as he pointed out one accent element after another. "These homes weren't built by contractors, or even carpenters, they were crafted by *artisans.* And *that's* what I want to preserve here," he said with conviction.

He was surprised, and a little embarrassed when Rose laughed unexpectedly. "I apologize. I probably got carried away because – "

" – because you're describing something that you're passionate about," she said with an understanding smile. "Because you can look at a 150-year-old building that a thousand other people would call a rundown dump and see its intrinsic beauty, and what it *can* be instead of what it *is*. Now I *get* it!" Tim went from pleased and gratified to confused and clueless in less than a nanosecond.

"Get what?"

"Now I know how my family and friends feel when I try to convince them that I'm not just following a daydream or... or imagining... an improbable possibility. Oh, I'm not making any sense..."

"No! I mean, yes! You are. That's *exactly* how I feel." He guided her slowly down the hall to the library where wood-paneled walls and empty bookcases provided the faintest echoes of a by-gone era. "Can you see it, Rose? A well-worn, leather wing back chair pulled up before a warm coal fire on a dark winter evening..."

"...with heavy draperies drawn to keep out cold drafts and... a... a..." Before Rose could think up another layer to add to the picture, Tim took up the tale.

"...and a desk lamp, turned down low, casting eerie shadows over the rows of book spines lined up neatly upon the shelves."

Thoroughly enjoying their foray into the realms of fancy, Rose looked appreciatively at Tim and added with mock seriousness, "The book lover sitting there would be wearing a richly brocade dressing gown, *of course*."

"Of course. With a glass of... malt whiskey..."

"...warm milk..."

He made a face and shuddered before concluding, "...on the inlaid occasional table next to him."

Without thinking, Rose leaned her head against his arm as she conjured up the vision before her. "I *can* see it," she said softly. Then she abruptly broke the enchantment of a shared daydream when she stepped in front of Tim and said firmly, "I want to help."

How does she shift gears so fast? he wondered, not sure what she meant. "You want to help…?"

"With this," she said, looking up and down the wide corridor from the grand front entry to the French doors leading into the conservatory, her arms spread from end to end. "With all of this. I want to help in any way I can to bring that scene to life in the library; to see a dining room table set for 14, loaded with a rich harvest; to hear carols played on a piano in the parlor while a family trims a Christmas tree in front of the bay window." Then she added simply, "I want to help you realize your vision."

Oh, my darling Rose, Tim wanted to say, *if only you* could *see my vision*. While she had been floating along in the false dream of Simon Atherton's feigned affection, Tim had been falling head over heels in love with her. He knew she only regarded him as a trusted friend, but he could dream too, and his dreams regarding Rose were wholly honorable. Whether they would ever enjoy a shared future, God only knew, but her desire to support his calling touched him – deeply. It also blind-sided him. He had obligations to clients. He would be gone two weeks in late July for Annual Training. He had already made commitments to start new projects when he returned. It was futile to think of undertaking any large-scale projects at the big house anywhere in the near future – impossible to even consider it… unthinkable to disappoint Rose.

Misunderstanding his hesitation, she offered humbly, "I know I don't have any real skills, but there must be plenty of tasks for unskilled labor that I could assist with. I've helped my dad with things like sanding and painting and stripping the finish off old furniture. There must be miles of wood trim here that need to be polished or refinished. Or maybe I could learn to run a floor stripper…"

"Rose – "

"…surely, it's not as hard to operate as the power auger we used on the garden project. And then there's the demo part…"

"Rose – "

"I can haul out old cabinets or remove busted blinds or…"

"*Rose!*" At the sight of her injured expression, Tim placed his hands on her shoulders and spoke quickly. "I can't tell you how much it means to me that you're willing to give up so much of your time to be a part of…," mirroring her gesture, he spread his arms out, "…all this. And I *know* you could do *any* of those jobs and probably a whole lot more, but this is an enormous undertaking. Why, the time alone would be – "

"Time is the *one* thing I have in abundance," she said, cutting in eagerly. "And I want to fill it doing something… worthwhile." She then added almost pleadingly, "I *need* to fill it."

That was Tim's undoing. He didn't know how he would make it all work, but he knew he had to. "Then I'll find the time, and we'll do something worthwhile… together."

CHAPTER 2

"Trudy, will you call the house on your cell phone?"

Gert, busy putting the breakfast dishes away, waddled around the kitchen on chunky legs that struggled to support her squat frame. Looking down her sizeable nose at her friend she argued, "Why would you want me to do a thing like that when I'm standing right next to you?"

Aletha smiled slyly and answered, "I'm conducting an experiment." Aletha's delicate, guileless features and fluffy white hair sometimes fooled people into underestimating her intelligence and lively sense of humor. The call, duly put through, ended as Angelica's had earlier – with a voicemail message, but no audible ring. "Now I find that very interesting."

"You mean…" Gert began, excitement in her voice.

"That horrid man must have found a few minutes when not…" Aletha's naturally gentle voice had taken on an edge. "No, I will not think about… Prince." Swallowing the lump in her throat she started over. "As I was saying, he must have tampered with my phone. When did you say he was here for his movie night with Rose?"

Gert snorted and said, "Movie night my eye! It was Friday and I know for a fact that he was alone for a while because he 'sent' Rose to inform me he was here. He had plenty of time then. That is, when he wasn't drugging her tea."

"Quite right. He was a thoroughly bad lot, and now that we've established his window of opportunity, will you place the call again and this time I'll listen."

Obediently complying, Gert waited for Aletha's reaction.

"Just as I thought. Those are my words, spoken in my voice. Very cleverly contrived from his 'interview' of me on Monday last, I should think. Now, as you remember, we met with Mr. Thurston, the bank manager, later that day. I think it's time to alert him to go ahead with the rest of our plan. And if the abominable Simon is still intent on completing his mysterious mission, I sincerely hope we lead him a merry dance!"

At that moment, the abominable Simon was anything but merry. Forced to leave the immediate area of Tinkers Well for the more remote environs of Kansas City, he had nearly exhausted his options. Still stinging from a painful physical encounter with Tim Ludlow, Simon was nearing the end of his tether.

There was clearly no hope of ever penetrating the fastness of *Fern Cottage* again after his fatal exposure. That meant that any plan to find and make use of the old woman's safe deposit key must be discarded, despite two days of painstaking work to set up a perfect avenue of access to the box's contents during previous visits to the Midwest Union Bank. He had but one desperate play left, and it depended heavily on the gullibility of far too many players in Simon's little drama, regardless of their apparent aptitude for their assigned roles. He adopted the guise of the geeky, nervous Floyd Paulson (used during his first foray of exploration at the bank) for one final assessment of the designated stage.

After quickly scanning the lobby, Paulson waited in line to be called to the cubby hole of Trix, the voluptuous teller who had been so forthcoming with information on that first occasion.

He hesitantly pushed a check toward the buxom blonde. "Hello again, T-T-Trix."

"Why if it isn't… now let me think… Mr. Palmer…no …Hallston?… no…Paulson!" She glanced at his check and grinned, blowing a bubble through her teeth. "I *was* right."

"M-my, what m-memory."

"Oh, it's not that big a deal. We don't see too many new faces around here. Need another check cashed, sugar?"

"Why, yes. B-but I'm also interested in op-pening an ac-c-count here. I would just p-prefer n-not to work with the D-d-dragon Lady." He giggled a little at the use of the nickname, supplied by Trix, for the formidable Mrs. Simmons, New Accounts Manager.

"So, you've decided to move here after all. Well, that's just fine, but I suggest you wait until Thursday for the account business. Mr. Thurston starts his vacation that day, so Dragon Lady will be acting bank manager while he's out, and if you think she'll do that from her puny little desk in the lobby when she could be occupying his gold-plated office upstairs, you've got another thing coming."

"Oh, that's g-good to know. Will the other young lady…"

"…Lindsey Morton…"

"…Ms. Morton b-be assisting all the n-new ac-count holders b-both days?"

"That's right, darlin'. But only on those two days. She's on *her* vacation through Wednesday. You come back when she does, and you'll be just fine. Now here's your money, and I hope you have a real nice day." With an encouraging wink, Trix was on to the next customer.

Thursday was cutting it uncomfortably close, but Simon knew there was no hope of getting past the no-nonsense Simmons. Rehearsing his script for an unsuspecting Ms. Morton, he tried to suppress the memory of his latest conversation with his increasingly impatient client, Miles Hawthorne. He had only met the wealthy real estate mogul once, but one meeting was sufficient for Simon to recognize in the other man the same ruthlessness he himself possessed. Hawthorne had made the comment that they would "deal splendidly together," and Simon had believed that to be so. But as Hawthorne's need for results grew greater his ill temper increased exponentially, leaving Simon to question their working compatibility.

Powerful men in the public eye maintain a retinue of staff to manage acquisitions and daily business dealings. But when it comes to delicate matters kept close to the vest, an unknown, discreet private investigator can prove invaluable. The Landrum Agency, with whom Simon was technically employed, maintained the mantle of respectability that drew men like Miles Hawthorne to its door. An agreement with the agency had been brokered before Simon ever came on the scene, though experience had taught him that fees could be renegotiated if the client was motivated enough. Desperate men make excellent clients. Simon hinted at such an arrangement during his first meeting with Miles but soon found that Hawthorne was made of sterner stuff than most of his class. There would be no negotiation, though Simon had been assured he would be well-compensated when he delivered a certain document.

The document in question was the deed to a parcel of parkland in the center of Brooklyn, originally purchased in the early 20th century by a self-made millionaire and philanthropist named Joshua Strong. The land had been passed down to each successive generation to either sell or maintain as greenspace, just as their ancestor had intended.

Over a four-year period, Miles Hawthorne had been putting together a massive development deal, having secured most of the property surrounding the park. But the deal was contingent on inclusion of the large two block parcel in the center of the area in question. Hawthorne had located the current deed-holder for the property but had been unsuccessful in getting her to agree to sell. He met with more success after tracking down her heir who was willing to part with the property if Hawthorne could secure the deed. Enter Simon Atherton.

Simon had learned over years of dealing with seemingly reasonable clients that their congeniality became more brittle as pressure for results became more immediate. He had recognized in Hawthorne's voice, during their last communication, a note of desperation. The words still burned in his mind. He had been on his way out the door on Saturday evening to discover some amusement or diversion, after the disastrous events of the day, when Hawthorne called. Simon nearly threw the hateful phone off the ten-story balcony of his new operating base in the city. Realizing, however, that he must keep Hawthorne on the hook to have any hope of being paid a very sizeable commission, he took the call. He took a tongue-lashing, as well, allowing the verbal abuse to roll off his hardened emotional armor, until Hawthorne accused him of having done nothing to earn a penny for his time.

Simon Atherton was many things – devious, clever, ruthless, inventive, charming, sinister – whatever quality the job at hand required. He had no conscience, a healthy avoidance of – rather than respect for – the law, and the ability of a wily fox to circumvent whatever obstacles might crop up in the course of his investigations. He had no moral compass, seeking to gratify his own desires at the expense of his clients or any ancillary persons involved in a case. Simon would probably not have balked at defilement, though prior to meeting Rose Thompson, he'd never met a woman not willing to gladly offer herself to him without reservation, even if she had no helpful information to impart. Though a hedonist of the first order, enjoying the finer things in life whatever the cost, he was also meticulously thorough. He could not command the exorbitant fees he was paid had he not earned a reputation for getting the job done. So, when Miles Hawthorne had the temerity to accuse Simon of having done nothing, the infuriated P.I. responded with predictable indignation.

"Nothing? *Nothing?!* Let me tell you what *nothing* I have done, *Mr.* Hawthorne." He then proceeded to pour into his client's ear all the evils he had suffered at the hands of the unsophisticated residents of Tinkers Well, and the residents of *Fern Cottage*, in particular. "I came to this god-forsaken hamlet to find your miserable land deed so you could make your millions and pass on a mere token of it to me. You made it sound like there would be deeds dropping from trees here, but *no*. I spent a *week* going through every shred of paper contained in over *50* boxes of ancient, meaningless historical files. A pretty, young, impressionable lass, who promised to be both a delightfully intimate partner and my entrée to anything I wanted from the old Mason woman, turned out to be a prude of the highest degree. And she brought her lovesick, muscle-bound boyfriend down on me with all the finesse of a sledgehammer." No need to mention that during an evening spent with the delightful partner, who had quickly been dispatched with a strong narcotic in her tea, he had stumbled on a different document – one that Simon could produce as a bargaining chip should Hawthorne prove difficult.

"I have been summarily banished from the state of Kansas with a split lip and the blood of that black beast on my hands... What am I *talking about*? The *dog!* The blind woman's great, snarling German Shepherd. He attacked me when I attempted to gain entry to the cottage at a time it should have been empty... Yes, he attacked me. And to prevent the alarm being raised, I was forced to dispatch him as quickly as possible and dispose of the body." The fact that Simon had misunderstood the dog's advances and had allowed the horror of a traumatic childhood incident to overpower his reason, was something he would never disclose to Miles Hawthorne, or anyone else for that matter. Simon could still scarcely believe it himself. Even after several days, he never felt as if he had sufficiently washed the sticky blood from his fingers.

At the mention of the dog's death, Simon was somewhat surprised at Hawthorne's response. He was obliged to move the phone some two feet from his ear to avoid permanent hearing loss. The people lounging around the pool ten stories below probably heard Hawthorne's bellow. "*You did what?!*"

"I merely rid the world of a detestable animal. Why would you care?" Simon asked provocatively. The man on the other end of the line was mute for so long, Simon thought he must have hung up. Then a voice suddenly spoke out of the silent void in tones of ice.

"You have until Friday, Atherton, to present the document in my office or you forfeit your fee, payment of all your, no doubt, excessive expenses — oh yes, the charges on the credit card will be forwarded to the Landrum Agency unless I clear them for payment – and your good-standing with your employer or any other reputable investigative agency in the city. I suggest you curtail whatever personal entertainment you have planned for the remainder of the week and *get me that deed!*"

Simon ground his teeth, ignored Hawthorne's warning, and engaged in every form of wild excess available in a Midwestern city. If Friday he was to die, then by God, he would live it up until then.

Tim was at a complete loss. He had done the calculations over and over again in his head on the way to *Milly's Diner* after spending the morning with Rose. There just wasn't enough of him, or time, or all of *Three Brothers Construction, Inc.* combined to meet all their business demands *and* begin serious renovation of the big house. He was still trying to think of a way to let Rose and her dreams down gently when he walked into the diner, and was surprised to find that Derek Warner had already returned from his visit to the VA.

"Tim! Just the man I wanted to see," he said as the two friends shook hands. "Have I got an idea for you."

"Wait. First things first. How did your evaluation go?"

"I'd rather tell you about my idea, but I will tell you that I was really lucky and got in on a cancellation this morning which, I guess, almost never happens. And I'm set up for regular talk therapy sessions every two weeks starting next week. The way God answers prayer is pretty crazy!"

"That's awesome, man!" Tim said, gripping his friend's shoulder.

"It is, but that's not the best part. Wait till I tell you about *my idea.*"

Tim buckled his tool belt and slipped on his work gloves. "Can you tell me while we're working? We have *got* to get this job done," he said, the stress evident in his voice.

Abe Yousef walked in just then with a box of hardware needed to install the new breakfast counter, so Derek had to repeat his report. Tim, though supportive, was obviously impatient to get started. "Look, we're both really glad you're getting help and that everything went well for you today, but could we just cut the chatter and get to work." Derek and Abe exchanged glances as Tim organized the hardware.

"What's happened with Rose?" Derek asked bluntly.

Tim said curtly, "Nothing!" After a brief silence, while he grappled with his thoughts, he blurted out, "Everything!" His friends waited patiently for him to continue, knowing Tim did not respond well to prodding. When he reached a mental dead end, he would unburden himself. Throwing the hardware back into the box, he looked at Derek and Abe in defeat.

"Just when we're really connecting and I'm earning her trust, like an idiot I promised Rose her heart's desire, and now I can't deliver. So, I become another jerk who disappoints her. What is *wrong* with me?" he said in despair.

"Okay. One, I think there are a whole lot of blanks you need to fill in, and two, you could *never* be anything like that jack wagon, Atherton," Derek observed calmly.

They had each perched on a crate containing booth sections awaiting installation. Tim frowned at his calloused hands as he recounted the morning's events – Rose's instant response to the essence of the house and her unexpected offer. "She *gets* it. She can see it like I do and wants to be a part of bringing it back to life. Man, if you could've seen her face." The image of her trusting eyes, looking so hopefully into his, floated before him. "I think she needs this as her own kind of… therapy. She said she wanted to be part of something 'worthwhile.' How could I say no to that? All the way here I've been trying to figure out a way to find the time," he said, looking up with a dejected expression, "but we barely have enough manpower to handle the projects we're already working."

Derek jumped up, holding his hands out to his sides in an emphatic gesture. "That's why you need to listen to *the idea I've been trying to tell you about.*" He finally had Tim's attention. "While I was at the VA hospital, someone mentioned a jobs board where guys can look for employment in the area and where prospective employers can post jobs. There's an actual, physical board in the main lobby – I know it's pretty old school – but there's also an online option. I had a few minutes to kill before my appointment, so I checked it out. Brother, there are lots of vets out there looking for work, and I'll bet you if the genius here," he said, indicating Abe, "can figure out how to post something online, we could hire a crew or at least three or four guys who have some construction experience to help us out so we can get you and Miss Rose to work on – "

Derek's comment was cut short when Tim engulfed him in a bear hug. "Brother, *you're* the genius!"

"*Hey*, I thought *I* was the genius," Abe interjected.

"And my new best friend," Tim added, the weight of the world suddenly lifted from his shoulders.

Derek's face split into a wide grin quickly followed by a frown. "Wait. I thought I was your *old* best friend."

"Abe, how soon can you put a job description together?"

"As soon as I get back to the office, boss. But I'll run it by you before I post it. *You're* the construction expert. I'm just the techno wizard."

"That you are. I'll contact the families and businesses we have scheduled a few weeks out to see if we can adjust start dates until we can get some help on board and see how they work out. We can do this, right?" Tim asked of his two brothers, a hint of doubt still in his voice.

"We may not be able to, but it seems to me that we have a higher boss who is doing quite well at working things out all around," Abe said. "I talked to my little brother, Husam, this morning, and he is coming to see me in August before starting university. Our God truly is a God of miracles!"

"But, Abraham, I couldn't possibly accept such a generous gift," protested Aletha.

"Mrs. Mason, I have given this much thought. I believe your need for Scout's presence to be far greater than mine," Abe said, and ruffled the golden coat of the retriever at his side. "If he comes to you now, you will have the rest of the summer to become better acquainted before Rose and Mrs. Gunn return to Kentucky."

Everyone sitting in the living room of *Fern Cottage* felt a little misty eyed. Derek, until then a silent observer, stood as if he had come to a decision and addressed the ladies of the house, including Angelica, who was present at his request. "I can't let you do it, man." Surprised by such a statement, all eyes, even those that could not see, were on Derek. "I can't let you cover for me anymore." Considerably mystified, the ladies waited for him to continue. He pulled up a footstool before Aletha and placed his hand over hers resting on the arm of her chair.

"It's me who is giving Scout to you, Aletha. You see, I was so… stubborn and… and prideful that I refused to admit I had a problem when I left the Army. I was the strong, tough man of the family, so I decided I could handle anything – everything, by myself. I was wrong. And when Abe came to live with Mama and me, he saw that. So, he requested a therapy dog for himself – his injuries are pretty obvious – but he did it so that Scout might help *me*." Derek looked at his friend, his face a study in humility. His grave expression seemed out of place where a broad grin usually resided. "And he did help me… more than he knows." Addressing Aletha once more, he said, "But I've finally manned up enough to get real help so I…"

he glanced at Abe who nodded, "…*we* want you to have Scout. We know he'll have a good home here."

"But surely the agency that trained and provided him for your use would object to just handing him over to me?"

"It is all taken care of," Abe said as he stood next to Derek. "I called them this afternoon and explained the situation. There is some paperwork to be completed, but you needn't worry about that. Scout is yours."

Aletha dabbed at her eyes with a delicate lace-edged handkerchief and said, "I don't deserve such kindness, but I gladly accept your gift with a grateful heart. Bless you." She reached out to touch Derek's face and lifted her other hand as if searching for Abe. He bent over the old woman's chair. "Bless you both." Granny Gert blew her nose loudly while Angelica smiled through her tears. Rose hugged both her friends and kissed each one soundly on the cheek.

"If I'd known you were going to do that, I'd have suggested this yesterday," Derek said, setting everyone at ease to enjoy the sight of Aletha extending her hand to Scout. The dog sniffed in discovery then laid his head on her knee where the old woman could greet her new companion with gentle strokes of welcome.

Watching the touching tableau, Rose glanced from Abe to Derek and thought, *These really are two of the best men I have ever known!*

CHAPTER 3

The words of his mouth are iniquity and deceit: He hath ceased to be wise and to do good.

Psalm 36:3, ASV

Additional help for Tim's scheduling dilemma came from an unexpected quarter.

"Honey, do you think Rose would be interested in serving on the organizing committee for the church picnic? I know she's feeling a little lost now, but I don't want to intrude on her time if *you've* made plans to…" Marilyn Ludlow left the sentence unfinished while she watched in awe as Tim inhaled his dinner like a human vacuum.

"Oh, I've made all *kinds* of plans," Tim replied, between bites. "You know, Mom, you're *terrible* at subtlety."

"Well, enquiring minds want to know. Besides, I thought if you paused long enough to answer me, I might spare you trying to swallow that steak whole. I'm afraid I don't know the Heimlich maneuver…" she added casually.

As Tim chose that precise moment to take a drink, he went off in a coughing fit that alternated between gasping for air and laughing.

"I *suppose* it's better to aspirate your water than an entire steak," his mother observed calmly.

When he could talk again, Tim put his fork down, folded his arms and said, "Okay. I get the message. It's just that I've got a lot of calls to make tonight. And as for your question, I don't know if *Rose* would be interested, but anything that keeps her busy for the next few days would help me enormously."

"Now that *is* interesting," Marilyn commented, putting her elbows on the table, and leaning toward her son. She and Tim shared the same fair coloring, but their facial similarity was merely superficial. Her countenance was soft and rounded where his was hard and chiseled. Her slightly downturned eyes, which dipped a little at the outside edge giving them a winsome, dreamy quality, were her most striking feature. They twinkled at him now, teasing him for a response.

Resuming his meal, but at a more sedate pace, he ignored his mother's statement and said nonchalantly, "Have I mentioned that I think it's time I got my own place?"

"Touché!" she replied, laughing appreciatively. "I promise I will not be the interfering mother, but seriously, if there's anything I can do to help…"

Tim reached out to pat her arm. "I know you will, and you can." He filled her in on all that had happened earlier: his plan to augment his work force, and his ultimate goal of finally digging into the big house renovation.

"Oh, Tim, I think it's a great idea to hire veterans to work for you, but that's an awful lot to take on all at once…"

"I know, and I promise I won't overextend myself or the business. But I just can't disappoint Rose," he said with worry lines between his eyes.

"Then I'll call her right now. I'm going to invite Aletha and Gertie to join us too. I think it will do them all good to get away from the cottage for a few hours after what has passed recently, and it will give Scout the opportunity to get used to being around new people."

As Tim rose from the table, he grinned at Marilyn and said, "You're the best mom *ever.*"

"Flatterer. Now get to work. I've got things to do."

He reached for his phone. "Chuck? Tim Ludlow here. Have you got a minute? I need to talk to you about adjusting your project start date…"

"We'll need a couple of canopies: one to cover the food tables and one to provide shaded seating for those desiring a respite from the sun," Marilyn suggested.

"After the heat debacle at last year's picnic by the lake, the Parish Council purchased a used pole canopy, and I'm sure they'll let us use it for seating. It's pretty big – 20'x30'," said Lisa Lindeman, pastor's wife and all-around problem solver.

"And we've got a 12'x12' pop-up that can house the food," Lucy Bennett added. "Rose, you remember it from the pool party you came to with Tim, don't you?" Though she mostly remembered the delicious smoked BBQ she had discovered *under* the canopy, Rose nodded her head obligingly.

Four generations of Community Church ladies sat around Marilyn's open and inviting living room. Rose never ceased to marvel at the artistic cohesiveness of thrift store finds mingled with tailored window treatments and fine furniture mixed with rustic pieces. The room was both welcoming and beautiful and always a favorite gathering place for committees and small groups. Those present for the meeting were no different. Lucy had brought her youngest granddaughter, Ellie, who contributed little to the conversation but the soft breathing of a cherub at sleep. The others nibbled on Angelica's delicate pastries while one after another chimed in with their own, novel ideas. Rose became a little alarmed at the mention of a four-legged race, a horse-shoe pit, a duck pond, an egg-throwing contest, and a scavenger hunt. Visions of trampled flower beds, uprooted shrubs and dislodged rolls of sod caused her to fear for the survival of her beautiful garden. Marilyn, correctly interpreting her candid misgivings, hastened to clarify.

"Of course, anything that requires a lot of running or possible damage to the ground will be held *behind* the house or over by the old barn. The grass there isn't exactly lawn, but perhaps we can find someone to mow it to a useable height."

"Tom can take care of that," Lucy announced, blithely volunteering her husband's services.

"Perfect. Then we can preserve the garden and provide a place for those who prefer to sit in the shade and chat while they enjoy the serenity around them." Rose gave a silent sigh of relief.

The discussion continued, covering numbers attending, the amount of meat and drink needed to feed such a crowd, potluck sign-ups for sides and desserts, transport of tables and folding chairs, parking, extension power cords for a makeshift P.A. system, and the list went on and on. Rose had never really given thought to all the details involved in hosting an event for nearly 100 people. So far, her part had *only* required that she finish the formal garden in time. She began to feel as if that herculean effort paled in comparison to the growing list of puzzle pieces that needed to fit together by Sunday afternoon. But by the time baby Ellie awoke from her afternoon nap, demanding attention, and a bottle – not necessarily in that order – the ladies had handily addressed all the logistical details for the picnic as if they routinely planned the strategic movements of large armies. Rose was happy to cement an earlier invitation from Amy, church violinist and sister gardener, to join her for lunch on Thursday. They planned to spend the morning gathering all the necessary paper products for the picnic, prompting Lisa, sitting next to them, to announce loudly,

"Don't forget to save your receipts for any expenses so the church treasurer can reimburse you."

"Nonsense!" The single word was spoken with such authority that everyone stopped in mid-conversation to look at Aletha who had been almost silent during the preceding discussion. "The picnic is being held at *my* house, by *my* invitation, and as I am *still* the mistress there, kindly retain your receipts and give them to Rose. *I* will reimburse you at the picnic. Rose, can you take care of that for me, child?" She spoke into the open.

"Of course, Aletha," said Rose, hurrying to her side. "I'll set up a spreadsheet to track everything. That way we'll have a record in case you want to make this an annual event. Maybe Granny Gert and I could come back again," she added somewhat wistfully.

"I do hope so. You and Trudy will *always* be welcome," Aletha replied graciously.

Rose might not have agreed so readily to Aletha's request if she'd had any notion of how exactly she was expected to pay picnic organizers. On Thursday morning, Aletha gave Rose specific instructions on who to speak with at the bank and provided her with an antiquated leather briefcase (it must have been at *least* 40 years old) in which to carry the funds. Rose assumed Aletha had worked out some payment method with the bank that involved cashier's checks or blank checks signed by some bank employee, requiring Rose to merely fill in the individual details as needed. Though she'd rarely written a check, all her banking being handled online or by card payment, she could always ask Granny Gert for pointers. "I suggest you wait until *after* your shopping trip and lunch with Amy to visit the bank. No sense in taking any chances. Now run along and enjoy your morning."

Rose and Amy Walker enjoyed hunting for bargains at the local market and general store. If they ended up with more than paper products, it was time and money well spent in forging a new friendship. They had both parked on the square, and after stuffing their purchases into the backseat of Rose's car, they wandered through Settler's Park to the *Early Bird Café.*

"I'm sorry we don't have any more options for lunch besides the fast-food places out on the bypass," Amy said apologetically. "I can't wait till *Milly's Diner* reopens."

"Tim Ludlow told me they're hoping to finish a little early. He's hiring some more workers – other veterans actually – which I think is really great. I get the feeling that *Three Brothers Construction, Inc.* has made such a name for themselves that they can't keep up with demand. They've got Abe doing a lot of the manual work even though he's supposed to just cover the logistics and record-keeping end of things. But after knowing him only a few weeks, I'd say he's equal to just about anything."

Amy responded a little too casually. "I hear he's some kind of computer wizard. Do you know if he ever does any free-lance work? You know, helping people troubleshoot their PCs or figure out how to use new software…" She left the open-ended sentence hanging and glanced at her new friend.

Rose, smiling at a delightful discovery, tried to remain nonchalant. "He's such a nice guy, I'm sure he'd be happy to help you with… anything." She tried not to look at Amy but was sure the other girl was blushing. "Why don't you just ask him? You must have talked to him at church or in your small group?"

Amy hesitated a little before admitting, "I haven't actually *talked* to him. We just exchange pleasantries and small talk. But I don't mind telling you that I was blown away by his faith conversion testimony, and he seems like such a good man and he's really cute, and… so… *tall*."

"Amy, you *like* him," Rose couldn't help herself. Even if her luck with romance was abysmal, she could still take pleasure in helping others find it.

"I don't even *know* him," Amy argued half-heartedly. "Besides, look at me. I'm not pretty like you are. I'm tall and lanky and built more like a boy than a girl. And I never know what to do with my hair, so I just put it in a ponytail like I did when I was playing basketball in high school and college. And the whole make-up thing just escapes me. So, unless he's scouting for the WNBA, he's never likely to notice me," she added, as if resigning herself to obscurity.

Rose stopped walking and pulled Amy to a halt. "Let me tell you what I see. I see a young woman with the figure of a fashion model – one that most women would die for. I see soft brown hair that has all kinds of style potential, and a beautiful smile and big doe eyes that, with the right shading, will grab the attention of anyone who sees them."

Amy laughed despite herself. "Boy, you've got some imagination!"

"You're right about that, but in your case, I'm absolutely sure it's not exaggerated. Do you trust me?"

Still doubtful but willing, Amy replied, "I guess I don't have anything to lose, so… yes?"

They resumed their walk as Rose explained, "I'll have to do a little research about a hair stylist. And no," she continued before Amy could interrupt, "just trimming the ends yourself is not the answer. Then I'll have a chat with Gayle at the boutique. She always looks classy and would probably enjoy turning you out in style." Amy cringed at the idea of being dressed up like a doll. As if reading her friend's thoughts, Rose said, "I promise that once you can see yourself in something flattering, you'll feel more confident, and you won't be afraid to hold your head high." She had noticed that Amy tended to roll her shoulders and head forward as if to diminish her height.

"I want to believe in what you're saying, but honestly, the thought of a makeover scares me to death."

"Then we'll just have to do something about that, though it may have to wait until after the picnic," Rose replied, as they entered the café and found a table.

"Well, if it isn't the luckiest girl in the world," a familiar, tired voice drawled.

Rose turned quickly to encounter Sunny, who unwittingly interposed the unwelcome presence of Simon into an otherwise lovely day.

"Where's your boyfriend?" asked the inquisitive waitress who had served Simon and Rose on an earlier visit. "I haven't seen him in here for a week. What a dreamboat."

Rose, ignoring Amy's obvious curiosity, tried frantically to stem the flow of humiliating reminiscences.

How could I not have foreseen this? Rose chided herself. Simon had left his irresistible impression on every soft-headed woman in town – and she had helped him!

Keeping her eyes glued to her menu, she answered as offhandedly as possible. "Oh, Mr. Applegate wasn't my boyfriend. I was just acting as his temporary assistant while he was in Tinkers Well, but he has moved on now." *Well done, Rose!* She was congratulating herself on making it safely over dangerous ground when Sunny turned to Amy for a more satisfying answer.

"Did you ever get to be Simon's 'assistant?'" Rose sat with her eyes downcast, mortified by the implication.

"I'm sorry, but I'm afraid I don't know anyone named Simon," Amy replied.

"That's too bad. Believe me, you'd remember him if you'd ever met him. I'm sorry I won't be seeing that sexy smile anymore, and girl, could he tip!" she added, hoping his former 'assistant' would take the hint. She didn't.

Once safely outside again, and walking through the relative privacy of the park, Amy said, "I know we haven't known each other very long, but I've already made a romantic confession to you so it's your turn. Spill."

Rose had been so grateful for Amy's reticence in the café, under the listening ear of Sunny, that she enlightened her new friend with a condensed version of her own sordid history with one Simon Atherton. Recognizing Rose's distress, Amy mercifully kept any desire for details to herself, merely commenting, "Sounds like you're rid of a bad bargain. I say put him behind you and move on. I suspect he's not worth the effort of regretting."

"He's not. And thank you for not asking any questions. I… it's still just a little too… raw, if you know what I mean, but I promise I'll tell you more… when I can."

"Rose, you're the first real friend – single friend anyway – that I've made since I moved here last year after grad school. My roommate told me so many stories about visiting her grandparents in Tinkers Well when she was a kid that I never thought twice about moving here when I saw a posting for the position of small-town school music teacher. I chucked my job in a dysfunctional city school district and never looked back. I've really loved living in Tinkers Well, but there aren't many single working women, so I'm always kind of the third wheel when I'm invited to hang out with young married couples. It's nice to have a girl friend to talk to. I really hope you'll stay."

Rose didn't have the heart to tell her that she and Granny Gert would be leaving in the middle of August. "Thanks, Amy. That is so sweet. I've made three great guy friends in Tim, Derek, and Abe, but you're right, I haven't met any other single women. I'm really glad you invited me to hang out with you today."

They reached their cars and bid each other farewell until meeting again on Saturday for set-up duty. Rose waved as Amy drove away, then she walked, briefcase in hand, the short distance to the Midwest Union Bank. Thankfully, the bank was one local establishment she had never visited and, therefore, had no fear of any uncomfortable inquiries about her nemesis.

Per Aletha's instructions Rose went to the new accounts desk where she found a very business-like young woman with her hair twisted in a tight bun, and wearing horned rim glasses that dwarfed her face. She stood and greeted Rose in a highly professional manner, introducing herself as Lindsey Morton, and motioned Rose to a seat opposite her. The young woman's perfect composure deserted her, however, when she failed to realize the rolling chair she occupied had rolled out of range when she stood. Resuming her seat meant landing unceremoniously on the floor with her feet over her head, leaving her glasses cockeyed across her face and her tight bun a dangling mess. Ms. Morton, burning with embarrassment, rolled onto all fours before attempting to stand, while Rose ran around the desk to help her.

"Oh, my Gosh! Are you all right? Here, let me help you." Rose, assisting the disheveled young banker to stand, realized that the girl must be even younger than she was. She empathized immediately with the poor girl, especially when she saw tears of acute anguish appear. Doing her best to make light of the situation, she said, "Don't worry about it. I doubt anyone else even noticed. Let me just straighten your glasses for you." After providing that small service, she smiled encouragingly at the girl and launched into her request, hoping to help Ms. Morton focus on something besides her own distress.

"Ms. Morton…"

"Please call me Lindsey. I'm afraid I don't feel much like trying to maintain any formality now," she said with a rueful smile.

"Oh, I love that name. My best friend in high school was named Lindsey. Anyway, my name is Rose Thompson, and my grandmother and I are guests of Aletha Mason."

"Of course. I'm so happy to meet you." Then in a lowered tone, she added, "And so happy that you're really nice." In a voice approaching normal, she continued, "Mrs. Mason called this morning, and we have everything ready for you. Will you come with me, please? Trix has been working here since I was a little girl. She'll take care of your transaction." As she stood, Lindsey replaced her skittish chair under her desk. Arriving at the teller's window, she introduced Rose and left her after another word of thanks.

"So, you're staying with Mrs. Mason. I guess she's just about the most important person in town and just about the only one who still does her personal payments this way. Have you got a briefcase, angel?" Taking the case, Trix opened it on a table behind her and began filling it with cash – a lot of cash. Rose's eyes grew as big as saucers while she watched Trix put what looked like a million dollars in the briefcase. The teller turned and slid a receipt for $500 through the window and asked Rose to sign for receipt of the funds.

"I apologize for the small bills, but Mrs. Mason specifically requested mostly tens, fives, and ones – something about reimbursing expenses that would most likely be in small amounts. Now, just about anybody else would want to count everything again themselves, but I could tell you were watching me pretty closely so I'm guessing you're okay with the count?"

"Yes." Rose said in a dry squeak.

"That's fine then. I'm going to put your copy of the receipt in here, and there you go." Handing Rose the significantly heavier briefcase, Trix gave the girl a wink that Floyd Paulson would have recognized, and said in her good-natured way, "Now don't spend that all in one place."

As a bemused Rose turned to leave, she noticed a distinguished looking man in a pin-striped suit taking a seat across from Lindsey Morton. Lindsey must have been somewhat bemused, too, for she seemed to have already forgotten the faulty chair and was about to give a repeat performance of her tumbling act when Rose, waving wildly, caught the other girl's eye just in time. Lindsey retrieved her illusive perch and shot Rose a look fraught with gratitude.

The distinguished man seemed put out. *This chit of a girl should have been upended by now in an acutely compromising position. How could anyone have gotten to her and warned her in the past ten minutes? I put enough grease on those loosened wheels to send her chair into the next county,* he thought grimly. Then he caught Lindsey's expression and followed it to the object of all his woes. *It's not possible,* he cursed inwardly. *The gods must all be in league against me. How could that wretched, pestilential Rose have managed to unseat my well-laid plan yet again?"*

Rose, passing Lindsey's desk, looked at the distinguished man as he turned in her direction. He must have been in his late forties. His hair was brushed back from attractively graying temples over smallish ears. A short, neatly trimmed beard obscured his jawline and made his lips appear unusually thin. A single signet ring adorned his long, thin right hand. Gray eyes, peering at her through thick lenses set in fine wire frames, seemed to bore into her. Rose caught her breath. She had the oddest sensation of recognition while at the same time being absolutely certain that she had never seen the man before in her life. As their eyes locked, she felt a perceptible wave of pure hatred directed at her.

You're being foolish and fanciful. Stop it! she told herself firmly. Just then the man looked away and the feeling of intense malevolence was gone, but the nagging feeling of recognition lingered. Rose tightened her grip on the loaded briefcase and walked quickly to her car. She had had quite enough of the Midwest Union Bank for one day.

Losing the advantage in a game of liar takes all inadvertently worked to Simon's advantage. His initial brusque but polite manner became downright rude and condescending.

"Young woman, I have taken great pains to explain who I am, and my purpose here. If you are unwilling or incapable of assisting me, please contact your bank manager. I believe his name is Thurston." Having been forewarned by Trix, Simon knew himself to be safe from both Thurston and the formidable Mrs. Simmons who was sitting in for him as acting bank president. Simon had also gleaned enough from his previous dealings with Lindsey Morton, under the guise of Allan Pinkerton, to know that she would suffer the indignities of a thousand tumbles rather than resort to asking the Dragon Lady for help of any kind.

"Oh, I d-don't think that will be necessary. It's just that… that is… we didn't know Mrs. Mason *had* a nephew. I'm… I'm not sure *anybody* in town did."

"And I'm not sure why it should be anyone's business but mine and hers. As I told you earlier, though clearly you were unable to comprehend my explanation, I have spent my entire career abroad, only visiting Uncle Martin, for whom I am named, on rare occasions and then solely at his residence in Chicago. I am Mrs. Mason's relative by marriage only, but per a stipulation in my uncle's will, I have assumed the duties of Aunt Aletha's designated guardian. As such, I am required to take possession of a certain document currently located in her safe deposit box at this institution. I was obliged to penetrate the wilds of Kansas this morning to retrieve it because she felt it unwise to send said document by post. I must say I felt rather *de trop* when I arrived to discover that she was entertaining house guests. Or I suppose I should have said 'guest' as the young lady was absent at the time, having left the cottage earlier on some sort of errand."

"Oh, yes. I met Rose just before you arrived at the bank. Isn't she nice?"

"I wouldn't know now, would I, as she wasn't present at the cottage," Mason pointed out with a mirthless smile.

"Oh, you're right. I guess that makes sense."

"I'm so gratified to know that we have come to the same conclusion. Now, can we please get on with it, Ms. Morton?" Mason asked with barely concealed impatience.

"Of course, Mr. Mason. I assume you have Mrs. Mason's deposit box key," Lindsey said timidly. The planned diversion of unseating Ms. Morton, thus allowing Simon to capitalize on her discomfiture and blame the missing key on the ensuing chaos, had come to naught. Thanks to the meddling Rose, he was forced to invent another plausible excuse for its disappearance. But then, Simon was so adept at improvisation.

"Though you are quite young, I'm sure you are able to grasp the vagaries of the elderly. I'm afraid my aunt becomes quite… er… scattered from time to time, shall we say. It seems she cannot remember where she secreted it. After a thorough search of the cottage, I was unable to unearth it. Perhaps you would like to call Aunt Aletha yourself to verify my credentials. I assume you keep a record of her contact information."

Obviously relieved by the suggestion, Lindsey called the cottage but received the same message that had been left on the answering machine the week before. "I'm so sorry, but she doesn't seem to be at home. I just got a message. Perhaps you would like to come back later when she can come with you," Lindsey suggested hopefully.

"I would not like to come back at any time!" He snapped, then spoke as if remembering something. "Please forgive my rudeness. I find this whole business quite irritating, but this time it is I who am in error. I just recalled that I found her phone to be faulty when I tried calling her yesterday to apprise her of my arrival, so I took the liberty of acquiring a cellular phone for her use. Much more practical and reliable. Here, I have the number in my own phone."

Lindsey had never actually met Aletha Mason, so she had no way of knowing that the person on the other end of the call was an actress and close personal acquaintance of the resourceful Simon Atherton. The accommodating Clarice was happy to impersonate women's voices or perform any other kind of favor at Simon's request provided he promise something to her liking in return. He had so promised.

"Who did you say this was?" asked a fluttery voice. "Oh, Miss Morton is it from Midwest Union? I've been a friend of Mr. Thurston's for years… What's that?... My nephew… Oh, yes. Young Martin is picking something up for me at the bank today. I hope it won't be a problem. You, see, I can't seem to find the confounded key. To my box, you know… Oh, certainly, please open it for him." Then she added, as if sharing a confidence, "The sooner he gets that silly piece of paper, the sooner I'll be rid of him!... Thank you, dear. Good-bye."

"Well, Mr. Mason," Lindsey said smiling as she hung up the phone, "It seems that everything is in order. I just need to notify the acting bank manager, and then I can open Mrs. Mason's box for you."

"Excuse me. I thought you said everything was settled. What possible reason could you have for bothering a busy man like Mr. Thurston, unless you feel unequal to the task without his blessing…" Mason commented, with a sneer in his voice. But Rose was not the only young woman to have received very specific instructions from an elder that morning.

"Oh no. I mean that's not it at all. It's simply bank protocol. I'm sure you understand." Lindsey smiled shyly at the obviously perturbed Mr.

Mason and dialed a number scribbled on a card in her desk drawer. It was a pity for Simon that he allowed his annoyance to distract his thoughts, or he might have wondered at the girl dialing a ten-digit number rather than merely punching a bank extension. He was a bit surprised at her temerity in bearding the Dragon Lady in her den, but apparently it *was* merely a matter of protocol.

"Mrs. Simmons, this is Lindsey Morton… Yes ma'am. I'm sorry to bother you, but I just wanted to let you know that I will be opening Mrs. Mason's box for her nephew… Yes, ma'am, I have received her verbal approval and have verified his identification… Yes ma'am. I'll email a memo to Mr. Thurston… Yes ma'am. Thank you."

The person on the other end of the call smiled, well pleased. He idly tossed a key in the air for a few seconds before depositing it in the vest pocket of his pin-striped suit. From the bank's upper gallery, Mr. Thurston watched the farce play out before his amused gaze.

Lindsey smiled at Mr. Mason as she rose carefully from her chair. "Right this way, please."

It was almost too easy.

It took every ounce of Simon's considerable cunning to maintain an attitude of bored aloofness when he spied a worn document headed in ornate script: *The State of New York, Deed of Ownership*. His hands shook slightly as he lifted the paper from among other contents that might have drawn his attention at any other time – gold and silver coins, what appeared to be jewelry boxes, and a ring of keys. Simon tucked the paper in his inside breast pocket, took brief leave of Miss Morton, and walked straight out of the bank into a golden future.

"Hello… Oh, hello, Mr. Thurston." Aletha spoke on Gert's cell phone, not wanting to disturb the obviously rigged land line until its purpose was fully disclosed. "My *nephew*, you say… And Miss Morton allowed him access as we arranged?... No, I really don't know what it means precisely, but I believe I may receive a visit very shortly from someone I haven't seen in… a number of years."

As Aletha returned Gert's phone, her agitated manner caused her friend to take umbrage with whoever was responsible for causing it. Unmasking the villainous Simon Atherton had seemed like a game until Prince's death, but Aletha was handling that better than might have been expected with the help of Scout. No, there was something else – a deep-seated, long-buried shadow that was creeping over Aletha's heart. Gert would have done anything to spare her old chum more suffering, though she didn't know how that was possible without being able to identify its source. But at least she would be there to stand by Aletha through whatever was to come.

Simon Atherton waited impatiently in the antechamber outside the great Miles Hawthorne's office. Miss Limstock had called her employer to inform him of Mr. Atherton's arrival then prepared to leave for the weekend.

"Mr. Hawthorne will show you in shortly. I trust you will enjoy a pleasant evening." Her manner was cold and brisk. Simon wasted none of his charm on her behalf as he had on his first visit. He had no thought for anything but the two documents he held in his possession and the enormous wealth they represented.

It was fifteen minutes before Miles Hawthorne opened the door and bid Simon enter. Neither extended a hand in greeting because neither expected nor welcomed it. Simon took little notice of the lush appointments of the penthouse office he had enjoyed nearly a month earlier. He stood squarely in front of Hawthorne, whose calculating expression appeared more set and unyielding than usual.

"I see you are, as am I, inclined to dispense with pleasantries. The document please," Hawthorne said coldly, reaching out in expectation. As

Simon placed the deed in his host's outstretched hand, he noticed that Hawthorne had begun to breathe a little faster. Moving to sit behind his imposing desk, he carefully removed the paper from its protective envelope and unfolded it. Just so might great scholars have reverently scrutinized the Scrolls of Qumran. But their reverent awe would never have transformed into astonished shock and dismay, much less in a matter of seconds.

Hawthorne's face, suffused with rage, stared in disbelief at the paper as the bewildered P.I. waited in trepidation for he knew not what. He hadn't long to wait.

"You fool! *You blundering, ignorant fool!* Did you never *read* this before daring to present it to me?"

"I'm no legal expert, *sir*, but it looked like a deed for land in New York City to me. I didn't exactly think you'd want me to seek authentication from Mrs. Mason," he added sarcastically, needled by Hawthorne's unexplained fury.

"You could have sought authentication from a *kindergarten teacher*, you dolt!" Hawthorne crumpled the paper in a ball, walked around his desk, and threw it in Simon's face.

Simon, still completely at sea, drew back instinctively, his fists clenched and his teeth set.

"Oh, I wouldn't advise that, my moronic friend. I have never felt nearer to murdering a man with my bare hands." Hawthorne almost spat the words in Simon's face. Gaining control of himself by a supreme effort, he walked to the window and into the past. After several minutes of silence, he finally spoke, in a bitter, introspective tone.

"That worthless *copied* piece of paper represents the land my father acquired to erect his company's first factory for the manufacture of electronic devices. It was in the mid-1960s, and TVs were already in every household, but people wanted to create their own version of the world. Transistor radios were quickly replaced by cassette tape players allowing everyone to become their own disc jockey. They could listen to music and forget the struggles of life for a while.

"I grew up listening to him extol the virtues of starting a business from the ground up through trial and error, success and failure, and the guiding hand of Providence. Dear old Dad was very business savvy, whether by his own merit or through the blessings of a beneficent Almighty. He had a sort of sixth sense about where product demand and the 'next big thing' would optimally intersect. That turned out to be microwaves and gourmet coffee machines.

"By the time I earned my MBA, he owned a Fortune 500 company, but he only offered me, *me* – a graduate of *Columbus Business School*, a paltry entry level position working *on the assembly line*. Oh, I was to progress by slow stages to ordering supplies, overseeing benefits packages in Human Resources, studying *under* the supervision of engineers in product development. My own father treated me like a drudge! So, I decided if I couldn't take my rightful place as a Vice President, I wanted no part of it. My mother sold the company after he died, but she held onto that worthless scrap of memory…"

"Your *mother*, I believe you said." Simon sneered at Hawthorne's unthinking disclosure. Turning to confront a cockier Simon, Hawthorne watched him draw a second envelope from his breast pocket. "You don't mean the same mother that you've tried to chouse out of a certain deed?" Noting Hawthorne's wary expression, he continued smoothly. "Now I wonder what the local press would pay to get wind of as ruthless a land deal as this city has seen in years." He spoke with great cunning and self-assurance.

Hawthorne said nothing. He merely held out his hand as before. Simon placed the second document in the outstretched hand with little concern. He had had several certified copies made before coming to Hawthorne's office. The false nature of the land deed had substantially deflated his confidence, but he knew he had the upper hand now. "'The State of New

York records the birth of a son to James and *Aletha* Hawthorne' I believe it reads. I can see the headlines now," he said, as if reading a large banner, "'Local businessman cheats elderly mother out of fabulous wealth in underhanded land deal.' It has a sort of ring to it, don't you think?" Simon smirked at Hawthorne, who merely sat quietly, perusing the 55-year-old birth certificate.

"I suppose it was still in the scrapbook with all my baby pictures," Hawthorne commented, glancing at Simon after seating himself once more at his desk. His manner-of-fact statement chiseled away at Simon's cocksure underpinnings.

Hawthorne continued in a voice almost devoid of emotion. "I don't think the press, local or otherwise, will pay you a red cent for such a story. I'm afraid you've overestimated your cleverness, you imbecile." The next words were spoken with decidedly more than a hint of disgust. "I walked away from my father's company and built... all of this," he said, his arms extended in a sweeping gesture, "with my ultimate success resting on the acquisition of a single piece of paper. I can't very well cheat my mother out of a land deal that *won't go through* without the deed that *you*, in your supreme incompetence, *failed to locate.*" Miles Hawthorne finally stood, his rising ire unchecked. "*Now can I?*" he yelled as he pounded his fist on the desk.

Simon felt the earth crumbling under his feet. He had nothing. The deed was worthless. The birth certificate was worthless. A month of tedium, insult, boredom, and botched plans for... nothing.

Hawthorne's voice, now a weapon of white-hot steel, shouted, "*Get out, you bungling idiot!*" When Simon, in a state of numb incredulity, failed to move, Hawthorne shouted even louder, "*Get out of my office!*" He grabbed the still immobile P.I. and pushed him toward the door. "You've wasted over three precious weeks, and now I'll see to it that you're *finished* in this town," he called after Simon, as he shoved the younger man through the open door. "*Finished!*" It took him several minutes to calm down enough to see through his blind rage. When he did, he observed the unruffled Miss Limstock sitting at her desk.

"I thought it best to postpone my departure in case you needed me for anything else this evening," she said calmly. "I waited until the young gentleman entered your office, then I returned to mine. Now, how can I be of service, sir?"

Hawthorne stood dumbfounded for a full minute. Then he felt a deep rumble in his abdomen that worked its way up his throat until it erupted into a shout of uncontrolled, hollow laughter, as surprising to him as it was to his shocked secretary.

"What would I do without the estimable Miss Limstock?" Noting her look of amazement, he rallied his wits and gave her succinct instructions. "With any luck I will return on Monday." He looked back as he walked toward his office and asked, "Everything is laid on for the investor's meeting tomorrow evening?" She answered with a dignified, if unnecessary, nod. Reentering his office, Miles frowned and said under his breath, "It's a pity my mother couldn't have been more like Miss Limstock."

CHAPTER 4

*The tempest comes out from its chamber, the cold from
the driving winds.*

Job 37:9, NIV

Women! Miles Hawthorne thought bitterly. Women had been the bane of his existence since striking out on his own. He had only ever loved two members of the fairer sex. One had cut him out of his inheritance and the other had cut him out of her heart. As he idly watched the elevated view of the metropolis fade away into open fields and smaller outcroppings of civilization, then disappear altogether under dense cloud cover, he allowed his mind to wander. His thoughts slipped back over thirty years to a time when he admired and trusted women.

Miles sipped a glass of champagne in the First-Class cabin of a plane bound for Kansas City, Missouri. It was a step he had hoped never to take. His mother, Aletha Hawthorne, nee Strong had loved him, supported him, and encouraged him through all the pitfalls of childhood and adolescence. She had also been a devoted wife. In the end, when Miles had needed her backing the most, she had deserted him to side with his father, James. It was they who had sent him to the best schools, ensuring he had a stellar education and all the tools necessary to make a mark for himself in life. Then, despite his gilt-edged pedigree, both had agreed that he should start at the bottom rung of the employment ladder, even in the family's own business.

How could she, who praised me for my intelligence and potential, stand with my father and tell me that I would appreciate success more if I had to earn it myself? Madness! thought Miles. *So many wasted years.*

Their decision had only made him more determined to show them he didn't need their help. He would make it on his own – he and his beloved bride.

His parents had both approved of his marriage choice and had loved her in her own right. But then, there was nothing unlovable about her. A sweet, caring disposition, an unwavering faith in a loving God – though Miles' parents had placed more value on that quality than he had – and a naïve belief in the inherent value of all people were her defining characteristics. She, too, had been a devoted wife. She adored her charismatic, driven young husband and tried to support him – even when he started to make less than honorable decisions about how to achieve wealth and advancement – though her devotion had only lasted so long. As Miles began to make a name for himself, to open doors for their future prosperity, she began to slowly withdrawn from him until one terrible night when he came home to find her packing her bags to leave him. He still remembered the anguish on her beautiful face, but he had long since relinquished any responsibility for putting it there. He only remembered his grief at her defection.

That unforgiveable act was the impetus that had sent him headlong into decades of non-stop deals, backroom negotiations, buying, selling, and emerging triumphant at any cost. Finally, he reached the summit of success. Miles Hawthorne was a force to be reckoned with in the business world – either through fear or respect. There had been other women along the way, but none that ever held a place in his heart. They had provided services for which they were amply rewarded. He required a hostess, a partner to share his bed, and they required money and jewels and all the trappings association with a wealthy man entailed. But when their acquisitive demands began to outstrip his patience, or he became bored with their commonplace offerings, he severed the relationships, usually long before there could be a claim for common law marriage. He had seen too many of his associates caught in the cyclical trap of marriage, divorce, and alimony to allow himself to again become so entangled. Though, to her credit, Miles admitted grudgingly, the wife of his youth had never asked anything of him – except his release. In all the intervening years, he had never been lonely, but at his core, he had always known himself to be completely alone.

He may have cut himself off from his family, but he had never fully let go of the emotions that bound them, however deep they were buried. When he heard Simon Atherton refer so callously to Aletha's blindness, the words struck at the very core of her unsuspecting son. He had suffered an unfamiliar twinge of conscience knowing she had had to walk into that darkness without any support from her only child. And when he learned of the death of her companion dog, another such twinge almost forced him into a decisive response, but his investors were breathing down his neck, so he had given Simon one last chance to find the deed, thereby negating any need to ever face his mother again. Simon had failed and therefore, so had Miles. He wondered if she would even know him now. Perhaps he could pass himself off as a company representative…

Sunday morning dawned hot and muggy with barely a breath of wind. Since all the set-up for the church picnic had been completed the day before, the ladies of *Fern Cottage* headed off to church with great anticipation of the day's festivities. The start time was set for one o'clock, allowing all the participants time to change clothes and pick up food after church before making their way to the big house. Derek and Abe directed parking in the large open field directly in front of the main façade, adjacent to the old, overgrown lane.

Rose stood at the gate of the picket fence bordering the front of the yard, freshly painted the day before. The exclamations of delight and wonder at the garden's transformation lifted an already greatly healed heart. As she greeted one new friend after another, she almost felt as if she was welcoming people to her home, and she allowed her fancy to picture just such a scenario: her children running under more mature shade trees, Granny Gert and Aletha sharing a swing on the veranda, and her husband walking toward her, impatient for her welcoming embrace. As he drew nearer, she still couldn't make out his features when suddenly Simon Atherton's face intruded on her thoughts, and she was jarred out of her pleasant reverie.

"Rose, are you okay? You look as if you'd seen a ghost," said Amy Walker as she approached her new friend.

"I'm sorry. I was just daydreaming. I'm fine – really." Amy accepted the response with some doubt. Since most everyone had arrived by then, she was able to convince Rose to walk with her to the food tent so she could drop off an enormous batch of potato salad in an old crockery bowl.

"Can you believe it? The bowl *and* the recipe are my grandmother's. I hope everybody's hungry. What would I do with all the leftovers?"

Rose said airily, "You could always invite Abe over to finish them off." Amy laughed a little self-consciously, while secretly applauding the suggestion.

The 12-foot canopy could only handle two long tables laden with everything from ham and fried chicken to baked beans, green beans and three bean salad. Various other salads, including the contents of Amy's big crock shared space with homemade biscuits, rolls, and sweet potato casserole topped with marshmallows. All the desserts were on display under the covering shade of the wrap around porch, now repaired and safe for foot traffic. The hot, midday sun was thankfully obscured by a building bank of clouds, so that dining conditions, even for those in lawn chairs or blankets spread around the yard, were fairly pleasant. Tim had placed an additional table and folding chairs beneath the spreading limbs of the willow tree. The table of honor was reserved for Aletha and the senior members of the church, and the briefcase of reimbursement cash was stashed underneath the table with Scout on guard duty.

The big house hadn't seen so much life and activity in over fifty years; not since Martin Mason had left the family home behind to follow his dreams and make a name for himself in the field of Agricultural Engineering and manufacturing. Rose could almost imagine that the grand old lady rising majestically above them was smiling down on the society gathered there.

When Rose was able to snatch a few moments alone with Tim on an unoccupied corner of the veranda the previous day, she had convinced him to set up a circle of lawn chairs for the young singles by the Japanese Wisteria.

"We've got to make sure there's an empty chair next to Abe tomorrow so Amy can sit there," she whispered to her fellow conspirator.

"Why are we whispering?" Tim asked, taking great delight in Rose's cloak and dagger air.

"Because they're both here today, and you never know when one of them will sneak up on us," she responded, keeping her eye on the lookout for either party.

"Okay, Mata Hari. If I have to, I'll toss whoever's sitting there when I see you two coming. Is that devious enough?" Rose had directed an adorable, exaggerated wink at him before intercepting Amy who was approaching from the other side of the porch.

True to his word, Tim had arranged the chairs as directed, and when Derek sat on one side of Abe, he planted himself on the other side until Rose and Amy approached from the food tent, loaded with plates and cups. Tim jumped up to help them, strategically guiding Rose to two adjacent seats, leaving only his vacated one for Amy. It was done so smoothly that she was left in doubt as to whether it was luck or a provident plan that placed her squarely in Abe's orbit. And since she chose to glance at Rose at the precise moment she turned to Tim to congratulate him on a flawless execution, Amy failed to catch any guilty expression on her friend's face, so she happily decided to err on the side of luck.

Rose sat quietly, content to listen to the usual comical dialogue between the three men, their outrageous banter producing an endless stream of laughter. She was especially pleased that Amy kept up her end in the conversation, inserting a few zingers of her own. The prior week had brought many similar moments of happiness and healing. Other than the unexpected reminder of Simon at the café and the odd encounter with the stranger in the bank to jar her fragile, newfound serenity, Rose had begun to enjoy the reality of life. She found it far more satisfying than wandering through a dreamlike fabrication. She had made a new friend, gotten involved with church event planning, and best of all, been introduced to the past *and* the future of the big house by her dearest friend. In fact, the only cloud looming on Rose's immediate horizon was the prospect of saying goodbye to Tim in six weeks. She would miss them all, but Tim was special. She couldn't say why, but she knew instinctively that theirs was a unique bond.

On the previous Thursday, when they met after delivering their respective charges to the Community Hall for Bingo Night, Tim had suggested that, rather than participate in what had become their weekly battle, they go to his place. He wanted to show Rose the original plans for the Victorian mansion and some preliminary sketches for his renovation ideas. Receiving Granny Gert's blessing, they spent two hours poring over the plans, with Rose contributing her mite. Tim was impressed by her quick grasp of his vision and even admitted that several of her suggestions actually improved on his original proposals. He reassured her several times that they would begin work on the house as soon as an added crew was in place, and he could focus his attention on the main project. He spoke in such earnest that Rose felt the need to reassure *him,* reminding him to take care of his business and not worry about her. She wasn't going anywhere in the immediate future. *If only that were true,* Tim thought. Both felt compelled to begin the project soon. Tim knew why. Rose only sensed that the success of the venture was somehow inexplicably tied to the success of her own future.

A burgeoning wind broke the stillness of the afternoon and the stream of thoughts passing through her mind. The breeze brought welcome relief from the stagnant air, but it also heralded the threat of a storm forecast for early evening. Diligent picnic organizers had duly checked the latest weather map that morning and all believed the day to be safe from interruption. The organized games were in full swing with winners announced periodically over the P.A. system. Kids and dogs ran hither and yon all over the lawn, but they managed to avoid the flower beds. The little girls, however, knelt beside the beautiful displays, admiring the wondrous color palette. What they didn't see was the flutter of hummingbirds or any of their winged cousins who had been largely absent all day.

The ladies under the willow tree chatted happily while the older men kept a weather eye on the sky to the southwest. Pastor Lindeman may have assured them that the worst of the elements would hold for a few more hours, but those who had repeatedly lived through the destructive power of a Kansas tornado weren't convinced.

Tim and Rose vied for honors in the three-legged race against Abe and Amy while Derek provided commentary from the sidelines. Marilyn and Angelica held the tape across the finish line. Granny Gert watched from the willow tree, giving Aletha a blow-by-blow account of the competition while they congratulated each other on the success of their matchmaking schemes. It was a perfect moment in time – a perfect gathering of family and friends in a perfect setting. And a prequel to the perfect storm.

*****

Miles Hawthorne set out for Tinkers Well despite words of caution from the service personnel at the rental car agency warning him of severe weather to the west. "I'm afraid I don't have time to waste waiting on the directional quirks of a storm. It may as easily break up or change direction. My business is far too urgent."

The young lady behind the counter looked at her co-worker and shook her head. "Can you say, '*He's not from around here.*'?"

Miles, intent on his mission and unsure of his reception, barely noticed the gathering clouds. Since he only had Simon's sketchy report descriptions of *Fern Cottage* and the larger main house to go by, he expected to find a serene setting in which a handful of women would be enjoying the quiet of a Sunday afternoon. When he arrived to find a large Victorian house almost overrun by an even larger group of strangers, he was not pleased. The last thing he desired was an audience for a completely unscripted, problematic meeting. He parked in the field, as seemed to be indicated, and removed his suitcoat and tie. In a tailored business suit, Miles would hardly blend into a crowd clad predominantly in shorts and T-shirts; no need to stand out any more than necessary. Rolling up his shirt sleeves, he moved into the milieu, conscious of curious glances in his direction. He walked around the less populated west side of the house just in time to see a young couple lunge across a finish line, tumbling into a laughing heap on the ground as those around them cheered. As he approached one of the women holding the remains of the tape, with her back to him, his and every other cell phone on the property went off simultaneously in a cacophony of sound that silenced everyone immediately. They collectively grabbed their phones then looked at each other, all signs of humor gone.

The young man of the sack race said, "The storm is moving a lot faster than predicted. We've got to get everyone out of here. Now!" he yelled and preceded to bark out orders like one born to command. Miles would have beat a hasty retreat to his vehicle, opting to return later, but someone grabbed him, pulling him in the direction of the seating tent, and told him to start loading chairs into the back of a waiting trailer. Men began razing the tent almost before the tables and chairs were removed. Women grabbed children and dishes, scrambling to load everything into their cars. Lawn chairs landed willy-nilly into the back of the closest truck, regardless of who owned it. Miles could see several elderly people being helped into cars, but he didn't have time to identify his mother. He had been summarily recruited to collect all the box fans, and the cords that powered them, with instructions to stow them in a van already stuffed with picnic paraphernalia.

From a distance, Miles could see the imperious young man, standing with an African American peer and one of what appeared to be Middle Eastern decent, telling everyone to "grab what you can and get the heck out of here!" The words were increasingly difficult to hear over the growing rumble from an approaching wall of clouds.

"Those of you who live in town should have plenty of time to get your families safely home, or to the church basement, but if you live west of here, you'll just have to ride out the storm in Aletha's cellar. You can park your cars in the garage. It may at least spare them hail damage – if it's still standing later."

Miles had no intention of gambling with the whims of Mother Nature in one of her angrier moments, so after grabbing his coat from his rental car, he followed the crowds headed for what must be *Fern Cottage*. He felt fairly safe in his anonymity among countless people forced to seek shelter in a crowded undergrown room presumably outfitted with marginal lighting. His dubious reunion would have to wait.

At Tim's insistence, Rose helped Granny Gert and Aletha into her car and drove them to *Fern Cottage,* giving no thought to the briefcase of cash under the table. By the time they arrived at the cottage, it had started to rain, so she hurried them inside as quickly as possible, getting them safely ensconced in the cellar before going in search of warm blankets to wrap around them. She had just gotten them calmed down and reassured that everyone would be safe when Aletha called for Scout and found that he was missing.

"Scout!" she called into the darkness. "Scout!" Rose saw the panic rising in the old woman and quickly intervened.

"I'm sure he's just a little disoriented with so many people around. He's probably upstairs looking for *you*," she said, trying to sound positive. "You just stay here with Granny Gert while I fetch him. All right?"

"Thank you, dear. If he's afraid of storms like my Prince was… well, I just don't know what could happen to him." Gert took over the job of chief comforter while Rose made her way back upstairs, feeling like a salmon swimming upstream among frightened families flooding the cellar.

Angelica and Marilyn, who had arrived at the cottage just minutes after Rose and the others, were busy ushering the now wet picnic goers into the cellar while trying to remain calm and cheerful. Each child who passed them received a hug and a reassuring smile. It was as well for Rose's plan that neither had time to give much thought to her. She dug a flashlight out of a kitchen drawer and disappeared out the back door after grabbing a raincoat from a nearby coat peg.

Rose had never really been completely honest with herself over Prince's death. She had been mortified by his *manner* of death and had cried countless tears of real mourning over his loss. But what she had never been able to face was her own self-imposed culpability in Prince's passing. Her saner self admitted that it was Simon alone who was responsible for that heinous act of murder. But her guilty conscience, though much relieved, still nagged at her. It enforced the notion that if she hadn't been such a fool, allowing herself to be led on by his false attentions, Simon might never have known about the daily lives of the *Fern Cottage* inhabitants. He would certainly not have had the opportunity to spend so much time there, searching for who knew what. Rose had witnessed Aletha's devastation at Prince's disappearance. She was not going to allow that to happen a second time. She meant to find Scout if it was the last thing she did.

Stomping their feet and flicking their arms to rid themselves of the worst of the rain before entering the cottage, Tim, Derek, and Abe looked more like bedraggled drowning survivors than able-bodied men. They cleared all the rooms upstairs to make sure they were vacant before joining the crowd in the cellar. Tim made his way over to his mother who was rubbing Aletha's hands, grown cold from wet and worry. He didn't see Rose next to her grandmother or anywhere else in the crowded space.

"Where's Rose?" Tim had to shout over the combination of competing voices and the growing roar from outside.

"Aletha told me she went upstairs to find Scout. Apparently, he got separated from Aletha when everyone was rushing to get into cars. Rose thought he was probably upstairs. She hasn't brought him back yet. I assumed she was waiting for you. Didn't you see them when you came in?" Marilyn shouted back.

Even in the dim light, she could see that Tim's face looked blanched. "She must have gone out in the storm to look for him." His mother had to strain to make out his words, but his expression of fear was far more eloquent. "I'm going after her." Marilyn saw his jaw harden and a look of steely determination settle over him, brooking no argument. Tim turned on his heel and stopped just long enough to make Abe and Derek promise they would stay and look after his mom and the others before he bounded up the stairs and out the back door.

Though tornados were not unheard of in Kentucky, Rose had never witnessed such a terrifying event first-hand. Any time severe storms had threatened, her father had insisted everyone move to the basement of their home. She remembered how, as a child, she had spent many nights sleeping on the den couch while raging winds howled outside. Ralph Thompson, alone, had remained awake to keep an anxious watch over his family. As a high school student, she had even participated in a "Homes for Humanity" rebuild project in West Liberty with her dad. An F3 tornado had cut a path through the center of the small Kentucky town, destroying several homes and businesses and leveling a church. The aftermath of that storm had been sobering enough. Now Rose confronted just such a force of nature head on.

She was immediately hit by a torrent of rain when she stepped out of the sheltering walls of the cottage. Even the thick rubber raincoat couldn't fully protect her from the punishing onslaught. She made it around to the front of the house where the east facing covered porch provided a modicum of protection. She called Scout's name, but the single syllable was engulfed by the swirling wind. Though It was only three o'clock in the afternoon, the sky had turned a dark, eerie shade of green. As she made her way to the line of trees along the driveway, in the hope that they would give her a semblance of direction, she looked over her shoulder to see a huge block of black clouds blotting out the sun. Terrified by the menacing spectacle, she was about to turn back when she thought she heard a dog bark.

"Scout! Scout! Is that you?" Rose called into the darkness, her flashlight barely cutting through the gloom. She heard another bark. *Was that from the end of the drive? Why does he not come closer?*

She moved from tree to tree and followed the sound until it seemed to veer to the left, away from the security of the driveway, into a dark unknown. She had to keep her head down against the lashing wind and rain, merely following the feeble light from her flashlight and the intermittent barking of the dog. When Rose finally looked up, she found that she had stumbled across the main drive, pushed by the wind into the line of Spartan junipers lining the edge of the yard on the west side of the big house. Lifting her flashlight, she saw the newly planted weeping willow bent double before it rose up in a frantic dance of swaying branches, then bowed once more to a powerful downdraft. Almost immobile with fear from the sights and sounds that drowned out her very thoughts, she heard Scout bark again.

Suddenly, she remembered the entrance to the storm cellar next to the kitchen porch on the northeast corner. Maybe some instinct had led Scout to that haven of safety. He had spent much time on the grounds with Abe and Derek. He may even have followed them down into the cellar on a tour of inspection.

Now who was rescuing whom? Rose gave thanks for the innate wisdom of her canine friend and crawled on all fours until she reached the cellar doors. It was an entrance built in the style of its day with double doors on an incline granting outside access to the underground foundation. One of the doors was laid back, and as she listened, she could hear Scout whining at the base of the interior stairs. She nearly cried with relief at the sound. Shining her light into the darkness beneath her, Rose began a wary descent into the gaping chasm.

"Dear God in Heaven, please keep her safe." Tim prayed the words repeatedly as he once again made his way into the storm, well aware that it could very well be his death sentence. But knowing that Rose was alone, and trying to fend for herself in the horror of a very real nightmare, was infinitely worse than the prospect of his own death. He struck out in the direction of the main house, sure that she would first look for Scout in the place she had last seen him. Tim switched off his flashlight for a few seconds, hoping to see another light somewhere in front of him, but the darkness was complete. No one at the cottage knew when Rose had left so there was no telling how much of a lead she had on him.

He followed the edge of the drive to keep his bearings, holding his arm across his forehead to allow optimal visibility against the slashing rain that turned to pelting hail when the temperature dropped precipitately. While he made painstakingly slow progress across the front of the house to the garden area where Aletha had been sitting, Tim suddenly felt the hail stop and the wind drop to an absolute calm. He looked sharply to the west and saw a massive funnel cloud moving across the open landscape with a sound like the roar of a freight train announcing its devastating approach. Tim was nearly disabled by a crippling fear – not for himself, but for Rose who was out there somewhere, vulnerable to the unchecked appetite of a monster of destruction. In his desperation he took one more frantic look around the yard and saw a light – a bright, glorious light – coming through an air vent in the stone foundation of the house. He had made sure all the power was turned off to the house before leaving the grounds during the evacuation, yet there was a light shining like a beacon. It could only be explained by the presence of a flashlight. Tim ran around to the back of the house and saw a single door to the storm cellar laid back like a welcome mat. He started down the stairs.

Rose flashed her light in the direction of the whining sound and spied Scout to her left, hunkered down by a shiny metal support post. She ran to him, speaking words of assurance.

"Scout, how did you get down here?"

Laying her flashlight on the ground, she hugged him while he frantically tried to lick her face, his tail wagging madly. When she sat back on her heels to stroke his damp coat, she made two curious discoveries. Scout was tied to the post, and a powerful battery powered lantern sat next to the foundation wall six feet away where there had been darkness only moments before. Struggling to process the full significance of the nonsensical details, Rose felt, rather than saw, the same concentrated evil she had experienced at the bank once again boring into her from the shadows.

"Hello, Rose." The dulcet voice, smooth as velvet, floated through the darkness, sending a chill down her spine. She made a frenzied attempt to untie Scout, but her shaking fingers were numb with fear.

"We can't have that now, can we, my sweet." Rose flinched as Simon Atherton pulled her hands away from Scout's collar. He hauled her roughly to her feet and forced her against the support post, his face only inches from hers with his back to the cellar steps. His breath reeked of alcohol.

Forcing herself to look at him, Rose thought her eyes were playing tricks on her in the lantern light. The voice was Simon's, but the face belonged to a stranger. Lindsey Morton would have recognized Allan Pinkerton immediately, another of Simon's aliases. Rose watched in fascinated horror as Simon slowly pulled off the false mustache and goatee, then removed the thick, blond wig, shaking his own short brown hair into place. He finished his transformation by peeling the deeply tinted blue contacts from his eyes.

"I thought I might blend in better at your little soiree as one of my alter egos. It seems I was successful. While you stood at the gate, greeting everyone like you were the Queen of the May, I walked past you and looked you directly in the eye. That shook you, but I'll wager you thought you were imagining things. You are, after all, so good at that."

"So *that's* why I thought of…" Rose began softly as the mental clouds cleared.

Simon laughed and tilted her head upwards with a commanding finger, then took her chin in a vice-like grip, forcing her to look at him. "Oh, you won't soon forget Simon Atherton. In fact, I can guarantee it," he added in a voice as hard as the stone that surrounded them. "Because of you, I had a league of suspicious women watching my every move. Because of you, I had to act circumspectly where any other woman would have fallen into my arms. That cost me precious time I could ill-afford. Because of you, my efforts to create a diversion for Ms. Morton came to naught. It was you who warned the blind woman against me, wasn't it? It was you who discovered I had tampered with the phone and you who led me to believe, falsely, that the cottage would be vacant the night that beastly wolf attacked me."

Rose tried in vain to deny the charges against her. But Simon had traveled too far down the path of irrational reflection to listen to any kind of reason.

"Because of you, I failed in my mission, costing me a substantial retainer, my reputation, and my livelihood. Because of you, I received a comprehensive beating from your muscle-bound boyfriend after you refused me – *Me!* I offered you – a priggish little bore – an introduction to the tantalizing realm of sensual pleasure, and you shoved me aside." Simon tightened his grip, causing her to wince in pain. "*No one* gets the better of Simon Atherton. I came all the way back from New York to this hell hole to exact my revenge."

Every instinct she possessed shrieked at Rose to fight back, but she was paralyzed into immobility by the searing evil in his eyes and the hypnotic timbre of his voice. Scout howled in frustration, pulling against the tight leash that bound him to the same prison Rose was forced against by Simon's body.

"Now I will take from you what you foolishly withheld from me." As he spoke, Simon slid the dripping raincoat off her shoulders and cast it aside to disappear into the impenetrable gloom of a far corner. Then he grabbed her sodden shirt and ripped it from top to bottom while running his mouth up and down her bare neck, his teeth exposed. The suddenness of the attack, coupled with the pain and revulsion of his touch, finally broke through her inertia. Rose started screaming and fighting back with her hands, her knees – anything that would keep the madman at bay. But even as she grasped the futility of her struggle, Simon's groping hands left her abruptly when he was spun around to receive a punishing blow to the jaw that sent him flying through the air to land in a heap ten feet away.

Though his head rang from the impact of the punch, Simon scrambled to his feet and rushed at his assailant, the lantern beam capturing the sheen from a blade in his right hand.

"Tim, he has a knife!" Rose yelled before sliding to the floor, her unsteady legs no longer able to support her. The warning came a split second too late. The sharp point missed Tim's abdomen when he stepped backwards, but the upward thrust cut deep into the muscle of his left upper arm. Tim grabbed Simon's right hand, squeezing the wrist until the knife fell to the ground then hit him across the jaw dispatching him to the dirt a second time. With his chest heaving, Tim watched Simon for a few seconds, ready for another attack, but Simon lay still. Believing his adversary to be permanently grounded, and almost out of his mind with worry for Rose, Tim turned toward her.

Through a tiny gap in his thick lashes, Simon saw Tim move away. In no mood to surrender tamely, and suddenly possessed with the strength born of an all-consuming hatred, he grabbed a heavy board laying near at hand with other discarded construction materials and crept up behind Tim. Fortunately, Tim's years of training in combat had developed in him a sixth sense for danger. In the act of bending down toward Rose, he heard the almost imperceptible sound of Simon's approach and straightened up to face him. The blow, aimed for the back of Tim's head hit him squarely across the back of the neck and shoulders instead. The movement probably saved his life, but the impact of a board wielded by a madman caused Tim's knees to buckle. He landed at Rose's feet, stunned and fighting to retain consciousness.

She was so intent on the battle raging around her amid the storm raging outside that Scout's silence went unnoticed. When Tim fell to his knees next to her, she instinctively moved between him and Simon, who had raised the board to strike again. An expression of unholy glee lit his face.

"No, Simon! *Please!*" She braced for the attack, willing to risk everything for Tim's sake because… because…

In a blinding flash, all the fragments of their relationship – their easy comradery, their shared vision, all the little kindnesses and mutual burdens – fell into one, crystal clear, indisputable truth for Rose. *I love him!*

The knowledge of her feelings, so long hidden from her by Simon's lies and her own emotional blinders, filled her with righteous anger. Simon had taken enough from her. Rose would not let him rob her of what she had sought for so long. For Tim represented not just romantic love, but a partnership in a future she believed in.

Her fear dissipated in that instant of absolute clarity. She drew her foot back and kicked Simon in the knee as hard as she could. It was all that was needed to disarm him. He dropped the board on Rose, but it lacked the momentum to do more than bruise her. He grabbed his throbbing leg, hopping around like a one-legged stork and cursing in cockney slang that she didn't understand – nor cared to. Scrambling to her feet, board in hand, she was ready to take on a world of Simon's if necessary. She might have saved herself the effort, for in a twinkling Scout finally chewed through the last strand of the leash that bound him. He rushed at Simon, knocking him down, and started barking ferociously enough to be heard over ten storms. Simon shivered at the vicious sound. He should have known the dog would turn out to be a miscalculation.

Earlier, a reckless Simon, bolstered by enough whiskey to give him Dutch courage, had managed to clip a lead onto Scout's collar during the pandemonium that ensued at the end of the picnic. Other dogs added to the chaos with their barking and howling so Simon was able to slip away unnoticed, keeping Scout under control through judicious use of a prod. Now, writhing in pain and fear on the dank earthen floor, he knew the game was up. Though he was no longer master of the situation, he refused to surrender without a final attack. Drawing on the emotional power he still believed to hold over Rose, he bragged of his own cunning while deriding her for her weakness. But he was powerless to penetrate her newfound strength and security. His biting insults failed to cause so much as a flicker of her lovely eyelashes.

"I hid in the garage until 'Field Marshall Ludlow' and his flunkies were engaged in getting rid of the last of the guests, then made a run for the cottage with that godforsaken dog in tow. Oh yes, I snatched the dog, but it took all my efforts to manage him, which meant leaving behind a promising briefcase. Then I waited for you, Rose, the soft-hearted, altruistic fool that you are! I waited in the miserable rain and wind for you to emerge in search of this blasted animal who would surely be missed. By the time I saw you on the front porch, visibility was so bad I felt little care over being spotted and brought you along in short stages, goading the dog when necessary to do his part. It was all so easy, but I should have known you would ruin everything!"

During his impotent tirade, Simon had been dragging himself toward the cellar steps with Scout growling at his heels. In one final, desperate movement, he scrambled up the steps and made good his escape. Just before slamming the cellar door, he yelled against the wind, "I beat you! I win! The three of you can stay down there until you *rot!*"

The last Rose and Tim heard of Simon was the sound of hysterical laughter before the door slammed and the bar was dropped into place.

CHAPTER 5

Rose sat in disbelief, struggling to take in the fact that Simon was really gone. The nightmare was over. And though the thundering storm threatened from without, she felt safe and secure in her shadowy sanctuary, alone with the man who had rescued her a second time. She knew, in that moment, that he would be there to rescue her again and again – the man she had come to depend on as her dearest friend and soulmate. She couldn't stem the flow of tears that came in waves from a heart relieved of care and renewed with the life-affirming knowledge of love in its purest, most selfless form.

While she dragged herself back from contemplation of a bright future to the urgency of the present, Tim faced a more palpable struggle. The searing pain in his neck was almost unbearable, but it was dizziness that caused him to keep his eyes clamped tightly shut. He had found the support pole during the confusion caused by Scout's charge at Simon and managed to pull himself to a standing position, leaning against the solid metal for balance.

"Rose?" He heard nothing but soft weeping. "Rose?" He called sharply. "Sweetheart, I can't see you. Are you hurt?" He reached out his hands, desperate to find her.

"I'm here," she said and moved quickly to stand before him, placing her hands in his. "And other than a few bruises, I've never felt better in my life," she said through her tears. Reaching up to caress the hard line of his jaw, she said softly, "Say it again. You know, the word right before 'I can't see you.'"

Ignoring the intense throbbing in his neck and shoulders, Tim performed a colossal effort at memory, and whispered, "Sweetheart?" *Am I dreaming?*

"Say it again."

"Sweetheart. *My* sweetheart," Tim said in a voice thick with emotion. He forced his aching eyes open and looked into Rose's upturned face, glowing in the lantern light.

"I'm sorry it took me so long to figure it out. In fact," she said on a short laugh, "I didn't know until… Simon…" Tears of shame suddenly filled her eyes, and she looked away. Swallowing a lump in her throat, she looked at Tim once more and continued, "…until he raised the board to strike you again. I know he hurt you through me, and I… I just couldn't let him hurt you anymore. That's when I *knew.* So, *yes,* my love. *Your* sweetheart."

Tim emitted a single cry of joyful wonder and pulled Rose into his arms in a crushing embrace, burying his face against her shoulder. She gently caressed the back of his neck, sending shivers of pure delight down his spine, and momentarily blotting out the palpitating pain. He turned his face toward her cheek and found her lips through the supremely satisfying process of trial and error, closing eyes that still burned to lose himself in a miraculous moment of shared discovery. There are rare instances when sight is superfluous.

Scout, wagging his tail with the ferocity of a great warrior who has successfully routed the enemy, found the ensuing activity in the cellar quite tame. He lay down at the couple's feet, rather bored by the young lovers, but content to watch over them whether they noticed him or not.

Tim conveyed in that first kiss all the love, pent up desire, doubt and worry of the past three weeks. Rose knew no hesitation, having consigned to distant memory her resolution to be more guarded in response to any suitors following in Simon's disastrous wake. She answered Tim with unwavering certainty and assurance. When at last he lifted his head, he could see his darling Rose clearly. Tears of relief and happiness had worked their miracle.

"I love you, Rose Thompson," he whispered in her ear and laid his cheek against the velvet softness of her skin.

"I love *you*, and *only* you, Tim Ludlow. With all my heart."

Minutes later, they drew apart again, both shaken by their reaction to one another. He gently brushed the now dry ringlets away from her face then rested his forehead against hers. When he opened his downcast eyes, he abruptly dropped his arms and stepped aside, turning deep red from his neck to the top of his head. He moved so quickly he nearly tripped over Scout and was once again assailed by dizziness, forcing him to grab the pole for support.

"Rose, I am *so* sorry. I forgot about… you know," he said gesturing in her general direction.

Shocked out of her dreamlike state by Tim's hasty retreat, she looked down and was scandalized by the open display of her lacey undergarment exposed by Simon's earlier attack. She immediately turned her back on Tim to hide her own embarrassment. "Oh, my Gosh! I completely forgot about… you know… too."

"Here," he said, "take my shirt. You have more need of it than – " He stopped short, immediately reminded of the gash in his arm still oozing blood. Rose couldn't help turning around at his quick intake of breath. She experienced a moment of queasiness as she looked at the arm covered in blood – the same arm that had embraced her so tenderly just moments before.

"Oh, Tim. Your *arm*," she cried out in concern. She hurried up behind him and took the shirt held out to her. Quickly donning it, she tore what was left of her own into long strips. "Come sit on the steps so I can bandage that cut. Maybe you should lean against the stone. You don't look too good."

Rose steeled herself to pack the wound and wrap it tightly, trying not to notice when he flinched involuntarily. At least her work helped her avoid looking at the distraction of his bared torso. The pair inhabited a world so far removed from the torrent raging around them that the shaking of the cellar doors above their heads barely registered. All of her concentration was directed at trying to staunch the bleeding with as little additional pain inflicted on Tim as possible.

When she completed her task, he said, in an oddly weak voice, "Now I don't want you to worry, honey, but I think the loss of blood and aftermath of the adrenaline rush from the storm… and the fight… and us… I'm feeling a little… light-headed. Could you just… sit on the step below me – "

Rose had no sooner taken her place, than Tim fell heavily against her, his face as white as a sheet.

The crowd of roughly 30 people huddled in Aletha's cellar kept an almost silent vigil over their loved ones, partly from the daunting power of fear, and partly because it was difficult to hear anything over the roar from without. Even the normally boisterous children stood clinging mutely to their parents for comfort, some crying softly in an uncertainty they didn't understand. Miles Hawthorne made his way to a corner and sat on an old shipping crate, his face mostly obscured by the coat he held over his head. No one took any notice of him. They were all focused on their families and their own circle of friends. Each inhabited a tiny universe where that which was dearest to them was within arm's reach. For 20 minutes they waited, while the savagery of nature grew around them until it sounded as if it would devour even those who had sought shelter from its ravaging power. Nearby power lines became obvious victims of the storm. Overhead fixtures flickered and died, leaving only the glare from cell phones to create tiny beacons of light in the smothering darkness. The almost deafening roar gradually abated, and the sound of heavy rain blown by lesser winds was all that could be heard until the tornado blew itself out some four miles away.

Noting Gert and Aletha's expressions, which reflected shattered nerves and emotional exhaustion, Derek thought it best to allow guests to leave the cellar first so that he and Abe could help the ladies upstairs slowly. When Aletha's steps faltered, he simply picked her up in his arms as if she weighed less than a feather and carried her to her chair in the living room. Gert stumped up the stairs after her friend and collapsed on the couch. Marilyn brought a footstool for Aletha and wrapped her again in a warm blanket while Angelica tried to coax Gert to lay down. But the stubborn old woman refused, asking who would help her go out and look for Rose.

Just then Derek returned from firing up the generator, restoring power to the house. He looked at Abe who knew as well as he did that their search could either end in futility or horror. The two men tried to dissuade Granny Gert from leaving, explaining that they didn't even know if a vehicle had survived to carry her in. But she was adamant. She waited, sitting bolt upright, until she heard Derek drive up to the cottage. Thanks to knowledge of an extra key hidden under the dashboard of Tim's truck, it was the big crew cab pickup with 4-wheel drive that waited outside. Derek felt relieved when his mother insisted she go with them, but he didn't hold out much hope for a happy ending to their search.

Meanwhile, Miles, having left the cottage amid the same crowd that hid his entrance, found his rental car intact but liberally dented from the hailstorm. The windshield was cracked in several places, but the engine turned over. He followed the line of other survivors who had left their vehicles parked in the field, fishtailing a few times on the muddy ground before reaching solid pavement. Miles might have looked for somewhere in the nearby town to bide his time before seeking a private audience with his mother, but he met the big white pickup just as it turned up the driveway heading away from the cottage. It looked to be driven by the young black man and the Arab friend he had seen at the picnic. He also recognized a backseat passenger as one of the two women who had held the line tape for the three-legged race. He couldn't see the one beside her clearly, but Miles took a chance on the cottage being vacant except for Aletha.

Parking his car between fallen oak branches, he sat for a few minutes attempting to steady his breathing. Miles had imagined this moment a hundred times on the flight from New York but wasn't sure he was entirely prepared for what would follow. Unfortunately, time was of the essence, so he left the pallid security of the car and knocked on the front door.

"Scout!" Rose called frantically. "Help Tim!"

She wasn't sure how long she could remain upright under Tim's dead weight, but she was determined not to let him fall further forward and possibly injure himself even more. His head had fallen onto her right shoulder, and she reached up to hold it in place, with her elbow wedged against the thick foundation wall. Scout surveyed the situation then ran to her side. He put his front paws on Tim's knee and began licking the portion of his face that was visible. After a few seconds of non-responsiveness, Scout barked repeatedly in Tim's ear and licked the hand dangling at his side. Whether due to the warm touch of the dog's tongue or his ear-splitting yelps, Tim began to come around. It's possible that his head falling forward had allowed the blood to suffuse his upper extremities again. Whatever the reason, he was able to raise his head a few inches, resting his forehead on the top of Rose's head. Drawing his hands up to lay on her shoulders, he concentrated on conscious thought. She still strained under the mass of his body weight, but at least he was partially supporting himself, using her as a prop.

"Rose." His voice was so weak she could barely hear it.

"Tim, tell me what to do."

He swallowed the bile rising in his throat. "Help me to lay back on the steps. I can brace myself against the wall for a few seconds." Rose felt his weight shift. She turned quickly and caught the back of his head before it hit a step above him and lowered it as gently as she could.

"Tim, we're locked in here. I tried my cell phone, but the cell tower must have been damaged by the tornado. I would go for help, but I heard Simon drop the bar in place when he closed the door."

Tim remained silent for so long, Rose was afraid he had blacked out again, but eventually he opened his eyes and looked into the shadows over her shoulder. "Other stairs," he managed.

"Of course!" she said. "The added stairs from *inside* the house that you told me about the other night."

Smiling wanly, Tim whispered, "Good girl."

Rose ran to get the lantern and flashlight she had dropped nearby. Setting the lantern next to Tim, she went on an exploratory tour of the cellar. She found the discarded raincoat and brought it back to Tim, laying it over him like a blanket with the sleeves fashioned into a pillow for his head. Turning once more toward the dark shadows, she caught the outline of stairs with the beam of her flashlight.

"I found it!" she cried with excitement, but Tim only grunted in response. It wasn't until the silence of that moment that she realized the roaring winds outside had subsided, though she could still hear the sound of rain on the cellar doors above them. Leaning close to him, Rose reached out to stroke his brow. It was cold and clammy to her touch.

"Tim, can you hear me?" she asked anxiously.

"Yes," he said without opening his eyes. "I think... the worst of the storm... has passed. You'll have to go... for help."

"I know, but I hate to leave you."

"I'll be okay. But promise me… before you step into the kitchen… look at the ceiling and door frames. If there's any sagging… come back down here… and we'll wait."

"I promise." Rose dropped a kiss on his forehead then turned to speak firmly to Scout. "You stay right here next to Tim and keep him warm," she said, gently touching Tim's abdomen to show Scout where to rest his head. She hoped the dog's warmth would somehow offset the dampness of the stone steps under her wounded hero. When she was satisfied that the two were settled as well as could be expected, she walked purposely to the steps leading up to the ground floor, praying that she would find solid footing.

Miles had prepared himself for tears, recrimination, and manifest heartbreak from his mother. He had even resolved to beg her forgiveness, knowing in his heart of hearts that all the anger he expected he, in fact, had coming. But never in his wildest dreams had he prepared himself to see the door opened by a ghost from the past – a beautiful, kind, loving ghost who had haunted his dreams for 30 years. A ghost whose tender eyes a man could lose himself in. A ghost who had cast a shadow on all subsequent relationships, rendering them hollow and meaningless. He stood like a man turned to stone as he looked into the face of his wife.

Marilyn had gone quickly to answer the knock, hoping anxiously for news of her son. As she opened the door, she thought for a moment that her worried mind was producing hallucinations. There stood a man with the same square jaw and cleft chin, the same piercing blue eyes, the same athletic build, and the same thick hair that distinguished Tim's appearance. But there were fine lines around the eyes and a feathering of gray at the temples. Marilyn stared for a full minute at the newcomer, whispered one word, "Timothy," and would have crumpled in place but for the quick actions of the man who reached out to catch her. The gallant rescue almost came to naught, because he underestimated the effect her presence had had on him.

When he caught her, he found that his own legs had turned to rubber, and they both went down together. He hardly noticed the jarring impact of landing hard on his knees.

"Mari," he whispered as he touched her pale cheek in wonder. Miles Hawthorne felt something stir in the deepest caverns of his soul. It had been so long buried that he didn't even recognize it. An unfamiliar lump formed in his throat as he blinked moisture from his eyes. In the back of his mind, he thought he must have caught cold on the flight out. Marilyn stirred in his arms, opening her eyes to see his face hovering over hers. When the enormity of the moment finally dawned on them, they were both covered in embarrassment. Miles rocked back on his heels to stand, then helped her gently to her feet. But nothing was said. The gulf between them was so vast, mere words seemed futile as a means of traversing it. They might have stood there indefinitely, seeking some means of communicating 30 years of loss, but Aletha called from the living room.

"Marilyn. Marilyn, is that Tim? Did he find Rose?" Though her voice was feeble from strain, Miles recognized it immediately – the voice of the first woman he had loved and the one against whom he had perpetrated the greatest betrayal.

"No, Aletha," Marilyn answered. Her voice sounded odd, even to her ears. "It's... someone we weren't... expecting." She stepped back and bid Miles enter the house. He walked into the tastefully decorated cottage and memories of his childhood home came flooding in. The furniture was different, but the ambience was the same – old world elegance that was at once warm and welcoming. He walked as one in a trance, approaching his mother's chair with increasingly heavy steps.

"Hello, Mother," he said and braced for the anger and resentment that must come.

"Timothy? *My Timothy?*" Completely forgetting her worry over his suspected role in the events of the previous week, Aletha spoke not in anger, but in joyful awe, a smile hovering on her lips. She stretched out her hand to 'see' him. Miles sat in the chair Marilyn had placed beside Aletha's and took her frail hand in his own. He brought it to his face then brought her other hand to join it. As she explored his features, touched his hair, traced the line of his jaw, her lips began to quiver and quiet tears fell from her eyelashes. "Oh, my darling son. I never thought to see you again. God is truly good. He has answered my prayers at last."

Miles could have handled bitter rebuke or an unbridled diatribe against his conduct and character, but he was ill-equipped to receive unconditional love. It had become such a foreign concept that it completely undermined his self-control in a way that an attack of blatant indignation could not. His plan for a cool, calculated meeting, unencumbered by needless sentiment, dissolved into dust when confronted by his mother's genuine, unequivocal affection. As he sat looking at her, a woman trapped in darkness, left alone by all the men she had loved yet finding joy in being reunited with the only one who had left her by choice, Miles experienced the strangest sensation.

He began to shake, and he felt the lump rise in his throat again, but this time the moisture in his eyes overflowed as tears filled them beyond his ability to blink them away. He felt a curious sense of uncontrolled release as a deep well of suppressed emotion burst inside him, and he found himself on his knees once more, his head on his mother's lap, sobbing his remorse as she lovingly stroked his hair. Miles felt an arm come around his shoulders. Marilyn knelt next to him, her tears mingled with his.

"Oh, God, Mama. Please forgive me. Please forgive me," Miles pleaded through the tears.

"My dearest son. I forgave you long, long ago. And I'm so thankful that God has granted me the blessing of telling you so. Now, Timothy, you must learn to forgive yourself," she added gently.

While Rose was taking a tentative step into the kitchen, Derek and company were headed down the driveway looking in all directions for any sign of her or Tim. It was the only way Granny Gert could be included in the search. After exhausting that avenue, they would have to park the truck at the big house and proceed on foot. What they saw didn't encourage them much. Many of the redbuds lining the drive had been uprooted and hurled into the distance. The iron gate had been pulled out of its stone setting and a downed power pole lay alongside the main road. Thankfully, the lines had been snapped and pulled in the other direction, so those who had sheltered at Aletha's cottage had been able to access the road without danger.

Little was said as the import of the scene weighed heavily on everyone's mind. Derek drove back to the main house, noting the exterior of the old stone barn to his left as they passed it. Sections of the metal roof were curled up or missing altogether. He didn't say anything, hoping that Granny Gert had not noticed. When they reached the main house, everyone was cheered by the sight of the picket fence looking as fresh as it had an hour earlier. A few shingles were missing from the roof, but otherwise the old house seemed to have weathered the storm fairly well. The sight of the majestic structure still standing tall and largely unaffected by the tornado brought additional hope to the anxious group. Derek and Abe, with the help of Angelica, succeeded in keeping Gert in the truck while they walked around the yard. The rain had stopped, but piles of hail stones still littered the yard, melting slowly in the emerging sun. Just as they rounded the corner past the conservatory, they saw Rose running from the kitchen door toward them.

Derek gave a shout of triumph, hoping the ladies in the truck would hear. He ran to meet Rose, almost giddy with relief. But when Rose explained what had happened to Tim, Derek yelled at Abe to drive the truck around to the other side of the house then helped Rose open the doors to the storm cellar. Though he was greeted ecstatically by Scout, who started barking as soon as he heard Derek's voice, his focus was on Tim.

"Hey, buddy," he said lightly, even as he took in Tim's appearance with misgiving. "I hear you got yourself into a knife fight. Man, couldn't you think of anything better to do while you were trapped in a cellar with a pretty girl?"

His words elicited a weak grin that disappeared when Tim's teeth began chattering.

"Rose, why don't you stay with this lazy bum while Abe and I figure out how to get him out of here?" She tried to return his encouraging smile, but Tim's condition alarmed her even more now that she could see him in daylight.

After a short conference, Derek ran to the garage to find some kind of metal posts or poles while Abe dug a new tarp out of the back of the truck. The old one had been buried with Prince. The two men quickly fashioned a makeshift stretcher for their friend and laid it on the cellar steps next to him, then Derek took charge. He addressed Tim, but the instructions applied to all present.

"Now, brother, we've got to get your sorry butt out of here, and you're such a big guy, it'll have to be on this excellent hand-crafted stretcher put together by Abe and yours truly. Your fine Miss Rose is going to help us, too. So, you just cross your arms and let us move you. Maybe I should mention that this may hurt a little bit..."

It hurt a great deal.

Derek got behind Tim and wrapped his arms across Tim's chest. Rose and Abe each took a leg. Even with all of Derek's muscles in play it took several heaves to get Tim onto the stretcher, and despite every effort to avoid it, his wound began bleeding again. They finally hauled him up the steps with Derek and Abe on either side of his shoulders, bearing the bulk of his weight, while Rose and Angelica each grabbed a stretcher pole at his feet. Gert, no longer fretting over her granddaughter's well-being, and having delivered a sound reprimand to that young lady for worrying her granny half to death, took command of the situation. She told them to be mindful of Tim's arm, to wrap him up warmly, and to make sure he had plenty of room in the back of the pick-up.

"No sense in having anything falling on him, poor boy." Before the others braced themselves to lift Tim into the truck, she said to him in a rallying tone, "Sonny, you'll be back on your feet in no time. Because if you're not, you'll have me to answer to. I won't have you breaking my Rosie's heart now that you've both had the sense to figure out you were meant for each other."

With the shadow of a smile, he replied weakly, "Yes ma'am."

"That's the ticket," Gert said as she patted his good arm. Then she stepped back and said, "Up you go!"

They dropped Angelica, Gert, and Scout at the cottage to deliver the good news there, then made as much haste as safety allowed, given that Tim and Rose were in the truck bed with the tailgate down. Abe called ahead to the clinic in town, but as expected it was full to overflowing and all first responders had been called out on emergencies, so they opted to drive east to the hospital in Jefferson County since that populace had dodged the storm.

Rose held a shade over Tim's face to protect him from the sun now shining brightly in the west.

"Sweetheart?"

Will I ever tire of hearing that? Rose wondered. "I'm right here," she murmured in his ear.

"I promise our next date will be more fun," he said with a crooked smile.

She answered with a spontaneous gurgle of laughter. "I'll hold you to it, Ludlow," she said, leaning in to kiss him gently. Tim had been right after all. Rose recalled his comments on the first Sunday after they met. She *had* found beauty in the broken.

When his regret and sorrow were spent, Miles sat on the floor next to Aletha's chair. Marilyn still knelt next to him. It was a moment none of them could ever have foreseen. Miles, expert businessman, who controlled every situation he encountered, was at a complete loss. He had no idea how to proceed. He still needed to get the deed from his mother, but that somehow seemed less urgent now. Marilyn stepped hesitantly into the emotional void.

"Timothy, why don't you sit here again, and I'll get another chair."

But Miles wasn't so lost that he had forgotten his innate good manners.

"No, Mari, you take this chair, and *I'll* get another one." The gesture wasn't his typical imperious command. It was rather a man showing deference to one who deserved it.

Once seated, Miles looked from Aletha to Marilyn, amazement paramount in his expression. "I don't understand how… this happened," he said, indicating the obvious close relationship of the two ladies. "When you left…"

"Timothy, I'm *so* sorry. I didn't *want* to leave you. I *had* to leave you, though I know how much it hurt you…"

"No, Mari. It's I who hurt you. I knew it then, but I was too young and proud to admit that you and my parents were right about me, about my attitude, about my ambition. You have nothing with which to reproach yourself. Please forgive me, my dear. I was a fool to drive you away. I was an even bigger fool to not try and find you." He reached his hand to her then started to withdraw it as he realized that she probably wouldn't welcome it. Marilyn quickly took his hand in both of hers.

"The past is forgiven. This is a new beginning – for all of us," she said as she looked from him to Aletha. "We have both followed your career over the years so we know that you have become quite successful, but there is much you need to know – much that I should have told you years ago." Marilyn released his hand and walked over to the sofa where she idly rearranged the pillows to give herself time to gather her words. She continued to move about the room until she seemed to come to a decision about how to begin.

"The night I left you, I went to Aletha."

"*What?*" There was quiet incredulity in the single word.

"I knew my grandparents would never approve of divorce. They had warned me that if I married you and regretted my decision, I would be on my own. I was so alone and so unhappy. I went to the only person who would understand – Aletha.

"She knew how I was torn over our marriage. I loved you so much, but I was afraid of you, of what you had become." Miles said nothing, the full weight of her words tearing at his conscience. "She welcomed me. I felt like such a traitor to the Hawthorne family, but she welcomed me. I can't tell you how humbled and loved I felt at a time when I desperately needed reassurance."

"Oh, I think I can empathize with you on that point," Miles said, looking at his mother. She sat quietly. This was Marilyn's story to tell.

"I didn't know when I got there, that someone was in the study, and I was so upset, I just blurted out everything to Aletha as soon as I walked into the house. She soothed me down and settled me in the guest room where I cried myself to sleep." Miles cringed, but Marilyn wasn't looking at him. She was looking into the past. "The next morning, she told me that someone had called to see me. I was terrified that it was you." She paused when she saw Miles' disquiet. "I'm sorry, Timothy, I don't mean to hurt you by telling you these things, but you must understand how I felt. I was afraid that if I saw you again, felt your arms around me, I would lose my resolve. But it wasn't you. It was Peter Ludlow." She saw a flicker of recognition cross Miles' face.

"Ludlow. Wasn't there someone by that name who worked for my father? Wait... Peter Ludlow..." Miles looked up at her as the memory came to him. "He was that stuffed-shirt accountant who was always making sheep's eyes at you. I never could stand the fellow."

Marilyn winced at Miles' description. It wasn't completely off, though he had failed to mention that Peter Ludlow was also very kind and honorable. "He was 'the someone' in the library the night before, and he had heard my pitiful story. So, he came the next day to make me an offer."

"What kind of offer?" Miles asked, frowning.

"He had just been hired for a position in Chicago and told me that as soon as my divorce was final, he would like to marry me and give me a home and the opportunity to get away from New York – and you."

"The damned arrogance of the man!"

"Timothy" was all Aletha said, effactually silencing her son.

"He agreed that it was to be a marriage of convenience only until, or if ever, I wanted more." Marilyn glanced at Miles, but he had looked away, his lips clamped tightly together.

"I agreed, because he was kind and humble, and I needed a father… for my baby… your son."

Miles sat mute, shocked into silence, unable to say anything.

"Oh, Timothy, please forgive me. I was afraid that if you knew I was expecting a child, you would never have let him go, and I so wanted him to grow up in a… a normal household, without the lure of riches and power. That's why I left when I did. Please say you forgive me," Marilyn said as tears of remorse flowed down her cheeks.

Miles was silent for so long, she could almost sense him retreating into his shell as he had done so many times before, but she misunderstood his withdrawal. He had been called all manner of names by his business associates – ruthless, tough, barracuda, shark. He had taken pride in those descriptions, worn them like a badge of honor. But the knowledge that his bride had been so afraid of him and his eventual influence over their child, that she had hidden the baby from his own father was the final blow to Miles' already shattered ego. He rose and walked over to Marilyn where she stood with her back to him, fighting to control her tears. He put his arms around her and spoke gently into her soft hair that smelled of lilacs.

"Thank God, Mari. Thank God you were brave enough to take that step. You were right, you know. I would have tried to turn him into another… me." She looked into his face, marveling at his reaction. "Come, sit down and tell me about him. What did you name him?"

"Tim. Timothy James after you… and his grandfather," she said, glancing at Aletha. Marilyn tried to tell Miles all the details of a little boy, a teenager, and a man that a father would most want to hear. She told him of Tim's military service and of his stubborn resolve to take care of his mother after Peter died. "He's a good man, Timothy. I… I hope you'll want to meet him."

"I have a sneaking suspicion that I already have, or at least I saw him from a distance. Was he the young Galahad who won the three-legged race, then started barking orders like the Lord High Commander when all hell broke loose before the tornado hit?" Marilyn laughed at the apt description of her autocratic son. Then her face suddenly grew grave.

"What is it?" Miles asked sharply.

"It's Tim. He went out in the storm after Rose, and we haven't heard anything from him since. His friends went out to look for them, but they haven't come – "

Before she could complete the thought, Marilyn heard car doors slam outside. She ran to the door to see Tim's truck driven off by Derek, and Gert and Angelica walking toward the cottage accompanied by Scout. Angelica shouted, "He's all right. They're both all right. Heaven be praised!"

"Oh, thank *goodness!*" Marilyn nearly began crying again from another burden lifted. "Where were they?"

Between the two, Angelica and Gert gave a lively account of the afternoon's events, glossing over the nature of Tim's wound.

"Do you think I should go to the hospital?" Marilyn asked anxiously.

"Oh, I don't think so. He'll probably be home before you know it, pumped full of antibiotics and pain pills. Besides, he hasn't got eyes for anyone but my Rosie right now." Gert added with a wink.

"You mean…"

"I mean the Thompsons and the Ludlows will be planning a wedding before I'm much older."

Marilyn and Aletha were both delighted at the news. It was just what was needed to lighten the mood and help everyone turn their focus from the past to the future.

Miles had been standing in the background, enjoying the old woman's story. He had no trouble recognizing the 'gorgon' described by Simon Atherton. As the celebration died down, Aletha recalled her duties as hostess and introduced her son to Gert and Angelica.

"So, the prodigal has returned," Gert replied bluntly.

"Returned yes, but I'm sorry to say, must be leaving soon." Noting Aletha's obvious dismay, he hastened to add, "But I promise to return as soon as I complete a delicate business deal," he said, taking his mother's hand. "Now if you'll excuse us, I need to discuss something privately with my mother."

"Oh, no you don't, Sonny. I've got a feeling this is about that scoundrel Simon Atherton, so we'll all be staying right here. We'll just wheedle it out of Letha later, and it's always best to hear something firsthand," Gert said as she grabbed Angelica's hand and pulled her to a seat on the sofa next to her.

After the disclosures of the previous hour, Miles was sure nothing could shock him further. He was wrong. He hadn't been rendered speechless so many times in one day since he was in middle school. He turned to his mother with a look of utter amazement.

Almost as if she could see his expression, Aletha said, "It's true, Timothy. I can't imagine that you came all this way after 30 years by chance. Not that I'm not thankful, for it's the happiest day I've known in decades, but I believe I know what brought you here. And it's only because that scoundrel couldn't find it. I suppose I can at least be grateful to him for that, even if it has all been so unnecessary."

Miles sat down beside her, disturbed by her words and their implications.

"Mother, since you have guessed some of my tale, I won't beat around the bush. I've been putting together a land development deal for the past four years. I'm mortgaged to the hilt because I had to acquire so many properties in the area to attract a potential developer - the right kind of developer. But the deal hinges on old Joshua Strong and the parkland parcel. I know it belongs to you now, but it will be mine someday, and I must be honest with you. I fully intend to sell it when I inherit the deed." He saw the disappointment in Aletha's face. "I'm sorry, but I have never understood why we continue to hold onto something worth a fortune just for the sake of a long dead idealist!" he said on an exasperated note.

"We keep it, Timothy, because it's the right thing to do," Aletha said simply. "Your father understood that, but we were afraid of what that kind of temptation might do to you."

"Mother, I'm a grown man, now. I know you don't approve of the decisions I've made, and I've finally come to realize that I have made some terrible choices. Choices that cost me my love," he said, glancing at Marilyn, "my family, and yes, perhaps even my soul. But if this deal doesn't go through, I will lose *everything else*. I'll be washed up in New York. I won't be able to get so much as a newsstand built. So *please*, Mother, may I have the deed *now?*" he pleaded.

Aletha leaned forward, great sadness in her blank eyes. "I'm sorry, Timothy. But I told you. All the nonsense with representatives from shadow companies trying to buy me out over the years, and the futile efforts of Mr. Atherton, were tragically unnecessary. You see, my dear boy, I don't have the deed anymore. *You do.* I sent it to you not long after your father died, *over 30 years ago.*"

CHAPTER 6

He that trusteth in his riches shall fall; but the righteous shall flourish as the green leaf.

Proverbs 11:28, ASV

Miles' reaction upon meeting his ex-wife and mother had shocked him out of his customary rigid self-control. The news of a grown son had stunned him, rocking his world. But at his mother's final disclosure, Miles saw that world imploding and felt himself being sucked along with it into a gaping black hole. He fought valiantly against the gravitational pull while experiencing the equally odd sensation of floating above the room, detached from those around him. He registered amazement on the face of the Jamaican woman, gleeful surprise from the old friend, a thoughtful frown from Mari, as if she grappled with an elusive thought, and sorrowful resignation in his mother's wilting frame. As Miles struggled to take in the enormity of the revelation, his considerable mental faculties still in disarray, he only managed to speak a single word, and it sounded more like a hoarse croak.

"*What?*"

"I know you received it because I called Marilyn the day I sent it. I asked her to put all the contents of the box somewhere safe, so that you wouldn't discard anything out of anger. You see, I hoped that someday your resentment toward your father would pass, and you would want to go through his most prized belongings when you allowed yourself to remember how much you loved him."

Miles caught one phrase and spun around to look at Marilyn with hurt and disbelief. "You *knew*, Mari, and you never *told* me?"

"No, Timothy, of *course* I didn't know. That is, I remember receiving the box from your mother. I was with you when you opened it. It was two weeks after your father's funeral. Don't you remember? When you saw what was in it, you threw it across the room and told me to get rid of it. But I had promised Aletha to keep it safe. I put his Bible on the shelf with some other books he had given you, and everything else went into the basement storage unit. You rarely looked for anything there, so I didn't think you would notice. And even if you found the box, you might have cooled off by then and appreciated having something that reminded you of the father you had looked up to and admired so much. But I *promise* you, I *never* saw any deed." She ended on a helpless note, feeling as if she had somehow, unwittingly, kept something else of paramount importance from him.

Miles turned back to his mother in disbelief. "Do you mean to tell me that you sent a document worth a king's ransom in a box with a bunch of old trinkets?!" The anger that never lurked far beneath the surface of his calculated façade was bubbling up, threatening to undo all the good of his earlier emotional purge.

"Do you still have his Bible, Timothy?" Aletha asked.

"Do I still have his *Bible?* Mother, I've moved three or four times since then. Why would I keep track of an old Bible, and what difference could that possibly make?"

"Do you still have his Bible, Timothy?" Aletha asked again.

In the face of her insistent question and the implied import behind it, Miles sat silent for a moment before answering. "Yes," he said at last, more quietly, but with a hint of rebellious indignation. "I still have it, though I never felt the need to open it. But I knew it was his most valued possession, so I could never… bring myself to throw it out." After a moment's reflection he added with a puzzled look, "But I still don't see what it was to do with…" He stopped short as a horrifying thought occurred. "Oh please, *please* tell me you did not leave a multi-million-dollar piece of paper in a Bible that I was never likely to open. *Did you?*" The final words were a desperate plea.

"When your father grew so weak and ill, he told me that he didn't want me to bear the burden of the land's ownership any longer. You were a grown man. A man who had great potential, but equally great failings. You had already turned away from the faith of your youth, but we never stopped praying that you would return to it someday. At the time you and Marilyn were still married, and we had hopes that her influence might bring you around. But your spiritual darkness blocked out even her light. James realized that only God's perfect timing would bring you back to his perfect truth. Then, and only then, would you be ready to handle the decision about the disposition of Joshua Strong's land. So, we put the deed in James' Bible where he had marked a particular verse. If your soul was ever ready to seek out the Lord, we knew you would go to your father's Bible first. I suspect you don't own any others?"

"No," came the stupefied reply.

"I won't allow anymore grief or wasted lives over that foolish document. It is yours to do with as you see fit, Timothy. You will find it in Proverbs, Chapter 11."

Miles stood as one in a trance. Without another word he walked straight to the door, not looking at anyone. The four ladies sat in silence as they listened to him drive away.

The gash in Tim's arm was significant, requiring numerous stitches, but Granny Gert's prophecy had been accurate. After pumping IV fluids into him, boosted by a healthy dose of antibiotics, he was sent to Radiology for a CT scan to verify that there was no serious head trauma. Released from the ER to go home and rest, he was given strict instructions to keep his arm immobile and to change the dressing daily for at least a week. Suspecting that Tim would be a poor patient, resenting any forced inactivity, Rose resolved to enforce the doctor's orders with Marilyn's help.

She called Marilyn as soon as Tim was examined, alerting her to their promised return sometime that evening. If Marilyn's receipt of the good tidings was somewhat subdued, Rose attributed it to exhaustion from the events of the afternoon. Marilyn *was* exhausted, but the emotional turmoil went far beyond worry over Tim and the trauma of riding out a tornado. Miles was not the only one who had been shaken to the core that day.

When Marilyn married Peter Ludlow, she thought she had left Timothy's world behind. Ironically, it was through her own actions that his memory was kept continually close at hand, though only a pleasant, muted one. For it was Marilyn who invited Aletha to visit Chicago, knowing she would want to meet her baby grandson. And since Peter's new position was with Martin Mason's agricultural equipment company, Aletha was introduced to the middle-aged bachelor. She had been a widow for almost two years, doubly lonely for having lost not only a husband, but her only son as well. Martin appreciated her grasp of business, despite her aura of petite fragility, and surprised everyone by finally marrying late in life. It was a happy union for both. Martin became devoted to that which he never realized he had been missing – a loving wife and a welcoming home. Aletha found a new purpose in life and took solace in filling the aching void of lost motherhood with the joy of being a grandmother.

But it was a little boy, growing quickly into adolescence and manhood that brought Timothy's memory into such clear focus. Though fair-haired like his mother, Tim was the spitting image of his father, possessing the same determined spirit and work ethic that had been twisted into a lust for power in Timothy Miles Hawthorne. Marilyn credited Peter with teaching Tim integrity, moral courage, and a high regard for others, but his drive and ambition came straight from his Hawthorne genes.

The Ludlows were never able to have another child, despite her eventual willingness to be the wife that Peter deserved. Their marriage may have lacked the passion that she had known with Timothy, but it was filled with companionship, trust, and mutual affection. When Marilyn suggested they move to Tinkers Well so that she could be of comfort to Aletha as she aged, Peter happily supported the decision because of his own fondness for the Masons, and because he, too, was ready for retirement. He had no family ties of his own as his parents had died some years earlier – not surprising considering the 15-year age difference between himself and his wife.

Marilyn mourned Peter's passing with honest grief. She missed his friendship and comforting presence, but she found renewed direction in taking up the teaching career she had abandoned when she married Timothy. The work was both rewarding and affirming and helped her discover that she could stand on her own two feet without a man at her side, though she never quite adjusted to the loneliness of solitary living. The challenge of opening the minds of her inquisitive students, however, gave her purpose. Her courage and confidence reaffirmed, Marilyn was perfectly content to follow that course until Tim insisted on leaving the Army to take care of her after Peter's death. Despite repeatedly attempting to convince him that she was perfectly capable of taking care of herself, he came to Kansas. She could hardly fault him for his sense of duty to her and Aletha, and she had to admit that she found his presence welcome company. But even after Tim moved to Tinkers Well, looking more like his father every day, and determined to make a go of his construction business, Marilyn never imagined that she would ever again see the image her son so closely resembled.

Then she met Timothy face to face and every memory of their life together – and that terrible final parting – rushed into her mind, blotting out everything else, and overwhelming her to the point of collapse. When she witnessed the unimaginable, a Timothy broken by remorse, she was filled with thanksgiving and hope that the husband of her youth could be found once more in the shell of Miles Hawthorne. Timothy's response to her own plea for forgiveness over her long-held secret lifted the burden she had carried for 30 years and left her marveling at his transformation. She held no illusions that they could ever be more than friends again, but she yearned, for his sake, that he might return to the God he had forsaken as a young man, knowing that to be the only way his healing would be complete. Then Aletha revealed her shocking secret and Marilyn watched, as in a nightmare, Timothy's abrupt departure. Her hope-filled heart was pierced to the quick.

How she got through the rest of that day, she couldn't remember, though she felt almost driven to stay busy. Preparing for Tim's arrival spurred her into welcome activity. She put clean linens on his bed and prepared a big pot of homemade chicken noodle soup, not sure he would even want it.

Marilyn sat by his bed that night after he had fallen into fitful slumber, wondering how on earth she was to tell him about his father. He knew that Peter was not his biological father. She had disclosed that truth when Tim was a freshman leaving for college, allowing him to believe her pregnancy had been the result of a youthful indiscretion and that it was painful for her to talk about. He had respected her reserve, thankful only that she had given him a surrogate father he could love and respect. He did not know that Aletha was his grandmother, although she and Martin had filled the role of grandparents all his life. The simultaneous loss of Peter and Martin devastated Tim, removing his two staunch male role models and champions. It was ultimately the distraction of helping Abraham through his troubles that helped both Tim and Derek find new direction. Marilyn, too, was thankful for Abe's intervention; it allowed her to keep the secret of Timothy Hawthorne's existence to herself yet a while. That had been over a year ago.

But after all that had passed on a stormy afternoon filled with revelations and disappointments, Marilyn knew it was time to be done with secrets. If Tim and Rose were to begin a life together, they must begin with truth. The thought of that answered prayer lifted Marilyn's heavy spirit – momentarily at least.

As Rose had predicted, Tim was not content to lie around doing nothing just because of 'a little scratch on his arm.' "I'm going to drive over and see what kind of damage the big house took yesterday, and I'll pop in to see how Aletha and Mrs. Gunn are faring."

"And Rose?" Marilyn asked with artful indifference.

Tim grinned sheepishly. "I texted her earlier and told her I'd call when I started down the driveway so she can meet me there." With his right hand he searched the basket where keys were kept. Not finding the keys to his truck, he turned to see his mother dangling them from her finger.

"I think that's an excellent idea, but unless you plan on *pushing* the truck all the way there, which would be an even *greater* violation of doctor's orders, I will be your chauffeur today. Rose and I settled it between us last night."

"My girlfriend is in league against me with my *mother?*"

"Rose is a very sensible girl, when she's not walking on Cloud 9, and she is just as worried about your lack of patient compliance as I am."

"Oh, for Pete's sake! Can I at least go for a walk by myself for a while first? I'm feeling a little stiff this morning," he said, not meeting his mother's eyes.

"I'm sure a walk would do you good, but it will be a lot farther than from here to your truck," she said and held up the key Tim kept under the dashboard. "Derek showed me where you keep it when I drove everyone home last night."

"*Mom!*" Tim sounded, momentarily, like a 16-year-old arguing over being grounded for a minor infraction. "I am not a child. I think I know what I can and can't handle."

"Just because you're all grown up doesn't mean you have any more sense than that doorknob you're turning. You know you're not supposed to drive while you're still on pain meds."

"So next time, I'll just take some naproxen, okay?"

Taking pity on his obvious frustration, Marilyn said gently, "*Please* let me do this for you Tim." After a pause, she added diffidently, "Besides, there's something I need to discuss with you and Aletha... and Rose, because it concerns her too."

Curious over the change in his mother's attitude, he acquiesced to her wishes, wondering what could possibly be so important that she needed to talk to everybody at once.

Ten minutes later they were all gathered in the living room of *Fern Cottage*. Marilyn insisted Granny Gert stay to hear what she had to say, knowing how close Rose was to her grandmother. She couldn't help noticing how frail and withdrawn Aletha appeared, which wasn't surprising considering all that had happened the day before. She regretted the necessity of adding to the older woman's troubles, but the truth had to be told. Marilyn recounted the events prior to Tim's birth as calmly and succinctly as possible, but as she watched a host of emotions chase themselves across her son's countenance – incredulity, anger, resentment – her voice faltered. She saw the set line of his jaw grow more pronounced as she finished her story. Rose would ordinarily have appreciated the romantic nature of the tale, but seeing the pain on Tim's face, she felt anger toward someone she had never met simply for his sake. He sat silent for several minutes in a futile effort to process all he had heard.

"So, you *are* my grandmother. I've always thought of you that way." Tim spoke directly to the object of his observation who shrank from the unspoken condemnation in his words. Then turning to his mother, he said, "Why are you telling me this now? There must be a reason."

Though his voice was cold and unyielding, Marilyn was determined to bring everything into the open. She finally tied Tim's history to the present. This time he was shocked into abrupt speech when she disclosed the pivotal point involving the land deed.

"Are you telling me that my father was *here, in this house,* and you didn't think to *tell* me?"

"Tim, he appeared out of the blue, and I had no idea where you were. You'd gone out into the storm to find Rose. I didn't even know if you were still alive," she said, fighting back tears.

"Don't blame your mother, Tim. It's really all my fault," Aletha said in a voice weary from years of worry. "I should have disclosed the existence of that dreadful deed the day Rose found Prince. When Abe told us Simon Atherton had come from a detective agency in New York, I suspected Timothy might be behind it, but I so hoped it wasn't true that I kept my thoughts to myself. It was wrong of me. I should have warned you."

Tim sat with his head bent for several minutes. When he spoke again, he spoke quietly, though anger burned through every word.

"My father was such an ambitious monster that he drove you away without knowing you were carrying his child." Marilyn merely bowed her head. "My father was such a coward that he hired a *P.I.* to find a document rather than face the widowed mother he had abandoned." Aletha remained silent, though her tears spoke volumes. "My father's selfish greed ultimately caused the death of Prince, the humiliation and near ravaging of the woman I love, and this gash in my arm which was the result of a failed blow that was surely meant to be fatal. You both claim my father underwent some kind of spiritual transformation when he saw you, but he left without making *any effort* to see me, his son. Well ladies, thank you for sharing that charming fairytale. If you'll excuse me, I have work to do." He slammed the front door with such force that a delicate vase on the hall table fell with a crash on the wood floor.

Rose started after him, but Marilyn stopped her. "No, Rose. Let him be. He needs time to work this out on his own. I apologize for the shock all of this must be to you, too. Your grandmother met Timothy yesterday and learned about most of the whole sad story, but I asked her not to say anything until I could tell you and Tim together. Please forgive me." Rose went to the woman who had loved Tim so much longer than she had, and who had felt his pain more acutely because she blamed herself, in part, for bringing it upon him. Hugging Marilyn, Rose said gently, "You did what you did because you love him. I could *never* blame you for that. And I'm sure he won't either."

She waited an hour then slipped out of the house while Granny Gert and Marilyn directed their attention to drawing Aletha out of her depression. Rose knew where she would find Tim. When she let herself through the gate in the picket fence, she saw him sitting on the steps of the wrap-around porch where they had first met. His shoulders were slumped, and his head was bowed as if he bore a great weight. He looked up when he heard her approach. Not sure of her welcome, she was relieved to see him motion for her to join him. As she sat down, his right arm came around her, pulling her close. He turned his face into her soft hair, savoring her nearness.

"I'm sorry I stormed out on you, on everyone. I was just so... hurt – not by Mom or Aletha. I know they were only trying to protect me. It was knowing that my father – the man whose DNA I carry – thought some big business deal was more important than meeting a son he never knew existed. When Mom told me several years ago that Peter wasn't my biological father, I didn't really care. In fact, I respected him even more. He *chose* to raise me and love me when he had no obligation to do so. But this..." Tim stopped as his voice began to falter. When he felt more in control he continued, looking out over the garden, "And when I think of how his selfish desires affected you and Aletha... I'm not sure I *ever* want to meet him."

Rose gently turned his head to look at her. "You don't need to make that decision today. Besides, I can't believe any of the horrible attacks committed by Simon were on your father's orders."

"Maybe not," Tim admitted, grudgingly.

"And who knows, there might be more going on in his life than any of us realize. Perhaps the best answer is to pray for him. It couldn't hurt," she said in such an open, sincere way that Tim shook his head in wonder.

"Rose Thompson, what did I ever do to deserve the love of such an incredible woman?"

She replied thoughtfully, "Well, you *did* rescue me in the approved heroic fashion – twice." He couldn't help smiling. Then she added tenderly, "And you loved me in spite of all *my* failings, when I didn't even deserve your friendship." Tim's face grew serious once more, and he was about to respond when she added softly, "Maybe it's because God gave you a greater capacity for compassion and forgiveness."

"And maybe it's because he knew how much I needed you." He then proceeded to convince her of that need in the approved romantic fashion.

Later that day, Tim received a call from the county sheriff's office. During a thorough search of the tornados path, a body had been discovered in the twisted remains of a car two miles from the Mason property. A curious mix of identities was found on the body, one of which was recognized by the county clerk, Jim Hastings, who had met the man during a tour of the courthouse. The man in question had been in the company of a young woman who was a guest of Aletha Mason. Not wanting to worry the elderly woman unduly, and knowing of her close relationship with Tim, they called him to see if he would be able to identify the body.

Marilyn agreed to let him drive himself to the county morgue. It was a grim duty, but one that had to be done. Tim had seen dead and wounded men before in the course of combat deployments, but none whose face had been so lacerated by broken glass as to make it almost unrecognizable. He remembered, however, the western attire worn by Atherton as the two men were engaged in battle, and he noted the same long, thin hand he had shaken on their first meeting. A ring was still present on the fifth finger. He had every right to feel revenged on the man who had brought so much anguish to those he loved. But looking at the broken body, an empty shell that would probably never be truly missed or mourned, Tim felt only pity for a wasted life. He signed for a briefcase filled with cash, which he knew to belong to Aletha, and left the morgue. Finding a phone number for the Landrum Detective Agency, he called them on the drive home to notify them of the loss of one of their operatives. He decided to spare Rose the knowledge of Atherton's death until the nightmare elements of her interaction with Simon had faded into countless yesterdays.

Two days later the grandfather clock struck eight as the shadows lengthened across the yard outside. Gert answered the insistent phone in the living room, now working perfectly. Aletha pretended not to hear it. "Hello?" Gert put her hand over the phone's mouthpiece. "Letha, it's for you. I think it's that boy of yours."

Aletha became flustered, her hands twisting in agitation. "Oh, Trudy! What shall I say to him?"

"Well, you won't have to decide until you know what *he* has to say," Gert replied, thrusting the handset into her friend's hand, and sitting down next to her. Gert wasn't about to miss any of this conversation! When Aletha hesitated, Gert added in a thundering whisper, "Just remember that he's your only son, and you love him."

Aletha scowled before saying politely, "This is Aletha Mason. To whom am I speaking?" Her face paled as she repeated, "Timothy. I see. And did you find the deed?... I'm so glad to hear that it is still safe." Then a long pause ensued during which Aletha's jaw dropped, and she began to rock back and forth as tears filled her eyes. Gert started to become alarmed when Aletha said, "Timothy Miles Hawthorne, I have *never* been more proud to call you my son."

Now that sounds promising, thought Gert.

"Oh, my dear, dear boy, of course you will be welcome here at any time... in two months or so?... I can't tell you how happy you've made me. God is *very* good... Yes, my dear, and call me back when you have everything arranged."

CHAPTER 7

You are like a dove that hides in the crevice of a rock. Let
me see your lovely face and hear your enchanting voice.
                              Song of Solomon 2:14 (GNT)

In a reflection of the whole of creation, human life passes through seasons: times when the sun shines and growing things lift their faces toward heaven; times when the soft breeze of a cool day provides peace and rest; and times when storms gather and threaten to destroy hope, love, and life itself. Rose and Granny Gert and their friends had weathered that cycle in microcosm, and such had been the upheaval of their emotional and physical well-being that a period of relative calm inevitably followed. The steady beat of day following day in the score of eternity reminded all of God's provision and presence. Some dreams had been shattered, others had bloomed for a moment and faded away, but for Tim and Rose, unexpected dreams had been realized, while others waited in an unknown, yet promising future.

Tinkers Well had mercifully been spared much of the destructive power of the tornado. Its path had cut a swathe through mostly open fields. After leaving its debris in the harvested land just short of Tom and Lucy Bennett's newly remodeled farmhouse, it dissipated into nothingness. Ordinarily, Tim would have been the first in line to help with the clean-up effort, but Rose, seconded by Marilyn, insisted he leave that particular project to those not wearing a sling around their necks. Though he may have silently resented their interference, he was forced to admit they were both right. During the ensuing weeks, thanks largely to Rose's timely employment of an arched eyebrow whenever she caught Tim trying to violate what he called his 'terms of parole,' his arm healed quickly. However, the injury did prevent him from attending Annual Training with his Army Reserve unit, so he scheduled an alternate training option to occur after Rose's departure. It was the only time he ever had a grudging reason to be grateful for Simon Atherton's intervention in their lives.

Much happiness had emerged in the aftermath of the storm, but Rose saw, in unguarded moments, the hurt that still lurked in Tim's eyes. He never spoke about Miles Hawthorne, the father he had never met, but she knew the knowledge of his presence and subsequent silence had left an empty void in Tim's heart that even her love could not fill. She sometimes wondered if he had felt a similar sort of helplessness when he had watched her walking into Simon's web and been powerless to stop her. She continued to pray for some kind of resolution. Not hearing anything was the hardest burden for him to bear. She was glad that he was able to relieve that burden and the tedium of recuperation by focusing on the hiring of four other veterans to join the Three Brothers crew.

The first, a former Army transport driver and co-participant in Derek's VA hospital talking group, jumped at the opportunity. José Nuñez was a little shorter than Derek and had a grin that was almost as wide, but two gold-capped teeth set him apart – that and a full head of coarse black hair where Derek had none. Tim appreciated José's desire to learn more about the trade and found him to be both a quick study and a hard worker. He was a little concerned, though, when he first saw José stripped down to a sleeveless T-shirt and cut-off jeans. The man could have modeled for a tattoo parlor. Tim had to check out every inch of ink art to ensure there was nothing that might be offensive to clients. Thankfully, most were innocuous drawings of mythical creatures, with the odd exception of several Catholic saints. It seemed that José wanted to be covered, literally, by the patron saint of just about everything. "You can never be too careful, sir," he responded seriously when questioned about them. Tim imagined some interesting conversations in their future.

Jason Tyler Gaines and Jason Buchwald had both worked on construction crews before joining the Navy. Thankfully, Jason Gaines was happy to be hailed as JT which brought the confusion factor down several notches, especially given that they were both sun-bleached towheads, much the same height, who originally hailed from Savannah. JT left active duty after being assigned to desk duty at the Military Entrance Processing Center in Kansas City. He convinced his former shipmate Jason to join him there where both worked for a local construction company. Neither had ever really felt like they fit in with crews on other worksites, until they hired on with the Three Brothers Team in Tinkers Well.

The fourth was a pint-sized, but fierce, African American Marine named Jada Young. What she lacked in inches she more than made up for in attitude. While Tim was a bit concerned about her abrasive personality, she impressed them all with her craftsmanship using a prosthetic hook in the place of her left hand. Knowing she sustained the injury during a failed attempt to disarm an IED while serving as an explosive ordnance technician, Tim decided to give her a chance.

None of them were Christians, except José, whose faith was rooted more in cultural superstition than substance. Tim was upfront about his own faith, his Christian worldview, and the conduct expected of anyone representing his business. Because they met at the business office most mornings before leaving for their respective projects, the newcomers were invited by one of the original Three Brothers to join in a collective morning prayer. None, except José, actually participated, though from time to time the others made specific prayer requests, whether they admitted to believing in the God they were making requests of or not. They all respected Tim's integrity and leadership. The only pushback surfaced on a technical level.

The postponement of his Annual Training obligation not only allowed Tim to heal; it also gave him the opportunity to evaluate the capabilities of his new crew. Experience levels varied, but his commitment to excellence did not. On a surprise visit to the site of a carport addition, he caught JT and Jason cutting corners on materials and trying to pass off substandard structural support as satisfactory because that's the way they had been taught to do things. Tim set them straight when the two argued with him over the seemingly needless expense of following, or even exceeding, building codes, particularly if the discrepancies were in places no building inspector would ever notice.

"Look, you don't do it the right way based on whether you'll get caught or not. You do it that way because it's the right thing to do," he explained, allowing for no further argument. "I will pay you a fair wage for a fair day's work, and as much as I can use your help, if you're working for me, you'll work to code or not at all. Clear?"

Though JT and Jason were more embarrassed than either cared to admit when held to account for shoddy work, they initially responded with belligerence. JT argued, "We were, you know, just doing things the normal way, boss."

Wanting to encourage the two rather than engaging with them in a battle of wills, Tim thumped JT good-naturedly on the back and said, "Well, this is the new normal. And I promise you, once you start looking at the project as the owner does, when you recognize it as something of worth, no matter how small or seemingly insignificant, you'll *want* to do a better job. And you'll take pride in what you're doing." Whether it was Tim's ultimatum or his pep talk, or simply an intrinsic response to authority, some message got through, and the Jasons' shared attitude began to change. Tim was quick to point out positive progress and to offer suggestions for alternative construction methods. Once the two finally admitted to each other that Tim really did know his trade, they showed more interest in learning rather than just doing.

Meanwhile, Rose toiled to clean up the garden after the storm, then insisted she be allowed to help in any way possible with the projects inside the house. Tim, now even more protective of Rose, was inclined to think the work too hard for her, despite what he had said about her capabilities when she first suggested the idea. She found an unexpected ally in Jada who intentionally found jobs suited to Rose's strength and limited skills. Tim never had any problem giving Jada credit for her competence as a carpenter. When he saw her patiently coaching Rose on small projects until she was ready to take on more unsupervised tasks, his misgivings over the marine's temperament were also considerably mitigated.

He smiled as he thought to himself, *How could anyone have trouble working with Rose?* He would infinitely have preferred spending those precious moments with her himself, but he knew his time was better spent in his capacity as supervisor and resident expert carpenter.

Rose would have preferred Tim's coaching too, for as grateful as she was for Jada's tutelage and work advocacy, she found the short dynamo from the south side of Chicago a little difficult to get to know. Jada spoke little about her time in the Marine Corps and said almost nothing about her childhood and family – with the exception of numerous references to her brother, Jamal, who was two years her senior. Unlike his sister, whose formal education ended with a high school diploma earned chiefly because of outstanding grades in shop class, he held a Master's degree in Civil Engineering. Jada was inordinately proud of him and happily volunteered information about his celebrated accomplishments and current projects. Rose consistently greeted these disclosures with due admiration, but every time she attempted to steer the conversation into more personal or general channels, Jada shut her down in short order. One day Rose tried to introduce an idea she was sure would find favor with the other girl.

"Jada, did you know that Tim has a ski boat? We've talked about taking the whole crew and making a day of it at the lake when his arm is fully healed." Noting a marked lack of interest on Jada's part, Rose added,

"There's a really nice picnic area with a sandy beach where some of us can hang out while the others take turns in the boat," thinking that would clinch the deal.

"I *barely* passed my water safety test during basic training and that's as close as I *ever* need to get to water again." Jada's conversational style was, at all times, marked with an abrupt, edgy tone that reflected the essence of her personality, but when she felt especially strongly about anything her whole face emphasized her sentiments. Her vehement response to Rose's suggestion included bulging eyes and pursed lips. "Now, I can eat all day long," she said with a forceful nod of her head, "but you won't get me past the *picnic* table at the lake, *no* ma'am," and shook her finger emphatically. "So, I might as well just stay home with my brother."

Rose had given up in temporary defeat. She broached the subject with Tim later that day when he came to assess progress before walking her back to the cottage.

"Sweetheart, you have to realize that not everyone is as open and welcoming as you are. You and Jada are poles apart when it comes to childhood experiences and family life, whatever they might have been. Believe me when I tell you that it's nothing short of a miracle, growing up where she did, that she and her brother are not only alive but managed to thrive. For the time being, we need to simply accept her and the talents she brings to the job. I suspect she's a lot more wounded than outwardly obvious, and most of that probably happened *before* she became a marine."

They had reached the cottage porch, and Tim wasted no time in pulling Rose into his arms, sling and all. "For now, you just need to remember two things. One – I love you," he said, and bent to deposit a token of his affection on her eager lips. But he stopped short, merely leaving a chaste peck on her cheek before stepping quickly away. She was obviously disappointed and a little confused until Tim nodded in the direction of the front window. Even the most ardent of Romeos might be understandably put off by the sight of Granny Gert peering brazenly around the curtains at the young couple. Glancing over her shoulder, Rose giggled before demanding to know the other thing she was to remember. He answered, "Not every young woman you meet in Tinkers Well is going to be another Amy."

"I've never met anyone like Amy," Abe said a little wistfully. He and Derek locked up the diner for the day after José had driven off to his aunt and uncle's home in a nearby town.

"You've been talking about her for over a week. Is our Arabian sheik ready to set up his harem?" Derek asked with a smirk. The two had been discussing the events of the wild Sunday, ten days earlier, when everyone was blown a little off course, even as unforeseen opportunities opened before them.

"You mustn't let your feeble imagination run wild, my friend. Even if she noticed I was alive, I would never toss *any* woman across my saddlebow and ride off with her into the desert. I think you've been watching too many old movies," Abe responded with exaggerated dignity, hoping to hide his embarrassment.

"*If* she noticed you?" Derek said in disgust. "Dude, how could you have missed the way she kept looking at you at the picnic and always spoke in your direction even if she was talking to somebody else? Besides, she sat right next to you."

"It was the only seat left available. She was just being friendly. She's never really spoken to me at any of our small group events. I think she joined us at the picnic merely because of Rose, but at least I was able to enjoy her company for a short while. For that I am grateful."

They had just climbed into the cab of Derek's truck. "*Grateful?*" Derek said and stopped in the act of engaging the ignition. "I'm not starting this truck until you stop sitting there, acting like the world's last martyr, and call the girl." He removed the key and folded his arms.

"But what if I don't have her cell – "

" – her cell number? I saw Rose give it to you after church on Sunday. And that was only because Amy was out of town so you could chicken out and ask Rose for Amy's digits instead of asking the girl directly."

"Okay, so I'm a coward, but I have no real experience in the dating game. My parents had already approved of an acceptable bride for me before I joined the Army, and I suppose it might have been a suitable match, but with my change of faith and my injury and everything, it came to nothing," Abe said with a shrug.

"*Might have been a suitable match*? Man, that's what you say when you're buying a used car, not looking for the love of your life." Derek shook his head in disgust.

"I don't expect you to understand *that* particular difference in our cultures, but it really is rather a moot point now."

"Ex-*act*-ly! That girl is history so why don't you get to know *this* girl?" His raised eyebrows demanded an answer.

"But what would I *say*?"

"Man, you were talking just fine at the picnic," Derek pointed out.

"Yes, but that was in a group of people and…"

"Now you sound just like Tim. You know, for a guy who helped me practically throw him into Rose's arms, you're awfully slow off the starting block yourself."

"But I am no Tim," Abe argued feebly. "I don't have my own business."

"You have a degree in computer technology – you're the smartest guy I know."

"I don't have a home."

"You live in the room next to mine!"

Then Abe looked at Derek with restrained despair and said softly, "I don't have a leg, my friend. I am not even a whole man. What healthy young woman would want me?"

Derek waited before answering, not wanting his reply to sound flippant. "Look, brother, we are all broken. None of us is perfect, but it seems to me that if God goes to the trouble of putting a nice, godly woman in your path, that at the very least captures your attention, you ought to make an effort to get to know her. I'm not saying you have to marry the girl, just… talk to her."

He sensed Abe's continued insecurity and hesitation and wasn't sure how to help his friend when he was struck by a blinding flash of inspiration. He slapped the dashboard and said, "I've got it!" jarring Abe out of his self-imposed melancholy. Abe looked somewhat doubtfully at Derek who simply said, "The dinner."

"The dinner?"

"You know, the dinner Tim invited us to." Abe still looked confused. "To celebrate the future of Three Brothers and work out a plan for the next few months," Derek added, gesturing with both hands for emphasis.

"Well, yes, I know about the dinner this Friday, but what has that to do with Amy?"

Derek shook his head then spoke slowly to Abe as if trying to explain quantum physics to a three-year-old. "You can invite Amy to join us as your date." When he finally saw measured consideration dawn on Abe's face he said, "You know, for a genius you can be completely clueless sometimes."

Abe paid no heed to Derek's assessment of his character. "You are suggesting that I ask Amy to join us for dinner where there will be a group of people, and in particular her friend Rose, so that we may be more at ease just as we were at the church picnic? That is not a bad idea."

"That may be the *worst* reason I've ever heard for asking a girl out on a date."

Mimicking Abe's studied reaction to the suggestion, Derek said in exaggerated pedantic tones, "That is not a bad idea. Perhaps I would have thought of it myself in three or four years after careful review."

Abe grinned and drew out his cell phone while Derek started the truck and headed toward home. "Hello, Amy? This is Abraham Yousef... Yes, Abe. I would like to ask you..."

Everything was working out exactly as Rose had planned when she floated the idea of a celebratory dinner with Tim. It would have taken too long to wait for the opening of *Milly's Diner*, and she still hadn't eaten at *Louis' Bistro*, so she had convinced him that it was high time she was introduced to its culinary delights. The truth was, she really wanted to get the ball rolling as a matchmaker.

Rose had done her homework. On Tuesday morning she met Amy at *Shear Madness* salon and day spa occupying the basement of owner Tanya Miller's home. Rose had popped into the boutique on Commerce Street on Monday to pick Gayle Harwood's brain on the best local hairdresser in town. Gayle, who not only owned the boutique, but also a considerable mental catalog of all things necessary for turning women out in style, offered several suggestions. But, in the end, she confessed that she trusted her own stylish haircut to Tanya's skilled hands alone.

As Rose had hoped, when she disclosed her makeover mission, Gayle instantly offered her services as clothier. She took great pleasure in helping women to look their best, and the prospect of dressing a tall slender young woman who needed a boost of confidence and a touch of class served as welcome fodder for her creative soul. Reminding Gayle that Amy was a schoolteacher, and therefore not independently wealthy, Rose happily received the assurance that she would be amazed at what a few judicious wardrobe purchases could do for the ego without damaging the budget. "You just leave everything to me. Bring Amy by here on Wednesday afternoon and leave her in my hands. I promise you won't regret it."

Rose had taken Gayle at her word and started Amy's transformation from the ground up knowing that new clothes would display to best advantage on someone already made-up and polished.   Besides, Rose believed that there was nothing that made a woman feel more pampered than a mani-pedi. She had reckoned without Amy's total disregard for the state of her nails. Amy had never really given any thought to them at all. She cut her fingernails, when necessary, which meant when they interfered with playing the violin, and ignored their existence the rest of the time. Her toenails were merely coverings for the ends of her toes. Tanya changed all that. "Yes, it *is* necessary if you want to look like a well-groomed woman," she insisted when Amy protested.

In the end, the diamond in the rough surrendered to Tanya's mandate and Rose's coaxing. Fortunately, she found the experience more pleasant than she had anticipated and enjoyed sharing the latest town news tidbits with the other ladies present while relishing a heavenly foot massage. The eyebrow waxing was not as heavenly and might have ended the makeover process just as it was getting started. But a quick glance in the mirror showed Amy that the one newly arched brow made a huge difference in the way it complemented her eye. So, Amy gritted her teeth and steeled herself for removal of the second patch of wax.

"Owww! That hurts!"

"Well, you'll be happy to know that if you keep up with shaping them on a weekly basis, you probably won't have to go through that again for several months," Tanya reassured Amy. Turning her away from the mirror, Tanya tackled both the ponytail hanging down Amy's back and a face that offered a blank canvas for the hands of an artist. Forty-five minutes later, she swung Amy around to face the mirror. This time Amy had no words to say at all. She sat blinking in disbelief as she looked at the stranger staring back at her. Respecting Rose's admonition to keep everything as simple as possible so that there was more likelihood of Amy keeping up the enhanced beauty regimen, Tanya had, nonetheless, outdone herself. After surprising her client by rewetting her hair and gently removing all the make-up, Tanya patiently showed Amy how to replicate the effect by herself.

"You may be my grand-daughter's favorite teacher, but I don't plan to come by your house every day to help you get dolled up."

Her thoughts momentarily diverted, Amy said, "Miller. Not *Emily* Miller?"

"That's right. The one who's tone deaf and has two left thumbs. I don't know why she wants to play an instrument so badly, but she is determined to do it."

"She may not be very musical, but she's a fun kid. Besides it's important to learn to appreciate music, even if you're not great at creating it."

"I suppose you're right. But I promise *you'll* be able to create *this* look any time. Now let me show you…" And with that, a thorough tutorial, complete with a few failed attempts, gave Amy the confidence to tackle what most women would consider a simple task. Giving Tanya a generous tip in addition to a fervent hug, Amy walked out of the salon with her head held high.

And true to Rose's instructions, she presented herself fully made up at *Miles of Styles Boutique* the next day. It was the perfect setting for a Cinderella moment. Gayle had shrewdly managed the small-business loan from Aletha Mason the previous year and made much of the space occupying two shopfronts now combined into one larger establishment. She used standard industry display racks but surrounded them with details from vintage clothing stores to add a touch of class. A 60-year-old mannequin clad in a sequined black gown with long gloves and matching bag greeted visitors when they entered the store. The fact that the gown had numerous rows of missing sequins and the gloves had several rents in them was easily dismissed as insignificant minutiae. Simple shorts and tops were displayed on a utilitarian plastic table topped with a gingham tablecloth and an old-fashioned wicker picnic basket. Inexpensively framed posters of movie stars from the 1940s and 1950s looked down on the dress section reminding shoppers of a time when elegance and femininity were qualities to be emulated, not downplayed. The shop's adornments were not intrinsically valuable, but they inspired women with the belief that they would emerge from Gayle's boutique more confident and well-dressed than when they arrived.

Amy needed a lot of inspiration. She greeted the proprietress wearing her habitual summertime casualwear – basketball shorts and T-shirt. She had, however, fixed her hair and make-up just as Tanya had taught her, so Gayle wasn't as disheartened as she might have been.

After two hours of instructing Amy to "try on this" or "put that back" she was arguably as pleased with the final results as Rose or Amy. Believing that new customers make the best repeat customers if given a little financial incentive, Gayle presented a remarkably reasonable bill to Amy who looked at an enormous pile of separates and hanging clothes with wonder. Waving the two girls out of the store, Gayle gave herself a mental pat on the back for doing her part to transform the resident Eliza Doolittle with as much skill as any displayed by the characters in *My Fair Lady*. She had also convinced Rose, though it took little persuasion, to purchase a new dress for the social occasion. Rose agreed because it was a very feminine dress, and she looked forward to seeing the appreciation in Tim's eyes when he called for her on Friday. But she also wanted to rid her mind of the memory of a dreadful dress Simon had purchased for her, the one she had worn on the day he tried to seduce her and then humiliated her into the dust. Rose had ripped it into shreds in a moment of catharsis. Now she had a replacement that was more modest, more flattering, and one that she would be proud to wear.

Having laid all the groundwork for Amy's big reveal, Rose maneuvered the players for maximum effect. Amy had duly accepted Abe's gallantly worded though nervously proffered invitation for the evening. Acting on her friend's guidance, Amy told Abe she would have to meet him there due to a possible late return from a much-needed trip to Kansas City. This was, strictly speaking, the truth. Amy had been decked out from head to almost toe. Unfortunately, *Happy Soles* shoe store couldn't accommodate her need for fashionable shoes that fit a size 11, so a flying trip to the city was necessary to complete her ensemble. Rose had flatly refused to allow Amy to make her public debut in flip flops.

By the time Tim and Rose arrived at *Louis' Bistro*, the restaurant was filling up. The owners, Louis and Marie Thibodeaux, had set up a cozy table for five in the middle of the main floor. Though they catered primarily to couples and foursomes, the Thibodeauxs had been so pleased by the Three Brothers' conversion of the old railway station into an elegant little restaurant, they were happy to accommodate Tim's request.

The Thibodeaux family had fled New Orleans after Hurricane Katrina to join extended family members and fellow restauranteurs in Kansas City. The chance sighting of a realtor's sign, hanging outside the abandoned train station in Tinkers Well, had inspired them to retire to the country and open a part-time restaurant there. Even though they had only been in business for six months, they were already drawing clientele from at least five neighboring counties. Their bistro was a surprisingly popular venue, both because of the excellent food and because of the interior that took visitors on an effortless journey to the *Big Easy*. Snug booths lined the outside walls on a slightly elevated level a few steps above the main floor where intricate wrought iron railings evoked visions of New Orleans' French Quarter. Seating in the central dining area offered an equally romantic option where small intimate tables with delicate gilt chairs were scattered for maximum privacy. Linen tablecloths draped each dining surface and added elegance to fresh flowers in diminutive crystal vases. The muted warmth of gently flickering candlelight blended perfectly with the smooth jazz that accompanied quiet dinner conversation without dominating it. Rose found the setting enchanting.

And as she had hoped, Tim found *her* enchanting in the new dress that hugged her figure while lending her an ethereal quality with floating layers of ice blue gossamer fabric. In addition to her obvious delight in her surroundings, Tim noticed that Rose seemed to be hiding some secret. She kept an expectant eye on Abe. Tim kept a suspicious eye on Rose. And Abe kept a nervous eye on the door.

He was momentarily diverted by the entrance of a tall, willowy young woman with shining brown hair, cut in layers and curled in long, loose waves. The soft waves framed a face dominated by hypnotically beautiful eyes under delicately arched brows. She was dressed simply in a full, knee-length, cream-colored skirt that fell in graceful folds from a wide waistband. It was topped by a boat neck green satin blouse, loosely resembling a T-shirt, except for its exquisite cut and fit. Abe felt a little guilty for getting side-tracked by the newcomer and looked beyond her for any sign of Amy. But when the young woman turned and walked purposely in their direction his jaw dropped in utter amazement. The gorgeous super model with melting brown eyes *was* Amy! Momentary paralysis set in as Abe gazed at her in disbelief and wonder. Rose and Derek hurried to welcome her and invite her to be seated. After gallantly pulling out Amy's chair, Derek slapped Abe on the back of the head, jerking that bemused young man into the reality of sitting next to the loveliest woman he had ever seen.

"Oh, my goodness. You look so beautiful! I hardly recognized you," Abe said, then realized how that might be misinterpreted and fell all over himself trying to clarify his compliment. "I didn't mean… that is… you always look very nice, especially your smile. I have always admired it," he said simply and smiled shyly at Amy who had heard nothing after his initial comment. In a state of bemusement, she sat basking in the blatant admiration evident in his eyes. She couldn't help but notice that he had made a special effort too by wearing neatly creased dress slacks and a crisply ironed shirt complete with tie.

Rose watched them with happy gratification in the triumph of her achievement. Tim, watching Rose, leaned toward her under cover of drink orders being taken. "This whole thing," he said, gesturing with his forefinger in a wide circle, "was your doing, wasn't it?"

"I don't know what you mean." Her face was a portrait of innocence until, looking away from him at her menu, she allowed a satisfied smile to appear.

"*Rose...*" Tim said with an inflection in his voice that reminded her forcibly of her father when he had caught her out in a lie.

"Well," she whispered back defensively, "Don't we have something to celebrate?"

"Yes, but – "

"And doesn't your expanded business have something to celebrate?"

"Yes, but Rose – "

"Now it looks like our friends have something to celebrate, too." Tim was no match for her paths of reasoning.

Watching Abe and Amy as they progressed from shy, admiring acquaintances to two people comfortable with one another and confident in their conversation, Tim had to admit, "I don't know about Amy, but as someone who has recently gone through this process, I'd say Abe's got it pretty bad."

"Tim, you make romance sound like a disease!"

Taking Rose's hand, he raised it to his lips. "Well, if it is, I hope I never recover," he murmured in her ear, causing the color to bloom in her cheeks.

Derek might have felt like a fifth wheel, sitting at a table occupied by two couples rife with romance, except that he always believed himself to be the life of every party. He shared in Rose's satisfaction at getting Abe and Amy together and gave his confederate full marks for the makeover. Amy certainly eclipsed his expectations, and by the look on Abe's face, he wasn't likely to have eyes for any other woman even if a *real* super model walked through the door. Derek and Rose had already worked out a plausible excuse for her and Tim to take him home, leaving Abe with the keys to Derek's truck. At the end of a merry evening and a delicious meal, Derek convinced Tim that they needed to go over some plans for a Saturday project. Rose took her cue.

"That's a great idea Derek. That way Tim can join me at the big house first thing tomorrow. We can give you a ride home from the office," she added, beaming at Tim who regarded them both through narrowed eyes. He knew it was futile to argue.

"Then I guess we'll get going. Abe," he said, shaking his friend's hand, "Amy, enjoy the rest of your evening. It seems that duty calls." Derek tossed Abe the keys and waved goodbye. Rose gave Amy a quick hug then hurried after the two men.

Left alone, the objects of the evening's schemes felt momentarily self-conscious. Amy peeked at Abe as he shyly glanced at her, and they both started laughing.

"It would appear that I can now conveniently offer you a ride home. Shall we?" Abe asked, pulling her chair back.

As they left the restaurant, Amy put a restraining hand on Abe's arm. "Would you mind if we took a walk through the park first? It's such a nice evening." In truth, even at nine o'clock, it was oppressively hot but neither seemed to care. They strolled and chatted and laughed then sat in easy silence on a park bench, marveling at the simple pleasure of being together. Their fingers sought those of the other in the dark, and such was their mutual state of mind that the innocent gesture provided the same electric shock of pleasure that others might experience in a first kiss. Neither wanted to be the first to suggest leaving, so it was after midnight before Abe dropped Amy at the little duplex she called home, both conveniently forgetting her car parked at the restaurant.

Abe felt little need for Derek's truck. It was as if he flew on eagle's wings the short distance to the Warner home. If he could have, he would have captured that feeling and held on to it forever. But golden moments, like haunting melodies, are fleeting, meant to be savored only as long as they last.

CHAPTER 8

*There is an appointed time for everything. And there is a time for
every event under heaven – A time to be silent and a time to speak.*
Ecclesiastes 3: 1, 7b (NASB)

"Letha, don't be silly. Of course, he's going to ask her."

"Well, I have reason to believe that one obstacle to proposing has been removed, so I'm not sure what's taking him so long," Aletha replied with unwonted spirit.

Angelica, knowing that Aletha was feeling a little blue at the thought of her house guests' imminent departure, had joined forces with Marilyn to try to cheer her up. They planned a ladies' afternoon tea that coincided with their offspring and friends taking a day off to relax and do some waterskiing at the lake. Marilyn volunteered her home since it had a larger dining room than Angelica's. They invited several ladies from church to join them, including Lucy Bennet and Lisa Lindeman. There was much to discuss, and Gert and Aletha had wasted no time in coming to the point.

"And *I* happen to know that he's about to remove another," Gert said with a superior smile that Letha, though not able to see it, could, nonetheless, detect in her friend's voice.

"Trudy, what do you know that you're not telling us?" the gentle old lady demanded.

"Nope. I promised Tim I would keep it to myself, so just never you mind. You'll all find out soon enough, so let's move on." Marilyn had just freshened everyone's cup and passed around some heavenly scones dripping with butter. Gert snatched hers up, broke off a sizeable piece, and popped it in her mouth thus effectively rendering herself incapable of further speech.

Laughing, Lisa took the reins and suggested they consider wedding and reception venues. A pleasurable hour passed while those present examined the possibilities, but a chance remark caused Gert to withdraw from the lively discussion. She watched the faces of the residents of Tinkers Well that surrounded her, faces that would soon become Rose's new family, and she felt a sudden wave of sadness wash over her. No one seemed to notice accept Aletha, who knew her old friend so well and had guessed the reason for the change in Gert's usually outspoken manner. On the drive home, Aletha kept up a pleasant flow of conversation with Angelica to cover Gert's curious silence. After a terse thank you, Gert went immediately to the guest room where Aletha found her a few minutes later, sitting on one of the twin beds. Dabbing at unaccustomed tears, Gert contemplated the empty bed opposite her – the bed that Rose occupied while they shared a room for the summer. Taking a seat beside her, Aletha patted Gert's hand comfortingly.

" *'If she'd lived here longer, I'm sure Rose would already have set her mind on what she wanted, but I'll bet she'll be happy with whatever we suggest. She'll get to know the place better when she moves here permanently.'* Or words to that effect. It was Lucy's comment that made you think, wasn't it?" she asked gently.

Gert nodded her head silently.

"It's so much fun to plan a wedding, but we don't often look past the festivities to the way a marriage affects so many lives." She paused, waiting for a response, but Gert remained mute. "Tim and Rose will begin their journey together, and they won't need us as much anymore because they'll have each other. And even though we celebrate *their* happiness, it inevitably robs us a little of our own."

Gert drew a deep breath and said, finally, "I really *like* Tim and I know he's just the man for my Rosie, and Beth and Ralph will be tickled to death when they meet him. But she won't be able to hop in her car to spend the weekend with me anymore or take me to see a movie – not that there's much worth seeing these days. Oh, I know I'm just being a foolish, selfish old woman," she added crossly.

"You're being a loving, caring grandmother, and I would have been shocked if you hadn't felt as you do," Aletha said firmly.

"You would?" Gert asked doubtfully.

"I most certainly would. Now, why don't I take Scout outside for a few minutes while you pick out a really *good* movie, maybe one with Cary Grant or Rock Hudson, and get it loaded into the DVD player? Do you remember how Rose taught you to turn it on?"

They walked slowly down the hall behind Scout and stopped at the door to the library. The converted third bedroom offered the perfect setting for curling up with a good book or working at the computer that occupied the top of an elegant table desk in front of the window. The room also contained the only TV in the house, nestled among volumes of old classics on a tall shelf in the center bookcase. It had been Martin Mason's favorite room in the house – Rose's too.

"If I can keep those darned fool remotes straight. Hey, how did that get here?" As Gert moved into the room, she noticed Aletha's chair and footstool crammed in next to the only other seating option – a well-worn, overstuffed chair.

"I had Tim move it in here when he picked up Rose earlier. I thought this might be a good afternoon for a film – cheer us both up."

"Letha," Gert said gruffly, "You're one of the truest friends I've ever had. Can't think why I haven't come out to visit you sooner."

"Well, I think it was simply God's timing. If you'd come sooner, Rose might not have been able to accompany you, or Tim might still have been on active duty. And we might not have appreciated and needed one another so much. It's always best to trust in the Master's plans."

"Amen! Now let me see, I believe I noticed…" Gert scanned the shelf above the TV while Aletha walked to the back door with Scout. "Aha! Maybe we'll start with *Arsenic and Old Lace* and make it a double-feature with *Pillow Talk…*"

Tim had timed a crew R&R day at the lake perfectly. The sun was hot, the water was cool, and because it was a weekday, the picnic area and beach were almost deserted. Jada had been serious about her antipathy toward water and stayed 25 miles away in Kansas City. But JT, Jason, and José gladly accepted the invitation. Abe was not about to tackle waterskiing, but he had often driven the boat. And because Amy had mentioned that she enjoyed the sport during one of the countless outings they had shared since that magical evening in July, he acknowledged the many pointed hints dropped by Rose and invited Amy to join the crew. Tim was not the only one keeping an anxious eye on the calendar. While Tim grimly marked the days until Rose's departure, Abe became increasingly aware of the start of the school year right around the corner, and worried that his courting season would be seriously impeded when other demands claimed much of Amy's time. For courtship it was.

Still doubting his desirability as a husband, Abe nevertheless believed that he had found his life partner and pursued her with circumspect honor. Little did he know that his hesitation in overtly expressing himself, either verbally or physically, filled his equally smitten heart's desire with her own doubts.

Amy confided as much to Rose as the two girls sunned themselves on the little sandy beach while the men skied one end of the lake to the other. They had generously offered the ladies first dibs at the end of the rope. The experience left Rose feeling a bit water-logged, despite Tim's careful instruction. And though Amy's natural athleticism made even slalom skiing look easy, they graciously volunteered to go ashore and leave the skiing to the men. Knowing that was sure to be a few hours, they grabbed their towels and stretched out in the sun. A peaceful lassitude soon enveloped them both. The soft lap of water against the dock pylons mingled with the cry of darting water birds lulled them into a semi-doze from which Amy woke first. Her troubled thoughts sought council.

"I'm not exactly experienced in the romance department," she said, seeking reassurance from Rose, "but I really believe Abe cares for me. Or at least I thought so. Once we got over that initial awkwardness, everything became so easy between us. It was kind of funny when we finally figured out that each of us had been interested in the other for some time, but had both felt inadequate to say anything. Now we're able to talk about… everything. He even shared how much he misses his family and how he's constantly trying to reach out to them. I don't know how he carries such a burden yet still stays so positive and kind and funny and… and… *amazing*. Oh, Rose, I think I'm falling for him in a big way, and I don't know what to do about it," she finished on a note of desperation.

Sitting up to reach for some more sunblock, Rose looked at her friend and asked in disbelief, "Wait, you said you *think* he cares for you. How could you *doubt* that? Every time he looks at you his face lights up!" Sensitive to Amy's conflicted emotions, Rose added gently, "There must be something you're not telling me." She lay down again and closed her eyes, waiting patiently. Amy wrestled with her thoughts, attempting to put them into words while she unthinkingly rubbed in the sunblock handed to her by Rose.

"It's just that, well, he doesn't *show* me how he feels. I mean he's always a gentleman: opening doors for me, pulling out my chair, giving me his umbrella if we get caught out in the rain – that kind of thing, which is really nice," Amy hastened to add. "But he has never come out and told me how he feels or… or put his arms around me or so much as touched my hand again since the night of the dinner when we sat in the park and talked for hours. I know it sounds silly, but that was a magical moment. I was sure that more would follow, but I don't even know what *that* moment meant anymore…" Her voice trailed off in uncertainty.

"Well, I'm no expert either, but I wonder…"

"I mean, look at you and Tim," Amy said, as if Rose hadn't spoken at all. "Anyone can tell that you're in love – the way you speak to each other and the easy, familiar way you touch each other…" She stopped abruptly and added hastily, "Not that anything you do or say is inappropriate or anything like that, because I know you would never… well, you know," she finished in embarrassment.

Rose laughed as she sat up. "First of all, you can't compare you and Abe to Tim and me. The poor man had to rescue me *twice* from a treacherous villain and got *stabbed* on my account before I realized that I loved him. By then our first kiss was the most natural thing in the world, but I *don't* recommend that process as a way of learning to express your feelings!" Despite Amy's responsive smile, Rose hesitated before going on. "I know Abe has lived in the US since he was a boy, but I can't help thinking that he is still heavily influenced by the culture he grew up in. Could he be hesitant to declare himself because of some dating standards he's following that you don't even know about?"

As she considered Rose's words, Amy gazed out over the water with the deep blue of the sky reflected in its surface. She heard loud squawking and watched a pair of geese flying away in the distance. Nearer at hand, two squirrels chased each other across a clump of trees before disappearing into a bush. *Animals seem to navigate the road to romance without any trouble,* she thought. *I wonder why it's so difficult for humans.* After a few minutes she said aloud, "I guess I never thought of that. He *seems* so American and is a Christian now, but he is still Lebanese too, and he spent his whole life following Muslim traditions."

"Why don't you ask him?" Before Amy could protest Rose hurried on. "Maybe that's the only way to know. Though I must confess that that may not be as easy as it sounds. Believe it or not, as much as I know in my heart of hearts that Tim loves me, he hasn't said one word about *our* future and I'm leaving in less than two weeks." A shadow of doubt flitted across her face as if a drifting cloud momentarily blocked the sun.

Feeling guilty for dragging Rose into her own relationship troubles, thereby reminding her friend of those relationship problems closer to home, Amy jumped up, dusted the sand off her arms and legs, and suggested they get the charcoal going for lunch. The girls had also been left to unpack the bulging cooler and picnic basket waiting in the back of Abe's new SUV.

He had finally parted with a sizeable chunk of his savings to acquire his own set of wheels. The decision was due in part to his embarrassment at continually asking to borrow Derek's truck. But the real driving force was finally being able to see a future where he would have need of his own vehicle – and someone to share it with. Abe had intentionally included Amy in the process, wanting her input and approval but unable to tell her why.

Love may have filled the air of Tinkers Well that summer, but for those affected by its power, it might have functioned more efficiently as a clearly marked path rather than a nebulous, hazy sensation.

Tim and Rose knew they wanted to spend their lives together, but neither had broached the subject of when that might begin, though her scheduled departure date loomed large on the calendar. She had a taste of how much she would miss him when he was gone for a few days on what he called a treasure trip – a search for unique architectural pieces suited to the Victorian renovation. She begged to go with Tim, but Granny Gert put her foot down, saying she didn't care if they would have individual hotel rooms, no granddaughter of hers was going to go gallivanting across the country with a man. Gert had faithfully promised Tim to keep Rose from trying to join him. Rose didn't forgive her grandmother until the day he returned.

It was nearly dusk when Tim met Rose at the gate to the big house. She was attired in the dress he had admired so much the evening they dined at *Louis' Bistro*. He wore neatly pressed khaki slacks and a dress shirt –

practically formal attire for him. They embraced as if they'd been separated for three weeks instead of three days. After each had convinced the other of their unchanged affections, he led her slowly down the walk toward the veranda. There was such a glow about the young lovers it offered competition for the fireflies. Rose stopped abruptly in their walk to look back and forth between the east and west sides of the house where the willow branches swayed in the evening breeze.

"Tim! Look at the *willows*!"

"Okay…" He had no idea what she was so excited about.

"Don't you see? They're welcoming us to the house as we walk."

"Well, that's a nice thought…"

"Her name. I finally know her name!" Seeing his look of complete bewilderment, she said simply, "*Willow Walk*," and spread her arms wide. "Her name is *Willow Walk!*" Rose had spent the entire summer trying to think of a name worthy of the grand Victorian lady standing before them.

He looked at the house and caught up with her vision. "*Willow Walk*. Rose, my darling, you are brilliant." She smiled wistfully. At least she would have a name to remember her stately friend by. They continued their stroll to the front steps where Tim motioned for Rose to take a seat, then he pulled something out of his pocket and dropped to one knee. She suddenly felt her heart beating faster and waited breathlessly for him to speak.

"Rose Thompson, I love you so much that I need to tell you I have *not* been on a treasure trip as I described it. The only treasure I want now is you, so I flew to Kentucky to meet your family and to ask your father for your hand in marriage." She was crying now, the tears running over her beaming smile. "He said yes, by the way. Now I'm asking *you* if you would do me the great honor of agreeing to share your life with me. I know I'm asking you to leave your home – "

"Yes."

"…and live with a dusty carpenter – "

"Yes!" Rose was laughing and crying simultaneously.

"…in a small town where hardly anything ever happens, except when invaded by private eyes or uprooted by tornados – "

"*Yes! Yes! Yes!*" She threw herself into Tim's arms, putting her lips to much better use than merely mouthing words. When they were both able to catch their breath, he reached for her left hand and slid a dazzling pink sapphire surrounded by diamonds onto her ring finger.

"Oh, Tim. It's *gorgeous!*"

"Aletha gave it to me when I moved here. That was obviously before I knew my true parentage, but it was given to her by my grandfather, James Hawthorne. He couldn't afford an engagement ring at the time they married, so he presented this to her when she presented him with… a son." Rose winced at the evidence of Tim's ongoing struggle over the existence of his absent father, but she refused to allow that to cast a shadow over this shining moment. "She made me promise I would choose a bride worthy of wearing it. This ring was meant for your finger."

"Tim…" It was several minutes later.

"Mmm," he said, leaning his head against hers as they sat holding each other in the twilight.

"I want to be married at *Willow Walk*, in the garden. Or maybe we could take our vows here on the veranda…"

"…where I first verbally abused you? How romantic."

Rose giggled. "…where we first met, you goof…"

"…and where you just *promised* to put up with me for a lifetime. I mean to hold you to it, Thompson."

"I will – when my name is Ludlow." Rose was very late getting back to *Fern Cottage* that evening. Granny Gert didn't mind in the least.

Abe and Amy had been constantly in one another's thoughts and company for a month. They had both witnessed the joy that emanated from Tim and Rose when they announced their engagement and had shared in their friends' happiness. But for the first time in his life, Abe believed that such happiness could also be his. He could no longer look to his parents for guidance on a suitable marriage partner, but he could look to his Heavenly Father who had put Amy Walker squarely in his path. It was an idea that had been suggested by Derek (with whom Abe rarely agreed) but in this instance, he had been compelled to admit the wisdom of his friend's words.

Succumbing to the spell of her beauty and the power of soft moonlight, Abe had been so bold as to touch her hand, and the memory of her long, soft fingers intertwined with his still had the power to make him shiver. Not wanting to appear too bold, Abe had intentionally refrained from any further kind of touch or overt sign of his feelings, believing it to be the honorable way to conduct himself. He felt secure in asking Amy to spend time with him and believed her delight in his company to be unfeigned, but whenever he contemplated his next step in the courtship process, he fetched up on shaky ground.

He had been raised in a culture where the parents are heavily involved in the dating process. He knew for a fact that his own parents' marriage had been arranged, and that they had never been alone together before their wedding day. And though he knew his two married siblings had been much freer in their respective courtships, he had not been at home to witness either. Still, he believed them to have been far more temperate than that which he had observed in college, where intimacy between the sexes seemed to be a free-for-all. And when he was in the Army, the conduct of men toward women by his fellow soldiers could hardly be said to have reflected dignified restraint.

Abe's insecurity led him to seek out the one man he could trust for advice: one, because he would speak from a Christian perspective; and two, because he too was walking the same path. He was just further along the journey. Abe noted on the now substantially busier work schedule that Tim was finishing the trim at *Milly's Diner* preparatory to the grand opening on Friday, so he decided to tackle him there while he was working alone.

As he stepped through the door, Abe marveled again at the change in the place. The echoes of a 1960s-style diner were still evident in the booths lining the front windows and the swivel bar stools affixed permanently to the floor in front of the breakfast counter. But the old, stained Formica™ countertop had been replaced by granite, and a large flat-screen TV was mounted on the wall where a six-foot-wide plate glass mirror used to hang. The dinged and nicked black and white floor tiles had given way to engineered hardwood that worked in concert with a new gas stove to add warmth to the room. Abe found Tim on his hands and knees finishing the inside corner of baseboard trim in the large gathering room at the back of the diner. And being the master carpenter he was, he had cut the two pieces using the coping method, rather than cutting two 45° angles, thus ensuring the corner molding was a perfect fit. He knew his stuff about carpentry. Abe could only hope that he would provide expert dating advice as well.

"Now who's the genius?" Abe remarked in admiration.

Tim looked up, surprised at the sound of an unexpected voice. "Did I forget I needed to be somewhere else?" he asked, a little puzzled.

"Of course not. You are, obviously," Abe said, nodding his head at Tim's handiwork, "exactly where you need to be. No, I came to ask you for some… insight and direction."

Tim recognized the signs of worry and indecision in his friend's words. Knowing that men tend to be more forthcoming with their concerns if their hands are busy, he handed Abe a caulking gun already filled with a tube of trim sealant. "You do the chair rail molding, and I'll finish the baseboard. I promised Milly she could get in here tonight to restock and start decorating, so you showing up now is a godsend." After working in silence for a few moments, Tim asked casually, "So what's up?" while watching the other man out of the corner of his eye.

Abe wasn't sure how to begin, but eventually the words came and continued to come until he found it difficult to stop long enough for Tim to interject anything. When at last he came to a verbal standstill it was Tim who hesitated, wanting to respond honestly and accurately. "Wow," he said, shaking his head and looking directly at Abe. "You do realize that there is no easy answer to your situation. I mean, every couple has to decide for themselves how to conduct their courtship." He saw Abe's brows draw together and added quickly, "But if you are a Christ follower you want to honor him in all your relationships, right?" He waited for Abe's nod then continued, "And if you understand that physical human interaction, at whatever level, was created by God for our pleasure within the parameters he set for us, then you simply reflect that understanding in the way you live. Got it?"

"So, this is what it feels like to be Derek," Abe said, momentarily disheartened.

Tim laughed and asked, "What do you mean?"

"I have never felt more like an idiot – I hardly understood anything you said other than honoring God."

They had worked their way around the room to the counter where Abe ran out of molding. Tim continued to work on the baseboard. Pausing for a minute, he rocked back on his heels and looked up at his discouraged friend. "Okay. Look at it this way. The whole relationship thing between a man and woman starts before they ever touch each other or have their first date. You see a girl that catches your eye, and she smiles at you, and you feel something stir inside you. I don't know how else to describe it, but you know what I mean."

"Oh, yes. That I understand," Abe assured him.

"Then you see her when she's dressed really nice, you know for church or say, a dinner." Tim stole a glance at Abe who grinned in response. "And your heart kind of flip-flops, and you want to talk to her but suddenly your mouth goes dry, and you convince yourself that you have absolutely nothing to say that won't sound…" Tim searched for the right word.

"…sophomoric?" Abe supplied, as only he would. "You see. I knew you were the right man to talk to!"

"You might want to save your applause," Tim said ruefully. "Here's where it starts to get a little dicey. Because it's different for different people in different circumstances. You see, I felt that way about Rose at the same time she thought she was in love with someone else. In a way that took away some of the awkwardness because she just saw me as a friend, so we were free to get to know each other without any pressure to express ourselves in any way. She expected nothing from me but friendship, and I was determined not to let her know how I felt for fear of pushing her away, all the while trying to help her see what a jerk Atherton was.

"When everything came crashing in, there I was, still just her friend but someone she could trust. Mix in a tornado and a life and death struggle, and all the pieces fell into place for her. I had known all along. So, our first real physical contact was a kiss that, even now, can leave me running for a cold shower when I think about it. Since then I've committed to not crossing an invisible line that would tempt us to go further toward the kind of intimacy that was only ever intended to be shared by a husband and wife. As a man, I am compelled to protect her – even if it's from ourselves. There have been times when I've had to step away from Rose, because I didn't trust my own self-control."

"So, you're saying I must decide, with all that goes between that first glance and my wedding day, how to act so that Amy knows of my feelings for her without behaving ungentlemanly. You're right, there is no easy answer." Abe stood in thoughtful silence while he watched Tim work. Finally, he asked diffidently, "I know I may be impertinent in asking, but has Rose ever questioned your… pulling away?"

Tim finished applying a strip of caulk all the way to end of the baseboard before replying. "Worse. She looked hurt, like I was rejecting her or something. But when I told her why, and was honest about my own struggle, she understood." He laughed suddenly and added, "She told me about a saying her mom drummed into her and her sisters from the time they started noticing boys. '*No touching between the neck and the knees.*'

It's actually pretty good advice, except that it's kind of hard to hug a girl without putting your arms around her waist. But talking about every aspect of our relationship openly has helped us to help each other, because she's human too after all.

"The thing is, you have to remember that God hard-wired us — especially men — to desire intimacy with the woman we love, so it's natural to *experience* those feelings. But you must decide, *before* you face temptation, how to guard against surrendering to it in a moment of weakness. I've heard of some couples who only meet in groups with other people (Abe thought of his parents) and others who agree not to kiss until they're formally engaged. I even knew of one guy who didn't kiss his wife until their wedding ceremony, which I happen to think is a little extreme. I mean, a first kiss is a pretty personal moment — not one I'd care to share in front of a hundred or so people." He had finished his task and was capping the tube of sealant. "I don't know if that helped or not, but one thing I can tell you with absolute certainty is that you need to pray about this, and you need to be open with Amy — about everything. And whatever you do, don't look to mass media for advice. Hollywood and the music industry have been portraying a completely screwed up version of courtship for decades."

"Thank you, my friend. You have helped me more than you know."

Abe assisted Tim to gather tools and load them into the truck, signaling the end of another successful renovation. While he watched Milly's truck approach from the other end of the street, Tim said in a conspiratorial undertone,

"Don't you dare repeat this, but the truth is I'm kind of relieved that I won't see Rose for six weeks." At Abe's look of surprise, he grinned and added, "The more time I spend with that woman, the harder it is for me to fight that temptation. And by the time she gets back here, she'll be crazy busy with wedding prep, and I'll be putting the hammer down to finish several projects, so we probably won't have a lot of time alone together anyway. I would never willingly have planned to have Rose leave right now, and I know I'll miss her like crazy, but I believe this is God's timing. As hard as it is for me to admit sometimes, he really does know what's best for us!"

Granny Gert and Rose had their bags packed and loaded in Rose's car, except for what they would need for the next two days of travel. Angelica and Marilyn had been cooking all afternoon in preparation for the Farewell/Engagement Party now in full swing in the garden of *Willow Walk*. Tim and Rose opened gift after gift from their many friends who all rejoiced in the plans for their upcoming nuptials set for the end of October. Rose chose the time because there could potentially be some flowers still in bloom, but the air would be pleasantly cool, and Tim would have ample time to schedule future projects for Three Brothers around his absence for a honeymoon. She also wanted to make sure her oldest sister could be there, and with Violet's first baby due in early December, the wedding either had to happen by the end of October or not until the New Year. Tim flatly refused to entertain the second option, much to Rose's relief, declaring that her mother would just have to make the best of it.

Beth Thompson thought it a bit of a short timeline to get announcement lists coordinated and invitations sent, let alone making all the arrangements from 600 miles away. But Granny Gert stepped in to tell her daughter she was lucky they were willing to wait that long. "Why, they're nutty on each other! And they've already weathered more storms in two months than most couples face in their first ten years together, so I'd say they're more prepared than most." Pastor Lindeman agreed but insisted on a month of marriage counseling before the wedding. Tim would fly to Kentucky at the end of September to drive his fiancée to Tinkers Well where she would reside with Marilyn Ludlow. The original Three Brothers planned to move into *Willow Walk* as soon as the wood floors were refinished so they could devote more time to prepping the place for the big day.

Aletha waited until everyone had eaten, and all were sitting in relaxed fellowship before presenting her gift to the newly engaged couple. "Tim and Rose, I have something special for you, and I've selfishly kept it for last because I want everyone to share in what I hope will be your great pleasure. Here, my dear children," she said, holding out a long, decorative box, "please accept this from a joyful heart. You are the only two I could have given her to." Tim and Rose exchanged puzzled looks before opening the box. In it lay an old-fashioned key. Still mystified, they lifted a paper lying underneath the key. It was quite fragile and yellowed with age. They unfolded it carefully then stood in stunned silence as they read its contents. It was the deed to *Willow Walk* made over to them with a check adequate to renovate, remodel and revive the old beauty in style.

Tim and Rose began a vehement protest, declaring the gift to be too much, but Aletha raised her hand to stop them. Gesturing at the graceful building that she could no longer see with her eyes, but would always remember in her heart, Aletha said, "She needs to be a home again, to hear the sound of children's voices and the laughter of many guests. She needs to be loved and to shelter love, so please accept this gift with my blessing." Aletha received their enthusiastic thanks with a heart overflowing.

The morning of departure dawned all too soon. Most of their friends, Tom and Lucy Bennett, Pastor Lindeman and Lisa, the Thursday night Bingo crowd and the new crew from *Three Brothers Construction, Inc.* had bid Rose and Gert farewell the night before. But the dearest of Rose's new friends were there to see the travelers off. She hugged everyone as she said her goodbyes, happy in the knowledge that hellos would be said again soon enough. She was especially pleased to see Abe and Amy, who barely let go of each other's hands long enough to embrace her. Derek bowed, making Rose laugh, before crushing her in his arms and smiling at her with misty eyes. Marilyn kissed Rose's cheek, hugged her tightly, and told her she couldn't wait for the day she could call Rose her daughter. Angelica kissed the other cheek and thrust a bag of party leftovers into Rose's hands in case she and Gert got hungry along the way. When she got to Aletha, Granny Gert was standing by her old school chum.

"Did you ever imagine Trudy, all those years ago when our paths crossed, that our grandchildren would someday meet and fall in love in a place far removed from where either one of us began?"

"I'd call it a miracle. It's a good thing for them that we both lasted so long!"

"Well, we'd better last a little longer. I intend to see those two wed, so to speak" said the blind woman with a twinkle in her blank eyes. "And I want you by my side when they do."

"Don't you worry about that, Letha. I'll be here, and I'll make sure the Thompsons and Schmidts make it, too. So long old friend. Now don't *you* start crying…" The two embraced, then Gert got in the car, telling Tim, who was holding Rose like she was leaving forever, to get on with it. "We've got to get this show on the road!"

The others had walked to the end of the driveway to allow Tim and Rose some privacy. She raised her head from his shoulder and looked into his eyes, her own filled with the light of love.

"When I drove Granny Gert out here, I was running away from the past and afraid to face the future. I felt like I was looking for… something. At first, I thought it was self-confidence and faith in my own worth as a woman of God."

"And have you found that faith, my love?" Tim asked tenderly.

"I think I have. I know I have." Then, shaking her head, she added, "But I found so much more." Rose looked into the face of her beloved and said simply, "I believe God sent me here to find – you."

The penthouse office was empty save for a small, battered drop-leaf table in a corner by the window. On it sat a Bible and a legal document. The table had been the first desk used by James Hawthorne when he and his bride opened a start-up company manufacturing transistor radios in the 1960s. He had given it to his young son, Timothy, as a reminder that true success always begins with humility. Miles Hawthorne glanced at it, remembering the hours of homework he had completed at that desk. It was eventually relegated to storage after cutthroat determination had resulted in riches enough to buy ten far grander desks. But he had never gotten rid of it, just as he had kept his father's Bible. He walked over to the table and picked up the papers left by his attorney, tucking them into his inside coat pocket. He then dropped the leaves on the table and tucked the Bible under one arm. Picking up the table, Miles looked around the room then walked through the door and closed it for the last time.

Miss Limstock was waiting for him as he had requested. She sat at her desk – the only furniture left in the lobby. It would be picked up the following day. As much as any emotion registered on her very proper professional countenance, melancholy was foremost that day as she contemplated an uncertain future. She had been paid well by Mr. Hawthorne, but of late her income had been largely eaten up by nursing home bills for her bedridden mother. She had to work to support them both, but unattractive secretaries in their early 60s, though extremely efficient, were not in high demand. She was studying a list of inauspicious job postings when her employer appeared.

"Thank you for waiting on me, Miss Limstock. It would appear that we have reached the parting of the ways."

"Yes sir."

"May I enquire as to your plans?" Miles asked politely.

"I hope to find another position, sir. But you needn't concern yourself. Your letter of recommendation was very generous, so I'm sure something will turn up."

"May I suggest another option?"

"Another option?" Miss Limstock *never* considered options. She only followed well-thought-out plans.

"I believe you have a sister living somewhere upstate and that your mother is in a nursing home here in the city." Miss Limstock was amazed that the great Miles Hawthorne even knew she *had* a mother and a sister. He had made it his business to find out.

"Do you remember when you came to work for me – what was that, 20 odd years ago?" She merely nodded. "I never offered you a 401K option, but I did open a brokerage investment account for you and told you that I could only pay into it if I made a certain percentage of profit. I'm ashamed to confess that I made more than enough profit, and I did pay into it, but you never received any statements because they all came to me. You see, I set it up as a joint account with me as the other account holder. I must further confess that I had intended to keep all those shares for myself if you never asked about the account, and you never did." Miss Limstock dared not say anything.

Miles drew a statement from another pocket in his suit coat and handed it to her. "I think you will find that it has done very well." He pointed to a figure at the bottom of the page. Miss Limstock's eyes grew so large they nearly eclipsed the frames of her glasses. The total was well over $700,000!

"It is now, as it always should have been, yours. I only deducted what I paid in taxes over the years. I trust that will allow you to retire, if you so choose. It should also enable you to move you and your mother away from the expense of the city to somewhere closer to your extended family where this and your Social Security income will be sufficient." The staid, sober Miss Limstock then burst into tears, ran around her desk, and threw her arms around her astonished employer.

"There, there. No need for all of that. I am merely doing right by you and can only beg your forgiveness for withholding this from you for so long."

Still unable to formulate any words, Miss Limstock nodded her head, grinned from ear to ear (a sight Miles had never beheld in 20 years), and skipped off to the elevator with visions of a quaint cottage dancing through her whirling thoughts.

Miles smiled and said out loud, as he glanced at the Bible under his arm, "I guess you were right. It really *is* more blessed to give than to receive." He quoted that bit of scripture from Acts over and over to himself at his next stop. It was with a shaking hand that he signed over the greenspace parcel to the city of New York, under the agreement that it remain undeveloped and open for use by the people of the city for the next 50 years, and that it be given the name "Joshua Strong Park." Miles had insisted the legal transfer of ownership take place on the land he had sought for so long, a quest that had brought him nothing but headache and loss. After the signing, he strolled leisurely to the church founded by his ancestor where he handed the mortgage note stamped 'Paid in Full' to a stunned but grateful pastor. Then he got into his car, loaded with nothing but the little table, a few suitcases, and the box of his father's prized possessions, and turned his sights to the west.

Miles wondered if the early settlers of Tinkers Well had experienced the same sense of adventure and promise that road beside him as he turned his back on all that he had known in his lifetime. He was almost certain they had.

CHAPTER 9

Timothy!" Marilyn Ludlow felt the oddest sense of déjà vu. She
had come to *Fern Cottage* at Aletha's request. When the knock
sounded, she answered it. "You came back," she said, hardly
believing her eyes.

Miles Hawthorne was not surprised to see Marilyn, however. Having
made a clean break with New York, he needed to move on to the next phase
of his life. But that meant making amends in Kansas, so he had called his
mother the night before to ask for her help. "Yes, Mari. I came back."

He had seen her just two months before, but he was struck once more
by her timeless beauty. "May I come in?"

"Oh, goodness, yes. I... that is, we... was Aletha expecting you?" she
asked, a little breathlessly.

"She was... I mean... she is." Miles wondered why he felt like a tongue-
tied teenager.

"Oh, I see... no... I really don't see. I thought..."

"You thought that I had turned my back on my family again all for the
sake of the main chance?"

She blushed because he had read her thoughts so clearly.

"Mari, I know I don't deserve your indulgence, but will you let me explain what happened?" As she hesitated, doubt in her eyes, he pleaded, "*Please?*" She nodded and indicated a seat on the sofa. Before she could move to a nearby chair, he caught her wrist, gently pulling her to sit next to him.

Neither of them heard Tim enter through the kitchen door. He had arrived that morning precisely at 11 o'clock as Aletha had suggested. She had asked him the evening before to stop by and look at a kitchen cabinet drawer that kept jamming. Explaining that she might have a guest, she suggested he go to the back of the house and let himself in. Tim was missing Rose so much that her absence had almost become a chronic physical ache, so he gladly agreed to turn his thoughts and time to a carpentry puzzle. When he drove up to the cottage, he noticed an unfamiliar sedan parked next to his mother's car and assumed the visitor must be someone known to both his mom and Aletha. The name 'grandmother' still sounded odd to him, even in his thoughts. He located the drawer in question adjacent to the arched opening giving onto the hallway. But before he could diagnose the problem, he heard a man's voice in the living room. It was oddly familiar. Though a little embarrassed at listening to the conversation, he, nonetheless, felt compelled to draw nearer to hear what was being said. He heard someone take a deep breath, and the man's voice continued.

"I can't begin to describe how I felt that day, Mari. Breaking down like I did when I saw Mother, learning about you and Peter, and then being told I had a grown son named for me. I had every intention of waiting with you until Tim returned, but when Mother told me about that accursed deed, my mind just… snapped. I saw my whole career flash before my eyes, and I realized how futile it had all been — because I never learned the lesson of humility. My father tried to teach it to me, and you modeled it for me, but I was a damned fool. I turned my back on my family and on my faith. If I'd had the sense to hold onto either one, I might really have become a success.

But I sit here next to you, if not penniless, at least a far cry from where I was."

Tim leaned against the wall for support. The man speaking was his father. He wanted to step forward, to announce himself, to say something, *anything*. But he felt powerless to move.

In the living room Miles sat looking at his hands for a few minutes, avoiding Marilyn's eyes. Then he looked straight into their tender depths and spoke the unbelievable.

"I got rid of it all, Mari. I sold all the property I had accumulated for 'the deal of the century,' but I'd borrowed so much to purchase it, that I just about broke even after settling the debts I owed people I had cheated over the years. In the end, it was the tax write-off that saved me."

Marilyn stared at him, not quite comprehending.

"I found the deed. It was in Proverbs 11, just as Mother said it would be. But after I read the verse that Dad had highlighted, verse 28, I couldn't stop reading. I read that verse at least... 20 times. I even wrote it down on a scrap of paper and put it in my wallet. Then I stayed up all night reading Proverbs, all 150 Psalms and the four gospels. I finished Romans as the sun was rising."

Marilyn had unthinkingly reached out to take his hand.

"It was like I was seeing it all for the first time. Oh, Mari, I have been *so lost.*"

He was silent for a few minutes, wrestling with his past. She held his hand and waited. He drew it away to pull out his wallet before going on.

"You see," he said, and handed her a crumpled paper, written in a strong hand, with some words of the proverb underlined. "It was the wisdom I needed so desperately to hear. I got down on my knees and prayed for forgiveness. I offered my worthless, empty life to the Lord... and he welcomed me. He saved me, Mari."

She reached out and put her arms around him, not as a woman who had once loved him, but as a fellow believer sharing in a miracle. Miles pulled away, reluctantly, because he needed her to believe his testimony.

"I wish I could tell you that it has been easy, but I'd be lying, and I'm so tired of lies. I struggle every day, and when I do, I get this little scrap of paper out and read it.

He that trusteth in his riches shall fall; but the righteous shall flourish as the green leaf. (ASV)

"The hardest thing I've ever had to do in my professional life was to sign over the deed for a multi-million-dollar property to the city of New York." Marilyn gasped in surprise. "I donated the greenspace to the city as Joshua Strong Park."

"Timothy! You didn't!"

"I know I should have spoken to Tim about it first because he is next in line to inherit, but it has brought me nothing but misery, and if I am never able to do anything else for my son, I can at least spare him that. I hope he will understand and forgive me."

"I do forgive you." As if scripted, Tim stepped into the living room from the hall where he had heard most of his parents' exchange. "And I thank you."

"Oh, dear God," Miles cried as he stood and stared at himself in the mirror of his son's face. Marilyn looked uncertainly at her son and said in such a formal manner that the moment took on elements of the surreal, "Tim, I'd like you to meet… your father and your new brother in Christ, Timothy Miles Hawthorne."

Tim stood his ground in the doorway. "I didn't want to believe you had changed or that I would even *like* you," he confessed openly to the stranger who was his father, "but I'm marrying a woman who in many ways is far wiser than I am. She told me to have faith in you and to pray for you, so I did."

"I appreciate your candor and your prayers. And by the sound of it, you've found a woman in a million. Don't be the fool that I was and let her go."

"I don't intend to. You'll find that I am very protective of the women in my life," Tim replied in challenge as he moved to stand next to his mother, putting his arm around her shoulders.

Miles looked at the living portrait of honor and integrity, amazed that he could be of his own fallible seed. "I appreciate that, believe me. You have obviously taken much better care of them than I ever did." He was silent for a time while he and his son squared off. "Look, Tim," Miles began as if momentarily unsure of himself. "I have no right to give you advice or to claim you as my son. But I hope that, someday, I may be able to earn the respect I don't deserve now and be granted the privilege of calling you my friend."

Tim sifted through his own jumbled thoughts for the right words to express all that he was feeling. "I wish I could tell you that any relationship we may have will be easy and natural, but I just don't think that's possible given the massive chasm between us, which was none of my making. However, if you can be patient with me, I'm willing to try and bridge it."

Miles drug his eyes away from his son's face to find Tim's hand held out to him. He put his own in it, overwhelmed and humbled by the gesture. Smiling, he replied in a voice marked by evidence of the resurgent emotion he was growing accustomed to. "I'd like that."

Aletha, sitting in a corner of the dining room with Scout lying quietly at her feet, raised her hands in praise and thanksgiving. There would surely be many trials ahead, but it was a beginning.

Dear Rose,

For the first time since we agreed to the pastor's letter writing campaign, I find this process of putting my thoughts and feelings on paper somewhat helpful. It is forcing me to fully process all that has happened in the past few days. I know we are supposed to wait until we receive a letter from the other before responding, but I can't wait to get this to you. Just knowing you're thinking and praying about the situation steadies me. It's a pale second to having you with me, but I'm trying my best to believe that God is using this time of separation to teach me patience. I'm afraid he may be fighting an uphill battle! The crazy thing is that he had also been teaching me patience while you were here. Ask me to explain that later.

Where to begin. I met my father today – Timothy Miles Hawthorne. That sounds so strange, especially to me. I figured out later that Aletha had engineered the whole thing at Miles' request. I guess you were right. He really did want to meet me after all. And you were right about God working on his heart. I overheard him (as I was surely meant to) telling my mom about finding the land deed in my grandfather's Bible (the deed Simon Atherton was searching for), about reading scripture for hours and finally breaking down before the Lord. It was a very moving account of a transformed life. I just wish I could believe it. I can't put my finger on why I don't – fully, but it's almost too good to be true, if you know what I mean. I'm sure you would tell me, and rightly so, that I need to have a little faith. Believe me, I'm trying to! I think my skepticism may be tied to my mom's reaction to him.

I know she loved my dad – Peter Ludlow (this is getting really confusing), but in all the years they were married I never saw her look at him the way she looked at my biological father – Miles. I don't even think she realized she was doing it. Her whole manner changed. It was almost as if she dropped 30 years and was a young woman again. I don't mind telling you I found it all a bit unsettling. She's still Mom, but she has become "Mari" again – that's what Miles calls her. And she and Aletha both call him "Timothy." Apparently, it's the name we went by before reinventing himself as the ruthless businessman, "Miles Hawthorne."

I know what you're thinking, my love. I can hear those romantic wheels spinning from here, but let me tell you the rest of the story. It seems that he completely severed his ties with New York, selling all his holdings and donating that large parcel of land to the city of New York, which sounds pretty generous. But he also said something about a big tax break, which makes me wonder if the grand gesture was completely altruistic. Okay, okay, I'll give him the benefit of the doubt on that one, but get this – he's decided to open an office <u>in Kansas City!</u> Oh yeah. It gets better.

Miles ostensibly came to Aletha's house today to meet me and to ask us all if we approved of the idea. He said he would go anywhere else if any of us (meaning me, obviously) had misgivings about his proximity to Tinkers Well. That, of course, set off both Mom and Aletha, so I could hardly suggest that I thought it might not be a good idea. And you're right, (you see, I am fully capable of giving you credit for your superior insight) it wouldn't be fair to Aletha. She's so happy to have her son back after all these years, and who knows how many more they'll have to share. So, I jumped on the bandwagon.

I do want to know him better – he is my father after all – though I was up front about my reservations on that score. He can't expect us to be best friends overnight, but he was pretty decent about accepting our relationship on my terms. And if he has any idea of rekindling a romance with his ex-wife, my mother, I want to be around to make sure he treats her honorably. This is so weird – I sound like a character in a soap opera!

Before this becomes the great American novel, I'd better close and hit the sack. I'll keep you posted on further developments, but before I go, I need you to know:

I LOVE YOU!

And I miss you more than I can say.

I won't bother you with details about the town's newest officially dating couple. I'm sure you talk to Amy all the time. I am really happy for her and Abe, and since I know you played a big part in getting them together, I'm sure you're resting on your laurels now. I just have to wonder if everyone found us as nauseatingly devoted when you finally figured out that I was the most amazingly wonderful man on the planet, and you couldn't live without me. (Oh, how I long to hear that infectious giggle again…) You know, walking around hand in hand, spending hours together talking about absolutely nothing, floating along in a rosy haze. I hope you do remember because I fully intend to do exactly the same thing when I see you again. Good night, my love. I will sleep with the memory of your kiss on my lips.

   Yours ever,

   Tim

Marilyn Ludlow tweaked her hair and make-up several times before she heard the sound of a car pulling into her driveway. Glancing one last time at the hall mirror to ensure not a hair was out of place, she opened the door to see Miles Hawthorne, just as she expected. What she didn't expect was a bouquet of yellow roses (*He remembered!*) or a book held out to her. It was the signed first edition of *The Grand Sophy* by Georgette Heyer that he had given her on their first anniversary.

She gasped as she lifted the cover, "You kept it." She looked up to see Miles smiling at her surprise and pleasure. "All these years. I never thought to see it again." Marilyn reached out impulsively to take his hand. "Thank you, Timothy. I can hardly believe it."

He squeezed her hand then released it saying, "Neither could I when I found it in the back of a closet while cleaning out my condo. I remembered giving it to you and… and hoped you might accept it again as an olive branch."

"I accept it as a gift from a friend," she answered, looking at him with her clear, open gaze. "I don't know what else to say."

"Say that you're willing to wait until after dinner to re-read it for the 20th time." Marilyn laughed, grateful for the introduction of a lighter note.

She had agreed to join Miles for dinner with misgivings. Tim was spot on when he told Rose about the change in his mother's demeanor, but he was wrong in thinking that she was unaware of it.

She was, in fact, acutely aware of her response to her ex-husband. Since the moment Timothy stepped back into her life, the mature, level-headed Marilyn Ludlow seemed to be constantly engaged in battle with a younger, more trusting Mari Hawthorne.

Of course, you should rejoice in his evident change of heart. But it's been over 30 years since you spent any time with him. You don't really know anything about him, cautioned Marilyn.

But his remorse was so genuine, and you can see how delighted Aletha is to have her son back, countered Mari.

As she should be, but you need to guard your heart against disappointment and realize that he is simply a friend who needs encouragement in his newly rediscovered faith walk, argued Marilyn.

That may be true, but even you must have noticed how attractive he still is – even more so now with the gray in his hair and lines of life experience around his eyes. And hasn't he kept himself in excellent shape!

I believe it to be a commonly held maxim that men age better than women, particularly when they maintain a healthy physical condition. Mari was momentarily silenced.

In the end it was Marilyn who chose the cerulean blue cap-sleeved shirtdress with a wide belt for her evening out. She thought it practical and business-like. The fact that the dress's shape displayed her figure to best advantage, and the color had always been Timothy's favorite, never crossed her mind. Then she opened the door to see him wearing a tie of almost the same shade complimenting another of his expertly tailored suits. The sight of her favorite flowers and a cherished treasure, left behind with her old life, caused her a moment of indecision. But she knew she must learn to build a new relationship with him if he was to again be a part of her family. Marilyn told herself it was for the sake of the son they shared and for Aletha's happiness. Mari wondered if there was something more - something intangible and, as yet, undiscovered.

To the most amazingly wonderful man in the world who I simply can't live without (I can almost see your boyish grin), greetings. (We've been studying Paul's epistles in church. I thought the last word made my letter sound more ecclesiastical.)

I just got your letter about Miles Hawthorne. Wow! That must have been some meeting. I wish I could have been with you, but I know you handled it like the kind, considerate, godly man that you are. (There's a word of encouragement in that.) I am definitely praying for you and your whole family (who will shortly be my family!). I can't imagine how difficult this must be for you, but maybe you should look at it as a blessing. Not many people lose the father they love only to discover that they have another they never knew about.

You didn't say anything about what he looks like, but since you don't really look a lot like your mother, other than your coloring, I'm guessing you probably look more like Miles, which probably adds to the strangeness of the situation. I'm coming at this from a totally different place than you are. I will never know Peter Ludlow, but I am happy that I will have the opportunity to meet Miles Hawthorne. And not just for your sake, but also because he is a big part of your mother's and Aletha's pasts. Please know that I don't mean to make light of what you're going through – I know it's tough – but soon we'll be going through it together.

On another equally – I hope – important subject, I have some ideas about changes to the wedding that I'd like you to think about. My sisters have been helping me to plan things, and they made some suggestions that I think you'll be okay with. It won't be exactly what we envisioned, but maybe it will be better… We can talk about them when you get here in just 18 days!

I know you weren't crazy about the idea of communicating only by written correspondence during our separation. I smile every time I think about the look on your face when Pastor Lindeman suggested it. You'd think he had asked us to communicate by Morse code or carrier pigeon! I must admit that the idea was daunting at first, but I have found that it actually has helped the time pass more quickly, and I have the pleasure of curling up in bed every night and re-reading all your letters. I never tire of seeing every word and phrase as I imagine you writing each one by candlelight despite being exhausted after a long day of toil. Two words – fertile imagination.

Tim, I miss you so much. I miss feeling your strong arms around me. I miss hearing you call me "Sweetheart." I miss watching you work so hard to turn Willow Walk into our home. A few more return letters and we'll be together again. I can't wait. Good night, my love.

With all my heart,

Rose

Louis' Bistro was bustling as usual on a Saturday evening. Miles had specifically asked for a booth on the upper level when he called for a reservation. He was staying with his mother for the weekend, and though he had included her in the invitation for dinner, it was only Miles and Marilyn who took their seats at the intimate corner table overlooking the dining room. Aletha treasured every moment with her son but decided that there were times when her presence would be better for not being quite so present. Marilyn was well aware that Aletha had been included in the dinner plans and was equally well aware of the reason she was absent for the evening. She could hardly blame her former mother-in-law. That a reconnection between her son and his ex-wife was at the root of Aletha's actions, was patently obvious to Marilyn. Whether Miles guessed at the old woman's aim was less clear, but she decided to say nothing in order to avoid any awkward explanations. Instead, she looked forward to simply enjoying an evening out with a personable man at her favorite restaurant.

Miles was studying the menu, torn between the down-home Cajun classics and the more cultured Creole dishes. Marilyn assured him he couldn't go wrong with either. Each cuisine reflected the Thibodaux's colorful Louisiana roots whether prepared as a gumbo, etouffee, dirty rice, or jambalaya made with genuine andouille sausage shipped in from New Orleans. Miles made his selection quickly leaving him time to study Marilyn at his leisure while she studied the menu.

He knew enough of women's grooming rituals to know that the ash blonde hair free of any hint of gray was more a credit to science than nature. The confident carriage of her well-shaped head atop a slender neck, however, spoke of her noble character. The grace with which she moved across a room or sat with her shoulders back while her well-manicured hands held the menu, were evidence of her innate elegance and poise. The promise of these attributes had been present in a much younger Marilyn, but she had then lacked the self-assurance to bring them to fruition. Life, loss, and the unlooked-for freedom to discover her own strengths had allowed them to grow and flourish. She may have believed it was only men who aged well, but from where Miles sat, the years had been kind to her. He found her to be everything a woman should be yet rarely is.

They enjoyed the meal and the congenial company more than either had anticipated. Miles was at his urbane best, drawing Marilyn out and discovering real interest in her thoughtful answers to his questions. She was pleased by the consideration he showed for her contributions to the conversation and found that she was able to ask him about his life over the past 30 years without feeling any of the misgivings she might have experienced. Miles told her of his challenges in learning to do business from a base of honor and integrity, and Marilyn appreciated his openness. But when he asked her about her dreams and aspirations, she wasn't sure how to answer.

"Mari, if you could do anything you wanted to, change anything you wanted to, what would it be?"

She opened her eyes wide for a moment at such an impossible query, then stared thoughtfully at her coffee cup as she stirred its contents, watching the cream turn the liquid to a rich mocha color. After a few minutes she looked up and asked, "*Anything?*"

Amused by her reaction, Miles smiled and affirmed, "Anything."

He was completely unprepared for her answer.

"I've been very concerned for some time about the changes in curriculum in our schools. I had been away from education for so long when I took up teaching again that I was shocked by what is being fed to our children in the guise of education. You see, Tim attended a private school – did I tell you that?" Miles merely shook his head, his expression no longer one of amusement, but rather a reflection of his very real interest in what she had to say. "It was run on traditional lines with a heavy emphasis on mathematics, reading, writing, and American history – the true story of a nation founded on faith in God; its struggles, sacrifice, missteps, and shining achievements. All subjects were taught from a Christian worldview undergirded with a knowledge of God and biblical principles.

"But children in public schools today are taught revisionist history, which paints all of America's past in a negative light. Unless students who struggle with reading have parents who help them, they're being pushed through the system with minimal literacy skills because they've never learned to read phonetically. Other than an early delight in *Dr. Suess,* there is virtually no exposure to excellent poetry with complicated rhyme schemes or metric settings. It's all a sort of loose, descriptive prose. So, they're not challenged to expand their vocabularies or to learn the skill of memorization. I realize that normally happens in secondary school. I believe, however, that primary school children can benefit from the practice as well. You must still know some of the poetry our generation studied in school because I vaguely remember you quoting bits from time to time," Marilyn remarked hopefully.

> "*Theirs' not to make reply,*
> *Theirs' not to reason why,*
> *Theirs' but to do and die.*[2]

"As I recall, I often trotted out that Tennyson nugget when asked to empty the trash," he responded in a meditative tone. A look of indignation from Marilyn quickly melted into a crooked smile that pierced his heart. Warming to the reminiscent theme he volunteered,

> "*She walks in beauty, like the night*
> *Of cloudless climes and starry skies;*
> *And all that's best of dark and bright*
> *Meet in her aspect and her eyes;*
> *Thus mellowed to that tender light*
> *Which heaven to gaudy day denies.*"[3]

He sat in amused anticipation while Marilyn grappled with the poet.

"Wait… wait… Lord Byron!" she cried out at last. "Such a lovely poem," she commented then added quickly, "And then, of course, there is the brilliant nonsense of Lewis Carroll's *Jabberwocky*."

"Another fine choice. But I believe my favorite as a boy was the ballad by Robert Service." Miles looked at Marilyn expectantly, but she shook her head, at a loss.

"I'm afraid you have me there," she admitted reluctantly. Miles began,

> "*There are strange things done in the midnight sun by the men who moil for gold;*

---

[2] Alfred, Lord Tennyson, "The Charge of the Light Brigade" (Public Domain, 1854).
[3] George Gordon, Lord Byron, "She Walks in Beauty" (Public Domain, 1814).

The Arctic trails have their secret tales that would make your blood run cold;
The Northern Lights have seen queer sights, but the queerest they ever did see..."

Halfway through the verse Marilyn smiled and began nodding her head. Then to his delight, she chimed in as the words of the last line came to mind,

" Was that night on the marge of Lake Lebarge I cremated Sam McGee. "[4]

They laughed together, perfectly at ease. Marilyn, getting into the spirit, added her own favorites to poetry of the macabre.

"We can't forget *Annabel Lee* by Edgar Allan Poe or *The Raven,*" she pointed out.

"*Quoth the Raven 'Nevermore,* '"[5] Miles responded in sepulchral tones of deep foreboding. He leaned on the table and fixed his eyes, little more than slits on his dinner partner.

Laughing in appreciation, Marilyn rendered mock applause then asked in musing innocence, "Didn't you read Shakespeare's sonnets to me when we were young? Or was that someone else?"

"Oh, I am absolutely certain that no other swain was foolish enough to offer such drivel to his inamorata," Miles replied with a smirk.

"I will not allow you speak ill of the Bard." Marilyn said briskly. "Besides, I thought you read them very well and that they were quite beautiful."

"I thought you *bore* them rather well and that *you* were quite beautiful." Miles spoke with such unaffected sincerity that the two middle-aged ex-spouses were momentarily transported back to a time when their dreams

---

[4] Robert W. Service, "The Cremation of Sam McGee", (Public Domain, 1907).
[5] Edgar Allan Poe, "The Raven" (Public Domain 1845).

had been wrapped up in each other. Looking at one another in the present, it was as if each recognized the other for the first time. The transient discovery ended abruptly when the waiter appeared bearing two plates of Creole bread pudding. Marilyn was relieved by the interruption. Miles wasn't so sure.

"Oh, my goodness. I was having such a good time I forgot how we got onto classic poetry." She shook her head as if to clear her thoughts then continued where she left off before getting sidetracked. Miles would have preferred remaining in a vein of reminiscence, but he listened attentively.

"As I was saying, curriculum is concerning, and I have tried to augment where I can – as have many of the teachers I work with – but there are only so many hours in a day." She sighed, then went on, a frown on her face. "And added to all that there is an insidious, underlying theme that permeates everything. It is aimed at undermining the masculinity of boys. It's almost as if they're being taught that the qualities of strength and courage are character flaws, something to be ashamed of. At the same time, ironically, girls are encouraged to adopt those very qualities, and to embrace traditionally male roles. Don't get me wrong. I am all for opportunities for girls to excel and have career choices, but not at the expense of our boys or their own God-given femininity." Marilyn had been staring into her coffee cup again as she spoke. She looked up, an expression of rueful apology on her face. "I'm sorry Timothy. I'm afraid you hit a nerve when you asked me a question about what I wanted to change."

"Please, Mari, don't ever apologize for feeling passionate about something as important as the education of our young, though I'm afraid you have the advantage of me there. For obvious reasons, I can't say that I have ever taken much notice of current education practices other than to be aware of a growing tendency to push harmful, unnatural ideologies into the classroom. As lost as I was in my own spiritual darkness, I realized that things had taken a turn into what, even I, recognized as irrational and unholy. And I was hardly an arbiter of moral rectitude," he added with regret.

"That's just it, Timothy," Marilyn said urgently, and unconsciously reached out to touch his hand resting on the table. "*That* is the new horror, and I feel powerless to fight against it or to help parents protect their children from it."

"I'm afraid I don't quite follow," he said, regretfully watching her withdraw her hand. He helped himself to a bite of bread pudding and waited.

"It was bad enough when kids were exposed to the notion of families with two mommies or two daddies. I'm sure you are aware that it is now the 'trans' lunacy that is attempting to invade every facet of our society. Many states with progressive leadership support exposing children as young as *kindergarten* age to the idea that boys can become girls and girls can become boys. Books pushing this madness are mandatory reading. Why, there are well-documented cases of children experiencing great anxiety and bewilderment over these concepts where *none existed before*. And those students who believe these terrible lies are making medical decisions (with or without their parents' consent) that will have permanent, tragic effects on their mental and physical health. Some courageous states like Arkansas and Tennessee have legislated against allowing such actions by minors, but these perverse agendas have ever-increasing impact. Don't ask me to describe the filth our teens could potentially be exposed to in the name of tolerance and alternative lifestyles. It is truly unspeakable.[6]

"The worst aspect of the whole thing is that young parents, even those who are raising their children with Christian values are tragically unaware of how deeply embedded this twisted teaching has become in public education, or of its powerful influence. Can you imagine the potential

---

[6] Alliance Defending Freedom. 2019. "Students Don't Have to Leave Their Faith at Home." Accessed October 8, 2020. https://www.adflegal.org/issues/religious-freedom/k-12/key-issues/parent-rights

damage to children with parents none the wiser or simply willfully blind to the spreading madness?[7] Thanks to a school board populated largely by thinking, level-headed members, this insanity hasn't yet been afforded a voice in the rural bastion of Harrington County, but I'm afraid it may be inevitable."

Marilyn ended on such a note of despair that Miles had to restrain himself from reaching out to comfort her. He sought instead to divert her mind to more positive channels.

"This worry you have expressed – wholly justified, I might add – came pouring out because I asked you about *doing* something. What *would* you do, my dear?" He watched her face while she turned an idea over in her mind.

Finally taking a decisive breath, Marilyn looked squarely into Miles' eyes. "I would give families an alternative. Parents in these small rural communities have no option other than home schooling. And while I strongly support those families who educate their children at home with a robust, morally sound curriculum, it simply isn't realistic for all people. If I could do anything – you did say *anything* – I would build a faith-based school for at least kindergarten through eighth grade. The school would offer students a rigorous education and provide a place for teaching a wholesome, moral view of the divine purpose that God followed in creating boys and girls differently – a place where children can learn of his truth and his beautiful plan for *all* of creation.

"I know these are issues that should be taught in church and by parents, and to a certain extent they are. But not all kids attend church, and what is being pushed in public schools is undermining those teachings and causing children to question their parents' words. And then there is the issue of

---

[7] "Sex Ed Identity Crisis" Jeff Johnston, *The Daily Citizen,* Oct 2, 2019. Accessed September 15, 2020. https://dailycitizen.focusonthefamily.com/sex-ed-identity-crisis/

teachers being required to espouse something they believe to be false and harmful. I know I couldn't do it.

"So, the only alternative I can see is another school option. But even if I could figure out how to raise the funds to build it, this is a largely agrarian community. These people don't have the means to pay for private school tuition outright, but they are hard-working and determined to meet the needs of their families without government assistance. Few children would qualify for low-income student scholarships, and I'm not sure how far school vouchers would go in making up the difference."

Marilyn glanced at Miles who had opened his mouth to respond, but she cut him off.

"And don't suggest Aletha. She has already done so much for this town, besides leaving most of her wealth to a host of deserving charities including the School for the Blind in Kansas City." She sighed and dropped her eyes once again to her coffee cup, now nearly empty.

"I will continue to be an advocate for truth and the dignity of children, but what can one woman do?" Marilyn ended on a forlorn note.

When she stopped speaking the second time Miles reached out to clasp her hand. "First of all, having met only a few of the residents of your little town when I accompanied my mother to church a few weeks ago, I believe that you are probably not the only person who feels as you do." Marilyn showed the ghost of a smile. "And secondly, never underestimate what one person can do if sufficiently motivated." She still looked a little doubtful but was grateful for his encouragement.

Returning the pressure of his hand, Marilyn said ruefully, "I apologize again for adding such a discordant note to an otherwise lovely evening."

"Not at all," Miles replied. He tilted his head to one side and gazed at her in a considering way. "Do you know, Mari, I've never seen this fierce, impassioned side of you before. I find it rather intriguing." Marilyn could only respond with a telltale blush and an abrupt change of subject.

Later, after slipping into her pajamas and preparing to turn in for the night, she looked at herself in the mirror and found a rosy glow still present in her cheeks despite having thoroughly removed all make-up.

It was such a comfort to talk to Timothy about my worries. I believe he actually cares, Mari reflected.

Nonsense. He was just being polite, Marilyn stated firmly.

I don't know how you noticed one way or another, the way you were flirting so outrageously with him, Mari pointed out without any vestige of regret.

Don't be ridiculous!

Marilyn turned out the light and went to bed.

CHAPTER 10

*Many nations will come and say, "Come, let us go up to
the mountain of the LORD, to the temple of the God of
Jacob. He will teach us his ways, so that we may walk in
his paths."*

Micah 4:2a (NIV)

The second advent of Miles' Hawthorne was providential in many
ways. Occurring roughly midway through Rose's absence, it
provided Tim a distraction from missing her and an excuse for
taking an occasional break from the bruising work schedule he set for
himself. He didn't expect the rest of Three Brothers to follow suite, but
Derek helped out on projects at *Willow Walk* during their "down time,"
and Abe made an effort to add his assistance where he could, though his free
time was limited. He spent most of it with Amy. All three, however, were
adamant about keeping the Lord's Day as a day of rest.

Since Miles had made a habit of attending church with Aletha, if not
spending the entire weekend with her, Tim had ample opportunity to talk
to his father and watch with guarded interest the relationship between his
parents.

On the Sunday before Tim's departure for Kentucky to retrieve his
bride, he paid particular attention to Miles and Marilyn during church. In
the back of his mind, he could almost hear Rose pointing out that his time
would be better spent paying attention to the service. He only grinned

inwardly and continued his observation. Though still skeptical of Miles' apparent change in attitude, Tim had to admit that his father's emotional reaction to congregational singing appeared genuine. *Surely,* he thought, *no one could fabricate the thickened voice or misty eyes evident during the singing of the closing song.* Miles sang the words as if they were his own story.

> *Wonderful, merciful savior, precious redeemer and friend*
> *Who would have thought that a lamb could rescue the souls of men*
> *Oh, you rescue the souls of men*
>
> *You are the one that we praise, you are the one we adore.*
> *You give the healing and grace our hearts always hunger for*
> *Oh our hearts always hunger for.*
>
> *Counselor comforter keeper, spirit we long to embrace*
> *You offer hope when our hearts have hopelessly lost our way*
> *Oh we've hopelessly lost the way.*
>
> *Oh mighty infinite father faithfully loving your own*
> *Here in our weakness you find us falling before your throne*
> *Oh we're falling before your throne*[8]

There had been an equally obvious reaction by his mother to the presence of her former husband. Without a knowledge of their history, Tim might not have picked up on anything. But he did know. There was nothing overt to pin down, though he noticed a softened look in his mother's eyes. She appeared both confident and pleased to introduce Miles as an old friend. And at her potluck brunch, they worked like a well-oiled machine to serve guests, then cleaned up afterward with no indication that Marilyn found Miles' assistance intrusive or unwelcome. That, too, might not have

---

[8]Dawn Rogers and Eric Wise, *Wonderful, Merciful Savior,* Word Music/Dayspring Music, Adm. by Warner Chappell Music (Nashville, Tennessee, 1989) Used by permission.

raised any flags. However, Tim knew that it had usually been Angelica Warner who co-hosted the event. She had evidently stepped aside and suggested that Miles adopt the role.

Tim often felt like the chair umpire at a tennis match watching lob after lob of relationship volleys between his parents to determine which were at fault and which would be returned with equal energy. The exercise left him feeling careful, reassured, bewildered, and exhausted. He truly wanted to give Miles the benefit of the doubt, but so much hung in the balance if it was all a big charade: the possibility of his own looming disappointment; Marilyn's happiness; and Aletha's faith in a lost son who had been restored to her. Tim gladly shelved those worries, though, when his father asked that he be granted a tour of *Willow Walk*. He might have had lingering doubts about Miles, but he was at least gratified that his father showed an interest in his work.

The home tour also afforded father and son some rare one on one time. Believing that more intimate interaction might provide better insight into the man, Miles Hawthorne, than what he was able to observe of his father in company, Tim readily agreed.

"Of course," he said in response to the request. "I'd be happy to give you the grand tour, but remember, the place is still very much a work in progress and is currently inhabited by three bachelors."

"Enough said," Miles replied with a smile.

"You'll have to look at it through the eyes of your imagination." After a few moments of consideration, Tim added, "Though I suppose you've had to do a lot of that in your line of work. I wonder if that's where I – " He broke off in embarrassment as he was about to say, "– got my ability to see the potential in old buildings."

"I'd like to think so," Miles replied to the incomplete thought so calmly that Tim's self-consciousness was short-lived. The pair went through the house from the foundation up. Tim was impressed by Miles' general knowledge of construction and answered the older man's perceptive questions with more technical detail than he ordinarily would have. Miles' experience in construction was on a much larger scale – skyscrapers and entire city blocks, but his genuine interest in the updated structural, mechanical, and plumbing systems integrated into the old house pleased Tim. Likewise, Miles was impressed by Tim's expertise and attention to every architectural and functional detail. He could see through his son's eyes the pleasure and pride inherent in working on homes that had history and meaning for the people who dwelt in them. Tim was amazed to find that the completed tour, ending in the old carriage house turned garage, took over two hours despite avoiding the rooms inhabited by Derek and Abe. They might be pardoned for stretching anyone's imagination.

Miles looked back at the house and then at his son. "You're doing an absolutely terrific job, Tim. I know I don't have any real hands-on construction experience, but I'd like to help you sometime – that is if you think there's anything I could do to contribute to your progress."

"Do you own any beat-up old jeans, ratty tee-shirts or work boots?" Tim asked, smiling at Miles' silk suit.

"Point taken," Miles replied with an unaffected grin, "though I think that can be remedied easily enough."

"I can always use another set of hands, and I really appreciate your offer of help. There will be several jobs you can work on when I get a little further in the process. It might also give you an opportunity to get to know Rose. She's really looking forward to meeting you."

"Then I'll work on acquiring some appropriate attire," Miles said. "And I would be honored to be project assistant to your Rose." Tim could almost see the vast span between father and son growing incrementally narrower.

He shuffled his feet a few minutes then looked up and completed construction of his own personal bridge for the day. "There is something I could use your advice on. It's the old barn. Have you got enough time to walk down there with me? The ground's pretty dry right now so it shouldn't be a problem for your shoes," he said, glancing at Mile's expensive Italian loafers.

"I think my shoes can bear a short walk through the country," Miles replied affably, and the two set off.

The gravel pathway was overgrown with grass and weeds as little attention had been given to the barn other than doing some makeshift roof repairs following the tornado's destruction. The large structure, befitting the wealth and acreage of the founding Mason family, was a basement barn. Its solid windowed stone foundation had originally served as shelter for farm animals during the fiercest months of winter with a sunny southern exposure that provided warmth and light. Access to the lower level was by way of a door on the tallest side opening onto the lower slope of a natural undulation in the landscape.

"This old place is fairly unique as Kansas barns go," Tim explained. "It's sort of an amalgam of multiple architectural styles in use at the time it was built. Can you see how the raised stone foundation protrudes out on the ends to help support the cantilevered forebay overhanging the stable entrance? And the stone exterior continues partially up the gable ends of the main floor with vertical wood panels on the sides."

Amused by his son's obvious fascination with building techniques, even when applied to such a utilitarian structure, Miles asked, "And what makes these features so unusual?"

"Well, because the interior would ordinarily have been divided into three bays with hay lofts on either end, but... here, let me show you."

Digging some keys out of his pocket, Tim opened the padlock and pulled one of the doors aside. "It looks like there may have been corn cribs opposite the forebay side, but they were apparently converted into stables at some point. The hay lofts on the gable ends are more typical of a three-bay barn with side doors. However, this barn was built with doors on either end," he said, as if that explained everything. "In her own way, this old beauty is as novel and architecturally interesting as the main house, but if you tell Rose I said that..."

"My lips are sealed," Miles promised with a smile. He looked around again at the massive, hollow structure surrounding them and shook his head and sighed. "You know, I envy you your enthusiasm, Tim. I'm afraid I spent my youth chasing after fame and fortune rather than substance. Hold onto that zeal for your work, and you won't look back on your life with regret as I have." On a lighter note, he asked briskly, "Now, how exactly can I help you?"

Grateful for his father's shift to a more business-like attitude, Tim presented his dilemma. "I can remodel old houses, shore up foundations, and design period additions, but I'll be darned if I can figure out what to do with this monstrosity," he said as he and Miles walked the length of the nearly 60-x-30-foot building. "I thought that perhaps, since you deal in repurposing land and space, you might have some ideas about this barn. I had thought about moving our business office out here, but it's more convenient for our customers if we keep our headquarters in town, and this is really more room than we require." He shook his head and looked at Miles. "It seems a waste to let a place like this go unused, but Rose and I just don't need it."

Miles walked around the ground floor and peered up into the overhanging loft. "Is there water run to the building?"

"There's actually a spring fed well. The pump is below us in the basement, but Martin had it shut off years ago. I don't even know if it still works, though that wouldn't be a major issue to overcome provided the spring hasn't dried up."

Miles nodded his head. "Good. What about that pond we passed? Is it on your property?"

"Well... yes. But I don't see..."

"Never appraise the value of a property until you fully realize all its assets. Only then can you begin to visualize its possibilities." Miles continued his inspection as he spoke. "I can see that you have power here, though it's quite dated – knob and tube wiring. That will all need to be replaced. But it's all exposed so I shouldn't think you would find that too much of a challenge."

Tim nodded his head absent-mindedly. He was more interested in what Miles ultimately had in mind.

"You're the wood expert, Tim. What condition would you say it's in?"

"The structural wood is in great shape. The original builders used solid post and beam framing timbers and milled hardwoods which can last centuries if properly protected. The only damage is in the floor where watering troughs leaked, or rain seeped in through the shutter openings. I rented an industrial grade de-humidifier that I ran for weeks after the big storm once I'd patched up the roof. It was powered by a generator; you were right about the wiring." Shifting gears from assessment to application he finally pinned Miles down. "You obviously have something specific in mind, though I'm almost afraid to ask what that might be."

The professional developer rose to the challenge. "This would be an excellent site for a small manufacturing concern – say hand-crafted furniture or a pottery. It would make a great place to store farm equipment for a co-op, or to operate something like a veterinary clinic that could accommodate large animals on the spot." He paused to gauge Tim's reaction.

"I've thought of those, but this is a small community, and I just don't know of anyone looking for something like this," Tim said with regret. If Miles was disappointed, he gave no indication. Now astride the mount of his own specialty, he was prepared to produce a font of ideas.

"Ah, but have you considered looking farther afield for a client? Don't underestimate the willingness of the urbanite entrepreneur to stamp a genuine 'made in small town USA' label on his product." Duly noting Tim's dubious expression, he continued, "That leads me to my next suggestion – a wedding venue."

"A *wedding* venue? In *this* old barn?"

"Weddings and other events, yes," Miles replied, obviously unconcerned by Tim's skepticism.

"But there aren't enough weddings in three entire counties in any given *year* to make it worth the effort to renovate this place for guests. Besides, there are plenty of barns around here for people to get married in if they want to." Tim momentarily wondered how Miles had become so successful.

"Again, you're not thinking big enough, my boy. Why this could be a goldmine if marketed properly." Judging by his frown, Tim obviously required some convincing. "Wedding planners have made farm chic into the trendiest must have since boutonnieres – and the more bohemian the better: cowboy boots with $5,000 dresses, feed buckets full of flowers, or animals in the ceremony. And you've got fields, a pond, or for an extra fee, a Victorian mansion as backdrops for photographs. You can't get that in the city, and you're close enough to Kansas City to be a real draw if, as I mentioned, you can market this place well. I'm not saying that's the only option for this property, but I believe you have such a potential for success that I would be willing to sink some venture capital into the project myself."

"You're *serious*," Tim said, feeling like he'd just been drowned by a Madison Avenue tidal wave.

"I *never* joke about property development opportunities," Miles said solemnly. Tim wasn't sure, but he could have sworn he detected a twinkle in the older man's eye. "I'm not suggesting there won't be a great deal of work involved in transforming the space, but if you upgrade the *right* things... Add a rustic *cum* sleek kitchen and restrooms with up-to-date fixtures. Level the ground for a gravel parking lot and build a simple dock on the pond. With a little creativity you can advertise this place as down-home charm with uptown amenities. One of the hay lofts can become a musicians' gallery, and the other an open area, with a railing of course – plexiglass being the most practical – where parents can view the proceedings while allowing their children to play."

While Miles painted his picture a slow smile began to spread over Tim's face even as he shook his head. "All I have to say is, it's a good thing Rose isn't here. She'd probably already have me snapping chalk lines and configuring guest seating." He added doubtfully, "I suppose it might be profitable, but it would take a lot more of a financial investment than I can swing right now. You probably know that Aletha left us a very generous monetary gift in addition to the *Willow Walk* property, but it's meant to renovate and maintain the house, and I won't use it for anything else. This will just have to wait, and… well, I'd appreciate it if you didn't mention this to Rose – at least not until we've finished the house, and we can figure out where we stand financially."

"As you wish. But I meant it when I said I would be willing to invest in the venture, and I'm fairly certain I could find others to join me." He looked at his son and added ruefully, "Do you know, a year ago I would have advised you to juggle the money my mother gave you in order to finance this project. Of course, that would have left you gambling on its success while worrying about whether you could keep up with the house maintenance. As I told Mari, it's been a challenge to navigate the business world with scruples and integrity."

Tim replied with some diffidence, "I don't know if it matters or not, but I probably wouldn't have had much use for the man who might have made that suggestion a year ago."

"And the one who now struggles daily to live honorably?" Miles asked.

Tim smiled. "Him I'd like to know better."

They strolled back to the house in easy comradery, swapping functional and aesthetic ideas, content to have found some common ground.

Dear Rose,

I know I'll see you in a few days, but I wanted to send one last letter to you because it's the only way I can share time with you now, and I have so much I want to tell you. Besides, it's either this or I sit here feeling sorry for myself. Derek has already gone to bed and Abe isn't back from Amy's yet. He practically lives there when he's not working. I'm not passing judgement – I'm just envious. I can't imagine that it will be too long before they have an interesting announcement to make. But enough about other lovers, I'd rather focus on us.

Sometimes I miss you so much I can hardly breathe, which is one of the reasons I've been working so hard on Willow Walk. That and looking forward to the pleasure I hope to witness in your smile when you get back here next week. (Derek and Abe have vowed to have the place gleaming when you arrive, but I make no promises...)

I may be physically whipped by the end of every workday, but just thinking about you gets me fired up again. And I find that if I can concentrate that energy into something creative, it gets me through the evening hours until I can collapse into bed and dream about our life together. I hope that doesn't sound too corny. At least it's not as bad as the Shakespeare stuff Miles used to read to Mom when they were dating. She showed me some the other day because she thought you would appreciate the reference to a rose, but when the poet started going on and on about its odors, I could hardly keep a straight face. I didn't tell her what I really thought about it - I was afraid I might hurt her feelings. Who romances a girl by talking about her odors? When I asked Miles about it later, he glared at me and threatened to have me committed if I breathed a word to anyone.

He has this really dry sense of humor, and sometimes it's hard to tell if he's serious or not. I don't know how he does it, but his face may look sober as a judge while I'd swear his eyes are smiling. I know I'd hate to be sitting opposite him at the bargaining table or at a poker game. The truth is, I've been spending more time with Miles, and despite trying hard not too, I'm starting to like the guy. I don't know that I trust him yet – fully, but he's growing on me. He actually offered to get his hands dirty (I know, hard to imagine) and help with whatever projects he can on the house, even agreeing *to be your assistant. You will, of course, charm him with your beauty and mischievous smile. I know they worked on me!*

I'm still not sure about him and Mom. Sometimes I'm absolutely convinced that there's a spark there, but they are so courteous and circumspect when around other people that it's hard to tell if they share anything more than friendship. I can't help but feel protective of her, but I'm sure you will remind me (and rightly so) that they are both adults and perfectly capable of handling their own affairs of the heart.

Speaking of affairs of the heart, did I mention that:

I LOVE YOU!

I hope you never get tired of hearing that, because (full disclosure) I plan to bore you to death with ad nauseam repetitions of said sentiment for at least the next 50 years or so.

Good night, my love, and remember to get those beautiful lips in shape. I mean to put them to good use when I get to Kentucky, and I'm NOT referring to riveting conversation. We've had enough of words for the past six weeks. I'm ready for something a little more substantial. (Are you blushing yet?)

Yours ever,

Tim

Sitting at the table in Angelica's kitchen always filled Marilyn with peace and a sense of calm. The scent of aromatic spices mixed with the fragrance of exotic potted plants filled the room with a hint of the islands. And Angelica's lilting Jamaican accent inspired the listener with imaginary murmurs of tropical breezes and waves gently washing up on a beach. It was the place Marilyn turned to for friendship and sound advice. Now she felt in need of both. She could hardly go to Aletha since the source of her conflict was Miles Hawthorne.

Marilyn wasn't sure how it had happened, but she and Miles had slipped almost effortlessly into a relationship that was all at once comfortable, tentative, and exhilarating. The truth of Tim's parentage from their earlier marriage had become common knowledge. The disclosure was due in some measure to Miles' desire to be open about his past as it related to his miraculous new present, but also because the resemblance between father and son was so obvious, it would have been difficult to explain any other way. Marilyn's friends, especially those from church, were initially suspicious and concerned for her welfare. But when they witnessed first-hand Marilyn's calm acceptance of her former husband's presence and easy participation in her life, they graciously welcomed him also. Aletha's delight in sitting next to him in church almost every Sunday pleased *her* friends and, in less than no time, Miles was a regular at social events. Those closest to Marilyn and Miles agreed that general knowledge of his involvement with Simon "Applegate" Atherton served no purpose and was best buried with that unfortunate young man.

It was the unexpected rekindling of feelings for Miles, however, that left Marilyn in a quandary. And there was no better sounding board for her concerns than Angelica who demanded nothing of her friend but the simple gift of companionship. She sat patiently as Marilyn sipped her coffee, ready with a sympathetic ear and a commonsense response to whatever the other needed to share.

"Angelica," Marilyn began at last, "I don't know what to do about Timothy." Angelica said nothing, knowing more would come. "I never expected to see him again after I walked out on him all those years ago, and except for the sweet memories that floated back as I watched Tim grow more like his father every day, I honestly left all thoughts of him in the past." Seeing Angelica's skeptical look, she added, "Okay, *almost* all thoughts of him." Angelica merely nodded her head and waited.

"Then he showed up out of nowhere on that crazy day when we had to run for our lives from a tornado, and I was worried sick about Tim, and I lost it. I just… lost it. Seeing Miles like that completely knocked the stuffing out of me. I didn't know *what* to think. Then I saw *him* collapse in remorse, literally at his mother's feet. And I witnessed forbearance I could hardly believe he possessed when I told him about Tim. It was overwhelming. I felt like I'd been injected with some kind of weird mind-altering drug that left me flying high one minute and crashing into a wall the next. But when he walked out without a word after Aletha's bombshell about the land deed, I thought he was gone forever. I know I told you that I believed it was for the best even though I knew how disappointed Aletha was. I tried to convince myself that his absence wouldn't really make a difference to Tim all the while seeing the pain of rejection he worked so hard to hide. I felt like I was holding my breath, afraid to finally let go, and wondering if I would ever be able to breathe freely again without Timothy." Marilyn stopped to take another sip of coffee as if to bolster her courage before bringing everything out into the open.

"And then he came back," Angelica interjected succinctly.

"And then he came back," Marilyn echoed softly, staring into the depths of her cup for inspiration. But the only thoughts stirred up were as muddy as the liquid. She shook her head slightly while continuing to study the swirling fluid in her cup. "But he was… different. I could see it right away. All vestige of the hard shell he had wrapped himself in for so long was gone. He looked… vulnerable – vulnerable and… unsure of himself. I only vaguely remember him ever appearing less than supremely confident and self-assured, and that was when we were still dating. Back then, I vacillated between heeding my grandparents warning against him and succumbing to his irresistible magnetism. Once I agreed to marry him, any sign of weakness disappeared," she said, looking up at her friend. "That is, until I saw him a month ago, and it was as if I was meeting him for the first time – a kinder, more sincere and humble version of the Timothy I used to know."

Marilyn suddenly stood and began aimlessly puttering around the kitchen. Gathering their empty coffee cups, she rinsed them and stacked them in the drying rack, while keeping up a flow of one-sided conversation.

"But every time I attempt to build an emotional barrier between us, he reveals a previously unknown character trait that draws me to him all over again. He is thoughtful of others when he used to think only of his own interests. He spends hours talking with his mother when he used to brush off his parents with little attempt at civility. He makes himself indispensable at my Sunday brunches where he would previously have taken a seat and waited impatiently for others to serve him." Seated again at the table, Marilyn saw Angelica about to speak and hurried on. "Now I know what you're going to say – that he's acting like a man trying to impress a woman. But when he sings and speaks the words of the responsive reading in church, he's not trying to impress anyone, he's simply responding to God's love and forgiveness, and I honestly believe that his response is genuine. It's certainly often raw. I can't help but be moved by that."

Angelica reached out to cover her friend's restless hands, now void of occupation, and spoke words of comfort and wisdom. The lilting cadence of her phrases was balm to Marilyn's restless spirit.

"There's no reason to chide yourself for that, my friend. It's right to rejoice with him in his newfound faith."

She released Marilyn's hands and stood to move between counter and refrigerator as she gathered the ingredients needed to prepare meals for Derek, Abe, and Tim calculated to last through the week. It had become a Sunday evening ritual – one that Marilyn usually participated in. But she was so preoccupied that she watched the other woman working for some time before remembering her part in contributing to the weekly food haul. Eventually joining Angelica, she absent-mindedly began chopping onions, red peppers, and garlic to be added to the lasagna meat already browning on the stove.

While stirring the long, wide lasagna noodles boiling in a large pot of water, Angelica continued her observations. "But I think you know that. Now what exactly is it that worries you, for I can plainly see that somethin' specific is weighin' on your mind."

"How like you to see right through me," Marilyn replied with the hint of a wry smile. "Yes, I am worried," she confessed as she chopped potatoes, carrots, and celery for the beef stew. Taking advantage of the attention necessary for her work, she allowed her mind time to put into words what her heart was feeling. "I'm so afraid that I will allow myself to care for him again only to be disillusioned when the old Timothy surfaces. I just can't go through that disappointment again."

"Do you know, my friend, I think you're not bein' completely honest with yourself," Angelica stated candidly. Marilyn frowned as she held the colander over the sink while Angelica drained the noodles, a little wary of what the other might suggest. No one wants to face truth in lieu of sympathy, but Marilyn had no choice. Angelica looked directly at her friend and spoke gently. "I believe what you're *really* worried about is that Miles Hawthorne is *precisely* the man he appears to be, and you don't know what to do with *that* possibility."

Miles sat on an ottoman opposite his mother. He had found the seating position to be optimal for conversing with her since she often wanted to reach out to touch his hands or his face. Realizing early in their renewed relationship that touch was the only avenue open to Aletha for gauging his emotions or conveying her own, Miles had made a point of being within arm's reach whenever they talked.

"Tim was as good as his word when he said he was willing to try and bridge the gap between us. I believe that we are actually making some headway in our fragile relationship."

"Oh, I'm so happy to hear that, Timothy," Aletha said and squeezed his hand. "Tell me about it,"

He gently returned the pressure of her fingers and recounted the afternoon spent with his son. "We seem to have found some solid footing today. I thoroughly enjoyed my tour of *Willow Walk*, and he is obviously extremely proud of his work there. And justifiably so, I might add. I really know very little about the technicalities of remodeling, especially in a historical building, but Tim appears to be a very gifted carpenter and builder. Though I believe what pleased me most was him asking for my advice – did you hear that, Mother – he asked for *my advice* about disposition of the big barn behind *Willow Walk*. I promised not to say anything about the prospective project we have in mind, but I *can* tell you that for the first time since learning I had a son, I felt an inkling of what it means to be a father. I felt pride and humility and… and…" he paused, groping for the right words.

"…and affection for someone you hardly know without any expectation of his returning it?" Aletha suggested.

"Yes! That's it exactly. But how did you…"

"From the day you were born, when you were nothing but a helpless baby demanding everything, unable to offer anything but your precious existence, I loved you fiercely."

"And that love has never gone away," Miles said softly, finishing her thought.

"I'm beginning to think that being a father may be the making of you, my son" Aletha replied briskly. She could hear a smile in his voice mixed with a hint of irony when he replied,

"For what it's worth, I'm finding that learning to be a father is considerably easier than navigating the choppy waters of the ex-husband. I can dimly discern what a future with a son and daughter-in-law might look like, but I am at a complete loss when it comes to Mari." He sat silently for some minutes before standing and walking restlessly around the parlor. Aletha followed his movements with her ears.

"I knew this woman for four years. We were as close as two people can be and yet… I can spend an evening with her now and feel as if I don't know her at all. She is still everything she was but is now an entirely different person. Her whole essence is a dichotomy of past and present yet a perfection of the whole."

He continued his aimless pacing while he tried in vain to gain some mental traction through the exercise of thinking aloud. Aletha had almost ceased being a sympathetic listener and had become merely part of the background.

"There are times when I glimpse the trusting, innocent Mari that I married, and before my eyes she transforms into an independent, self-assured woman with determination and vision. She hugs me one minute with friendly affection then stands aloof the next, keeping me at a distance with polite conversation and gracious hospitality. She invited me to visit her classroom one day where I found her enthusiasm for teaching and inspiring her students infectious. She could be a strict disciplinarian if a student got out of line, then instantly switch gears to guide a student who struggled to understand a concept. She is 30 years older, but more beautiful than I remember. I find her fascinating in a way I never did before. Perhaps I was too young when we married to appreciate the qualities that truly make a woman desirable. I don't think I ever realized what those were until I met her again on that blessed, wretched day when our worlds collided. The day everything of value became worthless and that which I had despised and rejected became a treasure beyond price." Stopping in mid-stride, Miles opened the eyes of his soul to recognize that which he had been incapable of understanding before. He quickly regained his seat and took his mother's hands in his, desperately needing advice from the only person who knew him as well as he knew himself – probably better.

"I have been so focused on me for so long that I have never really seen her before, have I?"

"I'm afraid not, my dear," Aletha replied regretfully. That he had likewise failed to see his parents and others who had tried to guide him into paths of success in life hardly seemed worth mentioning.

"Even after moving here and reconnecting with her, I have always seen Mari in the light of a woman I was attracted to, someone I desired because I felt the need of her presence in my life. That can't be love. It smacks more of the selfishness that has defined my life."

"If your aim is to secure your own happiness without any thought as to how that goal will affect the object of your love, then yes." Aletha said, now hopeful that light was dawning at long last.

"I do love her, Mother." Miles spoke in wonder at the singular discovery. "I love Mari. I don't think I ever really stopped loving her, but it was always on my terms. Help me. Help me to understand how to love her for the sake of *her* happiness regardless of whether she returns my affection or not."

Miles' heartfelt plea gratified Aletha more than his remorse over his treatment of her. Though it had taken a lifetime, he finally seemed willing to sacrifice his own happiness for the well-being of someone else. She wanted to shout for joy but replied placidly enough, "I think the best place to begin is to stop thinking in terms of 'I want, I need, I desire' and start asking yourself: 'what does *she* want, what does *she* need, what does *she* desire.' The answers will show you the way."

Driving back to the city, Miles felt like a man on fire. He had direction, a mission, almost a divine purpose, and he was determined to waste no time in setting certain wheels in motion.

CHAPTER 11

Children, do what your parents tell you. This is only right. "Honor your father and mother" is the first commandment that has a promise attached to it, namely, "so you will live well and have a long life."

Ephesians 6:2-3, (MSG)

Abe threw his car keys on the hall table and flopped down on the worn couch in the parlor. (Rose had insisted the front living space be referred to by its original title.) Stretching his long legs out before him, he leaned his head against the wall in a weary gesture. The sound of footsteps approaching through the dining room from the kitchen heralded Derek's arrival after foraging for leftovers in the new stainless-steel fridge.

When he and Abe had taken up residence with Tim in *Willow Walk* to help move the renovation process along, they had been the willing beneficiaries of Angelica's belief that a house full of bachelors would starve to death without a woman's care. Despite the three telling her that they could fend for themselves, she – with Marilyn's help – had kept the refrigerator stocked with casseroles, homemade pot pies and Derek's and Abe's favorite Jamaican dishes. The ladies knew how much the hard-working trio were capable of consuming, though of late, Abe had taken many of his meals with Amy.

Derek greeted his friend through a mouthful of warmed up lasagna. He sat down in Tim's beat-up leather recliner, destined for the library before Rose returned, and asked Abe if Tim had gotten off to Kentucky all right.

"Yes," Abe replied. "He should be airborne by now."

"Man, I'd like to be a fly on the wall when those two see each other at the airport. They'll probably spontaneously combust! And I'll lay odds Granny Gert is there to make sure nobody gets in their way." Derek waited for Abe's answering grin. It wasn't until then that he noticed how quiet and preoccupied the other man appeared.

"Bro, is everything okay?"

"Yes, everything is… fine." Abe nearly spat out the last word.

"Well, it doesn't sound fine. You'll never get me to believe that you had a fight with Amy," Derek remarked before taking a swig from his water bottle, "so what gives?"

Abe stood up abruptly and walked over to the window, throwing a brusque reply over his shoulder as he moved. "Can we not talk about Amy right now?"

Derek watched Abe through narrowed eyes. He couldn't remember his friend ever looking so grim despite having lived through many devastating life experiences. "Well, what *do* you want to talk about? The supply order you filled today? The weather? Trying some of this awesome lasagna?"

Abe swung around, a look of desperation on his face. "Why do we have to talk about anything?"

If his unusually quarrelsome attitude hadn't gotten Derek's attention, Abe's total disregard for the best lasagna in the county would have. He never turned down food.

Setting his plate aside, Derek considered the other man's agitation then replied with unusual gravity, "Because you're one of the best friends I've ever had and because there's something obviously eating you up inside, and I want to help you if you'll let me."

Abe ran his fingers through his hair in a frustrated manner before replying, "No one can help me." He sat down again and stared at his fidgeting hands as if transferring to them his troubled thoughts. Presently he looked up and said with a smile gone horribly awry, "God finally answered my prayers today."

He returned to contemplation of his hands while he slowly unburdened his heart to Derek. "You of all people know how I have been praying for reconciliation with my family. You and Tim and everyone here in Tinkers Well have done such a splendid job of making me feel welcomed into your homes and lives that it helped take the edge off the pain I felt after being cut off by my parents. And then, of course, there is Amy." Abe's voice broke as he uttered her name, and he paused for a moment before going on. "But spending only a few days with Husam last month made me realize how much I still miss having my parents and my brothers and sisters in my life. When I looked at Husam I saw my father's eyes looking back at me, and I longed all the more to see each one of them again."

Derek could sense Abe's internal struggle but had no idea what event could possibly have brought about such a change in his normally even temperament.

When Abe spoke again it was as if the words were wrenched from the deepest reaches of his soul. He looked at Derek with tears in his eyes and cried out, "How could the Savior, whom I chose to follow at the expense of my family and everything that I held dear, answer my prayers in such a cruel fashion? Have I not suffered enough to honor his sacrifice on my behalf?"

Derek listened as the whole convoluted sequence of events came tumbling out – unexpected joy mingled with unbearable heartbreak. There was nothing he could do but remind Abe of God's goodness, even if it was hidden for a season.

Abe soon retreated to his room, though he found no comfort there and slept little that night.

The aerial view that had greeted Tim on his first visit to the Bluegrass State – lush green horse farms in all directions, marked out by miles of white fences – were ghosts in the darkness. At nearly ten o'clock at night, the view was limited to the glow from the city of Lexington and the welcome lights of the landing strip. But it mattered little what he could see from the air. The only sight he looked for was that of Rose waiting impatiently for him at the bottom of the escalator inside the terminal. If Derek's prediction of spontaneous combustion fell short of the mark, it was by a slim margin. As soon as Tim's feet hit the ground floor, Rose launched, as if from a catapult, into his arms. They held each other, barely moving, for what seemed like hours but was, in reality, only about 15 seconds. Tim's kiss was gentle and brief. A more substantial and satisfactory exchange would keep until they could find a few precious moments of privacy. For the time being, he was content to take in her beloved face beaming with happiness.

The Thompson clan gave them exactly one minute before rolling out the welcome wagon with hugs and handshakes all around. Since they lived in town not far from the airport, Violet and Lily, with husbands in tow, had joined their parents to greet their new brother. But it was only Ralph and Beth who escorted Tim and Rose to the family home in Winchester. Granny Gert was the only obvious absence, and Tim found that he actually missed seeing her. He had grown quite fond of Rose's grandmother because of, rather than in spite of, her unguarded tongue and sometimes outrageous antics. He assumed the late hour had kept her at home and that he would see her over the weekend before departing with Rose on Monday.

Friday was devoted to packing completion, stretching Tim's ability as a loadmaster to the limit. It didn't help that Rose, or more probably her mother Beth, continued to find small trinkets that were deemed essential for the success of the wedding or the marriage. Beth insisted her daughter take a pair of gigantic, hideous candle sticks simply because they'd been in the family for eons. Rose suspected it was more likely that her mother had failed to convince Violet or Lily to take them on the occasions of their respective weddings. Regardless of the reason, it was Tim's job to find room for them. Ralph Thompson merely stood on the sidelines out of the direct line of fire, amused by the spectacle of the bridegroom trying to maintain his patience while simultaneously running interference between mother and daughter. There wasn't another man alive who had more experience in trying to understand Schmidt and Thompson women than Ralph, but when a frazzled Tim sought him out for advice during a lull in the action, Ralph had to shake his head good-naturedly and admit his limitations. "Beth and I have been married almost 33 years, but I still haven't figured her out."

Saturday was a blur of last-minute wedding preparations. Though the actual ceremony was still over a month away, Beth insisted on Rose's final input before she left for Kansas. Violet and Lily freely contributed their unsolicited suggestions, as they had for the past six weeks, and they inevitably ran counter to what Rose wanted. For years they had asserted their Type-A personalities in what they considered helpful guidance for their younger sister. And since Rose was naturally inclined to try to please everyone, she had habitually given in to the wishes of her more assertive siblings. Her wedding seemed doomed to the same takeover, but she convinced herself that it didn't really matter – all she really cared about was marrying Tim. So even though she and Tim had planned on a simple afternoon ceremony in the garden at *Willow Walk* followed by light refreshments served buffet style on the broad veranda, Violet and Lily had other ideas. They insisted Rose consider a more lavish affair at a hotel in Kansas City, with ample seating for a larger guest list and room for a formal dinner following an early evening ceremony.

"Rose, you have to have candlelight..." Violet pointed out. Rose preferred sunshine.

"...and far more substantial music," Lily chimed in. "At the very least a string quartet and some brass for the processional." Rose thought wistfully of the simple guitar, flute and violin ensemble Amy Walker had coordinated.

"Sweetie, you know that gardenias are the *only* flower of choice for the really elegant bride," Violet stated as if declaring an undisputed fact. And Lily crowned Rose's serial disappointments when she commented that nobody wore lace or a veil if they wanted to look truly sophisticated.

Rose regrettably watched the lovely autumnal sprays of chrysanthemums fade into a lost dream. Forcing a smile, she sought to embrace the selection of a strapless shirred sheath and matching tulle blusher that her sisters agreed on for her. Fortunately for the happiness and sanity of the bride, Granny Gert had been invited on the dress shopping excursion. She quickly noticed that Rose's wishes were once again being sublimated to her bossy older sisters' wishes.

"Violet, you just put that skinny dress away. Why, Rosie won't be able to walk in that thing! And Lily, if you want to spend a $100 on a slip of netting that looks like it was cut from Grandpa Ernie's old fish catcher, you go right ahead. But Rose knows what she wants, and for my money, it suits her perfectly." Knowing that Rose's intense look of gratitude might easily turn into tears of relief, Granny Gert rallied her youngest granddaughter's courage and demanded that she get "gussied up" again in the dress and veil of her choice. Gert understood, as the others could not, Rose's desire to honor the Victorian era and the home that reflected its dignity and grace. Any important dress worn there must pay homage to its grand surroundings. Rose won a small victory for her special day, but she wondered how she would tell Tim of all the other changes. She had tried to hint at her struggles in her letters but hadn't wanted to worry him.

In the end it was Rose's father, Ralph, who helped Tim appreciate his bride's dilemma. While the ladies were engaged in a flurry of wedding details, the men escaped to the quiet refuge of Ralph's workshop in a corner of the backyard. Tim had been given a cursory tour during his earlier trip, but on that occasion his thoughts had been consumed with convincing

Ralph to consent to his marrying Rose. Now with an actual wedding date on the calendar and no real interest in the particulars attached to the event, the two men were free to get better acquainted.

"Tim, what do you know about dovetail joints? I'm building this changing table for Violet's baby, and I wanted to include two drawers for storage." Ralph motioned to an open framed table with an elevated rim around the top and a lower storage shelf near the bottom of the legs.

"Well, I haven't done much furniture carpentry since college. I'm usually too busy knocking down walls or reinforcing old structures to have much time for that, but let's have a look." Tim spent several minutes on detailed scrutiny of the shop. It had ample workspace and a surprisingly comprehensive inventory of hand tools, saws, and clamps for an amateur carpenter. "Given your range of tools – which I've got to say is pretty impressive – and the size of the project, you've got several options. You *could* make them by hand, but that's fairly time-consuming. Or you could use your table-saw to create joints with wider tails and narrower pins, *or* we could set up a jig using your router."

"If you don't mind, I'll leave it in the hands of the master while I finish some sanding." Wanting to stay in his prospective father-in-law's good graces, and because he enjoyed the novelty of being able to work on a furniture project for a change, Tim readily agreed. As he worked on the drawers, Ralph turned his attention to the tabletop and kept up a gentle stream of conversation, reminding Tim of his dad, Peter Ludlow. Such slow, deliberate speech used to frustrate a younger Tim, whose innate drive and restlessness had left little room for reflection or diligent attention to his dad's words. In retrospect he realized it was Peter's way of teaching him patience. He sometimes wondered what Miles Hawthorne would have taught him.

"Yes, Rose told me how much she enjoyed hanging out here with you, working on little projects," he replied in answer to Ralph's question.

"Ever since she was a little girl, she would come knocking on the door if she saw me slip out to my shop. My little Rosebud. I'll miss her, but I believe she's finally found some direction in her life, and I believe I have you, at least in part, to thank for it. You seem to have helped her to believe in her own opinions and self-worth, and from what I can see, you'll stand up for her when she lacks the confidence to stand up for herself. That's something she's struggled with all her life – especially around her sisters."

"You know, it's funny you should say that," Tim said, looking up momentarily from adjusting the router bit for the jig. "I feel like she's been trying to tell me something in her letters, but she never came right out and said what it was. Several times she's hinted that Violet and Lily have ideas about the wedding that might be better than hers. Is that what you mean?"

"Violet and Lily have *always* had better ideas than Rose, or at least *they* thought so. And because Rose has always been devoted to them and looked up to them as being more successful and clever than she is – which is nonsense, of course – she tended to give way to their opinions over her own. I suspect that's been happening with all the wedding planning too." Tim frowned as he mulled over Ralph's words. "No, I think Rose was born for a different kind of calling. I am inordinately proud of all my girls, and Rose is just as intelligent and capable as the other two. She could have followed some career path if she'd really wanted to, but I believe she will embrace the roles of wife, and eventually mother, as full-time occupations that will make her feel complete in themselves. I know women aren't taught to think that way anymore. It's 'old-fashioned', but I expect that's one of the reasons you love Rose. And the fact that you're smart enough to recognize that special gifting means a lot to me."

"There are about a hundred million reasons why I love Rose," said the man not given to hyperbole, "but yes, that's a big one."

Ralph stopped sanding and laid the gritty paper on the wood surface then walked across the shop to his future son-in-law. "As hard as it will be to see Rose move to Kansas permanently, I believe her future happiness lies there, with you. She needs the room to grow and blossom into the woman God meant her to be, out from under the shadow of her sisters and her own self-doubt. She is now *your* Rose, son. Treasure her as I do, and I believe you will have a long and rewarding marriage."

He extended his hand as he spoke, the emotion evident in his voice. Tim laid his in the older man's then Ralph covered it with his other hand as if conferring a blessing. In that moment, Tim realized for the first time the price Rose's family would pay for his joy and contentment. He was suddenly humbled by that sacrifice and the faith placed in him by the only other man who had her best interests at heart. It was a sobering reflection and a foretaste of the vows he would make in a few weeks.

"I will, sir. That's a promise."

Ralph lifted his hand to slap Tim on the shoulder and give it a playful shake. "Good. I'm glad we got that settled. Now, let's get this changing table finished. I shamelessly mean to get as much work out of you as I can while you're here!" Tim grinned in response and the bond between the two men was sealed.

By the time the carpentry project was finished, Tim barely had time to get cleaned up before he was bombarded by every Thompson and Schmidt relation within 100 miles. He met cousins, neighbors, former schoolteachers, and anyone that had even a fleeting interest in the man who had captured Rose's heart. Beth Thompson, aided by her sister Patty and the irrepressible Granny Gert, had outdone themselves with the feast prepared for the open house held to introduce Tim to what seemed like the entire state of Kentucky. He wondered if he should look around for a few state senators hidden somewhere among the crowd. The Thompsons' 1960s era split-level home was bursting at the seams with people wandering through the various levels. Newcomers greeted friends and family whose paths had not yet crossed in the crush of well-wishers.

Tim couldn't help but notice, on the rare occasions when he was able to catch a glimpse of Rose at all, that she looked a little subdued for a bride-to-be. But he was never granted the opportunity to speak with her that evening. Other than a stolen kiss outside her bedroom door just before the rest of the family trooped upstairs for the night, the young couple hadn't had a minute to call their own all day. Their time arrived following church on Sunday when Rose suggested they drive east to Natural Bridge State Park to enjoy one of her favorite hiking trails.

The peace and companionship of simply being together was a welcome relief after the chaos of nearly being smothered by the Thompsons' collective relatives and acquaintances. Both Tim and Rose were content to savor the silence, only commenting on random sights along the way. At the park, Tim steered old Betsy into an empty spot by Hemlock Lodge, where many of the trailheads were located. The intrepid duo trekked through dense woods comprised of soaring white pines determined to reach straight upwards despite the steep incline of their home. They wandered through lower layers of hemlock and tulip trees interspersed with rhododendron thickets. Finally, after climbing countless limestone steps and carefully negotiating sharp cliff edges, the determined pair arrived at the natural bridge: a 30-foot-wide sandstone arch overlooking the Daniel Boone National Forest. Tim and Rose stood in the center of the bridge to rest and take in the stunning views in every direction.

"Wow!" Tim said, attempting to catch his breath. "I can see why you love this place so much." He put his arm around Rose's shoulders and kissed the top of her head as they shared the beauty of nature all around them. He ran almost every day, but the natural Stairmaster® they had just completed had nearly mastered him. "I am *so* going to feel this in my calves and hamstrings tomorrow. I never knew you were such a climbing machine, Rose. I had trouble keeping up with you! And though I realize that you could probably keep going indefinitely, I'm going to wimp out and sit down." She laughed and joined him, glad of an excuse to take a break and rehydrate.

After drinking his fill, Tim stretched out on the warm rock surface and closed his eyes, soaking up the tranquility of the moment. An intense wave of love washed over Rose as she contemplated the man who had asked her to be his wife. She also felt a sense of betrayal for changing all their wedding plans without consulting him. Turning her gaze away from him to the vast acreage of forest before her, she sought inspiration on broaching the subject.

"He won't care – men don't," Violet had declared.

"They just want to be told where to be and what to do when they get there," Lily had assured her younger sister.

Rose knew Tim better. He didn't appreciate being told to do anything. She was spared the worry of trying to figure out how to tell him of her concerns when she felt his hand gently rubbing the rigid muscles of her back.

"Sweetheart, something is troubling you. I've wanted to ask you about it, but we haven't had a minute to ourselves until now. So please tell me what it is. You know I'm always here for you."

Rose momentarily shuddered as she remembered a similar, manipulative action by Simon Atherton. But the respectful touch of Tim's ministering hand and the sound of concern in his voice combined to pull the words from her heavy heart.

"Oh, Tim. I don't even know where to start." She turned to look at him and asked hesitantly, "How set are you on getting married in Tinkers Well?"

He quickly sat up to search her troubled countenance. "Rose, have you decided you'd rather be married in Winchester? Honey, if that's what you want, you *know* I'm fine with it."

"Of course not!" She dropped her eyes while making much of retying a bootlace. "But how would you feel about getting married in a banquet hall at a hotel in Kansas City?"

Tim certainly hadn't seen that coming. "Why would we want to get married in Kansas City?"

"Well, we… that is… *I* thought it would be – "

"Wait, wait, wait. You started to say 'we.' Who is 'we'?" He asked pointedly as he lifted her chin, forcing her to look into his stern, but not unkind eyes.

"Violet and Lily pointed out that we could have a bigger venue and invite more people if…"

"…If we got married in a large, impersonal room in some random hotel in a city where we know no one except three carpenters who work for us?" He would also have pointed out the inconvenience to elderly guests and families with young children but stopped himself when he saw her evident distress. Instead, he moved closer to Rose, put his arm around her, and pulled her head down on his shoulder, comforting her with the decisiveness she lacked.

"Sweetheart," he said, after brushing the hair from her forehead and dropping a kiss there, "I don't care if Lily and Violet think we should get married at the Taj Mahal – though I hear it's booked up *way* in advance." A stifled giggle encouraged him to continue. "Tinkers Well will be our home so that is where we will be married, just as we planned. Please tell me your parents haven't put a down-payment on the hall yet."

Rose raised her head and said quickly, "Yes, but we can cancel up to four weeks ahead for a full refund and that's not till next Saturday."

"Whew! Then that's taken care of. Now, what *else* haven't you told me?"

Almost limp with relief, Rose quickly went through the other suggested changes for flowers, photography, food, and music. She saw his eyebrows draw together in a frown and mistakenly thought he was disappointed in her.

"Disappointed in you? Rose the only way I could be disappointed in you is if you thought I needed to rob a bank to pay for all that nonsense." He dropped his arm and took both her hands in his. "Sweetheart, you are going to have the flowers you want, the music you want and whatever else you want regardless of what Lily and Violet think about it. This is our wedding – not theirs." Tim decided that those two had a lot to answer for.

"And we can take our vows on the veranda of *Willow Walk*. Tim, it will be *so* beautiful," she said, closing her eyes to picture the vision.

"Yeah, about that. Rose, I think we may need to find another way to incorporate the house in the wedding weekend."

"But, Tim, you just said – "

"I said that you can have whatever you want, and I mean that. Hey, I'm the guy who's been working his tail off to get the house ready by then, remember? I want to include her in the celebration too, but I've been thinking of some other options. My primary concern is the weather. If everything is outside and it rains or the temp drops, we'll be in trouble. Even if we set up a tent in the yard, we wouldn't be able to fit everyone under it or in one room inside the house either, and we've got to think of our older guests and young kids. I told you that I've asked one of my army buddies to be a groomsman…"

"Rick… Edgerson?" Rose asked, not sure she had remembered the name correctly.

"Beauty *and* brains," he said, smiling. "Yes, Rick Edgerson. His wife just had their second child last month. I can't imagine they'll want to keep a newborn outside if it's cold or wet."

"You're right, of course," she admitted reluctantly. "Once again I let my dreams overpower my reason." Rose looked out over the vista of forest and watched a hawk fly off into the distance as if taking her cherished vision with it. Determined to turn her disappointment into excitement, Tim unveiled his master plan.

"Rose, you have the most creative imagination of anyone I've ever met." He stated her somewhat problematic character flaw like it was a good thing. But at least he'd gotten her attention. "What if we get married in Community Church, with the altar rail brimming with baskets of mums and pumpkins and gourds from *Plants Aplenty.* Then we can have the reception in Settlers Park and serve the food from *Louis' Bistro* under cover of the bandstand. We can add some folding tables and chairs to the picnic tables already there, if need be, but we're just having light appetizers and cake so it's not like people need to be able to manage all the table settings for a full meal. I'm sure all the locals would be willing to bring their own lawn chairs. If the weather is bad, we can move everything into the bistro. Louis said he can remove all the tables on the main level for more space. It would be a tight squeeze, but doable. But I'm hoping for the park. The kids will be free to run around, and we can bring the portable PA system from the church and use it to make toasts or play music." Tim could see a spark of animation in Rose's eyes as she considered the possibilities.

"I guess we could have group pictures taken by the old well or on the steps of the bandstand…" She was thinking out loud, but when she got to the biggest stumbling block she turned to Tim and said blankly, "I still don't see how that incorporates *Willow Walk*."

"The rehearsal."

"The rehearsal," she echoed softly.

"The steps of the veranda are deep and wide just like those leading up to the main platform at the church. So, we *practice* taking our vows there and instead of holding the rehearsal dinner at *Milly's Diner*, we host the dinner at *Willow Walk*. It will only be the wedding party and anyone else that has come a distance so we should fit. I've measured the space, and we can add an additional ten-foot folding table perpendicular to the dining room table in the space between the big pocket doors, which should give us seating for at least 20." Tim watched Rose's face light up as he described his vision.

"And we'll have more time to visit and show everyone around…"

"…*and* we can have the photographer follow us to the house after the reception in the park, so we can still have our 'couple only' wedding photos at Willow Walk. What do you think?"

"I think you're a genius!" Rose cried and threw her arms around him in an impetuous hug, caring nothing for the other hikers who looked on with interest.

Relieved that each had helped the other to accept compromise and a better plan than they had envisioned before, Tim and Rose found renewed energy and continued their hike with carefree spirits. Tim had his own reasons for not wanting to host the wedding and reception at *Willow Walk*. The prospect of lingering guests populating the house on his wedding night had bothered him for some weeks until he hit on the alternate schedule of wedding events. But he kept those thoughts to himself.

"All I know is that she said something at the party about a surprise when we stop in Versailles to see her on our way to Kansas," Tim said as he traversed the traffic around Lexington after Ralph and Beth Thompson had waved the couple off on Monday morning.

"Hmm. There's no telling what she's up to," Rose replied. "She didn't say anything to me." After a short pause Rose mused, "You don't suppose she'll give us a *puppy* or something…"

"Oh, *please* tell me you're kidding," Tim replied, leveling a pointed stare at his fiancée. "That's the last thing we need to deal with on a 600-mile journey." Rose secretly thought it might be fun. She quickly realized, however, that she and Tim would never see eye to eye on *everything*.

They were both filled with excitement and anticipation when they turned toward the west with the morning sun shining into the back of the little hatchback. Rose smiled to herself when she considered that in only five short weeks they would be leaving on their honeymoon. She still didn't know where they were going. She knew only that she needed a current passport, clothes for warm weather and several swimsuits. Despite trying to cajole, trick or beg it out of him, Tim refused to tell her any more than that. Rose was still mentally reviewing the options – a cruise, a resort on the Yucatan coast, or maybe one of the Caribbean islands – when they pulled into her Aunt Patty's driveway. Since Grandpa Ernie's death, Granny Gert had resided with her oldest daughter, a spinster who worked at the state capital in Frankfort. Patty had taken the morning off, presumably to spend a little time with her niece when she and Tim stopped by to bid farewell to Granny Gert.

Tim and Rose had just gotten out of the car when they saw Gert hurrying out of the front door with a spring in her step and a suitcase in tow. Tim stopped in his tracks as dawning horror caused him to swear softly under his breath. "*This can't be happening...*" he muttered to himself. It was.

"Here's my escort right on time," Gert said as she gave her granddaughter a bracing hug.

"Your escort?" Rose asked with misgiving.

"I told young Mr. Ludlow," Gert said, giving Tim a knowing wink, "that I had a surprise for him this morning. And here I am!" she said, beaming from ear to ear.

"And here you are," Tim repeated faintly and glanced at Rose to find that she was as stunned as he was. Moving in a daze, he helped Gert into the car, his good-humor momentarily impaired. This was a surprise neither he nor Rose had anticipated. But knowing Granny Gert, they probably should have.

Patty pulled her niece aside and said in a gruff but kindly voice not unlike her mother's, "I tried to tell her you'd probably prefer to keep this trip to yourselves, but she was convinced you'd be tickled to have her join you. She and her friend, Aletha Mason, fixed it up between them. I'm sorry Rosie," she added with a sympathetic smile.

Rose hid her dismay and mustered enough enthusiasm to convince her misguided but well-intentioned grandmother that they would be delighted to include her on their journey west. Tim had hinted at a surprise when they left her parents' house earlier, and Rose couldn't help but wonder if one hadn't negated the other. It had. Tim's plan to spend three days on the road rather than two, with carefully selected stops on lesser traveled US and state highways, had just been derailed. He had spent hours researching quaint towns along the way where he and Rose could stroll and shop or pause for a coffee or light lunch. When the now augmented party stopped at the Indiana Welcome Center, Tim stayed in the car while Rose helped her grandmother into the building. He reluctantly called the B&B's where he had booked two rooms for each night and cancelled his reservations. As he replaced his phone in the cup holder, he shook his head and smiled ruefully despite his disappointment. Life with a woman from this unpredictable family line would certainly never be dull.

The jarring clang of the afternoon bell sent students clamoring for the door and waiting buses. Others hopped into the cars of parents in the pick-up que. Those who lived close enough to the school sought walking partners who might commiserate over the evils of homework and instrument practice during the walk home. A fire drill in the last hour of class had wreaked havoc on Amy's teaching schedule at a time when she was still sorting out instrumental aptitude while trying to teach basic note reading to students with no prior knowledge of music. The chaos that ensued following the last bell of the day left her with instruments and music stands scattered around the room.

This was the worst possible day to have the added necessity of setting things to rights when she had hoped to finish her lesson plan for Monday early and be ready to greet Abe when he called for her after school. He had texted her the evening before to say he needed to see her today as soon as she was through at school, so she had asked another teacher in her neighborhood for a lift to work in the anticipation of being driven home by Abe in the new SUV of her choosing.

Having taken mental notes of the recently added wardrobe ensembles that he seemed to appreciate the most, Amy had intentionally worn lose, navy pants and a drop-wasted pale peach-colored top. She tied a woven sash around her waist, leaving the tasseled ends dangling off one hip. The outfit had drawn a low whistle of approval from Abe at Sunday brunch, and Amy smiled in anticipation of another such response. She was tucking her make-up and hairbrush back into her purse when she looked up to see Abe walk through the door. The smile of welcome froze on her lips when she saw his bleak expression and the frown that he rarely allowed her to see.

She impulsively started toward him asking, "Abe, what is it? What's wrong?"

He stopped her with a gesture, leaving her to stand helplessly at a distance. The invisible wall between them was no less powerful than an electric fence.

"Amy… Amy, I…" he began haltingly. Then, as if trying to hide the anguish behind his words, he said as steadily as possible, "I had to see you. To tell you that I am leaving."

"Leaving?" she repeated blankly.

"My father called me yesterday while I was driving back after dropping Tim at the airport."

"Abe, that's wonderful…" Amy began impulsively, but Abe cut her off, reciting the speech he had rehearsed as if he wouldn't allow himself to be distracted from his dread task.

"He called to tell me it was time to come home. He said that he and Ommy wanted to mend the hurt that we all experienced after my injury." Noting her worried, questioning expression, Abe felt he must make her understand. "I know how much I disappointed them with my career decision after college, and then my rejection of their faith. Now my father is trying to reach out to me in the only way he knows how. I *must* respect his wishes."

"I still don't quite understand. Surely this is an answer to prayer?" Amy asked, not sure she wanted to hear his reply.

"Amy, I promise you, that all the times I have prayed for reconciliation with my family, I never imaged that it would come like this or occur at anyone's expense – especially yours." He spoke in such a voice of torment that she knew only an impulse to comfort him.

"But Abe, I am truly happy for you. How can this cause *anyone* pain?"

He moved toward her, his hands held out. She would gladly have walked into his arms, but he checked her movement by taking her hands and holding them tightly between his.

"Because, my *darling* girl," he said as if the words were wrung out of him, "other than to attend Tim and Rose's wedding – provided they still want me to – I may never return to Tinkers Well."

Amy felt her legs melting under her, but she valiantly fought to stand her ground, struggling to believe what she was hearing. As she stood there, she had a fleeting sense of what it must feel like to die, for she experienced the same instant flash of treasured memories stored up over the past two months she and Abe had been dating.

Their thoughts and spirits seemed to have been in such perfect sync. He taught her how to cook his favorite Mediterranean dishes. She helped him develop his skill on the guitar. He introduced her to popular sci-fi movies. She expanded his scope of hymns and worship songs. Their heated one-on-one meetings under the basketball hoop always began with challenging banter and ended in laughter, despite very real competition. A thousand little insignificant nothings amounted to all they had become together. And he had eagerly accepted an invitation from her parents for an upcoming weekend visit.

The words had never been spoken, but she loved this man. And she believed him to feel the same way about her, assuming his hesitation in verbalizing or demonstrating his affection to be tied to his desire to keep their courtship pure and untainted. She had honored his suggestion, believing it to protect the greater joy they would share when their love was formalized in the promise of a life together. Amy simply could not fathom that this was to be the end of all that had been their world. She was so overwhelmed by a sense of disbelief that she found it difficult to take in the full impact of Abe's words.

"Amy, my parents want me to come home for good. Aby has a friend who has offered me a job in his tech company. I will be able to see my brothers and sisters again, to be an uncle, to be part of all that I thought was lost to me forever. I honestly never believed that God would grant me this opportunity to share my faith in Christ with those dear people. But I also never believed how difficult it would be to leave this place and all the people here that I care about. In my wildest dreams I never imagined I would meet an amazing woman like you, only to have to leave you. But at least we shared nothing that either of us can regret. I could not have forgiven myself that."

Shared nothing? Amy thought in mute misery. *We have shared almost everything! Our hopes, our dreams, our worries, our triumphs! We have laughed together, prayed together, grown together. We became one in every possible way except that which we mutually agreed was meant only for the blessing of marriage.*

As much as she longed to experience it, she had yet to feel the touch of his lips on hers. She still dreamt of that moment when they would become officially engaged, and waited patiently. Now, in the space of a few moments, her dreams had become a nightmare that was only too real. As if from a distance Amy watched while Abe bent over her hands, pressing them to his forehead before kissing each one with more fervor than she had ever witnessed from him.

Without daring to look at the numb loss in Amy's expressive eyes, Abe turned on his good heel and left her standing in the middle of a classroom that suddenly felt like the dark side of eternity.

CHAPTER 12

*"I've commanded you to be strong and brave. Don't ever be afraid
or discouraged! I am the LORD your God, and I will be there to
help you wherever you go."*

Joshua 1:9, (CEV)

It took two and a half days on the road for Abe to reach the Yousef
family home in Spurlock, Virginia. Despite getting a late start on
Friday, after his gut-wrenching final meeting with Amy, he drove for
almost seven hours until mental and emotional exhaustion forced him to
seek accommodation for the night. He woke the next morning with swollen
eyes and a headache that marked the remnants of a restless night spent in
tortured prayer and doubt. But when he grabbed his phone and saw the
daily Bible verse pop up on the screen, he felt as if God was sending him a
badly needed word of encouragement.

*I bow before your holy Temple as I worship. I praise your name for your
unfailing love and faithfulness; for your promises are backed by all the honor
of your name. Psalm 138:2 (NLT)*

Abe felt his throat constrict again, but he was done with tears. He forced
himself instead to smile and cling to those promises like a lifeline. As he
drove further east, he tried to focus on what lay ahead, blotting out
memories of what he had left behind. Not giving much thought to his
proximity to the Thompson home in Winchester, he stopped the second
night less than 100 miles away in Ashland, Kentucky. While Tim's patience

and ability to remember countless names and faces were being pushed to their limits, Abe sought only the respite of sleep.

Dozing late into the morning on Sunday, he felt more physically refreshed than he had in days. He covered the final seven hours of his journey in better spirits, finding pleasure in familiar terrain and sights as he drew closer to his home. The thickly forested mountains of West Virginia were a far cry from the plains of Kansas. Abe only began to feel trepidation when he finally entered Lawson County and the city of Spurlock in the northern part of the state. When he turned into the driveway of his parents' mid-century modern house, he remembered them telling him that they had chosen the place because of its resemblance to their home in Lebanon. Cream-colored stucco covered the simple, angular lines of the building which was topped with a flat roof canted slightly on an angle to accommodate winter snows. High windows free of windowpanes added a sleek look to the single-story building spread out over a generous lot sparsely populated with a few large evergreens – a nod to the ancient cedars of Lebanon.

Stiff from hours of enforced inactivity, Abe took a few minutes to let the blood flow into his outer extremities before walking up the long drive to a wooden door so imposing, it might have guarded the residence of one of his Phoenician forebears. But before he could reach the handle, the heavy door swung inward, and he faced his father. Abe was almost afraid to breathe as the two men confronted each other, separated by an emotional barrier that neither knew how to cross. It was Mr. Yousef who moved first, and the impetus of movement somehow freed him to drop the mantle of reserve that had bound him. He placed his hands on Abe's shoulders, kissed each cheek soundly, and embraced his son with genuine affection.

The dam that had held the rest of the family in limbo pending the outcome of that initial encounter burst in an outpouring of welcome. Abe's mother, trying in vain to conceal her repulsion and grief at the sight of her son's prosthetic leg, hugged him all the harder to convey her regret and sympathy. His sisters greeted him with the eagerness and teasing banter they reserved for their favorite brother. It was the sibling nearest to him in age, Abe's brother Fahkir, who cast the only shadow on the otherwise jubilant homecoming. He stood in the doorway in an attitude of constraint and only bowed stiffly in recognition of his brother's return. His wife and their two-month-old baby were conspicuously absent from the family reunion.

Entering the house on a wave of otherwise goodwill, Abe tried to absorb details of the surroundings that had first been his home as a child and a youth, then his home base during his Army years. Some might have considered the minimalist interior austere. Plush leather upholstery and richly hued oriental carpets over polished wood floors, however, added warmth and helped define intimate living spaces. A sprawling openness spanned the area between the high front windows and the rear sliding glass doors that served to draw the inviting backyard inside. Simple, white-washed walls functioned as neutral backdrops for the beautiful photographic artwork adorning each vertical surface. Mr. Yousef had won numerous awards over the years for his amateur photography, and Abe enjoyed noting the new entries of local interest and older prized photographs of scenes from the Levant. During a lull in the almost overwhelming barrage of questions from the distaff side of the family, mercifully cut short by the need to finish dinner preparations, Abe stopped in front of what had always been one of his favorite pictures. He was surprised in his perusal by a remark from behind.

"*Unity and Strength Tempered with Humility.*" Fahkir said, as he moved to stand next to his brother. "I believe Aby got the idea for the title from you, if memory serves me. I can't help wondering if the image still inspires you?" He had scarcely spoken a word to his brother since his arrival. Now he spoke in challenge.

Abe continued to look at the photo with a heavy heart. It captured in stark, monochromatic tones, row upon row of devout Muslim men bowing in prayer. The ancient practice of repeating the standard prayers that had been recited by innumerable generations of ancestors had – until 18 months ago – always filled Abe with a sense of continuity, grounded in tradition. As he took in the countless "faithful," inevitably facing toward Mecca, he saw a gathering of lost sheep who did not know the true Shepherd or the forgiveness, mercy, and grace offered them through great sacrifice. The new perspective filled Abe with sadness. He was reminded of the conversation between Jesus and the Samaritan woman at the well. She believed that her people were to worship on their holy mountain and that Jews worshipped in Jerusalem, but Jesus had gently rebuked her telling her that the true worshiper would no longer be tied to any particular location.

"They are the kind of worshipers the Father seeks," Jesus said. *"God is spirit, and his worshipers must worship in the Spirit and in truth." John 4: 23b-24 (NIV)*

No one broached the subject of his conversion to Christianity as if all had agreed to put it aside for the time being in order to preserve harmony within the family. Fahkir's question and thinly veiled hostility showed that not everyone was willing to forgive and forget. It also made Abe realize how desperately he wanted to share the spirit of truth with them all, but he too must wait out of respect for his parents' efforts. "It is a very fine photo," was all he said in reply. His brother was obviously not satisfied with Abe's response but reluctantly joined him in the summons to the table.

An almost artificial dialogue ensued while everyone spoke in turn of everyday events as only people who live in close community can. Abe took advantage of the discussion about daily activities he had no part in to study his family members more closely. He thoroughly enjoyed watching his sister, Radeyah, trying to get her uncooperative, but adorable thirteen-month-old daughter, Mina, to ingest more food than she threw on the floor. It didn't help any that her uncle kept making faces, sending her off into giggling fits. Correctly interpreting a meaningful look from the frazzled young mother, Abe shifted his gaze to the quiet young man seated next to her.

Abe had been present at their wedding just months before his last deployment, but he had had little opportunity to speak with the reserved Asad. He and Fahkir were obviously in sympathy over the presence of the prodigal infidel. Abe wished Husam could have been there. At least in that brother he had an ally, even if they disagreed philosophically. But college fall break was still two weeks away. Samia, seated next to her oldest brother, pointed out that she and Ommy had made all his favorite dishes, that he obviously required a new wardrobe, and that he definitely needed a trip to the barber. She received half-hearted affirmation from her sister still trying to feed little Mina. While he watched them, Abe was reminded of the natural beauty of Lebanese women.

Both sisters favored their mother who was fair skinned with dark expressive eyes. The hijab each wore hid their thick, dark hair, and served to underscore their allegiance to the practices of Islam. Any hint of femininity was well-disguised under long-sleeved, loose-fitting tunics and ankle-length skirts.

Their father bore the features of his Arab ancestry, not uncommon in the ethnically diverse country of his birth. If Abe's nose was prominent, his father's was positively homeric in its proportions. Abe had also inherited his father's swarthy skin, though somewhat lightened to a smooth olive by the gene pool. Mr. Yousef spoke little during the meal, but Abe noticed several speaking glances between his parents, and he wondered at their meaning. The male members of the family retired to the living room while the ladies cleaned up after dinner, and Abe soon heard much that had been left unsaid earlier.

"It is good to have you home, Ahmad." Abe heard his name spoken as if the comment was directed to someone else. He had grown so accustomed to his adopted name that the familiar had become foreign. "It is good to have the family together once more. Husam will be home in a few weeks, then we will be whole again." Abe had a few minutes to ponder his father's choice of words while Samia served hot tea to the men lounging comfortably in the living room. Mr. Yousef received the cup almost without noticing it, but he reached out to lightly rub his daughter's cheek in a gesture of affection. He sipped his tea while the others respectfully waited for him to continue.

Presently he said, "I have had a long time to contemplate and regret my words and actions toward you, Ahmad, when we saw you in the hospital." Abe was so shocked by this unexpected admission, he could think of nothing to say in response. "I was disappointed – deeply disappointed, but I must take some of the blame for your actions on myself." Now Abe thought he must be dreaming. "It took me too long to fully understand that you were a grown man. I thought I could wait until you had finished university and taken a job in the area to explain so many things. But you joined the Army, against our wishes." Mr. Yousef paused long enough to give Abe a quick look of reproof before continuing. "And then we learned of your injury and your change of faith. It was too much to take in at once. We went from feeling deep pity and regret, to being overwhelmed by an even deeper feeling of betrayal. And even though we may have been justified in our anger at watching you make one rebellious choice after another, we abandoned you when you needed us most, and for that I ask your forgiveness," he said in an attitude of humility, and bowed his head in Abe's direction.

"But Aby, I never made any of my life choices to deliberately anger or disappoint you."

"That is of little importance now, Ahmad. What is done is done. Please, let me continue." His tone was hardly conciliatory. All signs of humility had vanished.

Abe noticed his brother looking somewhat smug. *Does he know what's coming?*

"I never disclosed to you the true reason that your mother and I chose to move to America, and I believe that if I had, you might have understood better the importance of our adherence to the faith of Muhammad."

"I thought you came because of a job opportunity, and to get us away from all the political tension…" Abe ground to a halt as he caught his father's eye and realized too late that his participation in the dialogue was neither required nor appreciated.

"…in the event that another civil war might break out during the tenuous peace? Yes, that is true – in part. But we, that is my Muslim brothers and I, could already see the strength of Islam taking hold over much of the population in Lebanon. It has also grown exponentially in European cities, especially in recent years, due to the influx of refugees. But the United States has always been more inaccessible simply because of geographic constraints.

"My brothers and I had also been following the role of the Christian faith in America. We watched with interest the gradual liberalizing of its congregational sects and the shift of focus to social justice rather than the teachings of their holy writings. At the same time, public schools had all but expunged any remnant of Christian influence, so that children were growing up in a religious void. Ironically, it was the demand for social justice that gave Islam a voice in America. Where traditional Christianity was seen as a threat to intellectual formation, Islam and other minority religions were given overt attention in the name of cultural pluralism and inclusivity. Couple that with a drop in the U.S. birthrate over the last three or four decades and the perfect scenario for a steady appropriation of religious influence became obvious. We, the faithful adherents to Islam, could simply move in, become productive members of the local community and quietly, without any violence, gradually take over the country."

"But Aby," Abe interjected, unable to take in what he was hearing, "I remember your anger at the attacks on 9/11. I know I was quite young, but I was sure you, and other leaders in our Muslim community, wanted a peaceful coexistence with the people of our new country."

"I was angry," Mr. Yousef replied with quiet, yet implacable conviction, "because those behind the attacks were blind zealots whose miscalculation set our cause back ten to twenty years. Any student of this culture would have realized that no matter how fractured the American ethos might become, a direct attack on the country would only result in people from all walks of life and belief systems coming together against a common enemy. Other, wiser heads had already recognized peace as the only pathway to success in America."

He stopped when he saw Abe frown. Mistaking his son's expression to reflect disbelief in such a possibility, Mr. Yousef added with triumphant zeal, "But yes, Ahmad, it is inevitable, and those same Americans have, unknowingly, opened the door. My citizen peers, Christians and non-believers alike, embraced the 'Zero Population Growth' mantra of globalists years ago. Those powerful voices convinced young couples that the responsible reproductive practice was to only replace themselves, or better yet, bear only one child. In that manner alone could the world population shrink to a more manageable, 'earth-friendly' size. So, while the gullible American populace was raising one or two children, we were raising four or five. I believe many young couples now choose to avoid having children altogether so that they might enjoy a more decadent lifestyle relatively free from financial sacrifice.

"The unbridled practice of abortion played into our goals also by eliminating tens of millions of babies before they could ever present any kind of competition for the populace. It will take time, but I believe that within the scope of three or four generations, Muslims will outnumber conservative Christians in America. And the growing number of politically correct Christian sects, and those who are simply ambivalent about matters of faith, won't raise a finger to stop us. Were it not for all the illegal immigrants flooding the country from the southern border, our goal would be even easier to achieve. Among those undesirables are a few who may bring their Catholic faith with them, but that too will eventually by watered down by a culture of misplaced tolerance, and the guiding hand of a weak pope.

"Then," Mr. Yousef's voice rose as he unveiled the pinnacle of his strategic plan, "then we will offer the purity of Islam to fill the resulting spiritual vacuum. Young men who have been vilified and emasculated for so long by the progressive American culture will be drawn to the true faith that raises men to be leaders. Women, exhausted from the demands of being perfect physical objects, will rejoice in the piety and freedom of modest clothing and the hijab. Muslims, raised to respect knowledge and diligent study, will command control of higher education, particularly in the medical professions and disciplines such as law and engineering. Such success will open doors in politics and government, allowing us to institute Sharia law and effectually bring about a peaceful jihad without spilling a single drop of blood. *Inshallah!*"

"*Inshallah!*" responded Fahkir and Asad in unison. They were both obviously familiar with Mr. Yousef's vision and completely in agreement with its implementation.

Abe felt sick inside. "I see," he said faintly. He *did* see. He had never before fully realized the impact his decision to follow Christ must have had on his father. Abe had grown up attending what he believed to be a peace-loving mosque, at odds with the aggressive Islam he encountered in college. Now he finally saw his father's actions in a new light. *Can there be any validity in this picture painted by Aby,* he wondered with horror.

"Yes, I feel that you must see now," his father responded. "Your misguided desire to follow your Jesus will come to nothing. Let that go, Ahmad, and join us in making the wisdom of the great prophet known to our fellow Americans. It is the most important legacy I can leave to you and your brothers." Mr. Yousef spoke as one who believed his point to have been won. He had heard awe in his son's quiet response, rather than dismay. "You have much to process. I know this knowledge will call you to reorder your thinking, but when you do, I am certain it will bring you peace."

Abe was already absolutely certain that the only peace he would ever find was in the person of Jesus Christ, but he refrained from verbalizing those thoughts. This was clearly not the time to share his testimony.

"Good. Here come the ladies so we may discuss lighter topics. I will speak to you of these things again in a few weeks."

The rest of the evening was blissfully free of any intrigue or conflict. While Abe was fully aware that the present goodwill could not last, he was content to live in the moment. He even joined in the laughter brought about by others sharing old memories – when his preoccupied mind allowed him a moment free of mental conflict. Abe begged his mother's forgiveness in asking to be excused early, however, claiming travel fatigue as an excuse.

As soon as he closed the door to his room, he sank into the reading chair by the window, his mind reeling from all that had passed in the previous four hours. Abe reluctantly had to admit the possibility that some of what his father had said was true when he spoke of slowing birth rates and the demonization of men across the culture. Having only attended one church, Abe believed it to be a model of *all* Christian churches. He recalled the many times Pastor Lindeman had called men in the congregation to leadership roles or invited them to participate in men's Bible studies or prayer groups. Though Abe had attended the church for just over a year, he remembered the pastor emphasizing the reasons God had adjured mankind to "be fruitful and multiply" during a study of Genesis.

But perhaps Community Church is an anomaly, he thought, *a fellowship of believers that honors and studies God's word as its ultimate authority. Can it be that other churches treat the Bible as a simple book of wisdom written for another time, only to be referenced when it suits a desired social narrative?* Abe felt inadequate to address all the accusations made by his father, but he trusted his Heavenly Father implicitly. So, when he came to the end of his own weak judgement he dropped to his knees and prayed for wisdom and assurance.

Abe fell into bed that night emotionally drained – torn between the blessed healing of reunion and the toll it might ultimately demand. He longed to discuss with Tim and Derek all that had transpired, but he didn't want to burden them with his problems. And although he knew Tim deserved an explanation for his departure, that conversation could wait until he and Rose had returned to Kansas. Abe would not rain on their parade any sooner than necessary. As he lay in the darkness, his thoughts in chaos, he fought valiantly against images of Amy that forced themselves repeatedly to the forefront of his mind. Memories of their effortless communion of spirits, born of their mutual affection, came flooding in leaving him feeling lonelier than he had in a very long time.

"Oh, Mama, I don't know what to do," Amy cried out in despair. Though her husband had already gone to bed, Joyce Walker stayed up to welcome her daughter on an unplanned trip home. Amy's emotional state had been only too obvious during a late afternoon phone call.

"Well, the first thing you're going to do is take your things to your room and get ready for bed while I fix you a nice cup of cocoa complete with marshmallows," Joyce said in her matter-of-fact voice. "You know that always made you feel better when you were a little girl, and some things never change." Seeing that Amy seemed disinclined to move, she added, "Now scoot!"

Fifteen minutes later, mother and daughter were seated on the old, battered couch in the family room. Clad in equally battered flannel pajamas, Joyce listened patiently as a flood of tears interspersed with disjointed phrases of explanation came pouring out of Amy's anxious heart. Joyce Walker had never met Abe, but based on Amy's previous glowing descriptions, he sounded like just the sort of man she had hoped her daughter might marry. Amy's father hadn't been so sure. He was openly concerned about the challenges inherent in the two attempting to build a life together when each came from such vastly different backgrounds. But he had been willing to withhold judgement until meeting the young man in question over an upcoming weekend visit. That day would never come now, and Joyce wondered that hers and Amy's intuition had been so far off.

All she could do was offer her daughter comfort and a place to gather herself for a few days before returning to Tinkers Well.

"I know it will be difficult, but I think you need to be honest with Abe when you see him again at your friend's wedding. I suspect there is a lot he left unsaid, though I don't want you to get your hopes up only to be disappointed again. It's out of your hands now, so go to bed and tell your troubles to someone far better able to guide your path than me." Joyce hugged her daughter and sent her off to bed.

On Sunday evening, as she neared the end of her return journey to Tinkers Well, Amy listened to her favorite radio station to fill the emptiness of her solitude. Because she had left home at the last possible moment, it was nearly 11:00 at night when she entered Harrington County. It was the end of the golden oldies request hour featuring the music Amy had grown up listening to. The songs, more than a generation behind the times, had been her mother's favorites. She wished she could stop and phone in a request that was a perfect rendering of her thoughts set to music, but she kept driving. Ironically, some other tortured soul must have been experiencing something that roused the same emotions for as she listened, the precise song she longed to hear began to float over the airwaves.

To alleviate the worry of all that he had been confronted with that evening and to ease the loneliness of being cut off from his friends – especially Amy – Abe opened the app for the Christian radio station she had introduced him to. He lay in the darkness listening to words that might have been written for them. Abe found comfort in believing that Amy, too, was listening, but he refused to face the notion that she might also be suffering. Employing willful blindness as a coping mechanism, Abe nonetheless prayed the richest of blessings for her, believing he could never be a part of God's answer.

All I see is that I don't see what's ahead of me
I'm afraid my life will never be all I hope for in the end
All I know is that I don't know where the road will go
If I dream, then will I find it so, will tomorrow be my friend?

Sing me a lullaby, sing me to sleep tonight
Sing me a tender lullaby 'cause all my heart can do is cry
Help me compose my soul, quietly take control
Sing me a lullaby, and tell me I'm your child

All my plans are falling through, and I don't understand
Lord, I know, my world is in your hands, but won't you tell me
once again?[9]

Amy pulled into her driveway and turned off the car while she sat with her eyes closed, listening to the repeat of the chorus. After the song ended, she switched off the radio and let the silence of the night envelope her. In the stillness she felt compelled to pray – not for her own pain and loss, but for Abe and all that he must be experiencing. She prayed that wisdom, courage, and grace would be poured out on him. And though she still carried a terrible ache in her heart, for the first time in days, she experienced a sense of peace.

By the time Abe made an appearance in the kitchen the next morning, his father and sister had already left for the day. He hadn't emerged from his room so late on purpose – or at least not consciously – but he had to

---

[9] Twila Paris, *"Sing Me a Lullaby,"* (Dayspring Music [administered by Capitol Music] 1980). Used by permission.

admit to a sense of relief that there would be no mention of the revelations from the previous day. Instead, he was greeted by the aroma of coffee and his mother's unaffected smile. He took a seat at the island breakfast bar in hopeful expectation of a favorite breakfast treat.

"Yes!" Abe cried triumphantly when his mother placed a plate before him laden with pieces of flatbread hot from the oven. They were spread with olive oil and covered in toppings of minced lamb, eggplant and *zaatar* – a mixture of sesame seeds, thyme and sumac. Melted cheese smothered the *manakish* in gooey goodness. Abe's cup overflowed when she added a basket of *zalabia* (sweet fritters) at his elbow. He was so excited, he had a fritter halfway to his mouth before he remembered to give thanks for the feast and for his mother's thoughtfulness. Without thinking, he prayed as he would at any other time – freely and straight from the heart.

"Dear Lord, I thank you for this delicious food, for Ommy who prepared it in love, and I ask that you bless it to the nourishment of my body for your service." Then he added a resounding "Amen!" before digging in with gusto.

Abe's mother looked at him curiously. The evening before, he had sat quietly at dinner while those around him recited the *du'a* before and after the meal. He had also eaten little, which had worried her. *But today he is a different man!* Mrs. Yousef wondered at the transformation and thought it was probably due to nothing more than the relaxed atmosphere of being alone with his mother. Gone was the emotional gravity of being bombarded by the whole family at once, with the memory of their previous parting still weighing on everyone. With maternal satisfaction, she watched her son empty a second plate of *manakish*. "I wonder who helped you regain your appetite after your… accident," she asked haltingly.

They had chatted so easily during the meal that Abe answered without hesitation. "Mostly Angelica," he responded with a mouthful of his last fritter.

"She is the young woman that Husam spoke of?"

Intentionally disregarding the reference to Amy, Abe laughed. "*Young?*" he said, then added quickly, "I suppose I shouldn't laugh – she's probably about your age." He grinned at his mother before continuing. "She is Derek Warner's mom and except for the past month or so, I've been living with them. Angelica is about the best cook – next to you, of course – that I've ever had the pleasure of being fed by. She was kind enough to learn how to make some Mediterranean dishes – did I mention that she's second only to you as a cook?" He looked politely at his mother, a mischievous smile playing at the corners of his mouth.

She pursed up her face and answered tersely, "Now you just stick to your story and spare me your nonsensical flattery." But her pleasure in his compliment was obvious.

"As I was saying, before I was interrupted," Abe commented, emboldened by his mother's smile, "Angelica also introduced me to the spice of the islands – Caribbean, that is. She's originally from Jamaica and made me her biggest jerk chicken fan, though Derek would probably argue with me – he usually does." His grin failed to elicit another answering smile. Instead, Mrs. Yousef abruptly started clearing the dishes, avoiding her son's eyes as she spoke words born of guilt and shame.

"I am truly grateful, Ahmad, that you found such good friends to take you in after your troubles." Still avoiding Abe's gaze, she rinsed the dishes and loaded them into the dishwasher. It was her way of getting through the difficult moment. "They helped you when they had no obligation to do so. We did not and we are your family." She finally looked at Abe, and added with a quivering lip, "Please forgive me."

Abe hurried to his mother and gently took her in his arms. "Mama," he said tenderly, calling her by the name he had used as a little boy, "of course I forgive you. Please don't cry. I didn't understand at the time, but it was God's way of teaching me to trust in his provision. I know it is not what you and Aby wanted for me, but your actions forced me to a place where I was grounded in my new faith."

She looked up quickly and said, "Please don't tell your father that. I'm afraid it might undo all the good that was accomplished yesterday." She turned again to her task of tidying the kitchen. While she wiped down the cooktop she said in a steadier voice, "My remorse is more personal. You see, I of all people, should have been more understanding."

"I don't understand…" Abe began with a puzzled expression.

"That's because you and your brothers and sisters were never told of my true heritage. Aby thought it best, so that you would have no doubt about being true followers of Islam." Abe was still in the dark. "When I was a little girl my family and I went to the central market in Beirut one day. It was only a few months after the Lebanese Civil War broke out in the 1970s. I remember a horrible sound as a bomb – or grenade or whatever it was – exploded nearby. My father threw me to the ground and covered me with his body. His action saved *my* life, but he and my mother and little sister were not so fortunate."

"But you don't *have* a younger sister…"

"No," his mother replied gravely. "She died that day with my parents. I was left alone to wander the streets. By some miracle a policeman took me to his home and gave me into the care of his wife. I was in such a state of shock I had no idea what was happening until many months later. I learned that the couple had lost their own daughter to a stray bullet when the conflict broke out. One child was taken by war, and another provided. They may have given me a home, but I believe my presence saved them too. We became a family.

"*What?*" Abe said in disbelief. "Are you telling me that the grandparents I knew my whole life were…"

"Not my real parents?" Mrs. Yousef finished the question and nodded. "They are the only parents I really remember. I was only seven at the time and so bewildered by a world exploding around me that I clung to them for stability. They were very kind to me and raised me in their faith – Islam. But I was not born a Muslim. My true parents were Maronite Christians."

"You were a *Christian?*" Abe wondered how many more earth-shaking disclosures his parents would spring on him.

"My parents were Christians, but I had not yet taken my first communion. One of the few memories I've held onto from that time, aside from losing my family, was that I never got to wear my beautiful white dress for that special day. I was instead introduced to the hijab when I was 11, a year before I… I became a woman." Reminiscences ended, she shook her head and returned to the present, adding with some constraint, "The point is, Ahmad, that even though I was just a child, I once knew of Jesus as you do. I should have had more compassion, but I followed your father's lead. It nearly broke my heart to leave you in that hospital." Her voice caught on a sob and her eyes misted over. Abe gave her another hug and kissed her cheek then reverted to the more formal form of 'Mother' to help them both gain some solid emotional footing. "Is that why you are so fair-skinned, Ommy? I never really gave it any thought before."

"Yes, I believe so. I know it is vain of me, but over the years I have sometimes looked at my reflection in the mirror without my hijab and tried to imagine what my real mother might have looked like – without the gray hair, of course."

"Then you must know that she was quite beautiful," Abe said gallantly. Mrs. Yousef responded with a laugh.

"Now you are talking nonsense again." She added diffidently, "Can we keep this between ourselves, Ahmad? I think it might be best for the present."

"I don't see how hiding our family history is good for anyone," he said, frowning. However, when he saw the obvious worry on her face, he agreed. "I will respect your wishes, Ommy."

She sighed in relief and said briskly, "Good. Now we have things to do." They spent an agreeable day running errands and talking about everything under the sun. Abe chauffeured his mother in his car, much to her delight. As he drove, she caught him up on details of his siblings' lives. He, in turn, told her about Tinkers Well, his friends, and their recent adventure involving Simon Atherton, and about their near misadventure with a tornado. He didn't mention Amy because he wasn't ready to face those questions, especially since he had no answers.

He manfully endured an exhausting mall crawl with his two sisters on Tuesday, agreeing to the prospect of an endless search for clothes he had little interest in, all for the sake of sibling accord. He was fairly certain that the two would never let the idea drop until he acquiesced to their wishes. He knew his sisters well. Samia and Radeyah seemed to know the mall well, even though it reflected the signs of the times in shuttered stores and "going out of business" notices. They insisted on dragging Abe to every haberdashery left in the apparently infinite span of retail space. They also insisted on a trip to Asad's barber who gave Abe's unruly mop some much-needed shape and style. Before Abe could stop him, the enterprising stylist also zipped a razor across Abe's soul patch and instructed him to let his beard grow for a few weeks before returning for more grooming tips. His sisters merely laughed when the long-suffering Abe complained about having been left to the mercies of Attila the Hun.

Returned once more to the relative sanctuary of the Yousef family home, Samia loaded her brother with their shopping spoils and instructed him in exactly what he was to change into for dinner that evening. After collecting little Mina, who had been duly spoiled by her doting grandmother, Radeyah and Samia left soon after. Abe was a little surprised by their abrupt departure but assumed they had made plans for the evening. That left him more than a little confused as to why his clothing choice for dinner mattered at all. He became even more suspicious when he noticed that his mother had set the table for six. Just then his father walked in the front door and held it open for the three others who quickly followed him.

"Ahmad, my son. I would like you to meet my work associate and his wife, Mr. and Mrs. Salam." Abe politely greeted the newcomers. "And this is their eldest daughter, Noor. She is completing a PhD program in nursing and is one of Samia's instructors." Abe's heart skipped a beat. A tall young woman with expressive eyes and generous lips smiled shyly while he stood rooted to the spot. He blinked a few times to ensure that the vision he saw was real. Staring at the silky brown hijab draped around her face, Abe thought for a heart-stopping moment that Amy had miraculously appeared in Virginia, and his jaw slackened accordingly. He quickly recognized his mistake, but his apparent admiration of their young guest filled his parents with satisfaction. Abe and Noor were seated next to each other at dinner, and when they offered to help clear the table later, both sets of parents shooed them away suggesting they take a stroll in the garden instead.

Oh, good grief! If they weren't so painfully transparent, their efforts might almost be comical, Abe thought to himself. Sneaking a glance at his companion, he realized that she was also embarrassed and sought to alleviate her distress.

"Well, you must admit, they managed that very smoothly," he said softly, with a rueful smile.

Noor laughed self-consciously and said in a voice only he could hear, "Perhaps we should at least put on a show of compliance, or they may think up an even more disconcerting scheme."

Abe signaled his agreement by opening the sliding door and gesturing Noor to proceed him outside. The Yousef and Salam elders nodded to one another over the success of their plan. Their offspring walked in silence until they reached a marble bench in a secluded spot beyond observation from the house. If Abe was nervous about what to say, he needn't have been. As soon as Noor felt they were free from prying eyes and ears, she turned quickly toward her escort and hurried into low, earnest speech.

"Ahmad, I must confess that the only reason I agreed to accompany my parents this evening was to meet you. Please don't think me forward, but I believe you may be the only person I can speak openly with." Completely taken aback, Abe merely sat quietly on a nearby bench while Noor disclosed her personal predicament and the role she hoped he would play in coming to her aid. As he listened his eyes began to glow, and the two became so engrossed in their discussion, they lost track of time. Their enterprising mothers, speaking nonchalantly but at an unnaturally loud level, came looking for them. Fortunately, plans for another meeting had already been set, and Abe made a point of mentioning the coffee shop date to everyone in parting. As he had expected, his parents took smiling notice as they bid their guests a hopeful farewell.

"Yes, Iffaa, I believe we made the right decision in calling Ahmad home at this time. Things appear to be working out exactly as we planned," Mr. Yousef commented as he and his wife watched their eldest son disappear down the hall. After an hour spent alone with Noor, Abe was determined to prolong that belief as long as possible. The unexpected verbal exchange in the garden left him with much to ponder.

CHAPTER 13

*When three of Job's friends heard of all the tragedy that had
befallen him, they got in touch with each other and traveled from
their homes to comfort and console him.*

Job 2:11a (TLB)

While Rose waited for Tim at the kitchen door of *Willow Walk,*
she felt a slight letdown; she had discovered that his was the
only vehicle in the garage behind the house. Derek and Abe
had apparently already left for the day. Though she had come to check
renovation progress with her favorite handyman, she had also looked
forward to seeing her other friends again and laughing at their good-natured
teasing. But it was only Tim who greeted her, giving her a brief kiss and
instructions to keep her eyes shut and her imagination warmed up. After
attempting, unsuccessfully, to get a glimpse of the kitchen beyond his
imposing bulk, Rose allowed him to cover her inquisitive eyes as he guided
her down the hall to the foyer.

When they stopped at the imposing ten-foot front doorway, Tim
dropped his hand and spun her around. Rose was immediately struck by the
obvious absence of the detail that had previously drawn the eye. Most of the
wooden baseboards and crown molding were gone. The "wooden lace" of
the hanging pendants across the hallway entrance looked lonely without the
other trim components. Wandering into the living room, she was dismayed
to find the seasonal mantle missing, and a quick peek into the adjoining
dining room showed its mate missing also. She couldn't tell what shape the

wood floors were in due to their protective coverings. Despite her best efforts to conceal her disappointment, Tim had come to know her too well to miss the signs.

"I know it doesn't exactly look very grand now," he said, "but I promise you it will all come together before the wedding. We had to get into just about every wall to update the wiring and run plumbing and vent pipes for all the added plumbing fixtures. We also had to replace insulation on the exterior walls which were full of nothing but matted down old newspapers. And replacing the lath and plaster walls with sheetrock required removing all the wood trim. Believe it or not, we've come a long way since we started the demo process."

Rose gave mental thanks for having been spared that part of the house's life cycle.

"I would have preferred to refinish the floors last, but since we had to move in enough furniture so Derek, Abe, and I could call this home, I started that process as soon as you left then covered every inch of flooring to protect it." Frowning, he looked around and added, "I sure hope we didn't rush that stage, or we'll have a mess when we uncover everything."

"But you *are* going to reuse all of the molding, aren't you?" Rose asked, trying to sound optimistic.

"I promise to do my level best not to waste anything. And I noticed that *you* noticed the missing mantles. I'm having them dipped and stripped so we can refinish them with whatever stain and varnish sheen you like. The carving on each one is so intricate it would have taken forever to strip them by hand, and I don't want you to feel like you're solely responsible for cleaning every inch of woodwork by yourself."

"Wait. I can see it all now," she said, as if looking into a vaguely discernable vision. "There I am, an old woman chained to the stair spindles as I scrub and scrape at the wood until my knuckles are raw and my back is numb from hours of painstaking labor on my knees."

He grinned and guided her through the dining room toward the kitchen. "I solemnly swear never to chain you to the stairs, you adorable nut."

"Can I get that in writing?" she asked politely. Thoughts of wood trim were quickly put to flight when she stepped through the pocket door that separated the dining room from the kitchen. Rose gasped when she saw the clean, white Shaker cabinets adorning the walls where grimy, dilapidated cabinets had hung before. She and Tim had agreed that there was little point in having the cupboards go all the way to the 12-foot ceiling since she would have needed an extension ladder to reach the upper shelves. Left with a good four feet of open space above the main L-shaped section of the kitchen, she itched to start collecting bric-a-brac to display there.

"Tim, they're perfect. I can't wait to see it all come together when the gray marble countertops are installed. And I love the long island with the raised breakfast bar. This is so much more functional than the old layout," she said and gave her private contractor an impulsive hug. "Oh! I just noticed. You made the window wider over the sink…" Rose swung around to look at the other exterior wall. "…and you *added* a window by the table. You are an absolute genius, my love," she said, as she looked around. "What a wonderful surprise."

"You haven't seen the best part yet. Come with me, my dear," he said. Taking her hand, he led her to the other side of the island.

"Is that…?" Rose began and looked at Tim, who grinned from ear to ear. "It's my stove!" Then realizing it was too good to be true she chided him, "I thought we had agreed not to spend so much on any one thing – even if it's exactly what we want." She gazed wistfully at the bright red, six-burner gas stove boasting two ovens and designed in a retro style. They had seen one in a home improvement chain store on a trip to Kansas City, but both had decided that the focal point of the store's kitchen display was too expensive. They were committed to being as frugal as possible, knowing that the total cost of renovations would quickly eat up Aletha's generous monetary gift if they chose high-end fittings for every room. Tim knew, none better, that the upkeep on a house of that antiquity could potentially be a constant drain on the budget even if renovated with the care and precision he employed.

"We did, but that was when it cost 9,000 dollars. Which, I have to admit, was pretty ridiculous. But, I had to see a stained-glass craftsman in Leavenworth for those little windows above the stairs, so I popped into their branch store for a few other things I needed, and guess what was sitting right there as I walked through the door – at half the original price!"

"Tim, you know I want to keep it, but that's still a lot of money…"

"Yes, but your savvy fiancé talked the store manager down another 1,000, and with my military discount taking it down even more, I just couldn't say no." He happily received a second impulsive hug followed by a volley of kisses.

Holding her by the shoulders he said sternly, "You keep that up, young lady, and I'll *never* get any work done today."

"Well, it looks like your crew beat you to it. I've got to say, I was kind of surprised – and disappointed – not to see Derek's old clunker or Abe's SUV outside when I drove up."

"Can you believe it? I haven't actually seen Abe yet at all. He must have come home really late last night and left early. I can't imagine what he's working on that's so urgent. Derek pleaded ignorance last night and barely said a word to me this morning before he ran out the door." Tim shook his head and frowned as he thought about the few words they had exchanged. "It was really weird. It was almost like he was avoiding me, and the only thing he said about Abe was that he had to take care of some problem and that he'll talk to me about it tonight." Shrugging his shoulders he said, "I guess I'll find out later. But enough about my housemates. I need to act like a building contractor, and you need to check in on Aletha and Granny Gert."

"This has been the best homecoming *ever*," Rose said, resting her head on his shoulder after insinuating herself once more (with little resistance) into his arms. "I wonder what other surprises await me today?"

She found out soon enough. After a brief visit to the matriarchs of their respective families, and promising to return later for lunch, Rose spent the rest of the morning getting reacquainted with Tinkers Well. She unearthed a large crockery pitcher with bright red accent edging from the dark recesses of the *Unique Antique.* Making her way down Commerce Street she found the ideal fabric to line the back of the library shelves on a remnant table in *Pins and Needles* and ended up at *Miles of Style Boutique* where she splurged on a very feminine, ruffled blouse. She assured Gayle Harwood that she would be back later to look at the new fall dresses, certain that she would find the perfect one for the rehearsal dinner among them.

Answering a text request by Amy to stop by the school that afternoon, Rose entered the classroom during the almost eerie calm that settled into the hallways after the clamor and chaos inspired by the end of day bell. Rose instinctively felt something was off when she walked in to find her friend clad in worn slacks and a shapeless sweater, with her hair once more pulled back into a lank ponytail and her face devoid of makeup. Amy had grown so assured and competent in her ability to turn herself out in style that her co-workers, and even students, had noticed. She had begun to hold her head high with her shoulders squared – all six feet of her radiating confidence. But when Rose peered through the door, she beheld a young woman who appeared defeated.

"Hi, friend," she called from the doorway. Looking up from the music on her desk, Amy saw Rose and her face crumbled.

"Hey," Rose said gently, hurrying to the desk, "what on earth is the matter? Are you all right?" A shake of the head and a quivering lip were Amy's only reply. "Has something happened to Abe?" At the mention of Abe's name Amy broke down completely. Between sobs, she haltingly shared her account of his departure with Rose, who simply couldn't believe what she heard. Despite her evident heartbreak, Amy still asserted that Abe was the best man she had ever known. Rose was beginning to have some doubt.

She heard the story behind Abe's abrupt exodus three hours before Tim did. Arriving late at *Willow Walk* the night before, he had been too tired to wonder about Abe's absence, having no thoughts of anything but sleep. The following morning, still suspecting nothing, Tim began the rounds of all the job sites on the schedule. He was immediately caught up in remodeling details and project specifications and worked so long he was almost late for dinner with his two favorite ladies. When he walked into his mom's kitchen, he saw Rose sitting at the counter looking like she'd lost her last friend.

"Sweetheart," he asked in concern, "what's wrong? Are you feeling okay?" Marilyn was never so proud of her son as when he showed himself to be gentle and considerate, reminding her of her late husband Peter.

"You haven't heard about Abe and Amy yet?" Rose asked in surprise.

"What about them?" Her only response was to look at her hostess for help.

Taking up where Rose had absent-mindedly quit on the salad prep, Marilyn explained, "When I didn't see Abe at church on Sunday, I asked Derek about him, but he was very evasive. All he said was that Abe had gone out of town, but since Amy wasn't there either, I just assumed that they had gone to visit her parents. I knew they had made plans to do so but thought it was not for a few more weeks. Mine and Amy's paths don't naturally cross very often at school, so I haven't seen her since… well, since…"

Tim looked expectantly at his mother, who was suddenly silent, then at Rose.

"…since he left," Rose said on a dejected note. "He's gone, Tim. Abe has left Tinkers Well and Amy and Three Brothers and gone back to Virginia."

"*What?* That doesn't make any sense. All the way to the airport last week he talked about nothing *but* him and Amy. I'm not kidding. I couldn't get a word in edgewise. What in the world could have happened since then?"

"All I could get out of Amy this afternoon, between weeping bouts, was a disjointed story about Abe's father calling him out of the blue on the way home from the airport, essentially demanding that Abe come home. He was trying to make amends or something. What I do know is that my best friend is heartbroken, and one of the people I've come to love and respect the most has let us all down." Her voice was so forlorn, Tim instinctively put his arm around Rose to comfort her, but he couldn't help thinking there was more to the story.

"Maybe that's what Amy understood him to say, but I just can't accept that Abe would behave in such a cavalier way. Trust me. He is *crazy* about her. And he *is* worthy of love and respect. Why don't we all just hold off on final judgement until I talk to him? Like I told you earlier, one of the few things Derek did tell me was that Abe was going through a rough patch and that he promised to talk to me tonight – the night I had originally planned to get back – and explain everyth – "

Tim was interrupted when his ringer went off. "It's Abe. I'll be back in a few minutes," he said. "Don't start without me," he added and disappeared into the living room.

When he walked back into the kitchen, he was obviously pre-occupied. The only recognition of one of his favorite meals was to comment that something smelled good. He took his place at the head of the table just as his mother placed a basket of fresh biscuits next to him and sat down. He offered a short blessing, then sat with his elbows on the table and a furrow between his brows, lost in thought. He finally took notice of the ladies serving themselves and shook himself back into the present.

"I can't tell you all that Abe said, but you need to know that this decision was very difficult for him. He told me he needed our prayers more than ever."

"That seems all the more reason to have explained the whole situation to Amy. He hasn't called, or texted, or emailed since he left even though she has tried to reach out to him. He just seems to have cut her out of his life," Rose said with resentment.

Tim reached out to take her hand. "Sweetheart, do you remember when I first learned about Miles, and I didn't want to have anything to do with him, didn't want to believe that he had undergone a heart change?"

"Yes," she replied warily.

"How can we, knowing Abe as we do, not give him the benefit of the doubt just as you encouraged me to do with Miles? How can we do less than have faith in him and pray for him?"

"You're right, of course," she admitted, though a little resentfully. She was quiet for a few minutes then turned fiercely on her unsuspecting fiancé.

"Do you know what one of your most annoying habits is, Ludlow?" Marilyn smiled, knowing Rose only ever called Tim "Ludlow" in fun. He bit his lip to hide a smile of anticipation. "It's the way you use my own words against me when I least want to hear them." Then she added with grudging humility, "And when I most need to hear them."

No one recognized that tactic better than Marilyn.

"Don't feel bad, Rose. He's been honing his technique on me for years." A soft laugh escaped Rose before she glared fiercely at Tim, who no longer made any effort to hide his grin. "The last person who would want us to waste good food on his account is Abraham Yousef, so let's eat before this gets cold," Marilyn said and filled Tim's bowl with a heaping ladle of beef stew.

"So, you're getting married," Mark Lindeman commented on the obvious as an opener for the first of four sessions of pre-marriage counseling. He sat in a scuffed leather chair next to a desk mounded with books and scattered papers. The bookshelves, common to every pastor's study, were filled with Bible commentaries, Greek and Hebrew language references, history books and publications by his favorite authors. His impressive library contained volumes by names prominent in the faith, as well as those more obscure writers whose words were few and treasured by even fewer. Tim and Rose sat opposite him on a small couch, eagerly awaiting the pastor's guidance.

"I'm so glad we are able to do this in person rather than by zooming or video calls. I think you'll find it allows for better interaction."

"Wait," Rose said, looking at Tim, whose face was turning red. "You never told me we had the option to do this online. You told me I had to be back here to do this in person. *Tim...*"

It's never a good sign when a single syllable name is pronounced in two.

"I thought you *wanted* to come back here as soon as possible so I didn't... bother to mention it," he ended lamely, avoiding her intent gaze.

"*Tim...*" Two syllables again, accompanied by an unwavering stare.

"Okay, okay," he said with a sheepish look. "I should have told you. I'm sorry. I had no right to make that decision for you. My only excuse is selfishness on my part because I knew I would miss you so badly."

Rose transformed from strict school mistress into happy fiancée instantly. "I'm so glad you did, because it gave me the excuse I needed for an early return. Well done," she said and patted his knee.

Tim turned to look at Rose indignantly, "Why did you just hold my feet to the fire if you agreed with my decision to begin with?"

"Because I need you to know that I need to know anything that requires a decision from both of us, even if you think you know what I know I'm going to say." Tim stared blankly at Rose for a full minute before shaking his head and turning helplessly to the pastor. Their spiritual guide couldn't have been more delighted. He clapped his hands and beamed happily at the couple.

"Excellent!" he said. "This is the perfect segue to our discussion tonight on communication. Men tend to be straightforward in their speech, while women are more apt to couch their messages in more obscure terms."

"I'm not even sure what Rose just said qualifies as obscure. I'm pretty sure she was speaking another language!" The pat on his knee wasn't as gentle the second time.

"Precisely," the pastor said. "Not only do you speak in different ways; you also hear what the other is saying differently. Now I'd like to run through a few exercises," he said, handing them each a clipboard and pencil. "There is no right or wrong. I simply want you to think about how to express a few concepts."

The remainder of the hour saw frowns, indignation, rolling eyes and a great deal of laughter. As they bid Pastor Lindeman goodbye, with homework in hand, Tim glanced at his watch and said, "How about dinner at the diner with my best girl?"

With a commendably straight face, Rose asked cordially, "Will she be joining us there?" Tim burst out laughing.

"No, you woefully, deficient listener. I'm bringing her with me," he said, and grabbing his best girl's hand, walked her through the park to their destination. He continued to chuckle softly, prompting Rose to demand to know what was so funny.

"I was just thinking that we may be the first couple *ever* who require remedial marriage counselling *before* we get married!"

"No, no, *no!*" Tim yelled into his cell phone. "You can't do this to me, Mike. I *need* those countertops… I know you told me it would be early October before you could get to them, and I distinctly remember telling you I could hold off as late as the 15th on delivery… I get that, and believe me, I can sympathize with a manpower shortage, but my fiancée will kill me if I don't have the kitchen finished by then… okay, okay, I know you're doing your best, but I absolutely have to have them not later than the 24th, and if you need me to come in and help you cut them – *call* me!"

Tim ran his fingers through his hair and immediately regretted his action. Despite wearing work gloves, he had managed to get drywall compound on his hands, and it now clung in clumps to his hair. He ran to the laundry room sink and washed the mud out while holding his head over a five-gallon bucket, not wanting the compound to drain into the pipes and harden. As he dried his hair with a filthy towel he thought grimly, *One of my best friends may or may not make it to my wedding, the kitchen might or might not be operational for the rehearsal dinner – what else can go wrong?*

Rose listened in a state of happy complacency to Milly Dixon go on and on about Tim's sterling qualities. She never tired of hearing others praise her fiancé and his work, though they were simply repeating what she already knew.

"He has a real gift for capturing the style of a place and recreating it with such detail. But he also understands the need to make the building or store or house relevant to the times. Rose, you've got yourself one honey of a man," Milly concluded as she stood to make way for Amy coming through the door. "You girls enjoy yourselves and let me know if there's anything you need."

Amy slid into the booth, still a bit pale, but determined to put on a brave face for the occasion. Rose was equally determined to help Amy take her mind off her troubles – two friends with good intentions whose efforts were doomed to end in lamentable failure.

"Didn't the diner turn out well?" Rose commented, striving for common ground. "Remember the first time we had lunch together? We had to listen to the waitress at the *Early Bird Café* grilling me about Simon

Applegate. I am so glad we have a nice place like this to come to now, a place where we can enjoy a meal without any painful memories."

"I know that day was hard for you, Rose, but it was also the day you encouraged me to think that Abe might actually like me. And you convinced me to get a makeover. I can't tell you how much that meant to me, but now it all seems so pointless," Amy said dejectedly.

"But Amy, you should want to look your best for your own sake. You truly are an attractive woman when you want to be." It was meant to be a compliment, but Amy heard her best friend tell her she wasn't trying hard enough to deal with Abe's absence.

Amy bit back a wounded reply and suggested they order. "I think I'll have a Rueben sandwich and onion rings." When it dawned on her that she had chosen that particular menu item simply because it was Abe's favorite, she changed her order to soup and salad. "I guess I'm not very hungry today after all."

Rose ordered the same out of a desire to show solidarity, then struck out on another tack. "Amy, you have to come by and see the new stove. It's even classier than I remembered from the store. It is the queen of the kitchen, and the one thing I thought I would never have. Tim finagled the price down to about a third of the original cost. I think he may have inherited more from Miles than he realizes." Her smile slowly faded when she saw Amy's brows draw together. Little did she know that mention of Tim's bargaining skills reminded Amy of the fun she had had watching Abe politely, but adroitly, haggling over the price of his new vehicle until the salesman had practically paid him to take it.

Despite making every effort to avoid mention of Abe or the wedding or *Three Brothers Construction, Inc.,* the lives of the two women had become so intertwined that whatever Rose talked about somehow led Amy's mind to thoughts of her lost love. When the food arrived, Amy sat contemplating it with growing distaste until she pushed it away from her and looked at Rose with tears in her eyes.

"I can't do it, Rose."

Rose couldn't imagine why a salad had upset Amy so.

"Well… I'm sure you could order something else. Let me call Milly," she offered. She lifted her hand, but Amy reached across the table and pulled it down, holding it tightly.

"It's not the food, Rose. It's the wedding. I just can't do it. Not now. I am *so, so* sorry," she said in a desperate undertone. Squeezing her friend's hand before letting it go, she left the diner as unobtrusively as possible to hide her grief.

CHAPTER 14

"Do not be worried and upset," Jesus told them. "Believe in God and believe also in me."

John 14:1 (GNT)

Rose drove up to *Fern Cottage* in a blue fog. The sight of Granny Gert and Aletha sitting on the porch swing snapping beans would ordinarily have filled her with a sense of peace and security. Two elderly ladies practicing the arts of food preparation and preservation lent an element of timelessness to an otherwise madcap world, which, at the moment, seemed to be disintegrating into chaos. Her usual light-hearted greeting failed to find its way to her lips. Instead, Rose waved listlessly to her grandmother as she walked toward the house.

Noticing the signs of worry, Gert chose to ignore them in favor of distracting her granddaughter. Rather than giving Rose a chance to fall further into an unknown well of self-pity, Granny Gert ordered her to a nearby chair and handed her an empty bowl and a basket of freshly picked green beans. Aletha had no need of the bumper end-of-season harvest, but the process of breaking and canning the beans gave her a feeling of purpose and supplied a modicum of provision for those truly in need during lean times.

"Is that you, Rose?" An answering peck on the cheek drew Aletha's brightest smile. "What a delightful surprise. Trudy and I were just discussing how much we miss your presence in the house, but we understand perfectly your desire to get to know Marilyn better before the wedding. I suppose if you still wish to marry a man after living with his mother, you must truly love him, though I of all people know her to be a dear."

Rose smiled wanly and began idly snapping beans, her mind a million miles away.

Granny Gert grabbed another handful of beans from her basket and plopped them in her own lap, then did the same for Aletha. Her expert fingers worked without thinking while she fixed her eyes on Rose. "I suppose you've been frittering away your time on a lot of nonsensical details for your wedding, young lady." Watching Rose's frown lines deepen, Gert took pity on her granddaughter and asked casually, "And how are things progressing? I take it Tim is still determined to marry you?" Her efforts were met with a half-hearted chuckle. "I think she must be ailing, Letha," Gert said, ostensibly addressing her old chum. "Have you ever heard of a bride walking around like she's headed for a funeral instead of the altar?"

"Oh, Granny Gert, you don't know!" Rose cried out in despair.

"Then I reckon you should tell me. Nothing looks half so grim when you give it voice."

Rose gathered her words carefully. She knew from experience that her grandmother had an uncanny knack of turning the most desperate of situations into mere stumbling blocks. Rose wasn't about to let Granny Gert paint in a more positive light the serious calamities that had befallen her, threatening to upset all her carefully laid wedding plans. "It all started with Abe leaving – "

"Oh, we know all about that, dear," Aletha interjected. "Marilyn filled us in on everything. We'll all miss him, but I'm sure he had good reasons for going."

"I'm sure he did too," Rose reluctantly agreed. "But don't you see, Tim has lost one of his groomsmen. He thinks Abe might be here for the wedding, but he isn't sure."

"And I take it," Granny Gert said, emptying her bowl into a large box of broken beans, "that he can only get married if he has three fellows standing up with him. I don't know Rosie. I wouldn't be too sure of a groom that needs that much encouraging."

"Granny Gert, this is serious," Rose said sternly, while trying to keep her treacherous smile under control.

"I'm sure it is," Gert replied calmly, as she walked over to retrieve another bushel basket from the stack on the end of the porch. "But I can't imagine you've decided the sky is falling over one missing groomsman. Now go on with whatever disaster has cropped up since then," she said, her hands already busy with a fresh pile of beans in her lap.

"It's not just one missing groomsman. Amy is in such a mess over Abe's departure that she doesn't want to be in the wedding anymore either. I think the knowledge that her wedding dreams drove off with her boyfriend has just overwhelmed her. She feels it would be too painful for her to be a part of someone else's happiness, knowing hers to be impossible. I met her for lunch today, but she was so upset, she ran out of the diner without touching her food."

"Well, I'm sorry for them both," Gert said in a brisk tone tinged with real sympathy. "I truly am. but you can't let other people's happiness dictate your own. I know you'll miss them both because they have been good friends to you, and good friends don't come along every day. Don't I know it!" She patted Aletha affectionately on the knee before adding, "What it boils down to is this – will a smaller wedding party keep you from marrying Tim?"

"Of course not!" Rose answered with spirit. "I would marry Tim if he and I were the only two people in the room. And the pastor, of course," she added as an afterthought.

"That's what I thought," Gert said, nodding her head in approval. "Though you might need a few witnesses. You can count on Letha and me. We wouldn't miss it for the world." Aletha beamed in agreement.

But Granny Gert was wrong in believing she had routed all of Rose's concerns. The despondent bride, whose face had once more fallen into lines of worry, declared, "But you haven't heard the worst of it yet!" Rose waited for a sympathetic query, but the two old ladies sat on the porch swing snapping beans like they were in the habit of solving major crises every day as a matter of course. A little disappointed by their lack of response, Rose hurried on with her final dire revelation. "We may have to cancel the rehearsal dinner at *Willow Walk!*" she announced tragically. She was annoyed when her grandmother merely lifted her eyebrows and peered over her glasses. "Tim told me the countertops may not be installed in time! And we can hardly serve dinner for over 20 people without a functional kitchen," she finished with dramatic flair.

Gert pursed her lips and sat snapping her beans in silence for a few minutes before turning once more to her friend. "Letha, have you heard the news?"

"What's that, Trudy?" Aletha asked innocently. She had enormous respect for the other woman's cleverness in handling any situation.

"Why it seems that there isn't a working kitchen in *all* of Tinkers Well."

"I never said – " Rose began.

"Because if there was," Gert continued, ignoring the interruption, "the food for Rosie's dinner could be prepared almost anywhere – say here, for instance – and taken to the big house. I guess we'll all just go hungry for a while." With that philosophic conclusion she sighed and went back to her work, only looking sideways at her granddaughter when she heard a telltale gurgle of laughter from the adjacent seat.

"Ugh! Granny Gert you always do that. You always make things look better than they appear to be. It's so… irritating!" Rose said and made a face at her grandmother.

"Well, I'm too old to waste time looking for things to be worse than they are. Now you just focus on making yourself so irresistible that Tim won't notice if there are three groomsmen or 30. That boy is so besotted, I don't think you'll have to work very hard." Another giggle confirmed her suspicions. "You need to start snapping faster, young lady. We've got to get through that whole pile of beans before Angelica and Marilyn get here to help us start canning. Now hop to it, and while you're here we can discuss the menu for your bridal shower. It's only two weeks away, and Letha and I mean to make sure everyone has a whale of a good time!"

"Ms. Walker?" Emily Miller approached Amy's desk hesitantly. The other students had left for the day, and Amy was busy reviewing practice records, frowning at the ridiculously small amount of time many students spent on practicing their instruments. It was no surprise. Those committed to regular daily practice performed infinitely better and progressed exponentially faster than those who only got their horns out once or twice a week to blow a little air through them. She sighed in resignation. There was only so much a teacher could do. She could hardly go home with each student to make sure they practiced. It was up to the parents, and those parents who failed to understand that music education requires as much homework as other academic disciplines made little effort to organize their child's practice time at home. Amy sighed again, feeling that she had somehow failed in another realm of her life. The joy she usually experienced in sharing her love of music with her students had been sadly lacking during the past few weeks.

"Ms. Walker?" Emily had to repeat herself before Amy looked up from her task.

"Emily!" Amy said, smiling at one of her favorite students. Emily had no real natural musicianship, but she tried hard and had mastered the skill of reading musical notation through sheer determination.

"Ms. Walker, are you all right?" Anxiety was evident in the girl's voice.

"I'm fine. Why do you ask?" Amy said, touched by Emily's concern.

"Well, it's just that, well you look different, lately."

Amy frowned. "How do I look different?" When the girl hesitated, she added with a reassuring smile, "It's okay, Emily. You can tell me. Really."

Emily shuffled her feet and spoke to the clock over Amy's head. "It's just that, well, you don't look so pretty anymore." The ensuing silence was so deafening, she thought it best to shift her attention to the bassoon laying across two neighboring chairs. "And when you're not talking to us – me and the other kids, I mean – well, you look… sad all the time. You never looked sad before." Emily took a deep breath and nerved herself to once more look directly at her teacher who seemed to have turned to stone. "Did we do something to make you sad? 'Cause if we did, we're real sorry." The girl looked as if she was near tears.

Amy had been so lost in her own troubles that she had given little thought to how she had let them affect others. She knew pulling out of Rose's wedding had hurt her friend, but all she could think about at the time was her own hurt. Sitting there, listening to a sweet, innocent girl take on the burden of worrying about her teacher, drove a stake through Amy's heart. Her relationship with Abe had been one of choice, in which each shared the other's burdens out of affection. But students, faced with all the demands of life in the 21st century, should never have to anguish over the well-being of their teachers to the point of assuming unnecessary and undeserved blame. Amy impulsively jumped up and hugged the girl.

"You know what, Emily," Amy said in a livelier voice than she had used since Abe had walked out of her life, "I *haven't* been feeling well lately. But since you were thoughtful enough to ask, I suddenly feel much better. Now you run on home and practice your trombone and stop worrying about me. I think you'll see a new teacher tomorrow." Amy winked and waved the suddenly light-hearted girl out of the room before making a few resolutions.

The first she accomplished immediately by calling Rose and asking her to get together for coffee. Over cups of hazelnut java, the two young women shared, cried, laughed, and recalculated the bridal party once again. The second resolution spoke for itself when Amy walked into her classroom the next day looking polished and confident. There was still sadness in her heart, but she refused to let her students see it ever again.

"Abe! Oh man, is it good to hear from you! Can you hold on a minute?" It was just a week before the wedding. Pausing in the process of installing refinished baseboard, Tim stopped to answer his phone. When he saw who the caller was, he had motioned for Derek, restoring the trim around the pocket doors, to join him on the porch. Tim put the phone on speaker so all three could talk.

"Okay, we're all set. Derek is here, too."

"You lazy bum," Derek said. "Leave it to you to run out just when the really *hard* work was starting. But seriously, how are you, man? I can't believe I'm saying this, but I've really missed you and your Abe-isms."

Abe laughed, though he was in anything but a laughing mood. "And I have missed you too, my friend – both of you – more than you know."

"Abe, I've got to ask. What's going on? Is everything okay?" Tim couldn't hide his concern.

"I am quite well. In fact, I have never felt better, but I am fairly certain that any day now I will no longer be welcome in my father's house. That's why I had to call. I know I walked out on... everyone, with little explanation, but I can tell you now that it was the right decision. And having accomplished what I believe God brought me here to do, I must move on. I know I have no right to ask, and you are under no obligation to show me your favor, but I wondered... hoped that you might consider..."

"Yes!" Derek and Tim shouted in unison.

"Of *course,* we want you back," Tim said. "Heck, it'll probably take you a month just to sort out all the invoices and payroll ledgers and update the inventory. And please tell me you're still willing to be in the wedding."

"*Willing?*" Abe asked humbly. "I would be honored to stand up beside you."

"I'll second that," Derek said, "but I think I should warn you that I will look so fabulous that it's not likely anyone will even notice you're there except Amy…"

"Please, Derek – and Tim too – don't say anything to Amy other than to let her know I will be there. I have so much to tell her, but it must be done in person. Will you promise me that?" he asked anxiously.

"We've got your back, brother. And Abe? You know Tim and I have been praying for you."

"Then please don't stop now. I'm afraid the next few days may be the most difficult of my life." Knowing him so well, Tim and Derek wondered how anything could compare with what he had already gone through, but they promised to do as he asked.

Rose was beside herself with joy when Tim told her the news that evening. "I can't believe it! Abe and Amy will be together again and – "

"Sweetheart, let me stop you right there," he said, gently placing his fingers over her lips. "We don't know what's going on with them. From what Abe told us, he's still going through a really rough time, and this whole silent separation has been just as hard on Amy. We can't put any expectations on them. Let's just be thankful that they'll both be with us for the wedding. They'll have to sort themselves out *by* themselves. Agreed?" Tim lifted Rose's chin so that she was forced to look into his intent gaze.

She sighed as she twined her arms around his neck. "Agreed. That is, if you promise that we'll get to sort out ourselves by ourselves."

Tim wrapped his arms around her, pulling her close. "I dare anyone to try and stop us."

Marilyn joined Rose to pick up the mother of the bride and her sister at the airport on Tuesday while Tim and his crew devoted the day to finishing the kitchen and bathrooms at *Willow Walk*. Through the providential timing of another wedding miracle, the countertops arrived a day before their scheduled drop-dead date. All the plumbing was hooked up, cabinet hardware installed, and hanging vent hood mounted over the stove. The only working sink in the house, before installing the new bathroom vanities the week before, had been the utility sink in the laundry room. It had worked for two bachelors, but it wasn't exactly convenient. Now a second powder room on the main floor, two full baths on the second floor and the master bath in the attic were fully functional. Two glass shower doors were yet to be installed, but that was merely a matter of drilling some holes – a lot of holes.

"It's coming together, man," Derek said and patted Tim on the back as they looked around at an unbelievable transformation. "What do say we break in this kitchen? It's after two, now, and I need my beauty food."

"I thought it was beauty *sleep*," Tim said with a grin.

"Well, you won't let me do that on the job."

"Fair enough. Order pizza for everybody and I'll spring for it. I feel like celebrating!"

"Oh, honey, it's just beautiful," Beth Thompson said as she looked her youngest daughter over from head to foot. "This is definitely the dress for you." Turning to her mother she said, "I'm so glad you were with us for the dress shopping. I'm afraid I don't fare as well as you do when it comes to arguing with Violet and Lily."

"That's because you're a pushover," Gert responded with fond, if somewhat brutal, candor.

"You do look lovely, Rosie, though I've got to say it's probably a good thing that I never married. I would never have fit into a contraption like that," commented Rose's Aunt Patty. Since she was built on the same square, stocky lines as her mother, no one offered any argument.

Marilyn hosted a luncheon for all the women closest to Rose upon the arrival of her mother and aunt. Angelica insisted on helping and she had driven Aletha and Granny Gert to the Ludlow home in town. Marilyn had taken a week of absence from teaching, but Amy sent her regrets. So, it was just six who gathered around the bride-to-be to get a sneak preview of the wedding dress.

"I believe it'll do," Granny Gert said, nodding her head in delight at the sight of her glowing granddaughter. "Now, do we have time before lunch to see Rose in the rehearsal dinner dress?" she asked her hostess eagerly.

"We have all the time we need. Let's leave Beth to help Rose change dresses, and she can come out to the living room in the other."

No one had seen the second dress yet. It certainly made an impression on the ladies present. Rose walked out and twirled in a knee-length satin dress with a flattering V-neck bodice and three-quarter length sleeves over a double-tiered skirt. The rich blue of the fabric reminded Grannie Gert to dig in her purse and hand Rose a small package.

"Grandpa Ernie gave these to me as a wedding present, and I was still wearing them when your mother married, but I've had a notion for some time that these would be just the thing for you. Violet and Lily would have called them old-fashioned, but I brought them out to Kansas with me thinking you might want to wear them. But don't feel you have to on my account," she added gruffly.

Rose unwrapped the package and opened the box. She gasped as the light from above was caught in the facets of glittering blue stones. "Your sapphires! I've always loved these," she said as she lifted the delicate necklace with a single stone surrounded by antique silver filigree. She handed it to her mother who fastened it around her daughter's neck while Rose donned matching drop earrings. "Granny Gert, they're perfect. I'm wearing Mother's pearls with my wedding dress, but I hadn't really given any thought to what jewelry would best suit this dress. It's all coming together so beautifully. Nothing can go wrong now."

The Three Brothers crew stretched out around the old farm table in the kitchen, lethargic from full stomachs and the aftermath of hard work. As usually happened, stories started flying, some of them more lewd than Tim thought appropriate for mixed company, but Jada, the tough little Marine, had become one of the guys. She contributed little but listened intently.

Someone had just shared an account of an unscrupulous builder in Kansas City who got caught by building inspectors, then had to pay through the nose in fines and added work to correct the deficiencies.

"I think I may have worked for that guy once," JT said. "He was a jerk. It's good to know that at least every now and again they get what's coming to them."

"Oh, that reminds me," Jason chimed in. "I saw a Facepage post from Dave Harrison," he said, looking at JT seated next to him, "You remember him? He posted a story about this 'legendary' real estate guru," he said with air quotes, "who is really the world's biggest sucker. Apparently, he's been trying to make the big score for years by buying up either worthless property, or land that is unusable because of some problem or other – methane gas, right of way requirements, whatever. It seems that he's been shooting his mouth off all over town about a big deal he made with some New York land developer, thinking he'd hoodwinked him into buying land for twice what it's worth."

Tim said nothing, but his jaw hardened as he listened.

"But it turns out the big city guy pulled a fast one and has a deal with some big manufacturing outfit back east to resell the land for 10 or 15 times what he paid for it. Everybody in the business is laughing at old Horace, but he's so clueless, he doesn't even know he's been taken for a ride," Jason said with a grin and slapped the table.

Tim's face looked so stern, he might have been mistaken for a hanging judge if anyone had bothered to look at him, but all eyes were on the storyteller.

"Oh, yeah. I remember reading that," JT said. "I think the guy's name was Hawkins, maybe…"

"No, it was more like Thorne or Thornton… something like that. Doesn't really matter, the guy's a genius. I think – " Jason stopped in mid-sentence when Tim stood up abruptly, grabbed his jacket and headed for the door.

"Derek," was all he said as he gestured with his head, indicating that his friend was to follow him. Once outside, he spoke tersely as he walked toward his truck parked in the garage. "You're in charge now. Make sure those shower doors get mounted today then send everybody home. I don't know when I'll be back."

"Tim, what is *wrong* with you? You look like somebody just shot your mother."

"He hasn't yet, and I mean to stop him before he succeeds," Tim said on a harsh laugh.

"You're not making any sense. I don't…"

Tim threw his jacket into the passenger seat and turned to Derek before climbing behind the wheel. "Hawkins? Thornton? *Hawthorne.* Derek, they were talking about my father, Miles Hawthorne, the lying, cheating, *&@%$!"

Derek grabbed Tim's arm, pulling him out of the truck. "Take your hand off me, Derek," Tim said through clenched teeth.

"Look, I don't care if you *think* you can beat the crap out of me or not. I'm not going to let you go off half-cocked because two guys are shooting their mouths off to their co-workers."

"Don't you *get it?* It all fits. His reticence to talk about his work, his frequent presence here, but never an invitation to visit him at his place of business. He has brilliantly kept us all at a distance from what he doesn't want us to know. How could I have been so *stupid?*" Tim said, shaking his head in anger and self-loathing. "I have to know the truth, Derek. Can't you see that?"

Derek's face was now set as hard as Tim's. "*P-lease,*" he said in disgust. The two had never been closer to coming to blows. "You don't want to *know* the truth; you want to have it out with him *regardless* of the truth. And you're basing your feelings on something somebody read on *Facepage?* Now there's a reliable source," he added with heavy sarcasm.

"Stay out of it, Derek. This is *my* business and I'll settle it *my* way."

Derek stepped back and held up his hands in surrender. "Okay. Let it be on your head." Then he leveled his finger at Tim. "But you're *wrong,* Cap'n, and you *know it!*"

Tim's final reply was a screech of tires and a cloud of dust.

It was the dust that caused Derek's eyes to tear up, but it was blind fury that caused Tim's to mist over so that he had to dash his hand across his eyes to see to drive. With every mile he covered, he dredged up yet another memory of his father's perfidy. Miles Hawthorne was a master of manipulation, and despite all his reservations, Tim had let his father past the barrier of mistrust he had built for himself. He remembered the comradery they had shared while attending a football game, something Tim had never done with Peter Ludlow who had had little interest in sports. He recalled Miles' willingness to help his son haul in and install new toilets in all the bathrooms on a perfect Autumn Saturday afternoon when he might otherwise have been playing golf. Tim ground his teeth when he thought of Miles charming Rose while they spent hours together refinishing wood trim.

But when the vision of his mother's trusting countenance came to mind, as she had looked at Miles with undisguised affection, Tim nearly swerved off the road. That was unforgivable. Aletha could go to her grave believing in the redemption of her son, but Tim would move heaven and earth to spare his mother from being so blinded.

Tim had never been to the Kansas City office, but Miles had mentioned the building's location on a recognizable street downtown. Tim closed in on it as if it was launching signal flares. He drove like a man possessed, and had the roads been better populated with traffic police, he might have been pulled over and his anger allowed to abate. But nothing impeded his progress toward his single-minded goal. He bore down on his father's office like a vengeful enemy storming the gates.

CHAPTER 15

The weeks in Virginia passed quickly for Abe, and to his relief,
neither his father nor brother ever broached the subject of his
expected return to Islam and the future they would share together.
A week after the return of the prodigal, Mr. Yousef had introduced Abe to
the perspective employer he had lined up. When Abe interviewed with Mr.
Mashnuq, he suggested beginning work on a part-time basis. Abe reasoned
that he had been away from the tech world for a few years and would need
some time to study and to catch up with the latest advances. That he had
been doing so on his own since leaving the Army, he chose not to mention.

Mr. Mashnuq knew of the rift within the Yousef family, and kindly
agreed to Abe's suggestion, believing the request to be attributed rather to a
desire to heal divisions in the home. The truth fell somewhere in between.
In any other circumstances, Abe would have welcomed the opportunity to
work with Mr. Mashnuq. He had no delusions, however, about the
possibility of his father changing his mind regarding his devotion to the God
of Christianity and Judaism, and he did not want his boss to be left short-
handed by the abrupt departure of a full-time employee. That his departure
was imminent, Abe believed to be a certainty. There were days when he felt

like he was balancing on a particularly thin tightrope, but he was determined to see his uncertain journey through, regardless of where it took him.

A fragile sort of peace reigned in the Yousef home during that time. Abe counted every day with his brothers and sisters a blessing, and the joy of a prolonged reunion took the edge off the very real ache he continued to carry for his friends and the life he left behind in Kansas. Amy was the hardest to put out of his mind. He thought of her with every battle under the basketball hoop with his brother, Husam, who had made it home to celebrate Abe's birthday during college fall break in early October. Abe thought of her when he watched a favorite movie with Samia – a movie riddled with memorable one-liners that he and Amy used to bandy back and forth like seasoned performers. He imagined her playing along with the string section during a symphony concert he attended with Noor Salam and both sets of parents.

Ironically, it was his time spent with Noor that drew Amy's image most forcibly to mind while at the time reminding him that, despite their superficial physical similarity, Noor was only a pale imitation of Amy. But the more time Abe spent with the serious nurse, the more he developed a real affection for her. Noor was far more intense than Amy and often failed to appreciate the humor behind his jokes. She was kind and thoughtful, though, and afforded him sympathetic friendship.

He was also acutely aware that his parents had developed an interest in Noor as she fit into their plans for him. They smiled indulgently when Abe excused himself to meet her for coffee or to share dinner away from the prying eyes of family. A week before the Thompson/Ludlow wedding, he informed his parents at breakfast that he would be escorting Noor to a lecture at the university that evening, which ordinarily would have drawn comments of support and indulgent smiles. But it was Friday, the holiest day of the week for the devout Muslim with much time devoted to prayer. It was certainly no time for following social pursuits. But having assured

Mr. Yousef that he had been on his knees for an hour that day already, Abe received a grudging pass for the evening.

During his stay in Spurlock, Abe attended the family mosque at his father's urging, though the images and practices that used to inspire blind devotion were now empty representations of his old life. He kept up the pretense because he needed time — time to prolong goodwill within the Yousef home and time to complete a mission he had not anticipated. Fortunately, his father was always so caught up in reciting the age-old prayers, he allotted little concern for the absence of Abe's voice among those of the other men. He merely assumed it was due to Ahmad's embarrassment over so much time having passed since last participating in the ritual. Regardless of the reason, his son's lips moved, which was enough for Mr. Yousef.

Abe's present assurance that he had followed the Friday traditions had likewise mollified his father. But had the elder Yousef known that it was the name of Jesus and not Allah that had sprung so fervently from his son's lips, the evening would not have ended on such a tranquil note. The fragile peace that had reigned during Abe's return to the home of his youth was drawing to a close.

While Miles Hawthorne had come down considerably in the world since leaving New York, he was far from enduring the blight of penury the description of his circumstances might have conjured up in the minds of his former wife and son. Gone were the days of penthouse office suites with luxurious appointments. Nevertheless, Hawthorne ascribed to the theory that one could not attract desirable clients without fostering at least the appearance of affluence and success. To that end, he invested wisely in a comfortable, if not commodious, set of rooms located in a relatively modest building housing everything from dentists, investment brokers, and internet-based start-ups to an upscale salon and coffee bar. The fortuitous acquisition of the stellar secretary to the previous occupant, and its now defunct business, enabled Miles to establish himself quickly and efficiently. Mrs. Castle, a singularly satisfactory adherent to detail, with five grandchildren and a penchant for no-nonsense verbal exchanges, organized the office as a master chef might organize a gourmet kitchen.

Miles' name and reputation were not unknown in the land development world even as far afield as Kansas City, so he soon found opportunities to put his considerable skills to use. He had his own particular end in sight regarding profits and their distribution. Nonetheless, such single-minded focus on financial advancement took second chair to his sincere desire to be as upfront and honest as someone with his background and history could hope to be.

Accordingly, he sat in the tastefully decorated yet understated sanctuary of his usually quiet office putting the final touches on the regrettable reversal of an extremely profitable business transaction. The afternoon sun glinted on an engraved plaque sitting atop the small drop-leaf desk in the corner, highlighting the text of Proverbs 11:28. It was Miles' constant reminder of his father's wisdom and the guiding principle contained in the words. Tim's wedding was only four days away, and Miles had planned to conclude the business matter that day so that he could devote himself to assisting Marilyn and Aletha with the entertainment of out-of-town guests, and any other wedding details that required last minute attention.

He was gathering his information prior to leaving for a meeting when he heard Mrs. Castle attempting to soothe an irate visitor demanding an audience with her employer. The voice carrying clearly through the closed door sounded familiar, though Miles couldn't imagine who he had offended in Kansas or Missouri to such a degree that it warranted the storming of his own particular citadel. Such occurrences had not been uncommon in New York, and he regarded the interruption as more of a nuisance than anything to cause him alarm. But when the door suddenly flew open and his visitor entered the room breathing fire and looking as if he was ready to do murder,

Miles dropped his usually sanguine attitude and stood to face his accuser. He winced as the slamming of the door seemed to shake the entire wall.

"You just couldn't help yourself, *could* you?" Tim shouted at his father, his chest heaving with barely controlled fury. The fact that his anger had been allowed to reach the boiling point with no vent available during the solitary drive to the city, and was therefore stretched to unreasonable proportions, he chose to disregard. He spoke almost without thinking, unwisely letting his feelings rule his reason – a practice uncommon in the usually level-headed Tim Ludlow.

"You've been here less than *two* months – *two months* – and you're already up to your old tricks again." Ignoring the total look of astonishment on Miles' face, Tim went on, his temper white hot. "I wanted so badly to trust you, to believe that you had genuinely changed, and I let my guard down – fool that I am. I allowed myself to be buffaloed by your… your… smooth words and practiced technique. I knew it was too good to be true – that I had a father again – my *real* father: someone I could look up to and talk to as I had Peter, someone I could be proud of, someone who could take an interest in my life and my accomplishments." Tim laughed harshly. "But I have never been more deceived."

"Was I just another gullible dupe to be used for your own ends? To get to Mom? Well, I want nothing more to do with you, and I don't want you to go near my mother again. I won't let you hurt her anymore." A note of pleading crept into his voice as he continued. "Please, Miles, if you have an ounce of decency in you, leave her alone. I know she's been drawn to you again. It's obvious to everyone except maybe her. And I know it'll hurt like hell, but if you leave now maybe she'll get over you a second time without too much damage done." His tone took on an edge again as he went on. "You can do what you want about Aletha. I can't stop you, but you'll do it without my blessing."

Miles' face had hardened during Tim's tirade, and a frown appeared between his eyes. He had ample experience in facing opponents over the bargaining table where his keener mind and cutthroat tactics had left him the victor. The anger of disgruntled foes bested on the field of make-or-break deals had rolled over his formerly arbitrary conscience as water off a duck's back. But he had fully understood the source of their anger, if indifferent to it. Now he stood in the pillory, absolutely mystified as to what had instigated the vicious attack. He may have been concerned over his son's obvious distress, but Miles would not allow Tim or anyone to speak to him with such disdain and not offer an explanation.

"Tim," Miles said firmly but calmly, determined to keep a tight rein on his usually volatile temper, "you are obviously upset about something, but I'm afraid you owe me an explanation for – "

"I owe *you* an explanation?" Tim fired back. "Oh, that's rich!"

"Tim." Miles spoke louder but to no avail.

"You worm your way into our collective confidence," Tim continued as if Miles hadn't said anything, "all the while taking gross advantage of someone who has never done you any harm, just to make a score so you could be the big man in town again."

"Tim!" Miles' shout almost matched Tim's elevated voice. His rising ire certainly did.

"Just take your filthy fortune and leave us alone." Tim fairly spat the next phrase. "I don't know how you live with your con – "

"Timothy James!" Miles roared and pounded his fist on the desk, startling Tim into momentary silence.

"You may be my son, but I'll be damned if I let you go on slandering me without telling me why," Miles said with heat. "Am I to be accused and sentenced without a trial? I had thought better of you," he added, his anger barely in check, "and you dare to speak of *my* conscience!"

The turnabout of accusations caught Tim completely off guard. He persisted in hurling indictments even as nagging doubt tickled his subconscious, causing him to wonder if he might have misunderstood the story recounted by JT and Jason. "Do you deny that you purchased a parcel of land from a Horace something-er-other for far less than it is actually worth? Or that you were able to do so because of insider knowledge you held regarding a large manufacturing concern moving to the area and requiring such a property?" Tim was somewhat reassured about his information source when he saw a look of surprise on his father's face.

Miles paused for a moment before replying, then spoke without hesitation or heat, anger having given way to curiosity. "I do not." He watched Tim speculatively with the hint of a smile at the corner of his mouth.

The smile threw Tim out of his stride and effectively damped the fire of his animosity to smoldering contempt. "So, you *do* admit it. And without any vestige of guilt, I see. Hardly the actions of a reformed man."

Miles looked at Tim intently for a few moments then seemed to make up his mind about something. Without saying a word, he finished putting the paperwork into his leather satchel and walked around the desk where he leaned against it, arms crossed. He nodded to the plaque in the corner. "Do you see those words? That was my father's advice to me, and believe it or not, I have learned to heed it. Now I think it's time I give you some advice, provided you are willing – "

"I hardly think I need advice from…" Tim began but was silenced by the mere lifting of his father's eyebrow.

Miles paused to assure himself that he had Tim's full attention before completing his interrupted statement. "…provided you are willing to reserve judgement until all has been made clear."

It was hardly the declaration Tim wanted. As much as he hated to admit it, he realized he might not have heard the entire truth and had based his judgements on misconceptions. And being an inherently fair man, he reluctantly agreed to Miles' proposition though still suspicious and guarded. Miles ushered them both into the presence of Mrs. Castle who gazed unflinchingly at Tim over the top of the reading glasses perched on the end of her nose. Suddenly recalling his rude entrance earlier, Tim offered a brief apology, to which she merely nodded her head before turning to look at Miles for enlightenment. Once again the smooth professional, he promptly offered an explanation and an introduction as if the presence of raging guests was an everyday occurrence.

"Mrs. Castle, this impassioned gladiator is… my son, Tim Ludlow." Tim's face reddened in embarrassment. "He stopped by to accompany me to the meeting you obligingly scheduled with Mr. Wiener for this afternoon. We were… discussing different approaches to conduct of the business. I trust we did not disturb you unduly."

Mrs. Castle's only recognition of Tim's relationship to Miles was to say, "You could learn a thing or two about manners from your father, young man." Tim turned red from head to toe as he stammered a further disjointed apology, making him feel like a student standing on the carpet before the principal's desk. Having discharged her observation, Mrs. Castle turned away, ignoring him altogether.

"Mr. Wiener did call during your… discussion," Mrs. Castle informed her employer with a pointed look. "He sounded rather impatient for your arrival. I advised him that you always arrive precisely when you mean to."

Miles smiled in appreciation of her tactics, especially as regarded her ability to reduce the imposing figure of his son to schoolboy status. "You must remind me to give you a raise, Mrs. Castle." His lips twitched as he watched her make a note. "I will not be returning this afternoon, and unless you have any tasks of great import, I suggest you make an early evening of it. And don't feel that you need to be here during my absence this week. Enjoy some time off – I know I shall."

"Thank you, sir." Then, as the two men prepared to leave, she called after them, "Mr. Ludlow."

Tim quickly hurried back to her desk. He was almost afraid not to. "Yes ma'am?"

Mrs. Castle squinted her eyes as she looked at him appraisingly. "I suppose you're the young fellow who's getting married this weekend."

"Uh… yes, ma'am."

"Are you good enough for her?" Mrs. Castle demanded, her piercing gaze boring into him like an x-ray.

As he thought of Rose, a smile slowly spread across Tim's face and he answered ruefully, "No ma'am, I'm not. But I mean to spend the rest of my life trying to be."

"Well, at least you have that figured out. Don't forget it and you just might make a decent husband. Now, go on with you. I've got work to do." Tim hastened to join Miles who had enjoyed watching the exchange. Mrs. Castle waited until the door closed behind them before allowing a crooked smile to appear. Shaking her head, she addressed the empty room, stating succinctly, "Men!"

After a brief scuffle over taking individual vehicles (Tim's preference) or traveling the short distance together, Miles graciously accepted victory and the two set off for the meeting despite Tim's lingering doubts.

The office of Horace P. Wiener was situated in a rather less dignified setting than that of Miles Hawthorne. Literally located just on the other side of railroad tracks in a one-story building, it hardly served to inspire visitors with confidence in the abilities of the lessee. The premises were virtually deserted except for a utility truck parked on the opposite end of the gravel lot in front of a tool and die outfit. Tim's scowl returned as he began to suspect that the proprietor of the land company had far greater need of a lucrative business deal than the New York land developer. But he was learning to hold his tongue.

When the door swung open, Tim half expected to see a gaunt elderly man with stooped shoulders and a worn suit. It was the total antithesis of that imaginary personage that waddled toward them. The closest their host came to a suit was a threadbare corduroy jacket with functional, rather than fashionable, elbow patches complimenting a dusty pair of blue jeans. The faded jeans appeared to be held up as if by magic under a belly so round it resembled a ball mounted on spindly sticks. Scuffed snakeskin cowboy boots with ridiculously pointed toes and three-inch heels failed to present their owner as anything but short and rotund. And if ten-gallon hats were the norm, the one adorning Mr. Wiener's head must have had room for at least 20 gallons. Tim watched the approach of the caricature come to life with something like fascinated horror. He caught a glimpse of an amused smile on Miles' face and thought, *He's enjoying this!*

Mr. Wiener stood a good eight inches shorter than his guests, which partly explained the enormous hat, but he carried himself with the aplomb of a king. After extending his chubby sausage fingers in greeting, he ushered the two men inside. The office was clearly only inhabited by one person. It was sparsely furnished with an ugly, dated metal desk facing chairs with rusted chrome frames. Torn and tattered maps adorned the cheaply paneled walls, while a nearly empty water dispenser in the corner burped a belated welcome. Tim struggled to keep a straight face.

"Now who might this young fellow be?" Wiener asked as he invited the men to be seated. He remained standing. It was a decades' long practice – a lame attempt to keep the physical upper hand.

Miles' elegant carriage bore no signs of unease. He crossed his long legs and leaned back as much as the uncomfortable chair allowed before answering. "This is my… er… associate, Tim Ludlow."

Wiener's smile took on a suspicious edge. "I didn't think you had any associates. You certainly never mentioned any to me."

"He is a recent… acquisition," Miles replied smoothly. "I brought him along today so that he might witness the conduct of a business transaction in the skillful hands of a master negotiator," he explained, and nodded his head in deference to his host. Tim wasn't sure if the words were spoken in mockery or if they were a calculated attempt to instill the other man with suspect superiority. Wiener obviously embraced the latter. Watching the little man practically preen himself like a peacock, any lingering resentment or anger on Tim's part quickly dissipated to be replaced by curiosity and a growing belief that he had grossly overestimated any villainy on Miles' part.

"You won't find a shrewder operator in Kansas City than old Horace P. Wiener, son," their host remarked proudly, addressing himself to Tim. "That's pronounced 'weener' – like the hot dog." Tim quickly feigned a cough to hide the choke of laughter that threatened to surface. But Wiener never noticed. He was well-away on his favorite subject – himself. "Hell, I've been making the big deals around here since Christ was a corporal. Just remember 'With Horace P. Wiener you're always a winner.'" Tim had to turn aside to hide another coughing fit. "Need some water son?" Tim merely waved his hand, not daring to speak.

"I have to confess that I was a little surprised when your secretary called to set up a meeting today, Hawthorne. I thought we agreed on a closing date in two weeks."

"You are correct as always, Mr. Wiener. But upon further review of the property, and the sale amount we agreed upon, I felt it necessary to apprise you of some information you may not have been privy to at the time, in the event that you wish to reconsider your offer to sell." The renegotiation of sale was so neatly proposed that Tim's suspicion momentarily reared its ugly head again. It was quickly vanquished.

Wiener leaned on his desk and stared at Miles through eyelids that had become slits covering his beady eyes. He shouted, "Ha! Do you take me for a fool, Mr. Hawthorne?" Assuming the question to be rhetorical, Miles made no effort to give voice to an affirmative reply. "I've been holding onto that property for nigh on ten years just waiting to unload… er… that is, waiting for the right buyer to come along. And I knew that was you as soon as I laid eyes on you. Now I *know* I wasn't wrong." Wiener's overblown good-old-boy schtick turned to less than jovial wariness as he kept his gaze fixed on Miles.

"And I also believe that I am the right buyer, but I feel duty-bound to inform you that I intend to sell the property to a manufacturing concern relocating to the area from New York. I am fairly certain I can sell it for at least ten times the sum I am paying you."

Wiener's mouth fell open and his eyes nearly started from their sockets. "Ten times," he croaked hoarsely before collapsing into his chair. He continued to stare at Miles, whose gaze remained unwavering, reflecting only calm. Gradually, surprise was replaced by a sly look that slowly spread over Wiener's face until he gave a loud guffaw. Regaining his roly-poly stance, he slapped the desk and made a show of putting a toothpick in his mouth, which he alternately chewed on or rolled around with his tongue in a revolting fashion.

"Oh, it's a real nice property, what with good road on one side and railway on t'other. Problem is, Mr. big-city Hawthorne, it's also surrounded by Crenshaw land." Wiener smiled when he saw Miles' eyebrows raised slightly as if in inquiry. "That's right. Jedidiah Crenshaw – that mean, buzzardly old coot – won't grant the right of way to allow the owner of your parcel to build an access road connecting it to the highway, so I reckon *you'll* be holding onto that parcel for the *next ten years*," he finished, going off in a laughing fit. He only stopped when he noticed that Miles didn't seem perturbed in the least.

"What if I told you that I *have* acquired the right of way from Mr. Crenshaw, both to the highway and the railhead?" Miles asked politely. He didn't bother to add that Mr. Crenshaw had done so only after Miles had inadvertently shared his personal testimony and ultimate purpose for the profits with the old man, giving Crenshaw hope for his own wayward son.

Miles had already confirmed that Crenshaw would also grant the right of way to Horace Wiener, though, as Crenshaw had put it, "That varmint's the biggest swindler this side of the Mississippi."

"I'd say I don't believe you. And don't try telling me I could force the issue through imminent domain. It don't apply for one rich land developer – only when it benefits the general public. Oh no, Mr. Hawthorne, you won't catch Horace P. Wiener with his pants down!" Tim fervently hoped not.

"I see that I am left to show you the documents verifying all I have told you," Miles said in a resigned fashion that in no way alleviated Wiener's skepticism, but seriously impressed Tim. He watched his father draw some papers from his briefcase and hand them to the little man who glanced over each page briefly while gnawing on his toothpick.

"Now just supposing I believed all this malarkey, which looks impressive but could be a lotta hogwash," Wiener said, indicating the documents. "Why on earth should I believe that a big shot like you would be willing to walk away from such a sure bet?"

Miles considered the young man sitting next to him, then addressed his host. "Let's just say that I'm doing it for the sake of a boy who wants desperately to believe in his father." Tim's undisguised astonishment spoke volumes.

Unfortunately for the less mentally adroit Wiener, who read the look in a completely different language, the message was misinterpreted. He saw a junior partner catching his superior in a lie and responded accordingly. After slamming both fists on the desk, he shook a stubby finger at Miles. "You almost had me going, you with your slick talk and fancy papers. Well, this is what I think of you and your tall tale." And with that he drew a lighter from his pocket and set the papers on fire, then dropped them into a nearby metal trash can. "There's the door, gents. Use it. And Hawthorne, I expect you at closing with the amount we agreed on, or I'll sue you and your silk suit till you've got nothing left but your silk drawers!"

"As you wish," Miles replied affably and picked up his briefcase to depart.

"Hey, sonny boy," Wiener called after them. Tim, correctly understanding that the hail was directed at him, turned politely to his host. With a knowing look that Tim itched to slap off the little man's face, Wiener said, "I expect you've learned something today about dealing with Horace P. Wiener."

Maintaining a straight face with an effort, Tim answered, "More than you realize," and followed Miles out of the building.

Abe had seen his father annoyed. He had seen his father angry. He had witnessed his father's disappointment, displeasure, and indignation. But never in his entire life had he ever beheld his father so livid with rage that his whole head turned a deep purplish red, making his nose appear to be glowing. His entire being was overcome by a fury so intense that his ability to speak was completely suspended. Abe watched in very real concern, afraid that he might be a firsthand witness to a stroke. Ultimately gaining control of his vocal cords, Mr. Yousef drew breath and unleashed such a blistering diatribe that it found voice in English, Arabic, *and* French, and covered every grievance against his son from forgotten childhood infractions to innumerable recent failings. Abe stood rooted to the floor, shocked at the scope of animus pouring from his father's lips in a stream of vitriol that was almost tangible in its intensity. After a full ten minutes of pacing back and forth, shaking his fist at his son and pointing to him like he was the damned prisoner at an inquisition, Mr. Yousef finally got to the catalyst that had set off the present verbal explosion.

"How dare you! How *dare* you, Ahmad! It is not enough that you chose to ruin your own life by an act of such wanton disregard for honor as to bring shame on yourself and your family. Oh, no. You had to bring an innocent young woman down with you. A young woman whose parents trusted you to protect and guard her against anything as destructive as loss of respect within the community. Had you only followed your own selfish desires among people unknown to us, it would have been bad enough, but you have now alienated a friend and colleague. Mr. Salam was beside himself with grief when I arrived at the office this morning. He could barely collect himself enough to confront me with the sad tidings before leaving to console his wife. You have brought shame upon us all. I can't even look at you right now." On those words Mr. Yousef turned around and grabbed the back of a chair for support while he shook with emotion.

"Then *listen* to me Aby," Abe said in a clear voice, his own anger stirred by his father's accusations. "I had never *heard* of Noor Salam until you introduced us. It was you and Mr. Salam who encouraged our meetings and displayed such open gratification at their regular occurrences. It was you who conspired to bring us into a closer relationship – "

"Yes! But not like this," Mr. Yousef cried as he swung around to confront his son again. "I offered you a place in history with a worthy woman at your side, and this is how you repay me! Had you no thought for me?"

"I have never *stopped* thinking of you!" Abe responded with heat. He wrestled for control over his exacerbated emotions before continuing more evenly, his anger now tempered by compassion for his father's feelings.

"I built a good life for myself in Kansas among people who welcomed me and loved me without question. Despite my deep gratitude and affection for them, I left everything behind when you called me home out of respect for you and your wishes. I hoped that *you* would welcome me and love me without question. But you never even asked me what I wanted. You laid out your vision, fully expecting me to embrace it, despite knowing of my change in faith. You offered me the opportunity to be *you* – to think like you, to act like you. But I cannot. I must be true to myself. My choices may not be yours, but I will always respect the way you have modeled for me the manner in which I am to be a good man, a husband and a father – how to live with honor."

"How can you possibly speak of honor or view your actions as those of an honorable man?" Mr. Yousef hurled back, but with less vigor. It was as if Abe's calmer tone took the fight out of his own.

"I will answer for my actions to the One who judges me. I am only sorry that this situation has caused you such pain. If only I could share with you the God I serve – tell you of his righteous mercy and forgiveness…"

"I want nothing to do with a God who encourages such treacherous behavior."

"But, Baba," Abe spoke the diminutive name out of the heart of a child who longed to be heard by his father, "if you only knew the freedom of salvation…"

"No more!" Mr. Yousef shouted. In a softer, weary voice he echoed, "No more." He then made his final pronouncement. "You no longer have a place in our home." Unable to ignore the sound of weeping coming from the kitchen, he told his son, "Gather your things, Ahmad. You will leave this house immediately. It is you alone who are responsible for your mother's distress."

"If this is the last time we are to speak, Aby," Abe said, unable to control the emotion in his voice, "let me say this. For the rest of my life, I will love you. But you also need to know that I will strive, with every breath I take, to spread the truth of Jesus Christ to the people of this country so that they may be saved from the vision that you and Fahkir share."

Anger flared once more in Mr. Yousef's eyes, and he swore an oath under his breath. Finally, shaking his head in disgust at his rebellious son, he turned his back on all that Ahmad Yousef represented and walked away. The closing of the front door sounded as a death knell.

After gaining control of the laughter that shook them both, Tim suddenly felt embarrassed. He fumbled over words of apology. "Miles, I didn't… that is… please forgive me… I mean… I was an even bigger idiot than Wiener, if that's possible," he ended feebly.

"Oh, I shouldn't imagine there's a bigger fool in the entirety of creation than Horace P. Wiener," Miles responded smoothly. "Like the hot dog," he added and smiled at his son. Tim laughed again but insisted on making a full apology.

"I don't know why I was so ready to believe the worst of you. I know you have no reason to trust me, but I promise that's not like me at all." Tim looked away, ashamed of his own behavior.

"I do trust you. You have never given me any reason to believe otherwise, even though I have given you ample reason to distrust me. Let it go, son." The use of the last word fell effortlessly from Miles' lips and caused not so much as a millisecond of awkwardness for Tim. "We can't hang on to our mistakes if we are to have any hope of moving ahead." Miles held out his hand to Tim who gripped it gladly.

"Agreed, though you must let me say that I was duly impressed by your handling of that fool Wiener. I may not fully understand the scope of your business, but I can recognize and appreciate expert craftsmanship in whatever form it takes. What you did in there – it bordered on sheer genius." Miles smiled and nodded his head in acknowledgement of the tribute. "In my opinion, jerks like that don't deserve a break if they can't even recognize a great deal when it is handed to them free and clear. Wiener doesn't need any help in being out-maneuvered – he is clearly his own worst enemy."

"At the risk of imbuing in you a ruthless spirit, I must agree with you." Miles started the car and pulled out of the parking lot while Tim continued his animadversions on the character of one Horace P. Wiener.

"Well, it didn't take me long to realize that you couldn't have dealt more honorably with that idiot if St. Peter himself had come down from heaven to vouch for you. I guess I'm not quite as well-versed in handling people and the quirks of human nature as I thought," Tim added with a sheepish grin. After a few minutes of companionable silence, Tim jerked his head in the direction they had just come and commented, "I assume all of that back there was true, but you must have made the decision to offer Wiener the deal of a lifetime *before* my ill-advised descent on your office this afternoon. I know the reason you gave in there, and while I appreciate the gesture, there must have been something else behind it. And I know it's none of my business, but would you mind sharing that something with me? I somehow feel it would help me to better understand you."

"That would be an accomplishment," Miles replied with a wry smile, "given that I scarcely understand myself these days." Pausing briefly, he attempted an explanation. "The long and the short of it is that I had to know if I was capable of sacrificing something of great value, knowing I might very well receive nothing in return." Tim remained in the dark.

"I have a very specific project in mind from which I will profit nothing – nothing tangible, that is. But it requires a great deal of capital up front. By the providence of God's timing, I recently received a tip from a former business associate in New York, Blake Hoskins. He told me of a door manufacturer desirous of moving his operation to the Midwest where operating costs are considerably lower, and transportation of goods can be better managed from the more centralized location. I'm sure you'll appreciate the irony of life imitating art as it relates to the unfortunate Simon Atherton's cover story.

"But I digress. As it happens, Hoskins was one of the people I had *not* dealt with ethically in the past, but in settling my accounts before leaving New York I repaid him, with interest, what I believed to be a debt of honor. The money came at a time when he was experiencing a cash flow crisis, and in gratitude, he passed on the information about *Drummond Doors.* I was able to acquire just the property needed to build their manufacturing concern here, and the deal was done. But you must understand that the price for the land was set by Mr. Wiener who, at the time, never mentioned any difficulty in securing a right of way for the needed access road. I accepted the price without question. I had, of course, already gained written permission from Mr. Crenshaw for the right of way before ever approaching Wiener about the land sale. Now you may believe that I should have been up front with Wiener about that information before – "

"Not on your life!" Tim cut in emphatically. "You're not responsible for doing his job for him. Having spent just 20 minutes with the wily Mr.

Wiener, I'd say you were more than generous and above board. In fact, I still can't quite understand why you would feel any obligation to give that crook the time of day."

Miles smiled at Tim's complete about-face in attitude but merely said, "So that I could sleep with a clear conscience. Besides, having taken his measure upon our first meeting, I hoped that he would refuse to consider a renegotiation, and he did not disappoint." Tim grinned and would have commented on Miles' methods, but he was distracted by the discovery that they had pulled up to the best steakhouse in the city.

"How did you know I was hungry? I just realized it myself." Tim looked suspiciously at Miles and said, "If you tell me you're clairvoyant, too, this relationship is doomed."

Miles' answering laugh was genuine, rich, and care-free. His own boyish grin matched that of his son's as he admitted to his own hunger. "I'd like to discuss my plans for the windfall I can now count on, but I'd much rather do it over a steak dinner," he said as the two men exited the car.

"I am happy to discuss just about *anything* over a steak dinner," Tim replied, then added, suddenly a little unsure of himself, "There's something I'd like to ask you about too… if you're willing."

Miles nodded, slapped his son on the back and cried, "*Lay on, McDuff, and damn'd be him who first cries 'Hold, enough!'*"[10]

Grinning at his father's histrionics, Tim mumbled, "I guess I'm going to have to bone up on my Shakespeare after all."

---

[10] William Shakespeare, *Macbeth*, act 5, scene 8 (Public Domain, 1606).

CHAPTER 16

*"For I know the plans I have for you," declares the LORD, "plans
to prosper you and not to harm you, plans to give you hope and a
future."*

Jeremiah 29:11 (NIV)

At Rose's request, Amy arrived at *Willow Walk* an hour ahead of
rehearsal time. The bride wanted all the bridesmaids to spend some
time together before the official part of the evening began. Amy
had met Violet and her husband Steve the day before when they arrived in
the company of Rose's dad. Like everyone else, Amy was struck by the
contrast between the two sisters – Violet's dark hair and penetrating violet
eyes versus Rose's softer auburn coloring and warmer, ever-changing hazel
eyes. A familial similarity in their features and vocal timbre, however, bound
them as sisters. With the addition of the fair, blue-eyed Lily, the mixed trio
could have been excused for taking anyone's breath away. Amy knew now
that she could look just as attractive as any other woman – especially in the
simple yet classy dark green midi dress with lantern sleeves that she had
chosen for the rehearsal dinner. But she felt a little like the ugly duckling
thrust into the center of a brood of some other species when surrounded by
the Thompson girls.

Only Violet, Lily, and Amy would be attending the bride, however,
since Rose's best friend from High School, Linsey Walsh, was out of the
country on a long-term mission trip to Haiti. Amy remembered how excited
she had been about the prospect of being paired with Abe for the ceremony

when Rose and Tim had announced their engagement. The foreshadowing of what lay ahead for the budding couple was a possibility to anticipate, but with Abe's departure the month before, Amy had begun to dread the festivities despite her affection for Rose. What had promised to be a day filled with hopes and dreams was looming as an event simply to be endured for the sake of her friend. And the biggest hurdle was yet to be faced.

Rose had taken Violet and their father on a brief tour of *Willow Walk* the day before, but now she proudly escorted both her sisters on a detailed walk through the old place. Amy took some understandable pride in the work accomplished there since Rose and Tim's engagement party. She had helped Rose choose furnishings, fixtures, and cabinetry via the internet after the bride-to-be left in August. With the start of school and an ever-increasing desire to spend time with Abe, she didn't contribute much to the project during her friend's absence. But because Rose's return coincided mercifully with Abe's departure, Amy found the tasks of cleaning, painting, and decorating welcome distractions from an aching heart. Both women had poured themselves into the work, though for different reasons, so it came as a disappointing surprise when Violet and Lily made so many critical comments about the resulting décor.

"It's a nice room, Rosie, but don't you think the paint over here is a little dark considering the only light source is that turret window?" Violet pointed out. She stood in the little reading nook which was actually just a corner of the large third floor master suite. Rose had chosen the contrasting wall color to add warmth to the inviting, cozy space.

"Oh, the color there is alright Vi," Lily argued, "But Rose, you might want to reconsider the scale of the furniture in the rest of the room. All these old Victorian pieces are so heavy. Maybe something with straight, clean lines would lighten things up a bit."

And so it continued from attic to kitchen, where the two sisters praised Rose for her choice of hardware one minute then wondered at her desire to include an old farm table in the corner. When Rose proudly pointed out the top-of-the-line, over-sized gas range, Violet and Lily questioned Rose's judgement in wanting to include the fire engine red appliance amid its otherwise sleek stainless-steel counterparts. Rose protested that she loved the cheery accent color, especially since it was Granny Gert's favorite. But Lily only laughed and quickly countered, "Our grandmother is hardly the person to look to for decorating advice!" They couldn't complain much about the parlor since it had obviously been rearranged from its standard configuration to accommodate the additional dining table for the rehearsal dinner. But they both found fault with Rose's treasured oil painting of *Willow Walk* proudly hung over the fireplace mantle.

Though Amy tried to bolster her friend's confidence with positive remarks to offset the others, she could see the bride beginning to wilt under her sisters' unguarded criticism. Amy's heart went out to Rose, momentarily taking her mind off her own troubles, but as soon as she heard Tim's voice from the foyer announcing Abe's arrival she hastily retreated to the sanctuary of the conservatory at the back of the house. Angelica and her army of volunteers from the church were so busy with meal preparation in the nearby kitchen, they didn't notice her slip into the neighboring room and close the door.

Rose, with the help of Marilyn's practiced eye, had furnished the designated music room with an array of simple but comfy occasional chairs. She filled the remaining space with potted plants liberally laced with twinkle lights, turning the whole into a sort of musical fairyland. Moving to the piano, a rather battered baby grand with a worn finish but surprisingly good sound, Amy idly ran her fingers over the scratched ivory surfaces, picking out a tune to quiet her churning thoughts.

She didn't know how she would get through the upcoming rehearsal on the veranda steps and hoped they would only have to go through the motions once. She had broached the idea with Rose that she be paired up with one of the other men, but Rose insisted that none of the others matched her in height. Not wanting to put any more worry on the already stressed-out bride, Amy had agreed, but she now waited for the inevitable reunion, wishing she had not been so accommodating. In an attempt to sooth her jangled nerves, she began softly singing a favorite hymn. As inevitably happened, she found reassurance in the music and the words.

> *Fear not, I am with thee; oh be not dismayed*
> *For I am thy God and will still give thee aid*
> *I'll strengthen thee, help thee, and cause thee to stand*
> *Upheld by My righteous, omnipotent hand*

Finishing the verse, Amy glanced up to see Abe gazing at her from the doorway looking more handsome than any man had a right to. In the five weeks he had been away, his soul patch had been replaced by a neatly trimmed goatee, and his thick, curly black hair was cut tight over his ears with classic sideburns that served to highlight the interesting planes of his face. He was dressed in a slim-cut black wool suit and white sweater. Both treacherously emphasized well-developed musculature in his arms and thighs. The random observations that his sisters must have taken him shopping, and that he had obviously kept up his weight-lifting regimen flitted through Amy's subconscious. She had never seen him look more attractive – or more unapproachable. The depths of his hooded eyes seemed to burn with the intensity of some emotion unfamiliar to her. She waited for his customary greeting, but none came. Amy sat motionless, unable to speak or to take her eyes from his face, though she realized in that moment that, regardless of how they had parted, she still loved him.

Not knowing how to break the strained silence, Amy turned back to the piano and sang another verse of the hymn in a shaky voice.

> *When through fiery trials thy pathway shall lie,*
> *My grace, all sufficient, shall be thy supply.*

She heard the barely perceptible closing of the door and thought she had been left alone in her emptiness, but when she reached the last two lines of the verse, Abe's voice joined hers.

The flame shall not hurt thee; I only design
Thy dross to consume and thy gold to refine.[11]

Amy sat with tears filling her eyes, not daring to look at him. The sight of her distress effectively broke down the last barrier of Abe's self-imposed restraint and he cried out from the doorway, "Amy, please don't cry. Please let me try to explain." She rose and walked over to a large expanse of windows, turning her back to him so that he could not see the tears now coursing down her cheeks. There was no hope of controlling the jerk of her shoulders as uncontrollable sobs shook her body.

"I wanted to tell you how I felt when I saw you that last day, but I believed I had no right to. I didn't know what I would find at home, but I had to try to reach out to them. You *must* have known that." When Amy failed to respond, he pleaded, "Please try to understand. I might never have been given that opportunity again. I missed them all so much, but more than that I worried for their souls. I reasoned that if I could be a part of the family again, I could show them the love of Jesus, explain about the miracles of forgiveness, and grace, and justice rooted in love." Abe stopped, feeling desperate to reach out to her. Finally, he continued in a voice of regret and defeat. "So, I left you to minister to them. It was the hardest decision I've ever had to make because in doing so I hurt the only woman I had ever loved."

Amy's quick intake of breath caught on a sob as she turned to look at him, disbelief in her eyes.

"Like a fool I never told you my true feelings, but when I was called home, I convinced myself that I had at least spared you the notion of having

---

[11] Attributed to Robert Keene, *How Firm a Foundation,* 1787.

been willingly forsaken. I thought in time you would forget me and find someone far more worthy of your devotion. And when I got home, I quickly discovered that that was precisely what my parents hoped, too." When her expression changed from disbelief to confusion, Abe hurried on. "Apparently, Husam had spoken of you so much after his visit here, they thought I was simply ready to take a wife. They believed that if they could get me home and introduce me to a nice Muslim girl, I might be persuaded to return to the faith and raise a family accordingly. It took less than a week for me to figure that out, but when I met her, I knew that I had to play along – at least for a while – for her sake."

Amy didn't know what to think. The joy that had leapt in her heart when Abe finally professed his feelings disintegrated to burning embers at the introduction of another woman. Not wanting her to get the wrong idea, Abe continued quickly, nervously moving about the room as he spoke.

"Her name is Noor Salam, and our fathers work together. Thinking her a good match for me – an educated woman who was one of my sister's nursing instructors – my parents invited her family for dinner soon after my arrival. When Ommy and Aby suggested we stroll in the garden after dinner, I knew what they were up to. So did she. But what *they* didn't know was that she was already seeing someone – a young Muslim doctor who was investigating Christianity because of a friend who had shared his faith."

"Like you and Derek!" Amy's tears slowed as she was drawn into Abe's unfolding tale.

He stopped in his pacing and smiled for the first time. She nearly started crying again from the sheer delight of seeing the smile she had missed so desperately.

"Exactly! So, I spent a lot of time with them both and shared the story of how I came to follow Jesus. It helped Noor to see that her doctor friend was not an anomaly, and by meeting regularly at a local coffee shop to study the Scriptures together, we kept both sets of parents at bay for a while. Kalil was much closer to making a decision after God spoke to him through a dream, but Noor needed a little more convincing. Last Friday I took them to hear a brilliant Christian apologist speak at the university, and afterwards they both made professions of faith. I tell you, it was thrilling! And it helped me to finally understand why God had called me home. I believe that the Lord used me to influence and encourage Noor and Kalil. I had been arrogant enough to think that I could change the hearts of my parents and siblings simply by crossing their threshold. Now I must humbly admit that that can only happen through the work of the Holy Spirit. But at least we were able to reconcile to a certain degree, and to laugh together again and share good memories – that is until my part in Noor's conversion was revealed.

"I have never seen my father so angry as he was the day he found out, but I believe it was also due to his disappointment in my rejection of his vision. The incredible thing is that as difficult as that whole confrontation was, it gave me absolute clarity about my own vision and the calling I now have on my life. I want so much to tell you about that, but it will keep for another time. Anyway, it became painfully clear that I could no longer be a part of the family in the way they had hoped."

Abe paused for a moment and his face grew grave again. "I will always love them, and I will continue to pray for them, but their home is no longer *my* home. I never saw my father after that evening. Kalil took me in for the night when Aby threw me out. Ommy and Samia came to see me off the next morning – I'm sure without my father's knowledge. As I was driving west, I began to wonder if I would ever have *anywhere* to call home again." He stepped toward Amy, but she abruptly turned away from him again to try to get a grip on the resurging hope that threatened to engulf her. The movement caught Abe off guard and effectively stalled him in his tracks.

"Amy, I know I hurt you when I left. I would have given my other *leg* to spare you that pain, and I deserve neither your forgiveness nor your compassion, but I'm *begging* you to give me another chance. I can't promise that I will never do anything stupid again, or disappoint you in some way, but if you will give me just a glimmer of hope, I will move heaven and earth to *try* to be worthy of you. I know I can never truly attain that goal, but… Amy, please, say *something…*"

"Granny Gert. Have you seen Rose?" Tim asked. While on a search for his fiancée, he found Rose's grandmother peering through the glass French door into the conservatory. "Mark Lindeman just arrived so we can begin the rehearsal."

"Shush!" demanded two voices in unison as Gert waved him back down the hallway.

"What are you up – "

He was interrupted by another loud "Shush!" Granny Gert frowned at him while Aletha stood behind her confederate looking the picture of innocence.

"We're trying to find out whether Abe and Amy have patched things up," Gert whispered, peeping around the corner of the door again. She thought she had spoken softly, but her whisper was more like the blast of wind heralding a Nor'easter.

"You can't just eavesdrop on someone's private affairs!" Though he felt ridiculous, Tim was compelled by Granny Gert's glare to respond in a whisper.

"There is no 'just' about it, dear boy," Aletha interjected in her soft, gentle voice, setting straight his misapprehension. "Gathering information surreptitiously is a highly developed art."

"Aletha, not you *too?*"

"Well don't you want to know if they're getting back together?" she asked artlessly.

Tim only shook his head, threw up his hands in disgust and continued his search for Rose.

"To my mind, there's too much talking," Gert remarked, looking boldly through the glass at the couple obviously engaged in heated conversation.

"Well, what are they saying? I can't see anything!" Aletha retorted.

"Shush! I can't *hear* anything," Gert responded sharply, straining to catch their words.

Amy and Abe were in a world apart, oblivious to anything but each other. Schooling her expression to impassivity, Amy turned around at the sound of desperation in Abe's voice. "You did hurt me, Abe, but it wasn't because you wanted to reach out to your family. You must have known that I could *never* fault you for that." She stopped to gain mastery over her voice which had begun to tremble. "I was hurt... because you never asked me what *I* wanted to do. Abe, I *love* you." Amy's studied control was fighting a losing battle against a wave of conflicting emotions and the devastating effect of his presence. "I would have gone with you, stood by you – comforted you if that's what you needed. But you made a unilateral decision about my future happiness – *our* future happiness – without even consulting me. Did you have so little faith in me?" Her tears began again, but she was powerless to stem the flow.

"Oh, Amy, it wasn't a question of faith. In fact, I was afraid you might have offered to accompany me if I had given you the chance. But I had no idea what I was getting into. I had nothing of substance to offer you. Surely you must see that," Abe said, trying to make her understand that he had acted on what he believed to be noble ideals.

"*Nothing to offer me?* Oh, my brilliant, foolish, blind Abraham," Amy chided lovingly. "You have given me laughter and the companionship of soul mates. You have shown me honor and courage like I have never seen before. And you made me feel *truly* beautiful for the first time in my life. Where on earth would I ever find another man like you?" She gave him a shy, tentative smile and watched his desolate look melt away, to be replaced first by wonder, then by the same burning intensity she had observed earlier.

"Amy, my darling, amazing Amy, are you telling me…" He left the question unasked.

Amy saw that his breath came more quickly and felt almost mesmerized by his hungry stare. She continued faintly, "If you *ever* walk away from me again, I won't forgive you so easily. And I won't tell you how much I have *ached* for the sight of you, to hear the sound of your voice…"

Abe made it across the room in two long strides. He pulled Amy roughly into his arms, and began feverishly kissing her forehead, her eyelids, her cheeks. Covering her parted lips with his own, he devoured their softness like a man who has been stranded in the desert without water and suddenly discovers the sweet, cool spring of an oasis. When at last he lifted his head, Amy gasped for air. "Abe! I… I had no idea. I mean… *wow!*" she said, gazing at him in awe. "Not that I'm complaining, mind y – " She was cut short by Abe convincing her that he was perfectly willing and able to repeat his lauded performance.

When Amy gasped for air the second time she looked intently at Abe's beloved face and marveled at the ferocity of his embrace when he had been so intentionally circumspect before. He had certainly wiped away any residual doubt about the depth of his desire for her. Not daring to look too long into the piercing intensity of his eyes, Amy focused rather on his chin just at her eye level.

Stroking the outline of his soft goatee, she inquired politely, as if clarifying a delicate point, "Mr. Yousef, did we not agree that the pleasure of a shared kiss was to be reserved for engaged couples?"

Captivated by her flirtatious words, Abe – still holding Amy securely – straightened his head and looked down his long nose at her. In feigned shock, he asked, "Ms. Walker, can it be that you are *proposing* to me? Not that I'm complaining, mind you…" Amy looked up at that, a provocative smile dawning. She threaded her fingers through his thick hair and pulled his head down to meet hers. Abe had his answer.

So did Granny Gert now peering unabashedly through the door at the couple locked in each other's arms. She let out a chortle of glee.

"What's happening?" asked Aletha in an urgent undertone.

Leaving the lovers to their own devices, Gert turned to her friend and said, "He just planted a big one on her!"

"Well, did she seem to like it?"

"I'll say. She did the same thing to him!"

"Now isn't that nice," Aletha said in the same tone she might have used when approving of a new doily for the coffee table. Satisfied with their efforts, the two made their way back to the front of the house where the rehearsal would soon begin.

"Best tell Rosie that Abe and Amy may be a few minutes late joining the rest of the bridal party, but I don't expect she'll mind," remarked Granny Gert.

"I should think she'll be delighted," agreed her accomplice.

At that precise moment, the emotion uppermost in Rose's thoughts was anything but delight. Tim had almost given up hope of ever finding his fiancée. After an exhaustive search of the house, he noticed her coat missing from the hall tree in the foyer. Grabbing his own jacket, he sought Rose in her favorite spot in the garden, a place of peace and serenity. She sat on the old stone wall under the ancient willow tree, it's draping tendrils now almost bare of leaves after a dry late summer and an early frost.

"Rose, I've been looking all over for you," he said as he neared his heart's desire. Light from the lamppost in the garden was reflected in her eyes, allowing him to catch the evidence of tears. He hurried to her side and sat down next to her, gently pulling her close with his circling arm. "Honey, what is it? *Please* say you're not having second thoughts," he said, half joking, half terrified.

Rose looked into his face in the gathering dusk and said, "About marrying you? *Never.* But I… it's just that…" She hesitated, trying to find the right words when she suddenly burst into speech. "Oh, Tim, I've been looking forward to this day for so long, and I've been so excited about welcoming our family and friends to *our* home, but now I wonder if maybe it's not ready. Maybe we should have gone with *Milly's Diner* instead. At least there we know it looks nice and has a… a fresh modern interior instead of being a carryover from another time."

"Hey, what is all this? Rose, you've done a magnificent job of taking a lot of huge, empty rooms, albeit brilliantly restored by yours truly…" He searched for a smile in her face but found only trouble and worry. "…and turned them into a home. You knew just which pieces to include from Aletha's collection and where to add more contemporary elements. I love every single room, and I can't wait until we have the house all to ourselves so we can finish the others."

"Do you really like it? Truly?" she asked, an unaccustomed furrow between her brows.

"Truly. Now where is this doubt coming from?"

Rose looked away to focus on her nervously twisting hands. "I was giving the bridesmaids a tour before the rehearsal, not that Amy doesn't know every inch of the place with all the help she's given me. But every time I attempted to draw attention to a special feature in each room, Violet or Lily pointed out some shortcoming or made suggestions about how I could improve the space. They didn't seem to approve of anything – especially the elements that are most dear to me like that oil painting of *Willow Walk* that your mom and I unearthed on one of our thrift store expeditions. I knew I had to have it as soon as I saw it, and when we discovered who painted the landscape – you know, that sweet old man in the assisted living home – I felt like the painting was almost a blessing or a stamp of approval."

She added in a disheartened tone, "But Violet pointed out that the shadows weren't consistent; she took an art class in college. And Lily thought that because the new garden isn't exactly like the original in the painting, it might be best to hang the oil in the hallway or a guest room and replace it with an Impressionist print or something more… fresh." Rose sighed and said uncertainly, "Maybe they're right – they usually are."

"Violet and Lily…" Tim muttered through clenched teeth. Placing his hands on Rose's shoulders, he turned her to face him. "Do you care what *I* think?"

"Well of *course* I do…" Rose began.

"Then let me give you *my* opinion. I think the house is perfect. I think you're perfect, and I think the rehearsal dinner will be perfect." Still detecting doubt in his fiancée's face, he added gently, "Rose, if I had met all three Thompson sisters when the others were single, I *still* would have chosen you because you're more beautiful, more thoughtful – and quite frankly – more fun than the other two combined." His comments finally elicited a hint of the winning smile he longed to see.

"Tim Ludlow, I love you," Rose said with simple certainty.

Kissing Rose swiftly, Tim pulled her to her feet and tucked her hand into the crook of his arm as they walked back toward the house. "Good. You had me worried there for a few minutes," he said, covering her hand with his and giving her fingers a reassuring squeeze. "Now that I have a willing bride, let's get this rehearsal started. I want to make sure I don't mess anything up tomorrow."

Rose answered with a saucy smile, "Well, if you keep your eyes fixed on me and remember 'love, honor, and cherish,' you'll do fine."

Tim returned her smile, wondering for the thousandth time how he got to be the luckiest man in the world. He asked her to gather everyone outside while he flipped the switch for the flood lights on the front of the house. "I'll be right there. I just need to take care of something first," he said when he spied Violet and Lily coming out of the library with their mother. They appeared to be trying to convince Beth Thompson that Rose needed to make some change to the room's furnishings, but Beth, for once, seemed disinclined to agree with them.

"Excuse me, Beth. May I borrow my two new sisters for a few minutes?"

Beth glanced at her watch before answering, "Really, Tim, I'm not sure there's time now. I believe the pastor is anxious to get the rehearsal started." Beth Thompson always appeared to be worried about something.

"It won't take long. I promise." With that he offered an arm to each sister and escorted them back to the library and shut the door. Violet and Lily looked at one another with conspiratorial smugness. Clearly Tim wanted their help with some surprise, and just as clearly, he realized that there were none better suited for the mission. A superior smile graced each face, but when Tim turned back after closing the door, the smiles faded. Gone was the genial host who had welcomed the Thompson sisters only hours earlier. In his place stood a stern young giant with folded arms and an unyielding expression.

"First let me say, that having grown up as an only child, I am really happy to finally have some siblings." He didn't appear happy at all. "Secondly, I realize that you girls are all very close, and that you love your little sister and only want what's best for her. Yes?" He looked at each sister in turn, demanding an answer.

"Oh, well… yes… of… of course we do," said Violet in some confusion.

"We've only ever wanted Rose to be happy," Lily hastened to add.

"I'm glad to hear it." Tim didn't look particularly glad to hear anything. "That will make what I have to say a little easier." He waited till he had their full attention, then moved his hands to his hips and leaned forward. "Knock it off!" The succinct directive left both sisters with their mouths gaping. "I apologize for being so blunt, but I'm afraid this is an instance of 'desperate times calling for desperate measures.' In your zeal to 'help' your sister, you two very nearly derailed her wedding, her justifiable pride in our home, and worst of all, her self-confidence to plan or do anything."

"But we only suggested…" Violet began, bristling in her own defense.

"…that everything Rose chose for her wedding was somehow inferior to your choices? Did you ever *listen* to her wishes or the reason for her preferences?"

"Of course, we did, but we simply have more experience at planning events and following fashion trends, and… and…" Lily stumbled to a halt.

"You have less than *no* experience in planning what suits *me*. You also, obviously, know nothing about Victorian architecture or period furnishings, yet you managed to convince your sister that all the hours of study, sweat, and love she has poured into turning this grand old house into a home for us is somehow in error."

Lily was not accustomed to having her opinions questioned, and had no answer for Tim's accusations. She was reminded unpleasantly of a professional trimming she suffered at the hands of a ruthless judge who pointed out all the rookie mistakes she had made following her first court appearance. Violet was also taken aback by Tim's remarks, but whether because she was more inclined to admit fault or because her pregnancy hormones were raging, she at least had the grace to blush and appear chastened.

"Look, I know you didn't mean any harm, but your lack of intent does not negate the outcome. However, if we work together, we can still make this right. Here's what I propose. One – we're all going outside for the rehearsal like we're the best of friends. Two – neither of you will question, nor suggest or otherwise contravene the directions of either Rose or Pastor Lindeman. And three – at the rehearsal dinner each of you will offer a toast, paying special tribute to the brilliant job Rose has done on the house, freely admitting that you could not have done better yourselves. Understood?"

The belligerence and indignation displayed by Lily at being taken to task had gradually given way to the same shame and regret felt by Violet. Noting their conscience-stricken expressions, Tim judged that his words had finally gotten through, and he spoke more gently, with the hint of a smile in his voice. "I think it's time you recognize that Rose is a grown woman – a wonderful, caring, competent grown woman. I don't really know either of you, but I'm sure that you're wonderful, caring women too, and I look forward to being part of your family. What do you say?" Tim then surprised the two by kissing their cheeks before giving each one a warm hug.

Lily, the first to recover, said in a rallying tone, "Well, Vi, should we give him our stamp of approval even if that means admitting we were wrong?"

Violet, in the act of wiping tears from her eyes, gave a watery chuckle before replying, "I suppose we'll have to. Rose seems to be crazy about him so he must have *some* redeeming qualities."

They faithfully followed Tim's "orders" to the letter and the rehearsal *almost* went off without a hitch, and they could hardly be blamed for the only glitch in the proceedings. Tim's army buddy, and third groomsman, had to cancel at the last minute due to both his son and wife coming down with the flu simultaneously, requiring him to take over "Daddy duty" full time for several days. As expected, Rose was worried at the suddenly uneven bridal party, but Tim assured her that he would take care of it. She was so relieved at her sisters' supportive participation that she gladly left Tim to solve the only problem looming for their big day. By the time dinner was over, Rose was fairly glowing from the tributes paid her by Violet and Lily. Her happiness was made complete with the knowledge that her friends, Amy and Abe, would be following her down the aisle in the near future.

After bidding their guests good night, Tim managed to steal a few minutes alone with his fiancée before she left to spend her last night as a single woman at Amy's place. The Thompsons had effectively taken over all the guest space in Marilyn's and Angelica's homes, and other out-of-town guests were hosted by Tom and Lucy Bennett. Though excitement filled the air all around Tinkers Well, none was so sweet or tender as that shared by Tim and Rose. The couple gazed at the stars from the vantage point of the garden wall, holding one another as if not willing to let an ounce of their happiness escape into the vast night sky.

"Do you realize that you won't see me again until I'm walking toward you in the church wearing my wedding dress?" Rose asked softly, her head nestled on Tim's shoulder. She felt his embrace grow tighter.

"I almost wish it was two o'clock tomorrow afternoon right now," he said and brushed her hair with his lips.

"*Almost?*" Rose was certain Tim wasn't having second thoughts.

"I don't want to miss a minute of the life that God has laid out for us to share, and if that means spending this time, right now, holding you and dreaming about everything we have to look forward to together, then this is where I want to be." Tim turned her face so that he could look into her eyes shining through the darkness. His kiss was tentative, almost guarded. He had succeeded in honoring the pledge he made to himself to keep their relationship pure and unspoiled until they could share the unalloyed joy and pleasure awaiting them on the morrow as Mr. and Mrs. Ludlow. He wasn't about to jeopardize that now.

"Do you realize that the next time I kiss you, we will be married?" he whispered against the softness of her cheek. Her responsive shiver told him everything he wanted to know. "Go now with Amy, my love. After tomorrow, I won't ever let you go again."

Tim watched Rose walk back to the house, then remained seated on the stone wall lost in thought. Derek and Abe found him there some 30 minutes later after the last of the guests had departed and the kitchen was left spotless and uninhabited by church ladies.

"What is the man of the hour doing hiding in the dark?" Derek asked as he and Abe approached the solitary groom. They sat down on either side of their friend.

Tim, roused from his reflections, shook his head and replied, "I guess I was trying to imagine how my life will change now. It's hard to wrap my head around the idea that I will never be alone again."

"Hey, you're not alone *now*, bro. And we've always had your back, haven't we?" Derek asked, trying unsuccessfully to sound offended.

"Derek is merely trying to make light of the fact that he alone among us has not been swept off his feet by a beautiful woman." Abe leaned forward quickly to avoid Derek's hand aimed at his head.

Laughing at their old antics Tim said, "Have I mentioned how good it is to have you back again, Abe?"

"Huh! Speak for yourself," said Derek. "And for your information, the only reason I'm not taken already is that I've been busy getting you two sorry clowns out of the way first. Ms. Right is bound to come waltzing along any day now and when she does, she'll have all of this," Derek stopped to flex his muscles, "all to herself."

Abe leaned toward Tim and said under his breath, "Do you think we should warn her?"

"*I like that* – after all I've done for you losers. Why if it wasn't for me, you'd have left Rose to the mercies of that jerk Atherton," Derek said to Tim. "And if I hadn't practically forced you to invite Amy to dinner, you would probably still be mooning over her like a lost puppy," he reminded Abe. He then sat in wounded silence while he watched his friends expectantly out of the corner of his eye.

"Shoot! You know he's got a point," Tim said to Abe, ignoring Derek.

"As much as it pains me to admit it, I fear that I must agree with you," Abe responded reluctantly.

"That's what I'm talking about. Show me some love, my brothers," Derek said with a smug smile. Tim immediately tipped Derek backward off the short wall and began piling layers of dead leaves over him while Abe pulled his shoes off and threw them to the other side of the garden. Tim collapsed in laughter next to his friend, who was spitting and sputtering leaf residue as he emerged from the pile of debris. It was left to Abe to pull the two to their feet.

Tim slapped his buddies on the back and said, "Man, it is so good to have Three Brothers together again. I can't tell you how much it means to me that you're both here."

"Well, it would mean even more if my feet weren't so cold," Derek said, and glared at Abe while hopping from foot to foot on the cold stone.

Shoes retrieved and peace once more restored, Tim made a request. "You two are the closest thing I've ever had to brothers." He said with emotion in his voice. "Would you pray for me that God would give me the wisdom and humility to be the husband that Rose deserves?"

Three brothers knelt on the damp grass, Derek and Abe each placing a hand on Tim's shoulders. Their friendship would never be the same again. Their roles, responsibilities, and priorities would change with every new chapter of their respective lives, but the bond they shared would last a lifetime.

CHAPTER 17

Come and look, sisters in Jerusalem. Oh, sisters of Zion,
don't miss this! My King-Lover, dressed and garlanded for
his wedding, his heart full, bursting with joy!
                                        Song of Solomon 3:11 (MSG)

Tim opened reluctant eyelids to morning light filtering through blinds across the skylight. When the light finally penetrated his brain, an irrepressible grin spread across his face. He jumped out of bed and sprinted for the door. Intentionally optimizing the sound created by each footfall on wooden steps, he came to a heavy stop on the second-floor landing just outside Derek's and Abe's doors and let out a cry that could have wakened the dead. He was satisfied with waking the undead who eventually staggered out of their respective bedrooms – one because he had to struggle into his artificial leg and the other because he had to struggle into consciousness.

"Is everything okay?" Abe asked faintly, leaning on the doorframe with his eyes once again closed.

"There had better be somebody dying out here," Derek growled as he emerged with anything but his perpetual grin.

"*I'm getting married today!*" Tim shouted joyfully and thumped each man on the back.

Abe opened one eye and glowered at him. "Couldn't you have waited a few more hours to remind us?"

"I'm going back to bed," mumbled Derek and turned to retreat into the dark recesses of his room. He wasn't quite fast enough. Tim threw an arm around each man and shook them until they were, if not more genial, at least more awake, the effect of talking late into the night loosening its hold. The three had stayed up till almost two a.m. sharing everything from rivalry over their favorite football teams, to upcoming projects, to the big news that, besides marrying Amy, Abe intended to enroll in seminary the next year and the events that brought about his decision.

"Dude, we were up 'til practically dawn. What time is it anyway?"

"Oh, quit your whining, Derek. It's almost seven." In response to Derek's moan Tim added, "You had considerably less sleep in the Army."

"Yes, but we are card-carrying civilians now," Abe pointed out.

"But guys, *I'm getting married today!*" Tim's infectious happiness began to seep through his companions' lethargy, arousing something akin to enthusiasm.

"Okay, okay," Abe conceded with a sleepy smile. "I suppose I will be just as obnoxious on my wedding day, whenever that may be – hopefully sooner rather than later."

"Yeah? Well, *I* intend to get married at nine o'clock at night so I can get *lots* of beauty sleep."

"Some of us do not require so much slumber to acquire maximum physical perfection," Abe replied with mock modesty.

"I'll show you maximum physical perfection," Derek countered, flexing his muscles.

A piercing whistle split the air in a determined attempt by Tim to keep his friends on task. "You've both got to finish packing; we have to load the table and chairs into my truck and return them to the church; and we all need to get cleaned up and be at Angelica's by nine for the huge breakfast she promised all the men. Oh, and don't forget to pick up Aletha and Granny Gert and Rose's Aunt Patty. You'll have to drop them off at Mom's house. Any questions?"

Derek and Abe both perked up at the mention of food and disappeared into their rooms while Tim bounded back up the stairs resolved to ensure everything went off without a hitch. But flawless weddings are rarely memorable. No one involved would soon forget the wedding of Tim and Rose Ludlow.

Rose and Amy also stayed up late talking, laughing, and marveling at the way every worry and doubt had been wiped away. But the sandman hit them earlier, aided by happiness and relief, so that the girls were up betimes, methodically gathering all the beauty paraphernalia necessary for an indulgent morning of pampering and preparation.

As expected, Marilyn served an excellent and elegant brunch for the ladies who overloaded Rose with more marriage advice than she was quite ready for. Her easy blush appeared with uncomfortable regularity, especially since her soon-to-be mother-in-law sat right next to her. Most of the more racy comments came from her sisters and, of course, Granny Gert, who declared with customary candor, "I may be old, but I'm not dead, and I remember more than you might think!" But they eventually took pity on the sorely tried bride. Amy, seated on Rose's other side, was almost sorry when her friend was allowed to steer the conversation into more general channels. She had been making mental notes for future reference.

Rose had no cousins on her mother's side, and her Thompson cousins were a good deal older so there were no small children from the family to include in the ceremony. She and Tim decided instead to invite the children of some friends in their small group to fill the roles of ring bearer and flower girl. The children were in fact siblings, but they were adopted from China so they both bore soft white skin, jet black hair, and the piquant smiles of clever, mischievous temperaments. Kenneth Cornelius and Katherine Evangeline, affectionately known as KC and Cookie, were thrilled to be so honored. Each took their roles as seriously as a six-and four-year-old could reasonably be expected to.

Not long after brunch had been cleared away, and the kitchen made ready for its transformation into a salon and day spa, master beautician Tanya Miller and her assistant, Grace, arrived. Angelica slipped in moments later having dispatched her platoon of able-bodied men, now replete with an abundance of coffee and breakfast, to fulfill their assigned duties.

Long before Rose had realized the fractured fairytale of Simon Atherton or the solid promise of Tim Ludlow, she had dreamt of having all the women dearest to her gathered together on her wedding day. So, she imagined, might her distant great-grandmothers have come together to send some other bride off on her journey as a young wife with well-wishes, humorous anecdotes of married life, and gentle instruction. Another dream was coming true. She watched the faces of the women present and listened to their chatter with genuine pleasure – now that she was no longer the brunt of their teasing! Tanya's skillful hands swept the bride's hair into an elegant up-do with trailing tendrils. But before applying make-up, Rose asked everyone to gather in the living room.

Addressing the group she said, "This is my wedding day," and immediately got choked up. Clearing her throat, she began again. "All of you have contributed in some way to bringing me to this point in my journey. I wanted to recognize and celebrate the special role that each of you has played in my life." She walked over to little Cookie and squatted down before her.

"Cookie, I am *so* glad you're my flower girl. You make my special day even more special."

Only too happy to be the center of attention, Cookie promptly responded, "An I hab a pwetty dwess an… an… an I'n gonna dwop fwowahs ah ober duh chuch an… an… an dance wike a faiwy pwincess!"

"Yes you are!" Rose replied with a twinkle. "Will you teach me how to dance?" Cookie's answer was a prolonged twirl that left her a little dizzy but delighted with the enthusiastic applause of her audience.

The bride then turned to two ladies standing next to the fireplace. "Aunt Patty and Aunt Chris," she said, addressing her mother's sister and her father's sister-in-law, "Thank you for being my surrogate mothers and the life of every family gathering. I hope you'll come back to Kansas when we can have a nice, long visit." With indulgent smiles, they gently pushed Rose along her way.

"Amy, I can't believe we've only known each other four months. I feel like we've been best friends our whole lives." Rose took her friend's hand. "Thanks for being so faithful to help me prepare for my wedding, especially since I know how difficult it must have been for you at times." Her eyes grew a little misty, but she was able to regain her composure as the next words were spoken with joy. "But now we can celebrate together knowing that not only will *we* be friends for a very long time, our husbands will too!" Amy blushed and hugged the bride, anxious for her own special day.

"Since you're now the expert," she warned in return, "I intend to put you in charge of helping me get ready for *my* wedding – now that I'm sure I'll have one!"

Turning to her sisters, Rose took each of their hands. "Wow, I'll bet you never thought you'd see this day! I have looked up to you two and tried to be like you all my life. And I know we haven't always seen eye to eye on everything, but I always knew I could count on you." In a thickened voice, she added, "I couldn't have gotten married without both of you by my side."

Violet gently shook her sister's shoulders. "Rosie, you never needed to be like us. You've become a pretty extraordinary woman all by yourself and I'm so proud of you," she said, giving her a sound kiss on the cheek and a tight hug.

"The truth is, little sis," Lily added, gripping Rose's hands tightly, "we're both just a little jealous that you found a man with so much backbone!" A little mystified by the remark, Rose, nevertheless, moved on and motioned for Angelica and Marilyn, who were standing in the doorway to the kitchen, to join the rest of ladies.

"Angelica, you are such a beautiful example of what it means to be generous, thoughtful, and selfless. I feel so blessed to call you my friend."

"Now isn't that just like you, child. You've made me smile and cry all at the same time! Give me a hug and be on with you," she said gruffly, while her face radiated affection.

Rose felt a little shy when she addressed Marilyn. "You have been so kind to me that I felt like we were friends long before I knew you would be my mother-in-law. Thank you for making me feel so much at home here."

Marilyn gently laid her hands on either side of Rose's face and kissed her on the forehead before saying tenderly, "You are the answer to prayer and the daughter I've always longed for. Welcome to the family, honey." The two women who loved Tim Ludlow best embraced one another in mutual appreciation and gratitude for the other.

Beth Thompson waited for her daughter's greeting, not sure of what to expect. She was almost the only person that Rose quarreled with regularly, but Beth was wise enough to understand that their differences of opinion sprang chiefly from their similarities. Both lacked self-confidence. Both harbored feelings of inferiority when compared to their sisters. Both wanted to please everyone and to do the right thing, even when they weren't sure what that was. But the affection they shared was deep and abiding. Rose clung to her mother tightly, not saying a word.

"I love you, baby girl," Beth whispered.

"I love you, too." Rose drew her head back to look into her mother's eyes. "Thank you for insisting I drive Grannie Gert to Tinkers Well."

"Now Rose, I didn't insist on anything of the sort..."

Rose leaned forward to whisper, "Don't think I don't know it was your idea. Bless you."

Beth winked at Rose, kissed her on the cheek and pointed her gently toward the matriarchs occupying the couch with Scout in attendance at their feet. Rose wedged herself in between the two and put an arm around each one.

"Grannie Gert and Aletha, you two defy description. You exhibit great wisdom one minute then do something crazy the next." The two elderly ladies beamed as if a singular honor had just been conferred on them. "You are both courageous and independent, yet you've taught me the importance of allowing others to support you. You've shown me that true friendship never dies and that you're never too old to have adventures. And most important of all, you are the greatest matchmakers *ever*." Gert reached over to squeeze Aletha's fingers. "I hope that if I live to a ripe old age I will be half as wonderful and willful and wise as you are." Rose's voice had begun to show emotion again. "I love you both so much," she concluded with tears in her eyes as she hugged each one in turn.

Granny Gert blew her nose like a trumpet and announced, "Now that was a very pretty speech, but unless you want to turn this into a weeping fest, you just dry your eyes, young lady, and start acting like a bride. Why, you've mussed your hair, and you haven't got a lick of war paint on yet. You don't want to greet your groom looking like an old hag!" Rose laughed, kissed her grandmother, and called out to Tanya, waiting in the kitchen, for emergency repairs.

When Abe and Derek heard the sound of a door closing, they turned to see Tim step purposefully into the hall where they were waiting to accompany him on the short walk to the park for pictures. Derek immediately snapped to attention and rendered a solemn salute before bowing low with both arms extended saying solemnly, "We are not worthy, we are not worthy!"

Abe gave a low whistle. "No one will have eyes for the bride if you walk out like that," he remarked. "They'll all be blinded by your magnificence."

Tim grinned and turned almost as scarlet as his lapels. He had kept his choice of attire a secret from everyone, including his bride and groomsmen. Rose would not be the only one making a fashion statement that day. Striking a pose, he allowed his two friends to fully take in his sartorial splendor. Having intended to make the Army a career, Tim had invested in a mess dress uniform just months before he received news of his dad's death and his subsequent move from active duty to an Army reserve unit. He had never even had the opportunity to wear it to a military ball or dining out, so he made his debut in the Army's most impressive uniform on the occasion of his wedding.

The short dinner jacket in navy blue boasted lapels of crimson satin reflecting the primary branch color of the Corps of Engineers. Gold braid looped up the sleeves with gold and crimson braid around each cuff just below the braided captain's bars. Colorful miniature medals adorned the left chest panel and golden looped epaulets rested on each shoulder. Wide gold braid ran down the outside of each pant leg fashioned from a lighter shade of deep blue. The black cummerbund encircling his waist brought the whole ensemble together where chained buttons held the jacket closed over a pleated dress shirt topped with a bow tie. Tim had made sure that Rose would have eyes for no one else.

"And here I was thinking we'd all be making an impression in our black suits and matching ties, and you have to go and turn yourself out like Prince Charming," Derek complained. "How are we supposed to compete with that?"

Shaking his head in disgust, Abe reminded Derek, "We're not supposed to! This is Tim's day, and I think he looks splendid."

"Well, I can't argue with that," Derek admitted grudgingly. "But if you plan to pull something like this when *you* get married, you can find yourself another best man!"

"But Derek, there *is* no better man than you," Abe replied with commendable solemnity.

"You know that's right," his friend replied and straightened his tie. "Now let's go warn the cameraman to protect his equipment from the glare off Tim's uniform." The three men might have constituted a parade the way traffic stopped when they stepped out on Church Street headed for the park. All of Tinkers Well seemed to stand up and take notice. This was no ordinary day.

A flurry of activity over the next few hours kept the ladies busy until it was time to leave for a photo session. Nails were polished, hair was styled, and make-up air-brushed to perfection. Rose, surrounded by her bridesmaids and the generations of women that loved her, stood before the cheval mirror Marilyn had moved to the living room. The bride hardly recognized herself. The gown she had chosen was a superb combination of elegance and understatement. The simple A-line strapless underdress with a sweetheart neckline hugged her curves with flawless accuracy, while the overlay of lace applique on tulle softened the lines with the illusion of modesty, providing maximum effect. Scalloped lace followed the line of her collarbone and shoulders to flow snugly down her arms, ending in narrow cuffs at the wrist. As Rose made a half turn in front of the mirror, the full skirt fell in graceful folds from her waist to a demi-train that added a touch of old-world elegance without being cumbersome. Tiny silk-covered buttons cascaded down her back ensuring that the bride was beautiful both coming and going.

Lily, standing next to her grandmother, said more to herself than anyone else, "I hate to admit it, but I was dead wrong about the dress."

Grannie Gert, perfectly able to hear anything she really wanted to, looked sideways at her grand-daughter and said sarcastically, "Will wonders never cease?" effectively reducing that young lady to embarrassed silence.

Fastening into Rose's hair the sheerest of veils, edged with a diminutive version of the lace that adorned the dress, Tanya cautioned the bride not to move too much. "Every time you put that veil on and take it off, it loosens your hair a little so grab a quick look now, and I'll remove it for the drive to the house." The full effect was stunning. The only element lacking was flowers, and the florist would meet them at *Willow Walk* to deliver the bouquets. For though Rose had happily agreed to the change in wedding venue and the promise of a postnuptial photo shoot with Tim at their new home, she insisted that photos of the female half of the wedding party also be taken there. According to the careful schedule worked out by Tim and Rose, the photographer would be waiting for the ladies, having completed the few poses required of (or tolerated by) the men. Everything was running precisely to plan.

After receiving last minute instructions from Pastor Lindeman, the ushers waited in the foyer for guests to arrive. A stack of potted mums adorned one corner, and a basket of multi-colored gourds claimed the lion's share of the welcome table with wedding programs stacked up on either side.

"I can't believe that Tim is *getting married* in less than 40 minutes." Derek said as if discovering a miracle of science.

"I can't believe you're the best man," Abe said with a grin.

"Hey! What happened to 'there is no better man than you?'"

"I was merely attempting to bolster your self-esteem earlier, my friend."

Miles, who had agreed to augment the usher team, was immensely entertained by the interchange and waited in amused anticipation for the second act.

"Hey, bro. Remember all your duties as *third* groomsman?" Derek taunted.

"Other than supporting the groom during his hour of need, I have but to escort the love of my life down the aisle at the conclusion of the ceremony. And you?" Abe asked politely.

"Well, as *best man* I not only escort the divine Lily, I *also* safeguard the rings and hand them over when requested." Derek responded pompously.

"And where are the rings now?"

Derek's cocky expression turned to one of comical dismay. "Oh, crap! I forgot I was supposed to tie them onto the ring bearer's pillow," he exclaimed as he dug into his pocket, but when he pulled out his hand – nothing. He searched the other pocket – nothing. In a growing state of panic, he checked his inside and outside coat pockets, only to find – nothing. Derek looked at Abe under lowered brows and said almost inaudibly, "I don't have the rings."

"*You don't ha –* " Abe began in disbelief.

"Shhh! Not so loud!"

Abe grabbed Derek by the lapels and demanded in a fierce whisper, "*You don't have the rings?*"

"Is anything the matter, gentlemen?" Miles asked politely after returning from seating the first guests.

Abe quickly released his friend and said with assumed calm, "No sir. All is quite well."

"No problems," Derek added with a forced smile before being drug aside for a more in-depth inquisition.

"Where did you leave them, Derek? Think!"

"I *am* thinking!" Derek responded with feeling. Their conversation was no less intense for being conducted *sotto voce*. "Let's see, I remember Tim handing them to me in his room right after we loaded the chairs and table into the truck so…"

Abe snapped his fingers. "…so you were still wearing jeans. You must have laid them down somewhere when you changed into your suit at the house."

Derek's grin returned wholesale. "Dude, you *are* a genius. We just need to run to the house and…"

"*We?*"

"Two sets of eyes are better than one," Derek asserted. Abe reluctantly agreed. Their conference concluded just as JT and Jason walked through the door. Despite protests of inexperience, the two newcomers were enlisted as substitute ushers under Miles' supervision. After explaining their dilemma to the others, Derek and Abe dashed out the door 30 minutes before show time.

"Letha, do you know anything about these?" Gert asked as she placed two rings into her friend's hand. The two family matriarchs were sitting in a large room dedicated for women's Bible studies. It also served as a staging area for bridal parties. Having been decorated by the ladies of the church, it was both comfortable and afforded easy access to the foyer.

A frown appeared on Aletha's face as she touched the objects. "Why, I believe these are the rings for the ceremony, but how on earth did you get them?"

"I saw them lying on the hall table when the boys picked us up this morning, so I just popped them into my purse. Derek had already walked you to the car. I just remembered I had them when I pulled my phone out to silence it for the ceremony."

"Thank you for reminding me. I'll just do that too while I'm thinking about it," Aletha said and dug in her little handbag for her cell phone.

"Yes, that's all well and good, but what should I do with these?"

"*Do* with them? Well, I suppose you should give them back to Derek."

"Now that's a good idea. Hopefully he won't misplace them again." Gert motioned to Lily who responded quickly to her grandmother's summons; she was still stinging from the rebuke she'd received earlier. "Lily, go and find Derek and tell him I need to talk to him. It's important," she added for emphasis.

"But, Grannie Gert, why do you need to see Derek?"

"That's my business, young lady. Now you just do as you're told. Shoo!" Gert remarked to Aletha with some asperity, "That girl certainly found her proper calling in life as a lawyer – she argues for a living!" Lily returned presently to report that Derek and Abe had disappeared some time earlier, and no one knew where they had gone.

"I wonder what those two are up to," Gert mused as she absently fingered the rings.

"Gran, aren't those the wedding rings? They're supposed to be tied onto the ring pillow!"

"Then get me the pillow! Do I have to think of everything?" Lily rolled her eyes, but complied, fetching the little satin pillow from the table by the door. The rings were duly attached, then Lily took advantage of the opportunity to admonish her grandmother.

"Grannie Gert, you must remember to give the pillow to KC so he can carry it down the aisle."

"Well, why don't you just give it to him now, so I don't have to remember," Gert replied tartly.

"I can't. He's not here either," Lily retorted.

"Isn't *anyone* coming to this wedding?" Gert asked, slightly perturbed. Lily quickly gave an excuse and made good her escape before her unpredictable grandmother issued any other commands. Gert sat the little pillow on the couch next to her, but after eyeing it for a few minutes she thought, *If I leave this sitting here until that little boy arrives, I probably won't remember to give it to him. Best keep it with me.* And with that she popped the pillow into a purse the size of Mary Poppins' carpet bag and promptly forgot its existence.

"You're getting dirt on my pant legs!" Abe remarked crossly.

"Do *you* want to climb up to the second story balcony, Slim?" Abe merely glared in response. "I didn't think so," Derek added as he moved one foot from Abe's thigh to his shoulder then brought the other up to balance precariously while reaching to grab the balcony railing. He came up lamentably short, only able to reach the bottom of the spindles. "Here, get your hands under my feet," he directed, lifting one foot at a time. "You'll have to give me a boost."

"I'll give you a boost, all right," Abe muttered, and thrust with all his might. His focused strength, considerably fueled by frustration and resentment, sent Derek flying over the railing to land in a heap on the balcony floor.

"Hey, Samson, you just messed up my suit!" Derek yelled after righting himself from the tumbled landing.

"Shut up and get the blasted rings!" Abe answered, brushing dirt from his pants and jacket. That normally even-tempered young man was quickly running out of patience. He had suggested asking Tim for a house key before leaving the church, but Derek had refused to let Tim know about the missing rings. He was not about to let one friend down, though he was sorely testing the patience of the other. Both front and back doors had been locked tight when the frenzied groomsmen arrived at the house, nor could they find an open window. Derek had assured Abe, though, that he had left the door open from his room onto the balcony over top of the kitchen greenhouse turned laundry room. At least in that detail he had been right, but he reappeared on the balcony a few minutes later to report failure.

"Oh, for the love of God, Derek!" Abe said in disgust.

"No, no, it's okay. I just remembered that when we stopped by the cottage this morning Aletha asked to hold the rings. Right after I handed them to her, Scout came in, so I had to kneel down and say hello to my old buddy. I'm pretty sure I heard her..."

"*Pretty* sure..."

"...I heard her lay them on the table, but I must have forgotten to pick them up because I was helping her to the car. So now all we have to do is run to the cottage..."

Abe didn't wait for Derek to finish his suggestion. Nor did he offer to help him down from the balcony. Without a word, he turned and walked back to the car.

Grannie Gert and Aletha had spurned the offer of male escort down the aisle when it was their turn to be seated as guests of honor.

"We are perfectly capable of getting there on our own, thanks all the same," Gert said before sallying forth with Aletha on her arm and Scout walking behind. "You just save your services for Marilyn." Miles merely bowed in amused acquiescence and watched the two make erratic progress to their seats, stopping to comment along the way.

"That's right, I'm Rose's grandmother."

"Trudy and I are also the matchmakers, you know."

"Why, those two youngsters have *us* to thank that there's a wedding today at all!"

"Yes, it was *such* delightful fun plotting the course of their romance."

Once they reached the front row, having provided unexpected entertainment for the other guests, they waved graciously and took their seats next to each other just as Gert had promised.

In the rear of the church Miles turned to his ex-wife, his eyes glowing in admiration. She was dressed in a knee-length silk sheath that few women of her age could wear successfully. Marilyn could, and Miles noticed. "You look stunning, my dear. How fortunate that your cerulean blue once again matches my tie – and your eyes," he added with more effortless charm then most men produce in a lifetime. She smiled in response, then grew momentarily serious.

"Timothy, I want you know how truly happy I am that you are here today."

"As am I, Mari," he replied, "As am I." He took her hand and, kissing it tenderly, tucked it into the crook of his arm. Miles Hawthorne knew himself to be the most privileged man in the world as he walked a luminous Marilyn to her seat. There were more than a few murmured comments about the obvious source of Tim's good looks. Marilyn gracefully took her seat next to Aletha, expecting Miles to join her, but he leaned over and whispered in her ear, "I'll see you in a bit." With a wink he walked to the back of the church. Knowing Ralph would escort Beth to her seat of honor as the bride's mother before presenting Rose, Marilyn wondered what he could possibly be doing.

A quick search of the cottage entryway convinced both Derek and Abe that the rings were not there.

"Someone else must have picked them up on the way out of the house," Derek said in defeat.

"Well, you had better get on the phone and try calling them, because we have less than ten minutes to get to the church before the wedding starts," Abe replied grimly. Derek was unsuccessful in his efforts, but Abe screeched to a halt in front of the church with two minutes to spare. "I don't care if I'm parked near a fire hydrant, I don't have time to look for a parking place. If I get a ticket, it will be my wedding present."

"But what am I going to tell Tim?" Derek asked dejectedly as the two walked quickly to a side entrance to the church.

"You're going to tell him what you *should* have told him half an hour ago – the truth. And don't argue with me," he said as Derek started to speak, "I am in no mood for it."

Derek didn't think Tim was in a mood for explanations either. When the two AWOL[12] groomsmen burst through the door of the antechamber, they found Tim sitting with his head in his hands looking like he was about to be sick. It turned out that his ailment was more mental than physical.

"*Where the heck have you two been?*" he demanded furiously. "I thought I was going to be the only guy in history to be left at the altar by his *groomsmen!*"

"It's kind of a funny story…" Derek began.

"Have you been *mud wrestling?*" Tim asked in disgust, eyeing the evidence of housebreaking. "Never mind, you can tell me later. Here, maybe this lint brush will help a little," he said and handed the brush to Derek. At that precise moment, Miles breezed into the room. He grabbed the brush and put it in Abe's hand, then dragged Derek over to the corner.

"Any luck?" As a dejected Derek shook his head, Miles pressed two metal objects into the younger man's hand.

Glancing down quickly, Derek's eyes widened in awe. "Where did you *get* these?" he asked softly, unable to believe that his salvation, temporarily at least, was at hand.

"One is *my* wedding ring. I wore it around my neck today as a token of solidarity. Thankfully, I've held onto it for over 30 years. Now I know why," he said while deftly tying a perfect Windsor knot in a newly donned tie. "The other is the signet ring I sometimes wear for special occasions. It may do for Rose. With any luck they'll be so engrossed in each other they won't notice anything is amiss until after the ceremony."

"Hey, what's going on over there? Are you two about ready?" Tim called from the other side of the room.

"Nothing to see here. It's all good," Derek assured him with a reassuring smile. Under his breath he said, "Miles Hawthorne, you are the *man!*" Then

---

12 AWOL – Absent without leave.

noticing the rich coral color of the other man's tie, he added with a grin, "*You're* the other groomsman. That's awesome!"

"Time to line up gentlemen," Pastor Lindeman announced with clerical promptness.

While walking to their respective marks, Miles heard a gasp from the front row and stole a look at Marilyn, who had covered her mouth while tears filled her eyes. He heard her gasp again when Tim took his place looking as handsome and proud as any groom in the history of weddings. His uniform was a revelation to her too. As she sat there, looking at the miracle of father and son together, the tears spilled over onto her cheeks. Only then did she realize that she had forgotten to tuck a tissue into her clutch. Granny Gert, who could have outfitted an ambulance from the contents of her purse, came to the rescue. In doing so, she found the little ring pillow she was supposed to have given the ring bearer.

"Letha, what should I do with this?" Gert asked urgently, in her typical penetrating whisper, and placed the pillow in her friend's hands.

"Well, you can't very well take it back there now. Here, I have an idea." Aletha held the pillow to Scout's mouth and instructed him to take it to Derek. Catching sight of the pillow and its precious cargo, that young man added his assistance in encouraging Scout to complete his mission.

Meanwhile, KC was near tears when his mother tried to convince him to accept a different pillow than the one he had carried at the rehearsal the day before. He took the pillow but flatly refused to walk down the aisle. Cookie, who was never loath to have all eyes on her, announced that she would walk without him, immediately setting up his hackles, and the two started off together. The disgruntled ring bearer walked grudgingly down the aisle next to his little sister who was tossing handfuls of chrysanthemum pedals willy-nilly while absorbing the smiles of onlookers as she passed by. Eventually lifting his head from contemplation of his shuffling feet, KC saw Scout stepping obediently up the platform steps with the ring pillow between his teeth.

"Hey, that's *my* pillow!" KC cried out indignantly and threw the unsatisfactory substitute into the face of the nearest guest before sprinting for the prize. Cookie, who refused to be outdone by her brother, dropped her basket and ran after him, having spotted her four-legged friend from earlier in the day.

"Puppy, Puppy!" she called out gleefully.

The musicians sped up to a rollicking gallop as the kids went tearing past their mortified parents seated near the front of the church. They played louder to cover the growing cacophony of sounds from the platform, wondering if order would ever be restored. Derek managed to say joyfully, "Who's a good dog?" when he knelt to welcome his deliverer. Before he could retrieve the pillow, however, KC snatched it out of Scout's slack jaw and started off down the steps. Derek ran after him, promising to let the little boy keep the pillow if the best man could keep the rings while Cookie happily petted the dog, ignoring her mother's frantic attempts to coax her off the platform. The frazzled musicians finally gave up all together and waited for the chaos to die down.

Pastor Lindeman assumed an attitude of blindness, believing it his duty to maintain a mien of decorum until the madness subsided while the groom stood in paralyzed dismay. Abe, almost doubled over with laughter, was no help at all, and the congregation stood and snapped photos like an international gathering of paparazzi. It was Miles who brilliantly rose to the occasion to restore order and carry off the interlude as if it had been originally scripted that way.

He scooped up Cookie in his arms before she could protest and grabbed Scout's collar, returning him to Aletha. Whispering something in the little girl's ear, he calmly walked her to the deserted basket and held it for her while she sprayed the aisle with petals. He even pointed out spots she had missed, while simultaneously signaling the musicians to resume the processional at a more sedate pace. Their mission completed, Miles restored the child to her mother, earning a hug and a kiss from Cookie and the undying respect and admiration of every man in the room. Marilyn, watching in awe from her vantage point on the front row, believed it to be his finest hour.

The bridesmaids, who had been waiting in the back of the sanctuary to make their appearance, were still laughing when they glided down the aisle in shades of peach, each wearing a knee-length dress of her choosing. The colors complimented the wide variety of mums, asters, and flowering kale spread around the room or perched on windowsills. When Amy reached her spot opposite Abe, he saw nothing else until the musicians struck up the intro for the bride.

Tim held his breath until he saw Rose approach on her father's arm then expelled the air in a silent "*Wow!*" He looked so impressive in his uniform that Rose had to blink her own eyes several times to ensure she wasn't seeing things. *Can that be* my *groom waiting for me?* She heard the opening words by the pastor in an almost surreal daze.

"Dearly beloved: We have come together in the presence of God to witness and bless the joining together of this man and this woman in Holy Matrimony. The bond and covenant of marriage was established by God in creation, and our Lord Jesus Christ adorned this manner of life by his presence and first miracle at a wedding in Cana of Galilee. It signifies to us the mystery of the union between Christ and his Church, and Holy Scripture commends it to be honored among all people."

It wasn't until Ralph lifted the veil from his daughter's glowing face and placed her hand in Tim's, when she felt the warmth and reassurance of his touch, that Rose knew *their* moment had come. Another pair of lovers entered into the sobering yet touching ceremony that would change the direction, meaning, and purpose of their lives forever. The practice of repeating words that had been spoken by millions of couples over centuries of time failed to rob them of their freshness, as if the words had been scripted especially for Tim and Rose. Pastor Lindeman insisted that all couples whose weddings he presided over incorporate traditional vows in their ceremonies. While they were welcome to make their own comments, the covenant promises contained in the ancient text held more power, depth, and endurance than all the flowery prose about feelings and romantic love ever written.

For those few treasured moments no one existed but Tim and Rose. The pastor was a guide and prompt apart from them. In her turn she spoke the words, *"In the Name of God, I, Rose Elizabeth, take you, Timothy James, to be my husband, to have and to hold from this day forward, for better for worse, for richer for poorer, in sickness and in health, to love and to cherish, until we are parted by death. This is my solemn vow."*

When directed, Tim slipped a ring (the *correct* ring) on his bride's finger and said, *"Rose, I give you this ring as a symbol of my vow, and with all that I am, and all that I have, I honor you."*

While the music, pastoral message, and order of service reflected the uniqueness of the couple they honored, the words most anticipated never failed to give joy to all who heard them.

"Now that Tim and Rose have given themselves to each other by solemn vows, with the joining of hands and the giving and receiving of rings, I pronounce that they are husband and wife, in the Name of the Father, and of the Son, and of the Holy Spirit. Those whom God has joined together let no one put asunder."

The guests responded with a resounding, *"Amen!"* followed by one of the pastor's most enjoyable moments of the service – turning to the groom and giving him the blessing to kiss his bride.

"Thank you," Tim responded pleasantly, "I believe I will," and suited action to words.

Addressing the congregation Pastor Lindeman made the first official introduction of the newlyweds. "It now gives me great pleasure, and a *tremendous* sense of accomplishment, to *finally* present to you Captain and Mrs. Tim and Rose Ludlow."

A crowd followed the happy couple across the street to Settlers Park where all enjoyed Louis' food, perfect weather, and the fellowship of celebration. It all passed in a happy, crazy, wonderful, funny, emotional blur for Tim and Rose until, alone at last, they sat on the front steps of *Willow Walk*. The photographer had captured their wedding portraits during the best of the golden hour and left them in blessed peace.

Rose had removed her veil and taken all the pins out of her hair, allowing the curls to fall loosely on her shoulders. She leaned back against Tim, sitting on the veranda step above, and pulled his arms around her. It was the magic hour just after sunset when the world is still, and the last remnants of sunshine cast an enchanting mix of shadow and light across the garden.

"Tim?"

"Mmm?"

"It was a perfect day, wasn't it?"

He paused in the process of moving his lips methodically from her shoulder up the pure line of her neck and murmured in her ear, "Well, if you set aside missing rings, disappearing groomsmen, adorable kids gone wild, and our grandmothers giving a command performance of the vaudeville sisters, then yes, it was a perfect day."

Rose giggled. He loved her giggle. "That's what made it perfect, silly, though I'm sorry to say, I missed all of that. I hope people took pictures."

"Are you kidding? It will probably be on the front cover of tomorrow's paper!"

She smiled, supremely content, and gazed at the lengthening shadows. "Tim?"

"Mmm?"

"Don't you wish we could stay like this forever?"

A little alarmed, Tim asked, "What exactly do you mean by 'this?'"

Rose turned in the circle of his arms to look into his eyes. "Just the two of us in a perfect moment with no one to come between us or pull us away from this beautiful place we call home."

A tender smile lit his face. "Rose, that's *exactly* what I want – to know that when I kiss you good night, you'll still be lying next to me in the morning, to hold you without reservation. I want you to be my wife," he concluded gently.

She responded with the saucy smile that drew him like a moth to flame, "Maybe I'm mistaken, but I could have *sworn* you were the gorgeous hunk standing next to me this afternoon when Mark Lindeman pronounced us husband and wife."

It was his turn to laugh, but his smile changed to an intense look that caused a strange stirring deep inside her. "Sweetheart, I want you to be more than my wife in name. I want to start our life together. Now."

"Then take me inside, husband," Rose whispered, her lips the brush of an angel's wings against his. "All that I am and all that I have – are yours."

Tim gathered his bride in his arms and held her like the precious gift she was. He carried her through the front door he had carefully left ajar and mounted the stairs to their attic sanctuary where they would honor their Creator by living together as he had designed and purposed. She laid her head on his shoulder, knowing herself to be blessed among women.

Rose had come a long way since an insecure girl had traveled west to find adventure, but she realized, as she rested in the security of her husband's arms, that the adventure was just beginning.

Excerpt from Intersecting Beliefs

While the young women were dancing, each man caught one of them. They took them away and married them. Then they went back to the land God had given them. They rebuilt their cities and lived there.

Judges 21:23b (ICB)

A warm breeze rustled the leaves of overhanging palms, creating a kaleidoscope of shadows on the sandy lawn. At its gentle urging, a few stray hairs escaped the colorful headband tied around Rose Ludlow's auburn curls as she sat up. Reaching out to lay her hand on the recumbent figure in a neighboring lounge chair, she said, "Tim…"

"Mmm?" he responded, not moving a muscle.

"Honey, it's almost time to get dressed for the banquet. Let's take another quick swim. It will probably be our last chance before we leave tomorrow morning."

"No," came the mono-syllabic reply.

"No, you don't want to swim?" persisted his patient wife.

Tim Ludlow finally turned his head in her direction. Without opening his eyes, he covered her hand with his and said in a slow drawl, "No, I don't want to leave here tomorrow. I want to stay and float along on a lazy river, surrounded by white sand beaches and exotic birds, where the most difficult decision we have to make each day is which swimsuit to wear. And by the

303

way," he said, opening one eye to look at his wife, "I'm a *big* fan of every one of yours." With eyes closed again, he continued in a faraway voice. "I want to spend every day in the sun snorkeling over a coral reef, or parasailing in the bay, or zip-lining through a tropical rain forest until we're old and gray and tired of each other's company. In other words: I'd like to stay forever."

A predictable giggle followed as Rose pulled him unwillingly to a sitting position. "Come on, you handsome slug, I'll race you to the beach," she said and took off running through the opening in a hedge of pink hibiscus. The vivid, living wall provided both a lush color palate and much-desired privacy between the cottages of their secluded Belize resort. Tim waited till she was almost to the water before hopping up to race after her. Catching her neatly in his arms, he tossed her into the breaking waves. She wiped the salt water from her eyes and pulled him in after her, and the two forgot about everything but one another. The banquet could wait.

The Ludlows shivered and pulled their light-weight jackets tighter as a cold blast of Missouri wind blew through a gap in the jet bridge.

"Brrr!" Tim said with feeling. "I think we're almost in Kansas again, Dorothy."

Rose reached up to touch her husband's bronzed cheek. "I believe I can actually see your tan fading."

"No, that's just the way my face looks when my teeth are chattering uncontrollably." He put his arm around his wife to pull her close as they shuffled toward the gate.

She arched an eyebrow and inquired softly, "Surely, you're not feeling romantic *now?*"

"Don't be ridiculous. I need you to block the draft."

Derek Warner and Amy Walker were waiting for them in the baggage claim area while Amy's fiancé, Abe, circled the airport to keep the SUV warm. They didn't want the newlyweds to catch a chill after their tropical honeymoon. With everyone soon loaded in the blissfully warm vehicle, the five friends headed to the place they called home – Tinkers Well, Kansas.

"We ran by the house before leaving for the airport to turn up the heat there for you, too. There are freeze warnings in the forecast for the next three nights. Welcome home!" Amy said gaily and moved her left hand behind Abe's headrest. Something caught the light from passing cars and twinkled as she wiggled her fingers.

Rose gasped and switched on the dome light in the back seat. "Amy, is that your…"

"Engagement ring? *Yes!* Isn't it beautiful?" Abe grinned silently in the driver's seat.

"It's gorgeous! We haven't even been gone a whole week. When did *this* happen?"

"Some of us do not benefit from the largesse of long-lost grandmothers, so *my* fiancée had the privilege of choosing her *own* ring," Abe declared proudly.

His fiancée punched him lovingly on the arm. "I had an in-service day on Wednesday, so we drove to Kansas City and came home with… this," she said simply. "I love it."

"I can certainly see why." Addressing herself to the driver, Rose said with spirit, "I'll have you know, Abraham Yousef, that I love mine, too. And I couldn't have found anything I'd like half as much as the ring Tim gave me."

"Way to stick up for your man, sweetheart," Tim said with a cocky smile.

"Don't you people ever think about anything but love and engagement rings and honeymoons?" Derek asked, folding his arms in disgust.

After short consideration four voices replied in unison, "No."

"But we'll be very happy for you when it's your turn, Derek," Rose said sweetly. "You're just waiting for a very special lady who deserves a wonderful man like you, right?"

"*Finally*, someone who understands the essence of Derek Warner. Rose, you can be my best man. These two losers aren't good enough."

Derek endured the rest of the drive to Tinkers Well subjected to wild speculation on the improbable accomplishments and sterling virtues of the future Mrs. Warner.

About the Author

Linda Edmister is a self-proclaimed lifelong vagabond. She has lived on four continents and made a home for her army husband and their two children in 13 different residences over a lifetime of globe-trotting. She is a former US Army Major, State Department Community Liaison Officer, and Church Music Director. Linda holds a Bachelor of Arts degree and a Master of Music. Her favorite authors and literary influences are Agatha Christie, Georgette Heyer, and Elizabeth Cadell. When not teaching piano lessons or volunteering in her church library, she enjoys gardening, travel, and Bible study.

www.misteredbooks.com